Granville County Library System

P O Box 339

Oxford, NC 27565

P9-DJK-367

DISCARD

PLEASE
SEE
US

PLEASE SEE US

CAITLIN MULLEN

GALLERY BOOKS

NEW YORK LONDON TORONTO SYDNEY NEW DELHI

Gallery Books
An Imprint of Simon & Schuster, Inc.
1230 Avenue of the Americas
New York, NY 10020

This book is a work of fiction. Any references to historical events, real people, or real places are used fictitiously. Other names, characters, places, and events are products of the author's imagination, and any resemblance to actual events or places or persons, living or dead, is entirely coincidental.

Copyright © 2020 by Caitlin Mullen

All rights reserved, including the right to reproduce this book or portions thereof in any form whatsoever. For information, address Gallery Books Subsidiary Rights Department, 1230 Avenue of the Americas, New York, NY 10020.

First Gallery Books hardcover edition March 2020

GALLERY BOOKS and colophon are registered trademarks of Simon & Schuster, Inc.

For information about special discounts for bulk purchases, please contact Simon & Schuster Special Sales at 1-866-506-1949 or business@simonandschuster.com.

The Simon & Schuster Speakers Bureau can bring authors to your live event. For more information or to book an event, contact the Simon & Schuster Speakers Bureau at 1-866-248-3049 or visit our website at www.simonspeakers.com.

Interior design by Michelle Marchese

Manufactured in the United States of America

10 9 8 7 6 5 4 3 2 1

Library of Congress Cataloging-in-Publication Data

Names: Mullen, Caitlin, author.
Title: Please see us / Caitlin Mullen.
Description: First Gallery Books hardcover edition. | New York : Gallery Books, 2020.
Identifiers: LCCN 2019015477| ISBN 9781982127480 (hardcover) | ISBN 9781982127497 (trade paper) | ISBN 9781982127503 (ebook)
Subjects: LCSH: Single women—Fiction. | Missing persons—Fiction.
Classification: LCC PS3613.U4455 P54 2020 | DDC 813/.6—dc23
LC record available at https://lccn.loc.gov/2019015477

ISBN 978-1-9821-2748-0
ISBN 978-1-9821-2750-3 (ebook)

For Spencer, and for our daughter, with great hope and love

PROLOGUE

BY THE SECOND WEEK IN June, there are two dead women laid out like tallies in the stretch of marsh just behind the Sunset Motel. They are so close to each other that their fingers nearly touch. The women can see everything with perfect clarity now, the man's entire design available to them as though they had thought of it themselves: by the end of eight weeks' time there will be five more women. He plans to use the city's symbols against it. Seven women, seven warnings. Not so lucky after all.

The motel sits on the western border of Atlantic City, where stretches of salt marsh buffer the space between land and ocean. Casinos line the shores on the eastern edge of town, along the boardwalk, and to the north, where pleasure boats slip in and out of the marina or dock long enough for a bottle of wine, a bit of sun, a swim. At night the skyline is gapped, like a child's smile: half of the casinos have shut down and their lights are turned out. The empty buildings hulk against the shoreline, mammoth and spectral as shipwrecked cruise liners.

In death, the women are still dressed to walk the streets. To attract clients with a slice of leg, cleavage. To mime desire with a cant of the hips, a toss of their hair. Dressed to be undressed. Their jewelry glints in the sun: gold hoop earrings and the delicate chains of ankle bracelets. Charms in the shape of four-leaf clovers, a pair of cherries, a cat's head. A stack of cheap metal bangles, the gilt coming off in tiny flakes. There is longing in the way their hands seem to reach toward one another, the aching *almost* of it. Bruises bloom on the skin of their arms, delicate blues and greens that could have been painted with watercolor. Except for their necks, which are marked with purple rings. The water seething in and out with the tide means they won't be preserved for long. Already dense, iridescent clumps of greenhead flies tickle along their limbs, their cheeks, their scalps; the flies' thick, segmented wings like stained glass.

Each day brings a new hope that someone will find them. Planes fly banners over the beach, advertising Corona. The pilots loop back over the marsh but never look down. Other days an employee from the motel rattles a bag of recycling to the dumpster. Some nights a couple stops in the motel's parking lot to fuck in the back seat of a rusted-out Ford Explorer. The car rocks on its frame for a little while, and after it goes still the man ambles out to light a joint. Sometimes the woman squats on the edge of the marsh to piss behind the cover of the reeds. The women call to her, the shush of the wind through the grass like a whisper. *Look*, they try to say. *Look. Look. Please see.*

Cars and buses thrum past on the Black Horse Pike, trucks delivering cuts of filet mignon and rib eye to the casino steak houses, or vans of fresh laundry for the hotels: sheets and pillowcases that have been boiled clean, napkins and tablecloths stiff with starch. At one point or another the women in the marsh have wished for that kind of a cleansing, a way to scald their secrets away, their pasts swirled down the drain.

The man has turned their heads so they both look in the same direction: east, toward the lights of Atlantic City. They have been placed there to watch, to warn. Their eyes are open. They wait.

CLARA

IT WAS THE HOTTEST DAY of the summer so far when the missing girl's uncle came to see me. I sat in one of our metal folding chairs, shifting every now and then to unpeel the flesh of my thighs from the seat. Des said we didn't have the money to run the window unit in the shop, so I always felt feverish and sticky. Sweat sluiced down my spine and my hair was heavy and damp on the back of my neck. I had just bought a fan the week before, one of the old metal kinds with a steel cage over the blades, from the pawnshop on Pacific Avenue. I'd made Zeg, the owner of the shop, test it so I could be sure it still worked. He grunted like he was put out, but together we pushed an old TV away from an outlet, plugged the fan in, and watched it rattle to life. I touched my fingers to the cage, their metallic, rusty smell practically in my mouth, like dirty nickels. There was still enough space to slip something small between the bars toward the blades—the end of a pencil, a fingertip—and it beckoned, a dare.

"Christ, don't do that!" Zeg said. "You know how sharp that metal is? That thing will slice your finger off."

"Okay, okay, don't get your panties in a bunch," I said. But I knew what I was up to. I did stupid things in front of him because it felt a little good to hear him scold me. A little bit like love.

The fan didn't do much for the heat, but every now and then the breeze shifted and a cool wind blew in off the ocean. Sometimes it was enough to make the sweat on my back go cold, and a shiver would work its way through my body. But relief, when it came, was brief.

It was the third week in June, and already I had the sense that that summer was going to be different from any other summer I had known. The weather had been warm for weeks, and still the tourists hadn't come. The boardwalk should have been crowded, crackling with carnival energy: people wearing heaps of purple and gold Mardi Gras beads from the Showboat, drinking hard lemonades from colorful plastic cups, groups of bachelorette parties, drunk girls screeching and teetering in their heels, their Mylar sashes glinting in the sun. But two more casinos had closed over the winter. The trams that rumbled by never had more than a passenger or two on board, and the rolling chair men pushed their empty wicker carriages up and down the boardwalk, the wheels thumping over the uneven planks. By noon each day the chocolate fudge samples on the trays in front of Fralinger's Candy Shop had melted into one sticky, indistinct mass. Atlantic City felt like it was waiting for something to happen or for something to be revealed, waiting for an answer or sign. Like in my books, Mercury in retrograde, blood on the moon. I hadn't had a single client all day when I saw the man standing outside the window, squinting through the chipped gold lettering on the hazy glass.

The man backed away and approached the chalkboard sign in front of the door. *Palm Reading Special $5*. He shook his head, shoved his hands into his pockets, took a few steps, and turned around again so that he stood behind the beaded curtain. I could hear his breath, the slight whistle of it through his front teeth. I didn't say anything. Des would have told me to greet him. Would have told me to hike my skirt up a little bit, to show some skin. *Entice them, Ava. Times are tough. We've got to use every-thing we've got.* But Des was waitressing at the club, so I slouched deeper into my chair. Something about him made me want to watch, to wait.

He reached, parted the curtain, and for a moment his hand seemed disembodied, nothing but grasping fingers and raised veins, blue and meandering across the back of his palm. Then the beads clattered and the rest of his body joined his hand inside the shop. He was a short, older man in khakis and boat shoes. Lips pressed into a grimace, forehead glistening with sweat. He cleared his throat once, then again, more loudly, as though he were trying to convince himself of something.

"Hello," I said. "How can I help you?"

"I'm uh . . . well. I'm here for a reading?"

"Why don't you have a seat?" I smiled. "What brings you here today?"

"Well. I've never done this before. That probably goes without saying. I, uh, no offense." He reached into his pocket for a handkerchief, staunched a bead at his temple.

"That's okay. Most people who come here haven't done this before."

"Oh, well. Okay. Okay, I see. Um. You're really the psychic?"

"I am."

"Excuse me, but you're so young."

"An old soul." I always tried to smile in a certain way when I said this. Magnanimously. Patiently. Like I believed it. "The gift runs in my family. I come from a very long line of seers. Please sit."

His fingers left a smeared sweat mark on the chair as he pulled it out, and he lowered himself gingerly, as though sitting down signified a commitment he wasn't sure he wanted to make. He stared into the clear plastic sphere that passed for our crystal ball—something Des had bought out of a catalogue a decade ago.

From the other side of the table I watched the way it distorted his face, made his eyes huge and extraterrestrial, his mouth puckered and small. I thought of the freak show at the end of the boardwalk, of the alien corpse they claimed to have, embalmed, and yours to look at for only $7. How I had saved up to see it when I was younger, but when I peered down into its casket it was clear that it was only a doll.

"So, please tell me more about what you're hoping to find out today." I noticed that his nails were clean and neatly trimmed. He wore a gold wedding band on his left hand. His hair was mostly gray and receding, but he looked like he took care of himself. Like someone who swam laps at the gym and had fruit for dessert and took walks around the neighborhood after dinner. He didn't look like someone who spent his weekends in Atlantic City, gorging himself at bottomless buffets and snapping his fingers at cocktail waitresses to bring drinks to the poker table. It was what I wanted, too—to seem like a person who didn't fit in here.

"It's my niece," he said. "She's missing. She's my sister's girl. I helped raise her from the time she was ten or so. My sister, you see, had some . . . issues. So did the girl's father. Sherri and I—Sherri is my wife—became her legal guardians. There were some, ah, difficulties at first. She had never had any discipline, any order in her life, but things got better. She did well in school, became the star of the track team." He paused and rubbed another bead of sweat from his temple. "She was supposed to graduate from high school this month, but she . . . she ran away. She left a note, and then there was one charge on her credit card from a hotel here in Atlantic City, two weeks ago. But other than that, nothing. I have no clue where she is. I know you might not be able to help me, but because she was eighteen the only thing the police can do is file a missing person's report. I just thought at this point anything is worth a try."

I realized that I had seen her before, the missing girl. Or at least I assumed it was the same girl—not in person, but on the posters that this uncle, I supposed, had put up all over town. Stapled to telephone poles, hung at entrances of the bus terminals in the casinos. She was thin, dark-haired, with a rhinestone stud in her nose, a small gap between her teeth—same as her uncle's. The picture looked like it might have been taken at a party or gathering. There was a glow underneath her face, like she was leaning over a bonfire or the lit candles of a birthday cake. It had caught my eye because whoever was looking for this girl—I still couldn't remember her name—was offering a $1,000 reward for any information that proved useful. I had daydreamed about what I could do with $1,000. How far I could travel with that kind of money. How free I would feel. I tried to picture the poster again. J. The girl's name began with a J. Jessica? Jamie? Jane?

"So, um, anyway . . ." He looked around the room again, as though he might still find an excuse to leave. "I don't know how this works. But if there's anything you can tell me, anything about where she might be, that would be appreciated."

This kind of thing had happened a few times before—a client looking for another person who had slipped out of their life. Usually it was a boyfriend or girlfriend, a spouse who had left in the middle of the night. But this was different. No one had ever asked for my help finding a missing girl. Other times, there was something that could keep me from feeling too sorry for those kinds of clients—they were harsh and demanding. They were brusque or otherwise they were weepy, had a quality about them that made me understand why a person would want to pry themselves from their grasp. But this man in front of me, with his apologetic smile, his nervousness, and the sadness that hung over him like an extra layer of clothing—I felt sorry for this man.

"Do you have anything of hers with you right now? It isn't crucial, but it may be helpful." I was making things up, of course, and it seemed like some sort of a prop might make whatever I was about to do a little easier. I didn't want to disappoint him with the truth: what I saw was limited, out of my control. I couldn't just call up information from the universe as easily as plugging a question into a Google search. He shifted and reached into his pocket, produced a purple bandana, and smoothed it on the table.

Julie, I remembered, from the poster. The girl's name was Julie Zale.

"She ran plenty of races, but her best event was the four-hundred-meter. She got a scholarship to University of Maryland and everything. But then she said she didn't want to run anymore. Wouldn't say why. She used to wear this for all her meets. Said it was good luck."

"And how long has Julie been missing?"

A new attention worked its way into his posture, his face. He sat up a little straighter. "I—Did I tell you her name?"

"No," I said. "You didn't." Maybe he would think of the posters eventually, but for now I could tell that he was surprised. His eyes met mine over the table and I almost winced at what I saw in them now, swimming along with sorrow: hope.

"May I?" I asked, gesturing toward the bandana.

"Of course, of course. Whatever you need. And it's been three months. That's how long she's been gone." His voice broke then and I didn't look up, but I could tell he was using his handkerchief to dab at his eyes.

I picked up the bandana and ran it through my fingers. The cotton was a little stiffer than it had looked. It felt intimate, to touch an object that someone had loved. That Julie Zale had believed in, something she thought gave her power or strength. I thought about what it would be like to be her, running in a track meet—her legs burning, lungs heaving the air in and out, people cheering as she surged past them. I wondered what it would

be like to have this man for an uncle, what could make someone be so cruel as to run away from him. Maybe Julie Zale and I
were alike. Maybe she knew there was something bad, something
grasping and greedy about her. And maybe it made her both love
and hate him, for his gentleness, for the boundless kindness that
she knew she didn't deserve. It was how I had felt about some of
my teachers at school before I dropped out. Mrs. Witz, who had
recommended that I skip ahead from Geometry to Precalc. Ms.
Connolly, who offered to loan me workbooks for the PSAT because she knew that I couldn't afford to buy my own.

I closed my eyes. Where did I think Julie was? I had witnessed what happens to girls who run away and wash up here,
like debris dragged in by the tide. She probably didn't look like
the picture in the posters anymore: Her once-smooth skin would
be rutted with acne scars. Her hair dull and stringy. The piercing
in her nose red and inflamed. I pictured her on a street corner,
holding out a plastic cup, begging for change. Julie crouched in
an alley, her skinny body swallowed up in a stained sweatshirt.
Julie with a strap around her arm, feeling for the right vein,
then her head lolling back on her neck. When I opened my eyes,
her uncle was leaning forward, waiting. Everything about him
made me feel guilty, sad. His polo shirt wrinkled from so many
hours in the car. His thin, gray hair rearranged by the wind.
Out on the pier, the roller coaster cranked up on its tracks. In a
moment we would hear it plunge down the first drop, the few
riders' screams.

I closed my eyes again and worked the bandana between the
tips of my fingers. I was buying time, trying to decide what I
would tell this man and how. It was true that I could see things
sometimes. Glimpses of a life, under the right conditions. But
mostly I felt afraid for him. He would get bad news, a phone call
in the middle of the night. A police officer on his porch, his hat
in his hands. A feeling crept into my throat, a fullness, a pressure,

like I had eaten too much too soon. It was hard to swallow, my throat raw like I'd been crying. I touched my fingers to my neck. The skin was tender, hot.

I looked at the uncle to see if he had noticed, but he was staring out the window. At the empty boardwalk, maybe, or the seagulls swooping out over the beach. The feeling was gone as quickly as it had come. I didn't really believe in spirits, in signs. But that feeling seemed like an omen. I didn't need to be a psychic to know that something bad had happened to Julie Zale.

JANES 1 AND 2

THE WOMEN PASS THE LONG days and nights working the past over, studying the mistakes they made, the bad luck that reached in like a hand and turned them away from the lives they should have had.

Both Jane #1 and Jane #2 are Jersey Girls. Not just Jersey Girls, but South Jersey Girls. It's a small state, but any Jersey Girl will tell you there is no comparing a girl from Cherry Hill to a girl from Ramsey to a girl from Sea Isle City. Local girls are known for the snap of their gum, the way their skin is always slick with coconut-scented tanning oil. They call water *wooder* and don't mind the grit of sand in their bedsheets. Jane #2 is old enough to be Jane #1's mother: forty-eight years to her eighteen. But they were the same in the ways that count: They're from here, shaped by this place. They both had jobs on the boardwalk when they were young. Jane #2 sold ride tickets down at Steel Pier. Jane #1 worked at the caramel corn stand and would snack on the hot popcorn all day until she was dizzy with sugar and the caramel left a tacky mass on her back teeth. They both loved driving along the back bays with the windows rolled down, and when a Springsteen song came on they cranked the volume as loud as it would go. Bruce sang about girls just like them. Girls whose beauty was too outsized for their dingy hometowns, whose passions were too big for their tiny little lives.

Jane Doe #2 is newer—she's only been in the marsh for two days. If you got close enough you might still be able to smell the traces of her perfume on her skin or the scent of the last cigarette she smoked lingering in her hair. She is still that close to life, like a door she could almost walk back through. Jane Doe #1 has been here for two weeks now. She is breaking down; her skin no longer holds her in. The mud beneath her is dense and cold, like pudding. When the tide pulls the water back, there is a thick, scatological stink as the sulfur at the bottom is exposed. As the casino junket buses pass by, the passengers will frown, scowl in the direction of the restroom, look around at one another to detect a glimmer of guilt on someone's face. The old women press their handkerchiefs over their noses, trying to stifle the gag that rises in their throats. But the smell is everywhere, impossible to escape.

Jane #1 had loved school, even though classes bored her. A straight C kind of girl who doodled on the backs of her hands during class. Her teachers sensed some intelligence, ambition, coiled deep in her and were always prodding her to try harder, but she figured there would always be time for seriousness, for duty, later on in her life. And she thrived in other ways. Homecoming court, winner of the Best Wardrobe award her senior year, Prom Queen. She had a smile that even the strictest teachers couldn't resist, a quick, crackling wit that made her a good flirt. She spent those four years feeling like the bright shining thing that other people orbited around.

The summer after she graduated was when the malaise crept in, when everything became blunted, gray. When the beers didn't seem to be as cold, the parties as fun, the songs as moving, the sun as hot. It was as though there were some kind of screen between her and the rest of the world, dimming the thing that made every moment pulse with energy, sparkle with promise and light. And then the kids she dismissed as losers, nerds, moved away for college. One of them even went to Yale, and the idea that something so monumental could happen to someone whom she had thought so little of occupied her mind for days. She felt as though she had made a fatal mistake—all this time she thought she had mastered the order of the world, and it made her sick to wonder if perhaps, maybe, she had not.

She took a job at the cage in the casino, where she counted out chips and cash all day. The polyester uniform made her sweat. She hated the tuxedo shirt she had to button to her chin, the horrible little paisley bow tie cinched around her neck. The mildewed smell of old dollar bills always on her hands. The dim light threw dark circles under her eyes. Her tan faded by Labor Day. The blonde streaks in her hair from the sun grew back dark, and before she knew it, she was unremarkable. In December she ran into the boy who had been Homecoming King her year, who had been hanging drywall since they graduated. She felt such contempt for his ordinariness that for days the thought of him filled her with rage. But then she realized, he could look at her and feel the same. She was so disgusted with herself, so bored when she looked out at her future, flat, her days filled with counting other people's money, nothing to call her own. She was mortified by how often she got her counts wrong, and how everything started to remind her of work: the sun and the moon nothing but dull coins in the sky. Meeting men was what made her feel something, her only chance at being admired, at pleasing people again. And at least they were something she couldn't predict, the one thing in her life that wasn't going to be the same. Even the last one had seemed intriguing, mysterious. As they drove to the Sunset Motel she noticed the ways his eyes caught on the outline of the ballpark, the banks of lights that had gone dark years ago. What was that about?

Granville County Library System

P O Box 339

Oxford, NC 27565

The tall reeds shutter and shush in the breeze around them. #2's mother always said it wasn't truly summer until the marsh changed from heather to green. It's a brilliant green now, fertile, thriving. This place is feeding off of her, growing strong off of her body, off of what she gives. The more she breaks down, the better it grows. Her family has been here for centuries. Her father told her that they were the descendants of the sea captain whose house still stands in Somers Point. Her grandfather helped run liquor during the Prohibition, told her stories of lowering crates of rum into the hatch at the back of Nucky Johnson's house in Ventnor in the middle of the night. But the stories about her grandmother were always her favorite. Her grandmother had been one of the diving girls.

She's studied the photos: the wooden platform sixty feet above the boardwalk. The horse being led up the narrow ramp. The elegant woman in the bathing suit and dark lipstick, waiting, crouching, springing up and getting a leg over the horse, and then the dive—woman and horse tucking their heads, falling face-first through the air. The splash as they hit the pool, the gasps forced from the crowd. The woman—ta-da!—throwing her hands in the air. *How good it must have felt to perform that way*, Jane #2 thinks. To have a moment in each day when you could raise your arms and demand to be praised.

JANE #1 doesn't remember a time before the casinos and the hotels. To her they had always been there, the same way the ocean had always been there, the sand, the marsh. But Jane #2 remembers when they went up, her older brother going off to help build them, the new shadows the towers cast on the streets. She rode her bicycle along the boardwalk to watch the ribbon cutting ceremony when Resorts opened in '78, pushed her way through the crowds and gripped the rails of the boardwalk tight. Before, it had been an old hotel, then a Quaker meeting house, a plain three-story structure made of wood, and now there was this: a palace, practically. Large and clean and white.

Jane #2's older cousin, Louisa, was one of the first women hired as a cocktail waitress, and she got to go into one of the ball rooms early, before the place opened, and practice carrying trays of drinks without spilling anything over the rims of the glasses.

She used to watch Louisa shimmy into her uniform: the bustier lined with so many black sequins it looked wet, the way she flicked her Zippo, ran her kohl pencil through the flame, and drew dark lines, slowly, patiently, around her eyes. The nude stockings that were like skin but prettier, satiny. Number 2 knew that this was what she wanted when she grew up: getting paid to be so glamorous, to play dress up.

And she did. By the time she was eighteen, six more casinos had opened. She got a job at the Taj Mahal. By then, things had changed a little. The newness had been buffed away and carpets had faded. The crystal chandeliers had lost some of their shine. But she liked the girls she worked with: they looked out for one another. Pitched in when one girl was swamped with orders. Loaned stockings whenever someone else had a run. Grumbled over salads and Diet Coke in the cafeteria. The casino had rules for them to follow: monthly weigh-ins if you were a cocktail server. Gain more than 10 percent of your weight and you got stuck on the day shift, when everyone knew the good money was in the 6 to 2 a.m. slot.

That's where the drugs were meant to help.

Ah, the coke. If #2 could take it back, turn the other way when a dealer first offered her a hit on a shift, would she? That first zip of energy. The confidence of holding a straw, the comforting script of ritual. The thump of her heart and the lightness of her body. The way the nights blurred by in a frenzy of flirtation and vodka and little bumps in the ladies' room, the surge of energy thrumming through her limbs, the thread of her pulse pulled a little more taut. She felt proud that she could keep up her figure—proud even when her shift supervisor would come and fit his hands around her waist, the fog of his breath on the back of her neck.

No. Even now. She wouldn't trade it. Not those nights when everyone seemed to be laughing together. When she could feel men watching her, wanting her, and she could hold herself just beyond their reach. She would be more careful, though. She wouldn't, the night when no one was holding, take the barback up on his offer of speed. She wouldn't let the speed slide into pills. She wouldn't get so high that she tripped during her shift, crashing on the marble floor with a full tray of drinks. She knocked her tooth so hard on the rim of a beer mug that it fell out and she felt it slide along the slick pocket of her cheek. Her mouth filled with the taste of blood, and once she sat up, she spat the tooth into her hand. She stared at it for a minute, thinking it was strangely pretty, this little piece of her. She probably had a concussion, along with the sweet buzz of the speed, and it made her thoughts tilt in strange ways, but she had been mesmerized by the bizarre beauty of it, the swirl of blood on her skin, the hard white square at the center of her palm. The next morning she was fired for being high on the job.

If she could do it again, she wouldn't pick up a needle after she was canned, wouldn't feel so relieved that heroin came cheap. When she got clean, like she did in '96, '98, '03, '07, she would stay that way. Leave town, go to school, learn a skill that didn't involve moving through dark places, handing out drinks, leaning over so men could get a better look at her breasts before deciding how much to tip her. She pictured herself in an office filled with plants and sunlight, the smell of paper and ink. But school would cost money. And what to do in the meantime? She was like everyone else: the grind of daily life, so many bills to pay.

A generation apart, but both of them feel betrayed by the mythology they grew up on: that Jersey girls are the most beautiful, the most carefree, the most fun. That they were meant for something big, that they had grand destinies to claim, that Atlantic City had enough energy, enough luck, enough money and glitter for everyone. That they would one day have their own stories to tell their grandchildren—serving a martini to Madonna. The limo ride with Muhammad Ali. The silk and satin of their uniforms, the hair spray and air kisses and twenty-dollar bills rolled into their bustiers. That's what he's taken from them.

They knew death was inevitable. Once they started with the needles, being surprised by death would have been like being surprised when you come to the other end of a piece of string. But he took their stories and changed the shape of them. Janes 1 and 2 share their greatest regret: that once they are found here, in the marsh, this will be the only story anyone will ever tell about them.

LILY

I GOT THE INTERVIEW AT the spa for one reason: my father worked as an electrician at the casino before he died and people still remembered his name. My mother made a phone call to a friend of Dad's from the union, who put in another call to the facilities manager, who forwarded my résumé to the hiring manager, Deidre. We set up my interview for a Friday morning, two weeks exactly since I boarded a Greyhound bus from Port Authority and got off in Atlantic City, my eyes red from crying, my suitcase filled with a few things from the apartment I'd shared with Matthew. My future, which had once felt sturdy and assured, a ship I was steering, revealed itself to be much more fragile than that: a candy dish that I had mishandled. Now I was sweeping the pieces back into my hands, trying not to get cut.

The day of my interview, I stopped at the bar near the penny slots. It was only 11 a.m. but the bartender didn't bat an eye when I ordered a vodka and soda. A slumped-over man two stools away glanced at me in a slow, side-eyed way that reminded me of a lizard, and the sweat from my palms left a stamp on the bar top. Already slot machines whirred around us. The lights' glow brought out the crevices around gamblers' mouths, the circles under their eyes, the sagging skin around their chins. Every now

and then, some coins crashed out a metal chute or a cocktail waitress clicked by in her heels with a tray of screwdrivers, but mostly
there was just the empty, meaningless dinging and the lethargic
dim of a large room designed to keep out natural light.

The vodka stilled my nerves, which had been shot since I left
the city. I checked my emails while I sipped my drink and saw
that another blogger had written me, to ask for a comment on
Matthew. I deleted the message. I had plenty to say about Matthew, but those were private, jilted thoughts, and I figured the
only way I could salvage even a shred of dignity from the whole
situation was to say nothing. The art world loved nothing as
much as a controversy, but I'd retreated home for a chance to be
someone else—a reprieve from humiliation as the central fact of
my life. The week before I'd clicked on a link someone sent me to
an article in *Jezebel*, only to be greeted with a photo of myself crying, my mouth hanging open in a dumb gape, mascara running
down my cheeks in thick rivulets. *Is This Art?* the titled asked.
I closed the browser window before I could read another word.

The vodka was cheap and had a sharp, medicinal taste, but
soon enough its blunting warmth crept into my throat. I wasn't
worried about the job interview, but it was unsettling to be in
Atlantic City again—coming home had filled me with an inar-
ticulate dread. It was in the atmosphere, suggestive and hazy. In
the feral cats that flattened themselves to shimmy through gaps in
boarded-up storefronts. In the empty casinos that loomed along
the boardwalk with darkened windows and chains slung across
their doors. It was in the patrons lugging their oxygen tanks behind them on little wheeled carts, clear tubes running into their
noses, and the tattered posters on the telephone poles pleading for
information about a missing teenage girl. The entire town was
like a dreamscape tilted toward nightmare.

I wanted a second drink but knew that would likely lead to a
third, and whatever pity was being extended to me would evap-

orate if I showed up to the interview drunk. And, as much as I hated to admit it, I needed the job, needed the money if I was ever going to start over. It was only my second week back home, living with my mother again, and I had already resolved to stay only as long as it took to save up for my first month's rent and security on a new place back in New York. By my math, if I scrimped, I could be back in the city by September. I tried not to imagine where I'd end up—a dingy sublet, a windowless closet, mice scrabbling in the walls. But I thought that even the worst of my options would feel like a small success.

I signaled for my check, and as I thumbed through my cash I stopped to finger the two-dollar bill I kept behind the plastic pane that held my driver's license. I took it out and laid it on the bar. My father had always carried it, claimed it gave him good luck.

The edges of the bill were velvet between my fingers, though now one of the corners was missing. On the back, where it showed the Trumbull painting of the Declaration being signed, my father had drawn a lightning bolt above Ben Franklin's head, though now it was covered with a splotch of dried glue. *The guy did a lot for electricity*, my father used to say. *I owe him.* When I was little it had made me so proud—to look across the water from our town three miles to the south and know that my father helped make Atlantic City glow.

I loaned the bill to Matthew for good luck before his last interview with *Artforum* four months ago, and I didn't see it again until it turned up in the center of a collage in his last show. I was charmed that it seemed to mean something to him and pleased with my own magnanimity. But underneath it all, maybe I felt a change in my grip on him. Maybe I thought that two-dollar bill bought me what I shouldn't need to purchase: His loyalty. His love.

In the collage, he had included it among a recent dry cleaning ticket, an electric bill, a hair tie, a grocery list on the back of an index card: *bread avocado butter lettuce detergent.* Layered underneath were slices of a photo of us. I recognized it right away—it was the first picture we had ever taken together as a couple, on the rooftop of a new hotel in DUMBO, the lights of the city sparkling behind us. I found a sliver of the image that contained my eye, another of Matthew's mouth, my fingers on the stem of a glass, a slice of Matthew's forehead. All the meaning and glitter obscured by the drudgery of daily life. It was a bad, crude piece, which only added to the insult—it only became *art* after I tore the bill away, hands shaking with rage, leaving just a corner, a single filigreed 2, behind. I read later that it was one of the first pieces to sell. People said I must have been in on it.

If only that was true.

I slapped a ten on the bar top and slid the two-dollar bill back in my wallet, climbed down from my stool. A woman at a slot machine behind me mumbled a curse as she watched the numbers spin and, one by one, roll to a halt. Her expression shifted, her dumb, openmouthed hope contracting into grim disappointment. She shoved more coins into the machine like she was trying to teach it a lesson.

I hadn't been inside the casino since the new tower had been completed. The ground floor of it was made up of a long, tunnellike hallway that curved around a swimming pool, which was capped off by a glass dome that was filled with rattan cabanas and lounge chairs, lush with imported palm trees and hibiscus. The casino had named it the Swim Club. Even from the outside, it reeked of something saccharine and something chemical: piña colada mix and chlorine, suntan lotion and canned pineapple. The cocktail waitresses wore aqua bikinis and delivered brightly colored drinks on wicker trays. The spa was just across the hall, the entrance a metal door installed in floor-to-ceiling plate glass. Maybe it was the effect of that quick drink, but between all the glass of the Swim Club and the spa's façade I was reminded of an aquarium, and I had the slightly unnerving, claustrophobic feeling of being underwater and being watched. I looked up to the ceiling, found the glossy eye of the nearest security camera, jerked my gaze away.

The spa door looked heavy but was light when I pulled on the handle, and I staggered back as it swung open. I looked up to the camera again, knowing my every misstep was being transmitted, recorded, noticed. Before Matthew's show, it might not have bothered me in the same way, but now the cameras felt pointed, their gaze transformed from omniscient and impersonal to invasive, judgmental.

Unlike the casino floor, with its layers of stimulation—chiming machines, clicking poker chips, dizzying spin of roulette wheels—there was a chastising hush in the spa. I was immediately conscious of the way my cheap polyester dress swished as I walked. I had left the city in a rush, not bothering to take much, and so the only interview-suitable clothes I had were things I'd left at my mother's years ago. I could've brought more from New York—the Alexander Wang cocktail dress Matthew bought me for my birthday, the Rachel Comey oxfords I treated myself to after my first raise—but the morning I left I'd looked into my closet and everything seemed like the wardrobe for a play I'd never even seen.

In the lobby of the spa, a tall blonde woman about my age stood behind a long, brushed steel desk. There was a partition of frosted glass behind her, and combined with the bank of lights that shined down from the ceiling, it seemed as though she were on a stage. She had a dancer's posture, shoulders back, chin high, her spine pulled up out of her hips. The kind of grace that looks effortless but demands great strength.

She looked up and offered me an obliging smile. "Are you checking in for an appointment?"

Her hair fell over her shoulder, and it was so shiny it practically gave off a glare.

"Hi. Um, no. I'm Lily Louten. I'm here for an interview with Deidre. We have an eleven-thirty?" I hated the way I sounded—as uncertain as someone trying out a foreign language.

"Sure. I'll let her know you've arrived. Please have a seat." She gestured to a gray slipper chair against the wall. There was a coffee table in front of it—more brushed steel—and a spread of fashion magazines arranged in a fan on top. Next to the magazines, a single white orchid drooped in a pink glazed pot. I sat and tried to smooth over the wrinkles in my dress. The blonde woman—*Emily*, according to the name tag clipped to her lapel—picked up the phone, said *mmhmm*, and *yes, of course,* several times, then clicked the receiver down again.

"She's ready for you. I'll walk you back to her office now."

I followed Emily behind the glass partition, into a boutique, where I caught a look at my face in a vanity mirror. The circles under my eyes were inky and jarring. My pores were gaping and dark. I immediately felt revealed, embarrassed. Emily, perhaps sensing this, stepped over to a row of lipstick testers and plucked one between her fingers.

"Here. Deidre has this thing about wanting staff to wear at least three types of makeup on their shift. You should go in there looking the part, right? Try this one." Emily held a tube out to me, the silver case as sleek as a bullet. I turned the tube until the lipstick swiveled out, a pinkish red. Philip Louis, my old boss, always said he preferred a clean look for his gallery girls, and so I never bothered with more than a swipe of taupe eye shadow and a bit of mascara.

"Go ahead," Emily prompted. As I leaned in and traced my mouth in a shaky scrawl, her eyes gleamed with amusement. Or maybe it was annoyance. Up to a few weeks ago I would have said I was good at reading people. I wasn't so sure anymore.

Emily tore a tissue from the vanity and held that out to me, too. The color bled onto my skin and I looked like a child who had just eaten a Popsicle. The red made my exhaustion more pronounced, brought out my tired-looking skin, my puffy eyes. Her expression was still inscrutable. I couldn't tell if she was mocking me or being kind. She had stepped close enough that I saw there was a spatter of freckles, softened by foundation and powder, across the bridge of her nose. "Good girl," Emily said, taking the tissue from me after I blotted what I could of the mess. "Now let's get this show on the road, huh?" She had a slight accent that emerged then, a Midwestern pull on her vowels. I wanted to ask her what *she* was doing here—at the spa, at the casino—but she had already turned and started to walk away.

Emily led me down a hallway that was as bright and sterile as a hospital. We passed through a small room that she called the color dispensary, which was filled with shelves of boxed hair dye. Rings of fake hair hung from hooks on the walls, swatches in every color from bleach blonde to blue-black. The ammoniac smell in the air and rows of small brushes laid out to dry next to the sink reminded me of Ramona. I wondered if she would still use the small room in Matthew's studio. Maybe now that she had made a name for herself she would rent a studio of her own. An old factory building with huge windows that flooded with light every morning. Exposed brick, wide plank wood floors. *Fuck her*, I thought. But I still couldn't make myself believe I really meant it.

Emily stopped so abruptly that I bumped into her back. My hands went out in front of me automatically and I felt the knobs of her spine through her jacket. Blood bloomed in my face, and I pulled my hands back as though I'd touched something hot.

"I'm . . . God. Sorry," I stammered.

"Relax, okay? I just wanted to warn you, she's a bitch to everyone, so don't take it personally. I'm cutting my hours this fall so I can take more classes, so you'll be picking up the slack a few days a week—she needs you. But this location has been under-performing since we opened, and it's her head on the chopping block, so she's wound especially tight right now. Heads up."

I must have looked pathetic, terrified. I wanted to ask her what, exactly, was so bad. What was I getting into? But she jerked her head in the direction of another door, paused in front of it, and rapped on the frame. A weary voice permitted us to come in.

Deidre stood to greet me. She was a tall, breastless, wiry woman with a dark, razor-cut bob who wore, like Emily, all black. She reminded me of the women who used to come into the SoHo art gallery where I worked: Ferragamo pumps, chunky gold jewelry, Barneys bags swinging at their sides.

"You must be Lily," she said, eyeing my dress, then my purse, then my shoes, as I stood to shake her hand. Her skin was so soft in mine it felt nearly liquid.

"Deidre Bergman, the Mid-Atlantic regional manager for the company. Please, have a seat. Thank you, Emily." Emily responded with a beatific smile. Deidre turned for a moment to draw a pen from a silver cup on her desk, and Emily took the opportunity to mouth *good luck* to me.

Deidre's office smelled like lemon verbena and was furnished in the same style as the front lobby: sleek, low-profile chairs made from chrome and covered with white leatherette, a glass-topped desk, another orchid. Deidre turned to my résumé and ran a long, bony finger down the page. She scanned it with a disconcerting quickness, looked up at me, and was silent for long enough that I felt anxious. A general air of disapproval, of rejection, had filled the room, and I'd barely spoken more than my name.

"Do you have any questions about my résumé?"

"You have an impressive work and educational history. Tell me, why here? Why now?"

I expected this question and had rehearsed the answer to it again and again in my head the night before, but hadn't landed on anything that spun things right. I needed an answer that seemed plausible but that wasn't the truth: I didn't have much of a choice.

"I want to start over," I blurted. So much for staying calm. But I was surprised to realize that I meant it. Deidre seemed amused by how earnest I was. I wasn't like Ramona and Matthew. Or even like Emily, who turned on such a generous, obliging smile for Deidre, even though, just seconds before, she had called her a bitch. I wasn't like any of them: able to dissemble, able to pretend.

"Why's that? An art history major at Vassar, lands a job with a prestigious gallery in New York, and leaves it all for a part-time job in Atlantic City. Just seems like an unusual path."

"It . . . it didn't feel like my world anymore." She stared at me, eyes flashing with what—mockery? knowledge? For all I knew she'd googled me the way I googled this spa; maybe she had read all the write-ups of the show, could trace my path from that life to this desk with as much precision as I could. But to my relief Deidre only held my gaze for a second or two before nodding, apparently satisfied.

"You should know that we are facing an unprecedented number of challenges at this location."

"What kind of challenges?"

"Well, the *demographic* here is quite different compared to our other locations. And you are surely aware of the economic conditions in Atlantic City overall. We are fighting an uphill battle in terms of launching a luxury enterprise."

"So why did you choose this location?" I was genuinely curious about that. Everyone else seemed to know that Atlantic City was a bad investment. Two more casinos had closed in the past year. Violent crime was on the rise. The billionaire who put his name on two of the largest beachfront properties thirty years ago had gone bankrupt twice. His insignia was scraped from or painted over on the doors and the sides of buildings where it had first been affixed in giant gold letters, now traced in grime. Two days ago I had walked through the luxury mall that had been built five years ago and seen that it had lost most of its original tenants: Gucci and Louis Vuitton—they were replaced with the kinds of junk shops that cluttered the boardwalk, the ones that sold T-shirts and key chains and little lopsided mobiles made of spray-painted seashells and fishing line. The spa was part of the expansion project everyone had called insane: a last-ditch effort to bring Vegas-grade entertainment to the city while customers were being drained off to slot parlors in Queens and the Poconos.

"We believe that the potential for luxury to elevate daily experience is important. People may not be investing in, say, luxury vehicles the way they used to, but will they still treat themselves to a new lipstick? A facial, on a special occasion? We think so. Our hope is that we will also draw a new sort of client, beyond the career gambler, by offering an alternative to the usual Atlantic City entertainment options. That said, this puts more pressure on how we conduct ourselves here, and more pressure on the value we provide for our guests. If clients with diminished disposable income decide to allot a portion of that income for an experience here and are let down in any way, they will feel not only disappointed. They will feel betrayed. What we offer is a chance to transcend ordinary life through the promise of beauty and clarity of mind."

"Well, it would be a great pleasure to be a part of that for the clients of the spa," I said, though inside I bristled at the facile logic behind her speech. It seemed so condescending, to say that women would forget their problems if they had the right haircut or fewer lines around their eyes. Men were never offered this same ridiculous promise: if you look good enough, everything else will be fine.

"Guests." She smiled. "We always refer to our clients as guests." At that she slid my résumé off her desk and slipped it into a drawer, and I understood that I had been dismissed.

I made my way back out through the hair salon, where a client—*guest*—sat in front of a timer like a piece of meat cooking. The fumes from the dye were thick in the air, a forceful chemical tang that hit me in the back of the throat. *What was she promised?* I wondered. What pain or desire was she trying to soothe with a half-head of highlights, a few new layers around her face?

As I approached the desk, Emily looked up and quickly jerked her mouse to click out of an internet browser window. Her face changed when she realized it was me.

"Oh, just you. How'd it go?"

"Fine, I think. Thanks for the lipstick and everything."

"Sure, it was nothing."

"Have a good day," I said, waving like an idiot, and right away I wanted to cringe. My voice echoed in the hush of the lobby, too eager. Too loud.

Emily sighed. "You've already got half the job down." But by the way she said it, I knew it wasn't a compliment.

When Deidre called me a day later to make me an offer, I thought of Emily's face as I left that afternoon, of the dread I had felt sipping my drink at the bar. A knot formed in my stomach, yet I heard myself saying *Thank you, yes, I'd like to accept. Yes, thank you. Monday is fine.*

CLARA

IN THE FOUR DAYS SINCE the man had come to the shop, the posters asking for information about Julie seemed to have doubled. I saw her face around every corner: in the window of the saltwater taffy store, at the bus shelter on Pacific and Kentucky, the door of Tony's Baltimore Grill. I couldn't look at her picture without thinking that there was something hidden in the riddle of her disappearance that I should have been able to see. I felt the same fluttering in my gut that usually meant I was about to have a vision—both uncomfortable and pleasant, almost like the tingle before a sneeze, but it took over my whole body, starting with the center of my forehead and spreading outward through my limbs. It reminded me of the sensation I got when I thought about my mother, tried to picture what she must look like now, or remember the way she smelled, the sound of her voice. But when I tried to picture what was waiting for Julie Zale, I only saw a dark shape, like a spill of black paint.

On Sunday morning, Des and I sat in beach chairs in front of the shop, waving paper fans at our faces. A feral cat crept up from under the boardwalk and splayed itself in the shade of our awning. I poured it a small dish of milk, but it wouldn't drink and the milk curdled in the heat. A middle-aged couple in matching khaki shorts approached from the candy store. A plastic sack of salt water taffy dangled from the woman's hands. She paused in front of the doorway and stared into the shop.

"Come in," Des called to them, in the voice she used for clients—honeyed and sweet—though she couldn't always keep it up. The gruff, cigarette-roughened Des eventually slipped through. "Come find out about your future. We do tarot readings, palm readings, anything you like."

The woman leaned into the man's shoulder, whispered something in his ear. He shook his head, took her hand, and they walked on. I watched the sweat stain on the back of his gray T-shirt move down the boardwalk until they disappeared.

"Fuckers," Des said. "I'll tell you what's in his future: heart disease. You see the gut on him?" I tried to hide my smile. Des was probably the last person who should be calling anyone out for a lack of self-control. After all, the pills kept her thin.

"Hey Des, have you heard anything about that missing girl?"

"What girl? There's always missing girls."

"The one whose poster is all over town. She was here, apparently."

Des shrugged. "Someone is wasting a lot of paper, if you ask me."

"Her uncle came in. For a reading. Wanted to know if I could help."

"Shit. What'd you tell him?"

"Nothing much. That I *could feel her presence in the air*." That had been true. That feeling, that pressure on my throat, the tears that had built behind my eyes—I had convinced myself that they meant something, that I should care about what happened to her. Maybe that's why I stole the bandana—I wanted to keep a piece of her close. "You don't know anything, do you?" I asked. Sometimes, Des had said, girls showed up at the club looking for jobs as dancers. Runaways, girls fresh off the bus from farm towns in Pennsylvania, the smell of hay and manure lingering in their hair. Girls who hadn't heard that any glitz had rubbed off Atlantic City years ago.

"Zilch. Though she better not trot out that young ass, looking for a job. I'm probably about to be canned any day now. All Larry needs is some fresh little thing with decent tits waltzing in there, and I'm out with the garbage."

"You say that every week."

"Gets more and more true all the time. You should probably be more worried."

"We've still got this." I spread my hands to indicate the front of the shop.

"You know that's not enough. It hasn't been, not for a long time. That's the problem with this town. Nothing good gets its due here, not anymore. Shit, I mean you're practically the real goddamned deal, and we still can't pay rent on time."

Des was right. We got word-of-mouth clients for readings every few weeks, but people didn't seem to want to know their futures anymore. They came to AC because they wanted to escape from the unrelenting predictability of it all—their boring jobs, their indifferent partners, the same meals they microwaved night after night and ate in front of the TV. I couldn't blame them for that.

"We need to be more proactive," I said. "We should try the spa again tomorrow. I think those are our people—these ladies pay two hundred bucks to let someone rub lotion on them and put a bunch of hot rocks on their backs; they should be able to cough up ten bucks for a reading here and there."

"We got blacklisted there, remember, little miss? They said they'd call security if we came back."

I crossed my arms. Last time, Des and I paid $20 each for a day pass and spent a few hours offering to read cards for women who came into the lounge. We made $50 off a woman from Binghamton before someone turned us in and an employee in a dark suit demanded that we leave.

"They didn't mean that," I said.

"What we need is to make friends with someone on the inside, someone on the staff who will work with us. Let's just try it. It'll beat sitting here, sweating, my goddamned cellulite sticking to this stupid chair."

"You don't have cellulite, Des."

She turned to look at me, slid her sunglasses down the bridge of her nose. "You know when you look like her the most?" I didn't need to ask whom she meant. Des almost never talked about my mother, so when she did, I tended to hold my breath. I could count the facts I knew about her on two hands: she liked mint chocolate chip ice cream; she and Des moved here in 1987 from Newark after their mother died; she had visions, too, just like me; and she left for California when I was a baby, to become a psychic to the stars. I received letters from her every year on my birthday until I turned twelve. The only other piece of her I had was the book she left behind: a heavy old hardcover with browned pages, called *The Wisdom of Tarot*. I liked to read it before I fell asleep, so that some of its magic, some of her, might sift through my dreams.

"You make the same face as my sister did when you tell a lie."

"What kinds of things did she lie about?" I asked.

But Des didn't answer, and I watched her stare out past the boardwalk and the beach to the thick blue line where the ocean met the horizon. The air above it shimmered in the heat.

"I have an idea I've been meaning to float by you," Des said.

"Shoot."

Her eyes were still locked on the water—she knew I wasn't going to like what she had to say. "There's this flier someone was passing around at the club. One of the other girls gave it to me. A business opportunity."

"Okay . . ."

"Well, it's this service, right? Where rich men are looking to . . . take care of young, attractive women."

"What do you mean, *take care of?*"

"They pay you to let them take you out on dates. Buy you nice things, take you out to good dinners."

"Men pay you to let them buy you stuff? Come on, Des, that's not all they're paying for." I had lived here my whole life; I'd seen how this kind of thing worked. Young women in short dresses getting into the back seats of strangers' cars, disappearing into the night. In this town full of people who wanted to win and drink and take? No way an opportunity for generosity was what they were paying for.

"I'm serious! There's all these online services, but with me at the club, we could do it that way."

"I'm underage."

"They'll like that even better, trust me."

"If it's so good, why don't you do it?"

"Ava, so many women do this, okay? It's how young girls pay for college these days. No one can afford that shit otherwise, and there's no harm in it. Let some moron buy you nice dresses, have a steak with someone here and there. I would love to do it, but no one wants to go out with an old hag like me."

"You're thirty-eight. That's not old. And I still don't see why anyone would want to do that—blow money on a stranger. What's in it for the guy?"

Des sighed, rolled her head in slow circles. The little bones in her neck popped. "Some guy, probably married ten years, bored out of his mind, gets to go to a restaurant with a pretty little thing on his arm, order a good bottle of wine? It makes them feel powerful, alive. Men are like that; they need their egos fed constantly, the poor, stupid louts. Try this, just once. You hate it, we'll try something else. But it sure as hell would be nice to pay the electric bill. To not have to hide when Bill comes knocking, right?"

Bill was our landlord. He had come around two weeks ago to collect rent. Two months' overdue. Des and I hid in the bathroom in our apartment above the shop until he stopped yelling. *I know you're in there. You need to give me my money or else, Desmina. I mean it this time.*

"Fine," I said. At least when I saw my mother again, I'd be able to tell her that I did whatever it took to keep the shop going. I could say that I had tried to preserve what she had started. I was going to do it even though the idea made my heart race. Even though I knew full well I was probably saying yes to more than Des had described.

Des squeezed my wrist. "That's my girl. You'll need this." She raised her hips off the chair so that she could wriggle something from the pocket of her shorts: a driver's license, with the name "Clara Voyant" on it and a photo of Des on the left-hand side. Of course. Of course she had already banked on the fact that I would say yes.

I lifted the ID to my eyes. "Des, come on. This won't work anywhere. And why didn't you use my real name?"

She ignored me. "Come upstairs."

"But what if a customer comes?"

"It's dead out there. And we'll be back in an hour, tops." She rose from her chair and thumped up the stairs.

I called after her. "Des, come on! How are we ever going to fix the shop if we just bail in the middle of the afternoon?" But she was already gone. I dragged our chalkboard inside, drew the red curtains across the windows, and locked the door.

I found her in the bathroom, mixing water and brown powder in a plastic bowl until it formed a muddy-looking concoction. She saw me watching and held up a box of henna hair dye.

"I need to change my hair? No way."

"You need to match the ID." Des shrugged. "You really like it brown?"

"It's just . . ." I had never thought about it, not really. Des had been dyeing her hair the same bright red my entire life. In the photos I had of my mother, her hair was the same color as mine, a medium brown. Nothing special, maybe, but it tied us together in a small way, and maybe I treasured that more that I'd thought. "Nothing."

"Well, sit down, then." She gestured to the toilet. I sat and closed my eyes as she rubbed the mixture into my hair with her fingers. She worked the color from my roots through the tips of my hair, pausing now and then to wipe a stray streak of dye from my skin. It was the gentlest she had ever been with me.

With my hair still wet, it looked the same, though I could make out a flare of color at the tips. I sat in front of the mirror and waited. Slowly, as the dampness lifted, I could see the change. Gradual, and then sudden, a new me sprang up, stepping into a new life. *It's only hair*, I tried to tell myself. But I also knew that wasn't exactly true. I didn't trust Des not to turn me into someone I wouldn't like.

AFTER DES left for the club—heat stifling and no appointments in the book— I locked the shop again and walked to the library. Des and I didn't have a computer and we used burner phones, adding minutes when we could, so when I needed to know something I walked the eight blocks to use the library's internet. On the way, I passed two more posters of Julie Zale: one tucked under the windshield wiper of a parked car, another taped to the library's front door. Even in the photocopied pictures, her smile seemed to shine. I felt the same tug in my gut as when her uncle came: What made her run? Here I was, hoping to run toward love— California, my mother. What about being loved had been intolerable to Julie Zale?

There were only three other patrons at the library, and no one seemed to be doing anything that looked like work. A woman read a day-old newspaper. One man had his feet up on the table, trimming his fingernails. Even the employee at the checkout counter was asleep with her chin in her hands. I had come to search about my mother—a habit I indulged once a week—but this time I googled Julie Zale first. Her uncle had made a website where people could leave information by sending in an anonymous form, if they thought they knew anything or if they'd seen her. It showed the photo from his posters, but others, too: Pictures of Julie running in a meet, her eyes narrowed on the finish line. Julie at junior prom in a beaded blue dress, a flower in her hair. Julie sticking her tongue out while wearing a pink feather boa. I found more websites that mentioned her name, mostly articles from the local papers bragging about her track meet wins, her nomination to All State, the way she broke the record in the 400-meter at an event last fall. Even though she was probably in trouble, and maybe even in worse trouble than me, I felt jealous of her. She had a talent that made people love her, a talent that a whole town was proud of. I had a talent, too, I guessed: I could see things now and then that most people couldn't, but it felt like a burden. Most of the time, I would have given it away.

Next, I found her Facebook page. More photos of her running track, her in a yellow sundress, eating an ice cream. A shot of her giving a piggyback ride to another girl in front of a pretty red-brick school, the kind that I had only ever seen on TV. I scrolled through the comments people had left behind.

Julez, we love you. Come back home, babe.

J, you are missed. I hope wherever you are, you are safe and sound.

I'm a stranger, but your story caught my eye. God Bless You.

I knew why I wanted to leave, but why would a girl like that just pick up and go? I took my tarot deck out of my bag, shook the cards from their red silk pouch. You weren't supposed to ask the cards a question about someone else's fate if they hadn't requested it, but I couldn't help it. I'd only pull one card. Just a hint, I bargained. *What really happened to Julie Zale?* I shuffled the deck and the cards stuck together in the humidity.

The card I drew was the Moon. The card for women. The card that meant mystery, confusion, even insanity. But it could also mean knowing, intuition, or a sign that you needed to face what scared you the most. When she taught me tarot, Des claimed it was mostly learning to bullshit, that the cards were just props, ways to tell a story. But I believed in what tarot could tell me, in letting the cards speak. I also *needed* to believe that magic and meaning sometimes reached into our world. Or else there was just my life—the high school diploma I would never get, the shop, the mangy feral cats, the mother who never wrote anymore. Des coming home from a shift at the club with her pupils huge and glossy, rubbing at her nose.

If I wanted to use magic, *The Wisdom of Tarot* was filled with rituals and spells that promised to guide you toward the information you desired. I could try making an offering—I had never done it before. The book claimed that these rituals were powerful, that if you wanted to cast one, you needed to take great care. I imagined working alongside my mother, grinding dried flowers into powders, lighting sacred candles, arranging crystals into circles. According to her last postcard, four years ago, she lived in the guesthouse of a movie producer: 518 Montvale Road, Los Angeles, California. The main house was pristine and white with a wide semicircle of a driveway, a sweeping green yard. I imagined myself there someday, my bare feet on the lush grass.

On the satellite image you could see the square of the guesthouse, its terra-cotta roof, next to the aqua rectangle of the pool. She wrote once that sometimes when the oranges ripened, they grew so heavy that they fell from the trees and splashed into the water, that a jacaranda tree bloomed with tiny violet flowers right outside her window. *I'll bring you here one day, my love, when the timing is right. When I see the sign.* I ran my finger over and over the words so many times that the ink was more faded than any other line. I was still waiting for her to tell me when she was ready for me, when I could join her and start my real life. I had written her so many letters over the years, letters full of questions: Which famous people have you met? What are the parties like? Does it ever rain?

I looked up other things, too: Bus tickets to Los Angeles: $313. A night at a cheap motel: $55. A taxi ride from the Greyhound station to Montvale Road: $45. I checked them against what I had written in my notebook a few months ago—plus money for rent, for food, for clothes—I needed to save enough so that when I found my mother I wouldn't be a burden to her, the way Des was always telling me I was. Two thousand dollars was the amount I came up with, the number that would make me feel safe.

I walked home and slid *The Wisdom of Tarot* from underneath my bed. Her handwriting was spidery and strange in the margins, like something that might crawl off the page. The book was heavy in my lap; I flipped through it, a musty smell rising from the mold-flecked pages, until I found the section on the Moon. The book said that the Moon represented what was in shadow, parts of ourselves or parts of others that had yet to be revealed. To learn the truth behind a mystery, it advised leaving a crystal out at night to charge in the moonlight or even a sliver of your finger-nail or a piece of your own hair. There were notes scribbled in the margins that I couldn't make out, but I assumed it meant the spell must be good, if my mother had done it before. I fingered a ribbon of hair at the back of my head, one that I wouldn't miss. Then I sliced it off with a pair of kitchen shears and stroked it in the palm of my hand.

When night fell, a half-moon low in the sky spread a stripe of white light over the ocean. I set the piece of hair on my window-sill and tamped it under a hunk of white quartz. I added the ban-dana, too, smoothing it alongside the hair—maybe there was a reason that I'd been compelled to take it, after all. Before I fell asleep, I felt for the place at the base of my skull where the hair had come from, the short spikes sharp to the touch. I dozed off looking at the quartz, bright in the moonlight, the hair a streak of red beneath it, and waited to see what the world would offer me in exchange for this little piece of myself, what kind of secrets it might tell.

AS SOON as I woke up the next morning a vision came over me. At first, the only thing I saw was a pale shape against a splotchy background. I couldn't make sense of it, nor could I push it away. The throbbing began in the middle of my forehead and spread behind my eyes. I tried to focus on whatever this vision was asking me to see. A whitish square. Smears of red around it. Crisscrossing lines, like wrinkles. Skin. My mouth filled with the slightly sweet, metallic taste of blood and my stomach lurched, which was how I realized that the pale shape was a tooth that had come loose.

I came to, feeling disoriented, dizzy. The vision didn't make sense to me. The bloody tooth had no origin, no context, no person attached to it, someone on the other side yearning to be seen or told something. There had always been rules, limits to how my gift worked. Some clients thought I could see their entire futures like a film reel—beginning, middle, end. But usually, what I saw was a glimpse of the past—a moment that pulsed with intensity for them. Something essential to their personalities, an instance in their life that shaped the way they thought. So what was this? Whose tooth?

And why? Once again, I ached for my mother. I reached for the letters I kept in a shoebox under the bed.

Dear Ava,

If you are anything like me, this is the year when you will come to realize the power of your intuition. You'll be able to see things

that no one else can see. Women like us have power, have a deeper
understanding, a greater capacity for attention than most. All you
have to do is step out of your own way and believe in it. There will
be things you know without reason or proof. You'll see things that
should be impossible for you to see. Don't be afraid. Embrace it.
You have more power than you can even imagine. You have more
to learn, and I can teach you.

The letter had come a little late. Starting that school year, my head had already begun spinning with images—I think it was something about all those bodies and hopes and worries crammed so close together. That was the year that Des started me in the shop after school and on weekends, when she decided to call me the Great Clara Voyant. Sometimes ideas and images came to me with the suddenness and clarity of magic, but most of the time it meant observing, thinking, trying to understand who someone was the old-fashioned way—watching them and waiting for them to reveal a particular desire or wish. To be honest, it had a lot in common with what Des taught me about stealing: understanding where a person's attention was, how much you could get away with, what to do if it went wrong.

I ran the tip of my tongue over my gums and winced as I imagined how much force it would take to knock a tooth loose.

The hair on the windowsill was red as a wound against the white paint. The morning was already hot, the air close and thick. But the drowsy, unreal feeling that had pervaded my days was gone. My senses were alert, my attention sharpened to worry. I wondered what exactly I had opened myself up to, what I had asked for.

DES ROSE at eleven, bleary-eyed and smelling like the club: baby oil, stale beer. It took her a while to get ready, to arrange her hair to hide the hickey on her neck, before we could go try our luck at the spa again.

We walked toward the jitney stop at Bally's, and on the way Des stopped to reach into a tourist's tote bag as the woman paused in front of the salt water taffy shop. Des was too slow and the woman felt her, wheeled on her heels.

"What the fuck?"

"Oh, it's such a pretty bag, I didn't want to bother you, just wanted to see if it was real leather." She put her hand on the woman's elbow, her smile sickly sweet, and the woman smiled back.

"It's actually from Target," she said.

"Get out of here," Des shrieked. "You'd never know!"

"Fucking piece of cheap trash," Des said, and huffed, as soon as we were out of hearing range. I could tell she was embarrassed. Maybe it was the hangover, or maybe she was losing her touch. Either way, I knew better than to say anything. We passed a poster of Julie Zale in the window of the arcade. *I should find a way to return the bandana*, I thought. Track down the uncle or put it in the mail. The air was so thick it was hard to breathe, and I felt that same tightness in my throat.

We weren't on the jitney for more than a minute when the tingle crept into my forehead, soft and slow, before it moved down my neck, to my shoulders. I heard music: that Bruce Springsteen song that people around here played all the time, that I couldn't help but know the words to. It was about being in love with a Jersey Girl, Springsteen's voice crackling through a staticky radio. A song about dancing all night, holding hands under the spangle of carnival lights. About how being in love made everything else seem okay. I looked around as the music got louder, then so loud that my ears throbbed.

"I wish he'd turn that down."

Des jumped and dug her nails into my arm. "Jesus! Turn *what* down? Why are you yelling?"

"Shit. Nothing," I said, trying to lower my voice, even though I couldn't hear myself over the wail of the saxophone. I leaned my head against the window, closed my eyes. The jitney smelled sour, like lemon cleaning solution, but for a moment I felt sun and fresh, cool air on my face. I was filled with a thrilling sense of speed, and of hope. I tasted caramel on my teeth.

The song fading to a tinny whine in my ears, I opened my eyes as the jitney lurched to a stop outside of the casino entrance. After I stepped off the bus, I stood in the sunlight and looked around, but there wasn't anyone else nearby, aside from the hot dog vendor who clanked his metal tongs against his cart. I dug the heels of my palms into my eyes. What had I done with that spell?

"What's with you?" Des asked. "This was your idea. I need you to be focused."

"Give me a second. I . . . I feel carsick."

"You don't get carsick."

I didn't want to tell Des about any of it. That I had done a spell in the first place. That I thought it might have worked, that now I was seeing things, hearing things, tasting things that I didn't understand. Des applied another coat of red lip gloss, air kissed the little circle of her compact mirror. Her mouth had the hard, wet sheen of patent leather. The song finally went quiet, but I didn't like the way Des was looking at me. Like I was making her nervous. I felt something against my thigh, a quick brush of sensation, like a bit of string or a hair stuck to the skin, but when I looked down there was nothing there. Des watched me scratch at it. I felt it again, on my shoulder blade, but ordered myself not to move.

"Okay," I said. "Let's go." I pushed the song and the skin-crawling feeling and the bloodied tooth from my mind, shook my hair from its ponytail, and we stepped inside, the dim of the casino familiar and cool.

LILY

WHEN I WOKE BEFORE MY first day at the spa, my throat felt strained, as though I'd been trying to scream in my sleep. My heart zinged, and I couldn't catch my breath. I tried to focus on the details of my bedroom, the inventory of familiar things: my old bookcases along the wall, lined with paperbacks. The watercolors I'd done in high school hung over the desk. The red ladder-backed chair that had once belonged to my great aunt. I could hear my mother moving through the kitchen below me, the whistle of the teakettle and the creak of her opening cabinets. I rose and sipped a glass of water. After a few minutes my breathing slowed to normal, but heat lingered in the tips of my ears, my cheeks.

I got in the shower and lowered myself to the floor, rested my head on my knees. I didn't have much time to spare—it was a twenty-minute drive from Margate through Ventnor to Atlantic City—but I closed my eyes and let the water hit the back of my neck. I had been the same way after my dad died: anxious and jumpy during the day, grinding my teeth in my sleep. It took all my strength to stand up and lather shampoo in my hair.

After the shower I washed my face, brushed mascara on my eyelashes, and a memory surged up: the last time Steffanie and I got ready together to get into the club at the Taj Mahal. Sixteen years old, taking swigs from a Poland Spring bottle filled with Stoli while her parents packed for a weekend trip to Cape May. I shook my head. Over the past few weeks my brain had gone vulnerable, all of my worst memories coming to the surface. I hadn't thought of that night in years. As I swished blush over my cheeks in a lazy arc, I remembered how painstaking we had been with our makeup and clothes that night. Then Steffanie's face a few hours later, bloodless, with black makeup smeared around her eyes. Her legs sticking out from underneath the bathroom stall, and how I knew they were hers because it had been field hockey preseason and I could make out the tan lines from our shin guards, pale shins and browned knees. I pushed the image away and pulled a brush through my hair.

You are only pretending, I told myself as I stepped into my pants, slid into the cheap black blazer I'd found at T.J.Maxx. Pretending to live at home for a few months. Pretending to care about this receptionist job. Pretending that New York and everyone in it didn't exist for now. Yet before I left I slipped on a little freshwater pearl bracelet that my grandmother had given me when I graduated from high school. I hadn't worn it in years but maybe it would bring me luck. Even if I was just pretending, I had, for better or worse, inherited my father's penchant for superstition, and with the way my thoughts were tilting, I needed all the help I could get.

I EXPECTED to see Emily at the desk again, but instead I was greeted by Deidre. She told me she usually took it upon herself to oversee training personally, as she liked to instill the spa's values into new hires. Though the things I learned from her couldn't be called values, exactly: more like dictums, or threats. *Never cross your arms in front of your chest. Never say "hi" instead of "hello." Never say "you're welcome"—it's always "my pleasure."*

At the spa, there was no hint that beauty could be dangerous, could be seen as a prize ripe to be seized. Instead, as Deidre
toured me through the spaces, I saw that everything about the spa
had the air of the sacrosanct, of mystery and ritual. The wall of
little glass vials of scrums, which were dispensed with droppers,
like medicine or poison. The sauna, with its cedary smell and
hard, bare benches that seemed built for prayer or penitence, the
vaguely threatening glow of the red coals in the corner. The bar
of teas and glass jars full of trail mix, banana chips round and
pale, like communion wafers.

We passed the ladies' restrooms on the way through the
women's lounge, and I found that I couldn't escape the thoughts
of Steffanie, even here. Her attacker had dropped her underwear
into the toilet bowl, a bloom of pink lace under a murk of water-
logged toilet paper. Earlier that night we'd felt admitted to a new
kind of existence, as the bouncers eyed our obviously fake IDs
and still slashed Xs on the backs of our hands with black marker,
and when the bartender poured us each a double shot of rum for
the price of a single. The memory made me dig my nails into my
palms. The world was always conspiring to make young women
vulnerable while labeling it as "fun." Made it seem like we were
in control, like we were making all the choices, and then it was
our fault when things went wrong. Us and our short skirts, our
makeup, our taste for rum, for liking the things we were told to
like, wanting what we were taught to want.

Deidre led me out to the lobby again, and I was relieved to
see that Emily had arrived. "Lily, I'll leave you in Emily's capable
hands for the time being. She will walk you through check-in
and scheduling procedures. At two o'clock please come to my office, and we will review the material from the training manual,
including etiquette, preferred language, and wardrobe expec-
tations. And please, for your next shift take care to apply some
powder."

"I will," I said, flushing as I brought my fingers to my forehead. Emily and I were silent as we listened to Deidre *click click click* away.

"So, you're here after all. Brave of you to join us. How's your morning with the Skeletor been?"

"Oh. She's not that bad . . ." I was already thinking of Deidre's bony wrists, how her upper arm was so narrow I could probably close my pointer finger and thumb around it.

"Bullshit," she said, smiling. Her real smile, as far as I could tell, was slyer than the one she saved for Deidre. Mouth closed, eyes crinkled, a slight wrinkling of her nose. "If by *not bad* you mean totally sadistic, sure. Anyway, if I'm supposed to show you check-in, let's get to it." She tapped a button on the keyboard in front of her, and the computer screen came to life. "Our software is from like 1994, so it sucks. This company invests everything in product research and marketing so they probably won't upgrade during either of our tenures here. For now we will just have to deal. Here's the check-in screen. Notice anything?"

I did. There was a lot of blank space next to each time slot.

"No one's coming in today. Mondays are the worst, but we are underbooked in a big way, even on the weekends. I think they should really be focusing on creating a more approachable brand image, attract younger clientele. But what do I know. I'm just chipping away at my BA one lousy class at a time. Anyway, enough about this joint. What's your deal? You new in town?"

"Sort of. I grew up here, lived in New York for a few years, now I'm back. Living in Margate with my mom."

"Jesus, why the hell would you come back?"

"Breakup." I didn't want to go through the whole story with Emily. She was so self-possessed. I risked becoming her counterpoint: a ridiculous hysteric, babbling about betrayal and performance art. *Breakup*. The word was so simple that it felt untrue.

"That's rough. Still should have stayed in the city."

"It wasn't . . . it wasn't really an option. What about you?"

"From a flyover state. Religious family. Ran away from all that shit, clearly. Went to L.A. when I was eighteen and tried to find work as an actress."

"Did you ever get any roles?"

"Some soft-core porn, but other than that, nothing. Waited in a lot of lines to try out for Coke commercials." She drummed her fingers on the counter. "I'm just kidding about the porn, you know. Thought about it but it actually doesn't pay shit. Not unless you're willing to let someone fuck you up the ass on camera, and you don't even get much for that. Oh, and speaking of cameras, you should know that Skeletor is crazy enough to actually review the footage—when she's not back there in her office watching it live."

She took me by the shoulders, forced me to pivot, and gave me a little shove.

"There. Memorize this spot right here. If you hold your phone out six inches, the cameras won't be able to see what you are doing, only that you are standing here reaching for something." She crouched, reached around my knee, swung a cabinet door open. "And here, behind the gift certificate boxes. That's where you'll want to stash any contraband. Soda, candy, gum, pills—whatever your jam is."

"Pills?"

"Hey, whatever gets you through the day. Anyway, you get one free meal in the cafeteria every shift, but they use the same vendor as that prison over in Delmont. That's all to say you'll want snacks. But whatever you do, don't buy a hot dog from that guy with the cart out front. I made that mistake when I was new and I shat my brains out for three days straight."

The guffaw I let out surprised me. I didn't recognize it as my own right away—it'd been so long since I'd really laughed.

Emily shrugged. "Just trying to tell you what I've learned the hard way."

AS EMILY went over the phone system I watched as a girl hanging on a man's arm left the Swim Club and walked toward the main lobby, her limbs loose. She leaned her head on his shoulder like it was too heavy to hold up. When the police questioned me about Steffanie's attacker, I tried to remember his face and his clothes through the haze of rum, the darkness of the club, and the fog that rolled out of machines, the buzz in my ears from the throb of the bass, but I couldn't say anything definitive. Had his shirt been gray or blue? His eyes brown or green? I remembered him as an outline: broad shoulders, muscular arms, a paper cutout of a man. I wasn't surprised that they never found him. I never mentioned to anyone that I had watched her leave the dance floor with him, and when I saw her stumble, I told myself it was only because of her heels. Or that she swayed into his shoulder on purpose. One of those girlish tricks we were always reading about in *Cosmo*: *make him feel needed*. I let myself believe that she was in control, that she wanted him to put his arm around her, so that she could have an excuse to get close to him and press against his side.

Steffanie quit the field hockey team after that night, and whenever we passed one another in the halls at school she gave me a look that I could only call pity—like there was something plain and obvious between us that I didn't understand.

All of it felt tied together—the spa and its rules about how we were allowed to act and look, Steffanie, Ramona. I thought back to the night Ramona showed me her first large-scale paintings, when I was trying to woo her to sign with me as my first client. The one I liked the most was of a woman reclined on a divan. In the background there were bouquets of flowers laced with razor blades, wolves or dogs baring their teeth. The woman's skin, pale with a blue cast to it, seemed to glow. Her nipples were midnight blue, her belly button cobalt, her pubic hair navy. We talked about what it meant to be a woman, to be looked at all the time, judged and measured and punished in a thousand different ways every day, to feel both undermined and empowered by your body. I thought we had agreed on something. I'd been wrong.

EMILY WAS teaching me how to process gift certificate sales when I looked up and saw two women making their way toward the spa.

I noticed their hair first as they came around the bend in the hall, the same jarring red on both of them. Not a natural red, but the color you'd get out of a Kool-Aid packet, concentrated and fruity. Ripe. Even from that distance their bodies hummed with want. They had the flashing, attentive eyes of stray dogs, of scavengers. I couldn't tell right away what they were hungry for. All I knew was that they seemed more intense, more alive, than anyone else around them. Next to them, the other casino patrons seemed as inanimate as furniture: the tripod stances of old men resting on their canes, the woolly-haired women pushing through on their walkers, the ends of the metal legs capped with tennis balls. It was in the way they moved down the long hallway, switching their matching boys' hips, narrow and square. Their tangled gold necklaces and clanking bracelets. The thick wedges of eyeliner that made them look haughty and exotic and bored, high priestesses displeased by their retinue. Right away I could recognize that part of that magic had to do with sex: their long legs exposed in tiny pairs of denim shorts, their concave midriffs revealed in crop tops, the WonderBra cleavage edged with lace. But they had something else, too, something interior, something the spa was trying to promise people could be found in a bottle of expensive serum or in a series of treatments. It was the particular confidence of knowing who you were and of knowing what you wanted. I recognized it right away because I'd lost it. Or maybe I'd never had it at all.

Emily paused, having felt my attention drift. She must have followed my stare. "Oh God, those two. And on your first day. Well, you better start getting used to this shit."

"Who are they?" The two redheads flipped their hair, pouted. They clearly relished the attention, even the looks that they got from the women nearby, women wearing terry-cloth visors and pleated khaki shorts cut to the knee. Women who sneered as they passed but then looked down at the paper cones of french fries in their hands with a little less pleasure than before.

"Scam artists, as far as we're concerned. One of them will try to read you your cards while the other slips products into her purse, or they buy a day pass and try to hustle the few clients we've got. You have to keep a close eye on them; they'll take any-thing and everything while you've got your back turned. Last time they were here the younger one managed to pry the hair-dryer off the wall in the ladies' lounge."

"How often do they come in?"

"Not as much as they used to. Deidre blacklisted them so we can call security if they refuse to leave. This is the first time they've been back since. I think they've got another hustle going on. Drugs or prostitution, probably. A few weeks ago I watched the older one flirting with this guy at the Swim Club, kept putting her hand on his leg, laughing at his jokes. Or maybe she stole his wallet."

I must have looked surprised.

"Oh, come on, didn't you say you grew up here? That kind of stuff happens all the time."

"Sure," I said. "I know that." But it still gave me the chills to think about it.

From far away the women had looked to be the same age, but I could see through the spa's door that one of them was older than I had first thought and the other much younger, just a girl.

"Hello, sunshine," the older one said, greeting Emily. "Long time no see. And look! You've got a new friend."

"Des, this is Lily. And she's not going to put up with any of your bullshit either, so don't even try."

The woman, Des, held out her hand. Up close I could see that her face was caked with makeup that had settled into the lines around her mouth, her eyes. She wore so much mascara that her eyelashes matted together in five distinct spikes. The younger one had wandered over to the magazines arranged on the coffee table. She picked one up, flipped through a few pages, and rubbed a perfume sample on her wrist. When I shook Des's hand, she clasped her other hand on top of mine and squeezed. It felt strange to be touched with such tenderness and intent by someone I had just met.

"Ooh, pretty!" she said, fingering my bracelet hungrily. I pulled my hand away.

"Okay, seriously, Desmina, beat it," Emily said. "Deidre is here today, and she won't hesitate to call security on you. Neither will I, for that matter."

Desmina turned to me wearing an exaggerated pout. "I'm so glad you're here. See how mean she is to me? And most of the time we just want to come by for a quick visit, a little chat." She turned over her shoulder. "Clara, come meet our new friend, Lily."

The girl looked up from her magazine and stared at me. Her mouth parted a little, and a strange blankness came over her face, like she had been waiting for a bus for a long time or watching a run of late-night infomercials on TV.

"Is she okay?" I asked.

"Oh, she's fine. She gets like this when she's having a vision, is all."

"A vision?" I asked. I felt Emily sigh.

"What? Your girlfriend here didn't tell you? She's doing you and us a disservice. We are the best psychic duo on the East Coast.

Ah!" She pointed one long-nailed finger at me. "You are intrigued. I can always tell." I hated that she was right.

"That doesn't make you psychic, Desmina," Emily said, rolling her eyes. "It just means you're not blind."

Clara's face had resumed its normal expression, and she skipped over to the desk, linked her arm with Des's—they had to be related, but I couldn't puzzle out how. Mother and daughter? Cousins? With her other arm she wriggled a business card out of the tiny front pocket of her jean shorts. She held it out to me. *Clara Voyant*, it said. *Seer and Fortune Teller.*

"Clara's the psychic, really. I have a different set of talents."

Emily coughed. "I'll bet."

Clara was silent, still staring at me. Nervous, I reached for a canister of pens, straightened them just to have something to do with my hands.

"So, Miss Lily, as a gesture of friendship, what do you say you give us a pass to the spa for the afternoon and in exchange, we'll read your palm."

"I'll do it," Clara said. She pulled on my wrist and turned my hand over, pinning it to the top of the desk.

"This is insane," Emily said. "You two don't leave in the next thirty seconds, I'm calling security. We are a private business, and we don't need to serve you."

Clara didn't look up but stroked my skin with her fingertips so softly that it tickled and I flinched. Both women giggled.

"Ah," she said, her catlike eyes scrunched in concentration. She pet my palm as though it were wounded. "You are recovering from a broken heart." I felt my face go hot. I pulled my hand away and crossed my arms behind my back.

"Well, aren't we all?" Emily said. "Especially around here." She pointed out the glass to the hallway, where an old man shuffled toward the swimming pool. "He's heartbroken. And her, too." She pointed at a woman on a jazzy scooter speeding in the direction of the buffet. "And her, too. I'm sure of it," she said, about the housekeeper pushing a cart of toilet paper in the direction of the restrooms. "And I am, too, for that matter. Heart break is the human condition in this town. Hell, on Earth. I don't need a psychic to tell me that. Come back when you've got something better."

Perhaps Deidre had, as Emily warned, been keeping an eye on the security footage. We all heard the *click click click* of her heels coming toward us. Des made for the door, her gold earrings clattering as she flipped her hair over her shoulder. Clara stepped toward me, crooked a finger, and beckoned me to lean forward. She cupped her hand around my ear, her breath warm on my earlobe as she whispered, "You've suffered a reversal in fortune. You've been through a tremendous amount of pain. You're lost, and you like having plans, knowing your way. I can help."

The jolt started in my tailbone, zinged up my spine. I tried to tell myself that it was just a good guess, that everyone could look at their lives and point to loss or pain. She could have said the same thing to Emily, who would have found her own truth in the—what? Prophecy? Even supplying that word in my head made me feel foolish. But what she had said seemed personal. I felt pulled between naïveté and skepticism—an arrow shot in two directions at once.

She backed away and the corners of her mouth tugged up into a smile. "Come to the shop and we can talk some more. The address is on the card. Boardwalk and Baltic." She turned away just as Deidre rounded the partition of frosted glass. Her mouth hardened when she saw Clara skipping away and Des slipping through the door. From the other side of the glass, Des blew Deidre a kiss and leaned over to exaggerate her cleavage. It took all my effort not to smirk.

Deidre made a sound of displeasure, cleared her throat. "Emily, I take it you've let Lily know about those two? Shrinkage has been quite high in this location in particular, and I would guess that they account for approximately half of it."

"I have," Emily said. "I don't think they managed to make off with anything this time. I kept my eyes on them. It helps to have two of us up here."

"Good. Lily, why don't you come with me to my office and we can review the manual and go over any questions you have regarding what you've learned so far."

"Sure," I said. My voice came out quiet, faint. I was surprised to feel a tear leak from my eye, and I hurried to wipe it away before Deidre could see. It was only then that I noticed that something felt different, lighter, and I pulled at the sleeve of my blazer to confirm it.

My bracelet was gone. Clara and Desmina were even better thieves than Emily gave them credit for.

THE DAY had left me ragged, aching for a drink, and after my mother went to bed I walked four blocks to the local dive, Maynard's, that I used to sneak into when I was a teenager. Inside, it smelled like stale beer and the sea, the whole place scummed with mildew and salt. When I sat on a stool near the door, the cracked upholstery scratched my thighs. It wasn't until my first drink arrived that I dared to look around. Right away a familiar pair of eyes snagged on mine: Brett Griffin. We had graduated in the same class in high school. He'd been that stoner-sage kid who slept through geometry yet aced every exam. He rose from his stool and slid his beer glass along the bar top.

"Lily Louten! Well, well, well. Long time no see! How's my sophomore year history buddy?"

"Hey, Brett. I'm fine." It hadn't even occurred to me when I left the house, but of course I couldn't have lasted one night at Maynard's without seeing someone I had gone to school with.

Brett settled onto the stool next to mine. I concentrated on the scrim of bumper stickers that had accumulated on the mirror behind the bar. *This Car Climbed Mount Washington, Welcome to Sea Isle City!*

"What are you doing here? In town for a visit?"

"For the summer."

"Wait, don't tell me you're a teacher, too? I'm doing eighth grade math at Bellevue. Thirteen and fourteen-year-olds are sort of insane, but I love it. Well, most days, you know. I could do without all the state testing bullshit."

"No, not teaching. I'm taking some time off right now. Figuring out what's next." I couldn't help but cringe at the way I was crutching along on platitudes. But it was easier than the truth: That I had crept home with nothing. That I didn't know who I was anymore.

"Last I heard you were doing some art stuff. Museums? Wait, no. You wanted to run one of those galleries or something! That was your thing, right? I always envied that about you. You were one of those people who just knew what you were going to do."

I finished the bourbon and signaled the bartender for another pour. "Well, you can rest easy. I'm not sure I have anything to envy anymore."

"No, man, it was cool. You were ambitious. I used to see the stuff you were doing on, like, Facebook, and it made me happy, you know? I know we weren't super-close or anything, but it was fun to see it. At all those fancy openings, all those paintings you'd post about. So you're not into art anymore?"

I willed Brett to get a phone call, run into someone else he knew. He meant well, but we were circling questions I wasn't ready for. All I knew was that I wanted to forget what had happened in New York, sock away enough cash to boomerang out of town at the end of the summer, and start over as someone new.

"You know, I'm trying to think of the last time I saw you," he said.

I knew right away. Steffanie's funeral. He remembered a second too late.

"Oh, shit. Yeah. Man. I'm sorry. You guys had been so close."

"Nothing to be sorry for."

"She was one of the first. I think there's something like ten kids from our class who have died from that shit?"

"Yeah, that sounds right."

"Ten, in a class of three hundred kids. Fucking heroin. I look at my eighth graders and I just worry about them so much—you never know what growing up is going to do to you, especially around here. AC, man, it gets into the way you think. You live somewhere where people come to get wasted and blow all their cash—you start to think that's how the rest of the world is, that that's what life is."

Try being a girl here, I wanted to say, *that will really fuck you up*. But of course I didn't. Mostly I was touched. His earnestness, that slow, surfery cadence to his voice. Brett took a long, thoughtful sip of his beer, and this time we both looked away.

"Well, I've got to run and meet some people, but hey, hope I see you around." He slapped me on the back, and as he left I felt a twist of guilt and relief. I was so self-pitying, and yet, look at all of the people who Brett and I knew who had sunk into depths I couldn't even imagine. When I blinked, I saw Steffanie's gaunt cheeks. I signaled the bartender for a third drink and willed the room to go hazy, for all the din and clatter to get reduced to one low hum, waited for my mind to go blank. The less I noticed about what was around me, the less I felt.

When I paid my bill, I found Clara's card in my wallet and stared at it as though it would help explain what she had said that afternoon. It was one of the last things I remembered before I blacked out—*you are recovering from a broken heart*, those crooked little crescent moons.

LUIS

HE SEES HER IN THE morning, during his shift. She's at the desk with the other girl, and her face is a face he knows, but he can't say why. It's the feeling of seeing someone in a photograph and then again, in another, wearing different clothes, their body in a new position, but still that thing that lights up about them, that says SAME SAME SAME. He watches her as he cleans the glass, when he walks past her on his way to lunch, when he comes back. He's studied so many women's faces, hands, teeth, hair, elbows, eyelashes. The shape of their jaws and the curves of their ears and the swish of their pony-tails and the dots of freckles on their noses and cheeks and arms. He stores her away in his brain, her dark brown hair and her brown eyes the color of chocolate. Her pale skin and the arches of her eyebrows.

After he clocks out, he waits around for a chance to look at her up close, but she doesn't come into the back hall, where all of the other women keep their things. He knows this will continue to bother him until he sorts it out, the itch of an understanding that's being withheld. His fingers curl into a fist.

HE'S ON his way home, to the boardinghouse, when he sees the men walking in his direction, on the opposite side of the street. The sight of their silhouettes gives him a squirming feeling in his guts, like he's eaten something bad. He stops and wonders whether he should turn around and circle the block or try to slip into a store until they pass, but before he can decide, the man with the shaved head cuts his eyes right to where Luis stands. He taps the dark-haired one on the arm, and smiles, his teeth so big and white and square they shine at him with mean delight—save for one of the teeth, which glints coppery-gold. They cross toward him, their chains thumping against their chests, and Luis braces for what's next. He could try to run, but last time they caught him, and it only made things worse. There's a cop car parked in front of a bodega, windows down, but the cops just watch and never help. Gold Tooth runs into him hard, in the chest, so hard that his teeth crash against one another. The dark-haired one grabs his arm tight, the way you might do to a friend, then closes his grip until it shoots a pain into his shoulder. He jerks his arm away, shakes his head, *no*. It's been like this for months now, ever since one of them caught Luis staring at a woman in a tight pink dress. She had reminded him of someone he knew once, a daughter of his grandmother's friend, but there was no way to tell them that. The next thing he knew, the men were shoving him to the ground, kicking him in the ribs. That's how it's become around here—there are certain women who belong to men, women who are owned.

The cops come out of the bodega with paper cups of coffee, see the scuffle, smile, and shake their heads. One of the officers calls out to them, which makes the other one throw his head back and laugh. He tries again to pass, but Gold Tooth hooks a foot behind Luis's knees, sends him crashing to the ground. Luis looks over at the cops, who stare at him, smiling. More rage surges through his limbs, and he extends a leg and kicks the bald man in the ankle. He knows to brace for it—bam—another slap upside the head. His jaw slides sideways. His temple throbs, and his whole spine feels bruised.

The men leave him on the sidewalk and one of the cops spits a chewed piece of gum out the window. Even with their eyes masked behind mirrored glasses, Luis can tell that they're laughing at him, the corners of their mouths curling up. His heart flutters like a bird trapped in his chest.

He brushes the gravel out of his palms. Out of the corner of his eye he sees a needle in the gutter, a busted plastic lighter, a shimmering film of cellophane. He shudders, stands, brushes more gravel from the knees of his pants. He's been thinking of ways to avoid the men and the cops who do nothing. But what he wants most is violence, to take a swing at those big, stupid grins, grind their faces into the ground, a swift kick to each of their guts. But he knows what would happen then: his hands twisted behind his back, the silver cuffs biting into his wrists. The rules are different for him. And it wouldn't be his first arrest—in the spring he was caught in the parking garage of the old Taj Mahal. They must have thought he was up to something bad, but he was only curious. What it looked like empty of all those cars. It makes him feel better to think it, that they don't know the half of it—if only they knew how often he is somewhere he isn't supposed to go. If only they knew how frequently he made himself invisible, how closely he could watch.

As he limps home, he thinks about the way the whole city is dying around anyone who is left; slowly, though, like a large animal falling to its knees. All he can see are the ghosts of the places they used to go when he was a boy. The shop where his grandmother bought meat for the week, the one where his grandfather bought him his first bike. He can still remember when the boardwalk was lined with old hotels, beautiful redbrick and decorations that reminded him of frosting on a cake. His grandfather had brought him to the beach to watch as one of the bigger ones was destroyed. He and his grandfather pressed up against the plastic fence and watched the old hotel slide out from under itself, bloom into a cloud of rubble and dust. Other people around him covered their ears. He felt the crash of brick and walls and roof move up from the ground, through his bones, into his jaw. Five years after that he watched another one get smashed by a giant metal ball, but by then neither of his grandparents were alive to watch with him.

Then, the casinos rose up with their horrible red lights that blare through the night sky, their dark insides, their huge, gray slabs of concrete. They teemed with people for a time, but now the people haven't come, not like before. Now the movie theater has closed, the letters dropped from its marquee. Forgotten playgrounds with rusted merry-go-rounds, swings that hang from one chain. There are fewer visitors, and more litter in the streets. He feels inside of him what it means to have grown up here. Another thing that has seeped into him and made him all wrong on the inside. It's in his hands, his blood, in his bones.

The next morning he senses the soreness before he opens his eyes. He's older now and feels things in ways he didn't use to. The injuries linger, stay in his skin. There have always been the men and the cops like this in his life, people who will use the way his voice is trapped in him against him. People who think it means he's stupid, that he moves through the world not just deaf and mute, but blind and numb. He goes into work feeling tired, battered, and bruised, his anger glowing in him like a hot coal. Once again he tries to puzzle out where he's seen the girl before. It chafes at him, but he knows that doesn't matter. He'll get it right eventually.

For now he'll only watch and wait.

CLARA

I TOOK THE BRACELET BECAUSE I could, but also because I wanted to make sure that girl Lily came to see me. I had a feeling about her, something about the way she looked at me, the way what I told her changed her posture, the way she flinched and then relaxed when I leaned close to touch her hand. I could use her. She could be our way in at the spa, if I played things right. She would probably be angry about the bracelet at first, but I was sure I could work on her, get her on our side. That guy she worked with noticed me take it—the janitor. I had seen him in town enough to know there was something off about him, too. Always skulking around on his own. I didn't usually slip up like that, leave a witness, but I could spot someone with secrets and I figured he'd keep mine.

The next morning, Des clunked down the stairs, and I could tell she was going to see her dealer. She had her shirt tied up above her belly button, knotted at the narrowest part of her waist, and her hair was brushed to a glossy sheen.

"Do we have any readings scheduled for today?" I asked.

"I think you probably already know the answer to that. But hey, take those business cards and hand them out, drum up a bit of publicity. Only don't do it in Bally's. I think security has flagged us over there." Sooner or later I would lose track of all the places we weren't allowed to go. "Why do you look so sullen? You don't want to hand out the business cards? Fine by me. Besides, things are looking up for us. I think I've lined up your first date."

I ignored her. I didn't want to know anything about this date.

"I'll hand out the cards," I said, and grabbed the stack from the counter.

Des ruffled my hair. "This color looks so hot on you, babes."

When she walked away, I felt again for the spiky hair at the base of my skull. I was still confused about the visions, but it felt good to have a secret, a piece of my life that she had no hand in.

I shoved the business cards in my purse but stopped in the arcade before handing them out. I played a round of Skee-Ball, rolling the scarred wooden balls up the ramp, arching them into the targets, stopping to listen to the dumb trill of the music that played when you hit the ten-thousand-point mark. The machine spit out a strip of pale pink tickets, which I carried to the counter in the back. The woman who worked there knew me, though she and I never talked much. She looked like she was in her sixties, with brown hair that was white at the temples and skin pale and doughy from all the time she spent inside.

Once, I'd had a vision as I stood in front of her, a quick flash: an old woman embroidering a design into a piece of cloth stretched taut in a hoop. A lot of the things I saw were violent, or sad, but sometimes they were straightforward. Sometimes what I saw was even comforting. I didn't know how it worked, exactly—what bits of a life came to me, how certain memories sifted to the top and opened up to me. It was another thing I wanted my mother to teach me. How to see what I wanted to, and how to keep out or let go of what I didn't want—or was afraid—to know. My "gift" still felt bigger than me, a force that moved through and around me like weather. Maybe one day it would make me feel powerful—if I could ever get it under control.

I pushed my tickets toward the woman, and she produced a bin of flimsy metal rings with plastic jewels at the center and a box of chocolate poker chips from the glass prize case. I pointed to the candy and she counted out four of them, paused, then reached in and added one more piece to the pile. I unwrapped one and let the chocolate melt slowly on my tongue. On my way out I tucked a business card into the screen of a Mortal Kombat console.

I held out cards to anyone I passed, chanting *Tarot cards palm reading, tarot cards palm reading* until the words lost their meaning, my mouth just making the same shapes over and over again. I watched people take cards then drop them on the ground a few steps later. At first, I tried to look people in the eye, tried to show them something about myself: That I was, like Des said, the real deal. That they could trust me. That I wanted to help. Some people took them, thinking it was an offer for a free drink or free Italian ice, like the other shops handed out, and then crumpled the cards in their palms.

After an hour of walking I still had more than half of the cards to give away. I stopped in front of the darkened doors of the Taj Mahal, where signs warned against trespassing. Des and I had gone to the liquidation sale, before they closed their doors for good. Men loaded the chandeliers into moving trucks and workers pried light fixtures off the walls. In every room, tables were stacked with empty cocktail glasses and giant serving platters, shelves full of clothing irons and telephones, piles of Bibles shucked from the drawers of bedside tables, and towers of metal champagne buckets. In another room, a cluster of disco balls sparkled in a corner. An entire hallway was lined with mattresses from the hotel, most of them covered in stains. It made me realize how easily the casinos, places I thought were fixed and permanent, could be reduced to debris.

I turned around to walk south again. A drunk man slurred at me—*Heyyy, baby*—and a pair of women shook their heads as

I approached, as though I was holding out a spider or a mouse. I thought I had imagined it when I heard a girlish voice calling my name. "Ava? Ava?" After the jitney ride yesterday, I second-guessed everything I heard.

They were leaning along the rails, passing a bottle of pink lemonade between them. Lucy Ellison, Noelle Cohen, and Nina Wright. We had gone to middle school together, until their parents sent them to private schools inland. We hadn't been friends, exactly—Noelle and Nina lived in Margate, in large houses with fountains in the front yards and high iron fences, and they always hung out together after school. Lucy lived in Marvin Gardens, in a pink Spanish-style house with her parents and two standard poodles—her life looked like something from a storybook. Des never wanted to give me bus fare, so I never met up with them on the weekends or after school, and after a while they stopped inviting me.

"I almost didn't recognize you. Your hair," Noelle said. She passed the bottle to Lucy, who grimaced when she took a sip—not just lemonade.

"Yeah," I said. "It's different."

"How's Atlantic City High?" Lucy asked. "Do girls really throw bleach at each other when they fight?"

"I heard there's a day care in the building, because so many girls have had babies," Noelle said.

"I—it's okay." It wasn't true, about the day care or about the bleach. But I didn't want to explain that I had dropped out. I'd had visions more frequently in school than anywhere else. It made me anxious, unable to concentrate. Des told me she wanted me to help out more in the shop, but it had been my idea to quit, once my sixteenth birthday came around and no one could report me to the state. I told myself it would just be easier that way.

"Want some?" Nina asked, holding out the bottle.

"What is it?" I asked.

"Some of my mom's vodka, with a packet of Crystal Light stirred in. Down here none of the cops even care, so we came to pregame."

I took the drink from her. It smelled like nail polish remover and SweeTarts. A ring of lip gloss shimmered around the mouth of the bottle. I took a sip, which made me cough. I had never had a drink before, but I hoped maybe it'd make me feel different—calmer or braver, or just less myself.

"What are those?" Lucy asked, reaching for my wrist. At first I thought she meant the pearls, but then she turned my palm over into hers, slid a business card out of my grip. My face got hot, and I could feel the mottled rash creep across my neck, the way it always did when I was embarrassed.

"Clara Voyant, Seer and Fortune Teller! Oh my god. Stop."

"It's just a . . . a project," I said. I thought of what Des had said the other day. My mother and I made the same face when we lied.

"What kind of project?" Her eyes gleamed with mean joy.

"Hard to explain."

"So you, like, tell people about their futures and stuff?" Nina asked.

"Oh! Do Noelle. Noelle, see if Ava knows whether Nick will finally ask you out."

"Shut up." Noelle elbowed Lucy in the ribs. "Nick Hart. You know him, Ava."

"Ava used to like Nick Hart!"

"No, I mean, maybe. He's fine. But I don't like him anymore, obviously." If only they knew what my life was like now—that in a few days I'd probably go out on a date with a strange, grown-up man. But for a second I let myself picture how Nick would look in the prep uniform, the navy blazer with brass buttons, a crisp blue button-down shirt the same color as his eyes.

"You and Ava have to duke it out, Noelle," Nina said.

Noelle's smile was small, catlike. "We'll probably see him at the party tonight. Actually, we should get going. I gotta do my hair."

"Yeah, I need to get home, too," I said. Around these girls, I felt like a sliver of myself. Maybe because they had known a different version of me: quiet, mousy brown hair, good at math. They could see the ways I'd changed, the versions of myself that I had left behind. That itchy, tingling feeling crept up my stomach, and I rubbed at my shirt, hoping they wouldn't see.

Noelle and Nina whispered back and forth to one another. Nina giggled. "You should come with us," Lucy said, which made Noelle snort.

"Really, I've got to go. Have fun, though." I hated them, their stupid, perfect, easy lives.

My face burned as I walked on. I turned once to see the girls recede down the boardwalk, their ponytails swinging. Noelle held up my card and the three of them exploded into laughter. I stomped to the closest trash can and threw the rest of the cards away, retreated to the shop without raising my eyes from the ground. Once I was back, I sat at the table, cutting the tarot deck and stacking it again, watching the people stream past, and out farther, to where the waves broke into white foam near the shoreline. Dark clouds collected in the sky above, and I pleaded for them to break into rain, but they blew past, and we were left with the skin-blistering heat.

The next day I was sitting at the table in the shop again—thinking about those messages I'd seen on Julie Zale's Facebook page—when I heard the *tap tap tap* on the doorframe, so faint that at first I thought I had imagined it. A woman stood behind the beaded curtain. I called to her to come in. "Are you here for a reading?"

Her face was younger than I'd thought it would be, based on her posture and the slumped, tired-seeming shadow she cast from behind the beads. She was pretty, petite, with straight blonde hair and big brown eyes that shifted around the room. In the light, I could see she had dark circles underneath them, like it had been weeks since she had slept well. She held out one of the business cards.

"I found this blowing down the street." Her voice was soft, with a trace of a Southern accent. The card trembled in her hands. She was afraid. Of what—who? Me?

I stood and pulled out a chair. She sat and fiddled with a silver locket around her neck, working her thumbnail into the charm so it opened just a sliver, then pinching it back into place with a tiny click.

"So you found the card. But you made the choice to visit. Why did you decide to come here today?"

She was quiet for so long that I wondered if she had heard me or if maybe she had only come in because she wanted a place to sit. I eyed her bag—a tooled leather purse with an oval-shaped piece of turquoise embedded in it—and immediately my mind went to the best way I could snatch her wallet. The clasp looked like it would slide open soundlessly. Then it was just a matter of getting under the flap and hoping her wallet was on top. She wasn't wearing any jewelry, other than the locket, though I noticed a pale space on her finger, maybe where a wedding band used to be. She was so distracted that it would have been easy. But I had a rule: no stealing from clients. Des might double-dip, but I tried to have a little more integrity, at least in the shop. I thought it was what my mother would want. Though I wondered if I had broken my own rule when I took Julie Zale's bandana.

I was trying to be patient but couldn't wait too long—that bag was calling to me. I had $200 saved, a long way from my goal. I was restless, watching her sit and stare. "There are benches out on the boardwalk, you know," I said.

"Huh?" Her mouth parted in surprise.

"If you're looking to rest. You seem tired."

"I'm sorry," she said. "I was wondering. Jesus. I was wondering about . . . maybe you could help me." I felt bad about snapping at her. Seeing those girls, Des mentioning that date, had messed with my mood. I made my voice soft again.

"Of course. I would be glad to help you. What are you hoping to find out?"

Her hand closed around her locket again, her fist swallowing up the heart-shaped charm.

"It's best to have a question in mind. It gives the reading focus. If you can't think of one, we could ask what you can expect for the next month or year." I tried to smile, to put her at ease, but by now she looked like she was going to be sick.

"You're just a kid," she said. "You're so young." Her hand crept across the table, as though she was going to touch me, but then she got up so fast that the chair tipped over. "I'm sorry. I'm sorry, but this was a mistake." She was almost out the door when she turned around, took a few steps toward the table, then pulled a ten-dollar bill from her purse and dropped it in front of me.

"But I didn't even do the reading," I said. "At least let me read your cards."

"I took your time. I'm sorry. I just . . . I'm sorry, I really am." She practically ran through the door and down the boardwalk, jostling a tourist holding a funnel cake, who turned to sneer at her back as she fled.

I felt guilty as I tucked the ten into my pocket, but I still took out my notebook, adjusted my savings: $210. Why had she run after all that? I was used to people being a little nervous around me, or embarrassed, like Julie Zale's uncle had been. But I wasn't used to people being scared. I cut the tarot deck, shuffled it three times, and pictured the woman again, the way her hand closed so tightly around that locket on her neck. It was the second time I had broken the rules—read cards for someone who hadn't exactly asked. But this woman hadn't come to me for no reason—she had found my card, she chose to come to the shop. And, she paid. Maybe the cards would tell me more about her, or at least I might learn what she sensed in the air, a fate she intuited but didn't want to see. I decided that would be my question for the cards. *What was she afraid to know?*

I chose a three-card spread—our standard reading. The first card represents the past. I drew the Four of Wands. Usually that card meant lovely things: Celebration. A harmonious home life. Family. Peace.

The second card, the present. King of Cups, reversed. It meant a lack of clarity, a lack of judgment and reason. "I could have told you that," I mumbled, and then felt unkind. The King of Cups usually was a sign that the emotions and the intellect were out of balance, that a person was swamped by their feelings, overwhelmed.

The third card is the future: the Seven of Swords. I always flinched at this one—it showed a thief creeping away, looking over his shoulder at someone catching him in the act. It meant you were going to try to sneak away from something, or it could be a warning that there was betrayal waiting for you ahead. It was a sign to trust your intuition if you suspected someone was going to wrong you. As far as I saw it, these cards were a warning. If they were accurate, then this woman's life had gone from stable to chaotic and was about to get worse.

I was always telling people that the cards weren't the future, necessarily—they were subtler than that. The cards were reminders that we could make choices, a reminder to look at your life and parse out how you needed to think about things, how you might act, what options were available to you. I didn't believe in fate coming down like a guillotine or sweeping you up out of your life like a hot air balloon. We were always somewhere in the middle: everyone had obstacles, but we also had free will.

If I saw the woman—I wished that I knew her name—again, I would warn her, but I'd have to tell her that, too: that she still had a choice.

A fly buzzed against the window of the shop, slow and drowsy in the heat. I realized what the feeling was, the one that had been creeping along my skin for days. It was the tickle of insect legs. I reached for a magazine, rolled it up, and smashed the fly against the glass. Its guts left behind a greasy smear. But a second later, I felt it again, the creep of a fly along the top of my ear, and when I reached to brush it away there was nothing there.

JANE 3

SHE CAN'T LOOK AT THE pictures on the slot machines—the pair of cherries joined at the stem with a single green leaf, the yellow sickle of a banana—without thinking of her daughter's picture books, the pages made of thick cardboard, the images simplified into the most perfect versions of themselves. The words she was supposed to read in a slow, sweet voice so the baby could repeat them back to her one day. She can't listen to the jingle of coins without thinking of the rattles she shook and shook above the baby's bassinet, pleading with her to be quiet. *Shhh, it's okay, it's okay, it's okay.*

But they both knew that it wasn't okay. The baby was right— she didn't know how to be a mother. Sometimes when her husband was at work, she let the baby cry and cry even if she wasn't doing anything but laying on the couch, watching poor people win things on daytime TV. Someone told her once that the biggest pawnshop in the world is right next door to where they film *The Price Is Right*—that they offer half of the value of whatever the contestants win. That's the kind of world she was bringing her daughter into, where getting more than you've been slated for is only an illusion, where someone else already has half a claim on your good luck. She couldn't make herself feel anything for the baby. When her husband asked about the diaper rash later, she lied. *Whose side are you on?* she thought at him. But she knew the answer to that.

She watches the slot machines whir from a stool in the corner of the bar, slowly sipping the house white wine she's allowed herself, even though her money is almost gone. The wine tastes like chilled vinegar, but she drinks it anyway.

It was stupid of her to blow $10 for a psychic reading she didn't even get. It means that tonight or tomorrow, she'll need to pick up a john. The thought makes her gulp the rest of the wine. She orders another and feels her options whittled down. A headache creeps into her temples, throbs along a fault line that splits the front of her forehead. After this second glass she's down to $9, and that's if she skimps on the tip. Tonight then. She should start looking for her next date. Some girls sleep with the manager of the Sunset Motel—Robert—in lieu of paying their room bill, but she's prided herself on always being able to cover that much, at least. It's a small thing, but she likes knowing she still has some kind of code.

She pictures Robert's stained Hanes T-shirt, always riding up to reveal a round, pale slice of belly, the acrid and stinging smell of his sweat, the compulsive way he licks his lips. She can tell he loves having something to hold over them—even a crumbling motel room that goes for $15 a night. Once, when she came upon him at the desk, his eyes were closed, and as she stepped closer she saw he had his hand on the back of a woman's head, his fingertips tense with pressure. He smiled up at her, pleased with himself, as though to say *One day I can demand this from you, too.* As she walked away, she imagined how the threadbare carpet must have bit into the woman's knees.

Thinking of this, of course she shouldn't have had the drinks, but she needs the buzz, the thing that makes the world go a little slant, so she can pretend that this new life is a fever she'll wake from, that one day she'll be returned to herself—whoever that

is anymore. Sometimes she puts a little money into the slots because it means free drinks: the waitresses will come around and
bring you cheap liquor, wine, or beer, but she's afraid she's too
familiar now. Most of them have caught on that she only plays a
buck or two, then milks it for four, five drinks at a time. Worse,
they could call security or even the cops, if they know she's here
picking up men. When she thinks back on the past few months it
is through the warped haze of a hangover, a blend of discomfort,
disgust, self hatred, but one that also feels slightly unreal.

Maybe that's why she ran away from the girl in the fortune-
teller's shop. At first the card had made her smile. The cheesy
illustrations, moons with eyes, the punny name. *Clara Voyant*. But
as she held it in her hand, it seemed more and more like an in-
vitation. Since she got to Atlantic City, she had avoided thinking
about the future, beyond what she needed to do to cover her room,
get a bit of food. But when she sat down with the fortune-teller,
that girl, suddenly the prospect of having to reckon with the
consequences of her decisions seemed like the most terrible possibility in the world—more terrible than the smell of strange men
on her skin, than the motel room where she has heard gunshots
ring out from the parking lot, where roaches scuttle out from the
shower drain.

The slot machine nearest to her stops at two halved watermel-
ons and a lemon. She's been here for three months and doesn't
know what this means—it's as though if she refuses to learn the
language of this place, then it can't claim her. She thinks about
how real fruit is bruised, never as good as it looks. Or when it
is, she can't think past the fact that ripeness is only something
close to death, a few days, or sometimes hours, away from rot.
The baby must have known this, too. Must have known to re-
ject all these images that the world hands you, the ones that are
meant to tell us we are safe, that we're all okay. Just sign on the
dotted line for this mortgage rate. Just wear Ann Taylor and

eat your free-range eggs and drive your Toyota and wash your clothes with Tide. But then your life can split open, your body, too. After the birth her husband reported to her how there had been so much blood. She didn't know whether that was true, but the sound of excitement in his voice confirmed what she had suspected—her mortality was thrilling to him. What we're most afraid of gives us a little jolt of joy, when we brush up against it, when it hovers too close.

She thinks that's what all these gamblers must be trying to hide from, here in these dark caverns, pulling on levers and spinning their savings away: mortality. No clocks anywhere in sight. Gamblers are the only people she knows who believe the future isn't the past. Sure, she remembers the statistics: One probability is not dependent on the other. A heads on the last flip of a coin doesn't increase the odds of tails on the next. A loss could yield to a win on the next spin. But what about here, where the odds are rigged? The odds are always rigged. She hates this place, but here, her thoughts come back to her, her memory feels like a room that's been tidied up. That thing about the coins, probability—she'd never have remembered that with the baby screaming through the night. Motherhood was nothing like what she had imagined, running her hand over her belly all those months, thumbing through paint swatches for the nursery. She thought there would be softness, joy. Instead there was this new soul who, with all her screaming, insisted she not forget how scary, how terrible it could be to be alive. She started to think about what she could do to silence her. A pillow. A few hard shakes, and she could believe in the illusion of safety again.

When she closes her eyes she can still smell her, powdery and sweet, skin pink from the bath. *I'm doing this for her*, she told her husband on the pay phone outside of Baltimore. He didn't understand and she couldn't bring herself to say it. All those times she thought about how much easier it would have been for everyone if she'd held the baby down under the surface of the water in the bathtub. She could have done it with one hand. She thinks about the girl in the shop again, with her practiced adult voice, the too-smooth assuredness of her gestures, her hands. What had happened to her, that she was working in that dingy little storefront? And those posters she kept seeing all over town, about the missing teenage girl? Were they girls whose mothers had ruined them, or ones who never had a chance because their mothers were like her—too afraid of screwing up to even stick around? It was a feeble gesture, leaving that $10 bill, but for a moment it had made her feel a little lighter. At least she could care for someone's girl.

A man takes a seat at the other end of the bar. She watches him order a drink and thumb through the cash in his wallet, waits for him to feel her stare. He is probably twenty years older than she is, wears a wedding ring—which, of course, doesn't mean anything—and the top three buttons of his shirt are undone to expose the glint of a gold chain tangled into a pelt of graying chest hair. He looks up at her and she tilts her head at him, but he breaks away when a woman brushes behind him, takes the seat next to his. She can tell by the tension in the woman's arm that she's wrapping a hand around his thigh. She had never felt compelled to touch her husband like that in public, to lay claim. Sometimes, when they were at parties together, she would watch a woman flirt with him—her husband laughing a little too loudly or leaning in a little too close—and would feel like it confirmed something. How easily she would be erased, cut out of the equation. It was useful information, she thought. She stored it up, to make the leaving easier.

If she didn't find a man for tonight, she still had her credit cards, though she didn't like the idea of using them, of sending up a little flare: *I am here*. She sold the car for $750 at a mechanic's shop on the way into Atlantic City, at a place with a strange tower made of scrap metal and hubcaps in the bare dirt yard. She was distracted, the way the light glinted off the hubcaps while she was trying to negotiate him up to $800. She was sure that a woman in her right mind would have waved the white flag, gone home, asked her husband for forgiveness, asked for help, for pills that would make her mind go right. She could go back and submit to the baby, to the laundry, to the endless diapers and scrubbing the grime between tiles in the bathroom. Instead she booked three nights at Harrah's and the next week she pawned her wedding ring for a fifth of what it was worth.

She doesn't know how long the man has been sitting next to her, but when she turns from the couple—the wife is now running her fingers through the man's chest hair—he's at her elbow, taking her in. He's got sun-worn skin, and his eyes are a clear, placid blue, but shadowed by the baseball cap he's got pulled low, the way so many of the blackjack players wear them. To hide. His eyes flash out from under the brim. Looking at them is like looking at a blue object sunk at the bottom of a glass of water. The contrast is startling, uncomfortable and attractive at once. She feels like he can see all of her—the place where the pawned wedding ring used to be, where she still runs her finger over the bare skin, the bruise on her thigh from where the last man whipped her with the cord from the clothing iron in the hotel room. He drinks a beer and then a club soda but buys her another glass of wine.

"Where are you from?" he asks.

She surprises herself by telling him the truth. McLean, Virginia. It feels good, purifying, this honesty. Like her first fresh breath of air in long time.

"So what are you doing here?"

Maybe it's the wine, or the dimness of the room, or the puzzling clarity of his eyes, but before she can stop herself she tells him about hearing the baby cry in the middle of the night, how she rose from her bed and stood outside of the nursery for a minute, how she couldn't make herself go in. Instead she walked past the door, put on a pair of shoes, took her purse down from the hook in the hall, got in the car, and drove away. With each mile, she pictured a length of thread being wound back around a spool, returning. Something being called in. She drove past the coffee shop and the preschool where they had talked about one day sending the baby. She passed the 24-hour Qwik Mart, and then there was a highway ramp spread before her like an offering. That night was daylight savings time, and she was still driving when the hour jumped ahead. It made what she was doing feel more unreal. She was no one, going nowhere. Just a woman in a box of steel and glass, like hundreds of others threaded along the highway, following the glow from her own headlights. Maybe she should have felt terror, or guilt, but she only felt free.

She took a bus from the mechanic to Atlantic City, passing billboards for eighties cover bands, a performance by Frank Sinatra Jr., Donnie and Marie Osmond. There was marsh on either side of the highway, the grass rippling in the breeze like a prairie. A few squat motels, the ones where she now spends her nights when she's not with a john, or when they need a place to go. When the bus growled into the depot, she couldn't remember the last time she had seen the ocean, so she followed its smell, the brine mixed in with the reek of overflowing garbage cans. She sat in the sand until the sun rose and the sweat began to slide along her spine. The exhilaration had yielded to something else. She felt scraped out, raw, exhausted. Used.

"Tell me more," he says. They're in his room. He had stood apart from her on the elevator, three people between them, so that she could only see him in the metal panels of the elevator car. She tried to study his face for what she had seen in the others'—greed, hunger, anger—but there was nothing like that. He knew what she was, but he seemed encouraging, kind. "What was that like?" he says, and a sense of confusion splices through her. Is this what he wants? Is he the kind of man who gets off on playing the hero? For some reason that makes her nervous, too. But she runs her hand over the bruises on her leg and pushes the thought away.

She decides to spare no details, partly because it feels good to talk, and because it seems that this is what he wants, the way the others wanted her to slap them or call them "Daddy" or "sir." She talks about the first time she slept with a man for money. When her cash from the car and the ring dwindled, she asked one of the cocktail waitresses where she might stay on the cheap. The woman told her that the Trump Plaza had been the cheapest room in town, until it shuttered. *Now it's just the motels over by the marsh. A girl like you doesn't want to stay there.*

No choice, she said.

Well, bring pepper spray. Make sure they give you a room with a door that locks.

She didn't even make it from the motel office to the room before a man propositioned her. She didn't say yes or no, only let him follow her to her door. Pointed to the bedside table until he peeled a few bills from a roll in his pocket. She hadn't even been with her husband since the baby. The pain made her vision go white. They had sewn her up, and she swore she had come back together crookedly, wrong. She bled, stained the white sheets.

Didn't tell me you had your fucking period, he said. Slammed a lamp to the ground on his way out.

"It was easier to keep doing it than to avoid it," she tells the man. She is oddly relieved at being able to unburden herself, but she's anxious, too. When will they get on with it—the thing he's brought her here for? Whatever way he's paid to use her. She's heard of men who just want to talk, from some of the other girls on the street, but never met one herself. So far she's only been with the ones who get their money's worth.

"Don't you think your daughter deserves to have a mother?" he asks her.

"It's better this way." She knows it's true, but still, her voice cracks. "Today, I went to a psychic, this little shop on the boardwalk near Caesars." She hears herself laugh a bitter little chuckle. "Not a psychic, really. Just this teenage girl. I wanted to know what she could see about my daughter. If . . . if . . . she might forgive me someday. A goddamned psychic. A kid, probably a fake. And even then I was too afraid to hear what she had to say. I'm too afraid to see how bad I've ruined everything."

He steps away from her and pulls a bottle from the mini fridge, disappears into the bathroom and pours it into a glass. She wonders if she's imagining it: the way his footfall has changed, the work boots stomping away. He returns from the bathroom, holds the glass out to her.

"Have another drink, it will make you feel better." She thinks for a moment about all of the rules you learn first as a girl: Don't talk to strangers. Don't go anywhere with someone you don't know. Keep an eye on your drinks. Don't dress like you're asking for it. Don't get too drunk. But she is so tired of rules. When she found out she was having a daughter, she worried that she would have to instill in her that same vigilance, and what was vigilance but a form of fear? *Screw it*, she thinks, and swallows half of the glass in a single gulp. She needs this, for the drink to do its loosening work. But still she can't help it. She doubles over, sobs until she gags. He stands over her—she watches his shadow on the floor.

"You said the Sunset Motel?"

What is it she hears in his voice? Anger? Excitement? She nods. She doesn't trust herself to speak, or else she'll start to cry again.

"I'll take you home."

She's failed. She's not sure she can ask for money, but she'll need to ask for at least $15 to cover her room. She tries to think of how to say it on the elevator ride down, but the booze has already gone to her head. She feels her stomach rise up into her throat

when the elevator drops, and she tries to tally up her drinks—
the math doesn't add up. She feels too drunk for the number of
drinks she's had, even with the way she gulped the last one down.
She chalks it up to the sobbing, and the way the sound of her
daughter's screams echoes in her mind.

By the time they are in the parking garage, her vision is fuzzy
at the edges. She tries to tell him that something is wrong, but
there is a drag on her words when she speaks. He helps her into
the car but that is not the right word—*help*. Help is what she
needs, something that feels impossible and very far away. Her
words retreat. Her arms go heavy at her sides. Along the road
the lit billboards hover over the marsh, ringed in a hazy purple
glow. They pass underneath the neon sign for the Sunset Motel
and into the darkness. He guides his car around the back of the
motel. She wants to tell him that this is not where she needs to go
but can only manage a groan.

And then his hands are on her, circling her neck, pressing
against her throat. She can't raise her arms to fight him off or
kick her feet. She can't scream, but the screams in her head are
louder now, that three-part wail of her daughter's that used to
make her dig her nails into her palms. Her lungs burn. When the
blackness comes, it is a relief that she no longer has to look into
his face, his teeth clenched, the pale blue eyes that now glow with
rage. The last thing Jane hears is the groan that escapes from between his teeth and the swish of the grass in the breeze.

CLARA

I WORE LILY'S PEARL BRACELET again when I got ready for my date—Des's word, not mine. As Des curled my hair, I looked at my wrist and pretended I was another kind of girl: One whose desk was stacked with books and brochures for colleges with redbrick buildings. One who sat in cafes with her friends, laughing over iced coffees and slices of cake. A girl who lived a careful life, whose mother kept a bowl of fresh fruit on the counter, whose closets were filled with soft towels and clean white sheets.

"Hey, what's this?" She reached for my hand, tapped the bracelet.

"From that girl. The new one at the spa."

Des laughed and I could see the dark fillings in the back of her mouth. Des hadn't asked about the vision I'd had at the spa, and maybe she had thought I had been faking it, spacing out for show. That was fine with me. I always tried to forget most of what I saw from other people's lives, but it tended to stick around, bits of memories that lingered in mine like scraps of strange dreams.

"You're quick as hell, Miss Clara Voyant. I might even say

you've surpassed your teacher. Take anything else this week you want to let me in on?"

I thought of Julie Zale's purple bandana. It was in my room, under my pillow. Her uncle probably thought he'd dropped it on the boardwalk, that it had been carried away by the breeze. One more piece of her he had lost.

"Nothing."

"You bring that bracelet over to Zeg tomorrow, okay? And tell him you won't take less than fifty. He's been a real tightwad lately, and we've got bills to pay." I nodded, but that wasn't a part of my plan.

"Lean closer," Des said. I waited for her to say something else. To ask if I was still willing to do this, to see if I was okay. She wiped her thumb underneath my eye and pulled a kohl pencil from her pocket. "Up," she said, and I raised my eyes to the ceiling while she ran the eyeliner back and forth, back and forth, rimming my eyes in black. I could feel tears building up but knew that I'd make a mess of my makeup if I let them fall. I told myself there was only one first time for everything. To think of it as one more con—some idiot wants to spend his money on me? Fine. As Des finished my makeup, I had that same feeling again, the fly, crawling across my chin. I tried to keep still, but I couldn't stand it and twitched to shake it free.

"What the hell?" Des said. She had drawn a black line down my cheek.

"You didn't see anything?"

"I saw you freaking out. What do you mean? See what?"

"Nothing," I said. "I'm sorry."

She licked her finger and rubbed at the mark on my skin. "I need you to be cool about this, okay? We need this cash."

"I know," I said. "I will." She brushed my cheeks with powder and stood back to look at me, smiling at what she had made of my face.

"Hot as hell," she said, air-kissing near my ear so she didn't smudge her lipstick. I sat on my hands so she wouldn't see that they had started to shake.

THE MAN, who I was supposed to call Tom, would pick me up in a black car so we could eat dinner at the Italian restaurant at the Tropicana. I made my way down the boardwalk ramp, careful to place my feet so I wouldn't get the heels stuck in the cracks, just like Des taught me. The driver got out and opened the door without looking at me. I took a breath and peered into the dark cavern of the back seat. I had seen moments like this a hundred times—the young woman who had been bought, ducking into an idling car that took her away. You could tell the ones who were new at it by the way they took one last glance over their shoulders before they shut the door, while the old hands smiled and pushed their chests out, a thousand-yard stare in their eyes. I decided I wouldn't look back.

Tom was slouched against the seat, his arms loose at his sides, like this was the most natural thing in the world—a strange young woman sliding into a car with him, someone a third of his age. "Hello," he said. "Lovely to meet you." His hair must have been thick and dark when he was younger, but it was thinning at the temples, spangled with gray. He wore a button-down shirt and khakis—he looked like someone's dad. I checked his hand. If he was married, he had decided to remove his ring. *One first time*, I said again, in my head. I forgot to hold out my hand, but he picked it up, brought it to his mouth, left a wet kiss on the back. When he wasn't looking, I wiped the place where his spit shimmered on my skin against the fabric of my dress. I wondered if the rest of the night would be like that—him putting a mark on me, me trying to rub it away.

He put his arm around me as we walked through the Quarter, and I felt myself tense up and go hot every place his body touched mine. The stores and restaurants around us were made to look like old Havana, and the corridors were decorated with fake palm trees that rose toward a pretend blue sky. I stopped to watch the fountain trickle, and remembered the first time Des walked me through Caesars. I thought it was the most beautiful place I'd ever seen—the columns in the lobby, the statues of helmeted men and their impossibly large horses, the slick sheen of the marble floors. I was six or seven, and she was teaching me how to slide a wallet from a woman's purse. My small hands would be an advantage, but I had gotten distracted by a fountain just like this one, the layer of coins glimmering under the water. I reached in and scooped up as many as I could take. I still remember the sensation of the cold wet coins in my hands, the way Des laughed when she saw the dampness spreading across my pockets. She used to laugh a lot more back then.

I was staring into the surface of the water when the feeling came to me, the pulse behind my forehead. It flared through my body faster than ever before, and then I tumbled into a vision, like I had hit a trip wire. Images exploded behind my eyes: the smear of streetlights, a pair of hands with little cuts around the knuckles and on the back of the palms, a dust ruffle that skimmed a few inches above a carpeted floor, the dark space underneath it dense with dirt. A sense of needing to scream, that pressure building in my throat. Then, a newborn baby's cry, high and shrill. The next thing I knew Tom's face was close to mine, leering, huge. I was too terrified and surprised to hide my gasp.

"Hey there, twitchy little thing, aren't you? Don't worry. I don't bite. Let's keep moving, shall we?" It took me a second to remember whose voice it was. His big teeth gleamed when he smiled. I forced myself to smile back. I was hot all over, and as we walked away, I reached down and dipped my fingers into the water, dabbed some of it on the back of my neck.

I felt exhausted, battered as though I'd taken a fall. As we walked in the direction of the restaurant, I looked back over my shoulder, to see if there was a child nearby. It actually wasn't unusual to see a baby in the casinos, a mother perched at the edge of the gaming floor, absentmindedly pushing the stroller back and forth with her foot while she played the slots. But I didn't see any children, only tourists posing for photos, the women making kissy faces, jutting their hips, awkward and wobbly in their too-tall heels.

Tom gave his name to the hostess, who narrowed her eyes at me, and I felt her measuring me as she studied my makeup, my hair, my dress, my heels, but she turned to Tom with a smile so wide it must have hurt. When we'd sat, Tom ordered a bottle of foreign-named red wine.

"Very good," the waiter said, like Tom had passed a test. I wondered if men everywhere congratulated one another on such stupid, trivial things. What did people enjoy about wine? I hated the bitter taste of it in my mouth, the way it made my limbs feel looser, my attention drifty and unpredictable. That was it? The feeling that people seemed to crave?

I tried to think of things to say, but all I could think about was how I wanted to leave. Des had already received half of his payment up front—$250—and I would get the second half from him at the end of the night. If I ran, we'd still be okay. But Des would be furious with me for losing out on the other half of that cash. Her moods snapped these days, as fast as rubber bands. Forming sentences felt impossible, my head filled with air. I watched Tom take a sip from his wineglass, watched his mouth move, but all I could hear was that shrill, horrible wail. I forced myself to smile, like an idiot, and right away he looked confused. My head hurt from the wine and from the noise. I couldn't concentrate on anything other than how I could make that sound stop. The wail rose into a shriek. It was so piercing that my hands jumped to my ears.

Tom frowned. "I didn't know I was so boring." This time he didn't look confused, only angry. I remembered what Des said, about men wanting to go out with women who make them feel important. I was failing, and we hadn't even gotten our dinners yet.

I jumped again when a busboy came to the table to fill our water glasses from a big silver pitcher. Des told me this restaurant would be fun, but everything felt alien and threatening. The way the waiter smiled at me, like he knew exactly who and what I was. The silverware that gleamed from every tabletop, bright slashes in the candlelight. The way a man came and briskly wiped the bread crumbs from the tablecloth, like I'd done something wrong. Tom's mouth was moving again, and I understood that I was meant to be not just listening, but flirting, touching, talking, and yet all I heard was the baby screaming. I spoke over him, excused myself to the bathroom, and he narrowed his eyes at me as I stood.

I locked myself in a stall and took deep breaths, as slowly as I could. I couldn't afford to mess this up. I splashed some water on my face and counted to ten, to twenty, to thirty. When I got to fifty-five seconds, the crying stopped. I could hear the bathroom attendant singing to herself. She had a low, pretty voice. She smiled up at me as I washed my hands, but as I smiled back it occurred to me that we might be alike: doomed to smile even when we were trapped.

Back at the table our food had arrived. Tom was sawing into his pork chop. The waiter came by to ask how we liked our dinner, and I hated the way he looked at me. I picked at my pasta—a dish that Tom had ordered for me—but I hadn't been tasting anything at all. I took another bite and nodded, hoped that would answer his question. I knew I was close to failure, that so far I had been anything but the kind of girl Tom wanted me to be, the kind of girl Des had sold him on—flirty and giggling, dumb and sweet. I had to force myself to meet his eye. I wondered what would happen if he wasn't happy with me, if he could ask for his money back. Or worse, if he could get Des and me in trouble. Everything was on my shoulders. I touched the pearls on my bracelet and reminded myself to breathe.

"What do you do?" I asked.

"What do I do?" he asked back. He smiled but his voice was snide.

"Uh, yeah. What's your job?"

"Insurance," he said.

"That sounds interesting."

"You're interested in insurance?" He raised his eyebrows and looked like he was trying not to laugh.

"No. I mean, yes. Maybe."

"Let's not talk about business, huh?"

"Okay," I said. He went back to his meat and I looked up, like instructions might be written on the ceiling. It was painted with a scene of angels sitting in fluffy clouds. Women in colorful tunics clutching harps, a temple with big beige columns at the entrance. Ugly cupids who seemed to smirk at me.

I looked back at Tom, knowing his real name must be something else. I guessed we had that in common. Both of us were pretending. Both of us wanted to escape from who and what we were. That was when I saw it—just a glimpse. Flat blue water, like a bay. Or a lake. He was watching a thin, blonde waitress balance a tray of drinks on her arm.

"What was it like, growing up by the water?" I asked. It was just a guess, really, but that's how the visions worked, most of the time. They were like the tarot. Clues you needed to puzzle out, create stories around. He turned to me, and I could tell I was close by the way his attention snapped back. He tilted his head and leaned, just a little bit, closer to me.

"Did I tell you I was from Michigan?"

"No, I just guessed." I tried to use the voice that I saved for clients in the shop, calm and serene, but with a little bit of sugar in it. "Something about you, I can just . . . tell."

Finally, he smiled. "My parents' house backed up to Elk Lake. Most beautiful place there is. You never find water like that out here. Not that color, not smooth as glass on a calm day." His face brightened, and I knew he was picturing it, the shade of the water, the expanse of it on the horizon, maybe the way it changed during a storm.

"Did you like to swim?"

"Sure do. Learned to swim right in my backyard, practically. And in the winter? You can go ice fishing. My brother and I used to skip school, hide our gear behind this old woodshed a few miles down the road from our house, and we'd spend all day out there. Of course, later, we brought some, uh, libations along."

As he went on, I realized he didn't really want me to talk. He wanted me to listen. He wanted me to smile and nod, to laugh or look pained when he recounted a memory that was nostalgic or sad. I could have been anyone, any young woman willing to sit across the table while he talked about his brother, the past—someone new who hadn't heard all his stories yet. I hardly had to do anything at all. His nostalgia reminded me of Des, how she was always going on about how great things were in Atlantic City when she and my mother first arrived. The parties, the glamorous clients, and there was always a new casino or new restaurant or new club to go to. The boardwalk crammed with tourists, buskers, street performers who filled the air with music. The money that came easily to the two of them. I was different, different from these people for whom the past was perfect, pristine. I knew I wouldn't get older and dream my way back to my childhood, the long hours in the apartment when Des left me alone, the microwaved trays of macaroni and cheese I burned my mouth on. It was the future that glimmered for me. California. My mother. Jasmine in the air, like she had described in her letters. A warm breeze gentle on my arms.

After dinner, Tom put his arm around me while we waited for our car, but this time instead of slinging it around my shoulders, he wrapped it around my waist, drew me close. I wouldn't do it, but I let myself imagine pulling away, breaking out into a run. On the drive home he moved across the seat, toward me, wrapped his fingers around my thigh. I looked out the window while he spoke.

"This was a lovely evening. I hope I can see you again the next time I'm in town." Even with my head turned away I could smell the wine on his breath, sour and hot. He had drank most of the bottle, but I still tasted it on my lips, where it had settled into the sun-scorched cracks.

"It was," I said. "And I hope you'll come back and visit soon." I stared straight ahead while his fingers tightened on me, pressed into my skin. I willed myself to think of our shop. The leak under the apartment sink that we couldn't afford to fix and that was slowly spreading a brown stain across the ceiling.

He turned my hand over, pressed a few bills into my palm.

"Thank you," I said. I remembered what Des had told me, about these men wanting to feel like saviors. How everything I did should be girlish, helpless, small. "This will help us keep ahead on the rent this month." He slid another bill from his wallet.

"Well, don't forget to treat yourself to something nice, too." I looked down this time—a hundred, with a small piece of paper tucked into it. For the first time that night, I felt hope bloom in my chest. If Des was going to sell me, maybe I could make it work for myself, too. "And if you ever want to extend the date, come relax in my suite at the hotel, you let me know. That's my number. Get in touch."

Before I got out of the car Tom put his hand on my jaw, turned my head toward his, and kissed me, pushing his tongue into my mouth. The kiss was forceful, wet, and salty. Nothing like the few spin-the-bottle pecks I had known. I closed my eyes and thought of the ocean. I saw it every single day, and I could hear the rumble of the waves from my bed at night. But it still always looked huge and beautiful and violent, full of unknowable things.

I walked the dark half block home, refusing to think. The boardwalk was quiet, but I inventoried everything around me, a way to keep my mind still. Out on Steel Pier, the circle of the Ferris wheel was bright against the sky, lit up red and yellow, spinning in its slow, lazy circles. A cat zipped out from the direction of the candy shop, its tail high in the air. A man stood underneath the awning, studying the poster of Julie Zale in the window. When I stopped in front of our door, I could feel him watch me draw my keys from my bag. In the dark I could only make out the coal of his cigarette and shape of smoke drifting toward the sky. He tossed his cigarette down, crushed the butt under the toe of his boot. I felt the creep of another fly, this one across the upper ridge of my lip. I couldn't help it, even if I knew it was just in my head—I raised my hand to shoo it away.

I was relieved that Des wasn't home when I got back. I didn't want to tell her what had happened, how I had almost messed everything up, how I was hearing things that weren't there. I didn't want to tell her it had gone well, either—what would being good at this mean? I put the rest of the money Tom owed us on her nightstand but saved the $100 for myself—each dollar another step toward my mother, toward my new life. I couldn't decide if I was proud or ashamed of that extra money, whether it meant I had done something wrong or something right. I smoothed the bill into the back pages of *The Wisdom of Tarot* and refused to think about it—it wasn't bad or good, only what needed to be done. From my bed, I watched the ceiling fan spin in lazy circles above my head and tried to sleep.

I must have drifted off, though I know I tossed and turned. I woke up at dawn. I'd dreamed of the woman who had run away from me: those big brown eyes, the soft voice. I thought of the reading I'd done after she'd gone. The Four of Wands. Family. Harmony. The King of Cups, the lack of clarity. The Seven of Wands. Betrayal just around the bend. And then I understood: the visions from the night before didn't have anything to do with Julie Zale—they had to do with her, the woman with the locket. I curled myself into a ball, another phantom fly working its way along my thigh.

LILY

I WOKE TO THE SCREECH of my alarm, and as soon as I sat up I felt the lurch in my stomach. *Oh,* I thought dully, as the bar, the bourbon came back to me. I looked at my phone. I had dialed Matthew's number five times. I even called Ramona twice. Based on the call log, it didn't seem like I had spoken to either of them: each call was between eight and ten seconds long. I wasn't sure whether that was a blessing or another humiliation.

It was 6:15. I'd need to be at the spa in an hour to learn opening procedures. I ran through all the things that needed to happen by then. Four types of makeup. Hair washed and styled. Press the wrinkles out of my jacket. Pepto-Bismol, water, gag down dry toast.

I showered, smeared a little eye shadow on. The swing of the vanity mirror in the bathroom made me dizzy as I opened it and rooted around for brushes, Q-tips, hair spray. Even with makeup I looked clammy, pale. I heard Brett's voice. *You wanted to start your own gallery, right?* I slunk out without ironing my blazer. When I started the car and backed out of the driveway, I wondered if I wasn't still too drunk to drive.

IN THE parking lot I took another swig of Pepto-Bismol before stepping out of the car, and the taste of chalk and fruit made my guts twist. I hurried down the stairs and through the crosswalk to the circular drive that led to the main lobby of the casino. The elaborate topiaries that flanked either side of the entrance had overgrown, become fuzzy and indistinct at their edges. A lone gardener watered a patch of red impatiens, holding out the hose in one hand and scrolling through his phone with another. As I passed him, I could smell the sweet, metallic scent of the water trickling from the hose, and it reminded me of my childhood. My father mowing the lawn while my mother planted in the garden, pulled weeds, mulched. The softness and idyll of the memory was like a pastel drawing preserved under glass.

At the top of the drive, near the valet stand, a woman in Lucite stilettos was hailing a cab. She wore a Lycra dress with cutouts that showed the notches of her ribs. A long, thin scar ran down the back of her calf, and there was a tattoo of a peach above her left breast. She must have felt my stare, because before she turned to get into the taxi she stopped and blew me a kiss, then gave me the finger. The man at the valet stand saw it all and laughed heartily. *I'm not a prude!* I wanted to shout. *I've seen things! I've done things! I lived in goddamned New York City!* But I stayed quiet, and as I passed, the valet tipped his cap, gave me a smug little smile. I thought again of Clara and Des, the things Emily had suggested about them. About Clara's rounded cheeks.

I hurried down the long hall that led to the new wing, past housekeepers vacuuming neat stripes in the carpet and janitors emptying ashtrays into garbage bags, but when I got to the spa the front door was locked. Through the glass, I watched as a man ran a rag over the top of the steel desk. I tapped on the glass, but he didn't turn. I tapped harder. The man had turned and was walking toward the coffee table with all of the magazines when he saw me. I waved like an idiot. He unlocked the door and opened it a crack.

"Hi, I'm Lily." I pointed to my name tag, panting from my jog down the hall. "I work here." He frowned. "Can I please come inside? It's the beginning of my shift. I'm new and don't want to be late."

He stared at me warily for another moment before stepping aside so I could pass. I walked as quickly as I could toward the back of the spa, where we were meant to clock in with our swipe cards. I rooted through my purse as I walked—it was 7:29, and I couldn't be marked as late on my second day. I was still looking down when I pushed through the double doors that led to the back hall and smacked into something—someone—and we both went sprawling onto the floor. Something cold and wet landed on my hand.

"What the fuck?" a woman's voice said. "Are you insane?"

"I'm sorry, I was late. Are you okay? Please, let me help you. I'm Lily, by the way."

"I'm Brittany and I don't really give a shit. I'll have to mix this mask all over again. Do you know how much that stuff costs? If Deidre finds out, she'll eat me for lunch."

"I'm really, really sorry."

"I don't have time for new girls running around like morons and then apologizing." I realized that the mask—a lumpy gray mixture—had gotten on my skirt and on the front of my blazer. I tried to wipe it away but ended up smearing it into the fabric. Was I just this person now? The one who screwed up all the time? Brittany dropped a pile of paper towels over the spilled mud.

"I'll get Luis to clean this up." She vanished through the double doors and came back with the man who had let me in. Brittany pointed to the spill, and he frowned at her. She pointed back at me. He gave me a mean look before getting on his knees to assess the mess.

"You must be my new girl," a voice said, from down the hall. I turned and saw a woman in a black dress. She disappeared into a doorway and yelled to me to come into her office. I looked back at the man, Luis, on the floor, mopping up the mud with paper towels.

"Are you sure you don't need any help?" I asked. He didn't look up.

I assumed that the woman in the black dress was the manager Deidre had mentioned: Carrie. I hadn't gotten a good look at her before, but I was surprised to see how different she was from Deidre: petite, with long dark hair streaked with caramel-colored highlights, and blue eyeliner smudged underneath her eyes. When I walked through the doorway, she was eating a glazed donut and guzzling a blended coffee drink, mid-melt into sludge.

"Hi, I'm Lily," I said.

"Hey," she said. I extended my hand. She gave me a limp little handshake and turned back to her computer.

"Um, is there anything in particular I should get started on?"

She laughed. I smiled, more out of nerves than anything else, and she noticed. "Sorry, not you." She laughed again and kept typing. "Just go make sure all the computers are on and unlock the door. I'll be up in a few minutes to help."

As I passed the dispensary, I could hear Brittany complaining about me to another technician. "And then this moron slams into me, practically breaks my tailbone, and it all goes *splat*, everywhere . . ."

"I don't know where they're getting these receptionists," the other woman said. "These girls just fuck everything up. You should see my books for the next two weeks. Disastrous."

I wanted to scream, *I went to Vassar! I've sold art to buyers in sixteen countries!* But I knew the inevitable question would be: How did you screw all that up?

I stepped behind the desk and had the feeling that I had been left to man a ship, steering the prow into a day I knew nothing about, with instruments I didn't understand how to use. The day before I had been so relieved to know I would have a few hours free from Deidre, her all-seeing gaze, but now I missed having directions, having rules. What if a guest came? What if someone had a question? What did I say if the phone rang? All that, and I was still feeling weak and disoriented from my hangover. I wished I could step out of my body for a few hours. I'd had that feeling often lately. I couldn't stand being in my own skin.

As I waited for Carrie to come train me, I watched a woman wearing what looked like a safari guide outfit—bucket hat, khaki shorts, hiking boots, khaki vest with lots of pockets—make her way through the Swim Club. She climbed into the bank of plants that ran along the edge of the dome and starting snipping leaves and branches, other times misting a plant with a spray bottle, cupping a leaf tenderly in her hand. I was so engaged watching her that I didn't see the woman approaching the spa until she had her hand on the door.

As she entered, I said, "Good morning," sounding girlish, a little shrill.

The woman was petite, smaller than me, with thin blonde hair that was nearly translucent. "I have a wax appointment," she said.

"Sure, the last name, please?"

"Greer. First name is Ellen."

She was booked for an 8 a.m. I checked her in the way Emily had showed me, slowly moving through the series of clicks and keys, trying to pass off my hesitation as intentional—the measured, calm way someone who worked in a spa should move, should speak. "Yes, Mrs. Greer, we have you with Brittany today for your Brazilian bikini wax. Follow me, please." The spa offered four types of waxes. According to Deidre, one finger-width in from the crease of your thighs was a touch-up. Two fingers in was a standard bikini wax. Three fingers in was a Brazilian, and they were doing something new now, she said, called an hourglass, which was two fingers down from the top of the bikini area. It helped elongate your stomach and make you look slimmer. I led Ellen Greer to the locker room and tried not to think of Deidre holding up six fingers side by side. I couldn't imagine starting my day by paying almost $100 to have a stranger rip off all my pubic hair. It was the kind of thing I would have loved to talk to Ramona about—how violent beauty could be, how misogynistic, how cruel. Mrs. Greer was petite, muscles toned with expensive barre and pilates classes, fat edited away by five-day cleanses, green juice, kale. A woman who was constantly negotiating with her body, thinking of it as something to be punished or tamed.

While Mrs. Greer was in for her service, the man who had cleaned up the mud—Luis—came back to the front desk.

I tried to start on a new foot. "Hi," I said. "Good morning." Again, he didn't even look at me. I understood. I would hate someone like me, too. He must have thought I was tremendously careless, someone who made messes and left them for other people to clean.

I wanted to look busy but wasn't sure what else I could do. The phone rang twice, both times people calling from their rooms to ask what time the buffet opened. Deidre said that the casino had programmed them incorrectly and so the button that was supposed to connect callers to other places within the hotel was accidentally routed to the spa, and so most of the calls we got were actually meant for other facilities. The company required a very specific greeting, which I garbled with my cottony, hungover tongue: "Thank you for calling the spa. This is Lily, how may I assist you?"

In front of me, Luis wiped down the brushed steel table in the magazine area, pausing to pick up an issue of *Glamour* and squint at the cover.

Maybe I needed to try a different tack. "Does this place always feel so creepy?" I asked him. "It's weird, right? It's just so bright and empty and stark. Like being inside a Josef Albers painting. The one with the white squares." No response. But that was wrong, too. I just sounded like more of a snob, some spoiled white girl babbling on about abstract art. I cleared my throat. "Look, I'm really sorry about this morning. I'm Lily," I said. "I just started." Still, he wouldn't turn around. I gave up and simply watched him work the paper towel in small, slow circles.

I doodled on the edge of a spa menu as I waited for Carrie to come and tell me what to do next. Time was creeping by. 8:31. 8:35. 8:37. I turned my back to the desk and pulled my phone out of a gift certificate box, held it the way Emily had showed me the day before. No new texts, no missed calls.

"Hey!" a voice said behind me. I jumped, and my phone slipped from my grip, landed with a sickening crunch on the marble floor. "Jesus, it's just me. I came through the back. I thought I'd get here early. I'm sure Carrie has been completely useless to you."

Emily. Just Emily. When I picked up my phone, I saw that the screen was spiderwebbed with cracks. I cradled it in my palm like I would have a small, injured animal.

"Oh shit, I'm really sorry. That sucks." She took the phone from my hand, grimaced, handed it back. "There's a guy over on the boardwalk who will fix it for twenty-five bucks. I went to him last month. Right near the Taj Mahal. Or what used to be the Taj Mahal, at least. Hey, are you okay? No offense, but you look like you've been hit by a truck."

"Hangover."

"Ah. You'll learn not to go out before you open."

"It's been a shitty morning either way." I told her about running into Brittany in the back hall.

"She's a total twat. Ignore her. They're like children. Just can't listen to their bullshit. You're the one with the power and don't forget it. You can pack their books with appointments if you like them, or if they piss you off, then you can punish them for it."

"What's the deal with that older guy who comes in and cleans and like takes the recycling out? He refuses to talk to me."

"You mean Luis?"

I nodded. "I tried to talk to him like three times and he's totally ignored me."

"Well, he's deaf. And mute. And he doesn't use sign language, but he can read and write. Sometimes I think he pretends to understand less than he does—he's smart enough to tune all of us out."

"Oh—that explains it." But I felt even worse than before. No wonder he didn't like me, yammering on and on at him, oblivious.

"You'll see. He's really observant—he notices a lot about people. Once, when I couldn't find Carrie, he could tell I was looking for her and he pretended to put a finger down his throat."

"Wait, why?"

"Oh, you don't know yet. Well, you would have found out soon enough anyway. She's bulimic. She uses that bathroom right next to her office. It's pretty disgusting."

"So what has he noticed about you?" I couldn't help myself. I was so curious about Emily, about what she was doing here. It seemed like my chance to ask more.

"Oh, probably that I'm a sinner, like my parents said when I left. Good as dead as far as they're concerned." She was smiling, but some of the mirth left her voice. "What about you? Your parents like your ex?" She gestured to my shattered phone.

"How did you know . . ."

"Come on. I could tell you were seriously pining when I came up to the desk. Let's hear it. What's the deal there?"

"He . . . well." I fumbled for the right words. God, how to describe what it had really been like? The recording of Ramona and Matthew in bed. The nude she painted of him, him looking smug, imperial, in an Eames rocking chair, every inch the *enfant terrible*. The text messages I sent. *Matthew, where are you? Matthew, what's going on?*

"He slept with someone else. She's a painter," I said. "She was someone I was hoping to represent at the gallery where I worked. Matthew was—is—one of their clients. He's a sculptor. Quite well known, actually." Something I had thought about a lot over the past few weeks was how Matthew had never wanted for anything—not attention, not money, not admiration, not fame. How it made sense that he thought he could do what he did and that I might stay. I thought of his mother, a tidy, brisk woman in her sleek, modern house nestled in the woods of New Canaan. The summer place on the cliffs of Newport. The father who flew in from London every few months, who hid his fondness for red meat and gin in bespoke Turnbull & Asser. It had been a part of my initial attraction to Matthew—not necessarily the money, but the self-assurance it gave him. The unassailable confidence touched his every movement, from the way he hailed a cab to the way he peeled an orange.

I remembered when I first started at the gallery, the clichés that were being bandied around about Matthew Whitehall, the twenty-nine-year-old wunderkind. The *rising star*. I had been skeptical until I saw one of his newer pieces, a bronze of a couple embracing—there was an athletic quality about the way Matthew had rendered them, something nearly violent, that I found captivating. The articulation of their tendons, the definition of their muscles, the sense of the energy coiled in their limbs, as though they might just as soon launch themselves at one another and collide. I studied the piece until I felt something else—the rubber-band ping of attention directed toward me. I looked to see Matthew across the room, his eyes on my face. The knowing way the corners of his mouth turned up. Now I couldn't help but wonder if, from that moment, he'd seen me as a pawn.

I wanted to ask Emily more about herself. Did she have a boyfriend? Girlfriend? Maybe that was how she ended up here, too, after her stint in L.A. Maybe she was also retreating, also biding her time at the spa. Though I wondered who wouldn't be totally devoted to Emily, with her humor and her beauty and her strange, endearing combination of craziness and restraint.

"Ah. You'll have to tell me more later. Deidre, incoming." Emily nodded her head in the direction of the front door. I was relieved, for now, to have my attention jerked out of the past. I was still at the point where I could lose hours inventorying every detail for a clue about our end: the first date at the Cuban restaurant in Williamsburg, when Matthew took me home and used the belt of his bathrobe to tie my hands above my head, perhaps testing me for pliability. My first lunch with Ramona, when she ordered a rare burger and I watched the bloody juice run over her hands as she ate.

Deidre gave Emily the rundown for the day, and I found myself looking past them both, through the glass and down the hall. I hated that I was waiting for them, Clara and Des. *You are recovering from a broken heart.* That meeting them had felt like the first thing that had really *happened* to me since I had been back. I was watching so intently that it took me a minute to hear Deidre saying my name.

"Lily? Lily. Please tell me how your training is coming along."

I GOT lost twice trying to remember Emily's directions to the cafeteria: take a left at the first turn in the back hall, then a quick right, then take the freight elevator, then at the third floor make another left and a quick right after that. The first time, I ended up in a dead-end hallway filled with linen carts heaped with damp towels. The second time, I pushed through a door that led to a loading dock. Three men in janitorial uniforms looked up from their cigarettes to eye me warily.

"Looking for a delivery, sweetheart?" one of them said. "I'd load you up all right." I was too stunned and insulted to say anything back, so I simply turned away as the three of them laughed.

I found the freight elevator on the third try. When the doors groaned closed, I leaned back against the far wall and shut my eyes. I willed the elevator to get stuck, so that I could stay like that for hours, alone and quiet, no one asking me for anything at all. But all too soon, the doors opened again.

The caf smelled depressing, even from a distance. All of the hot food had an overcooked, stewed quality. I let a grim-faced woman splatter a scoop of mashed potatoes onto my tray and helped myself to a pile of iceberg lettuce, brown at the edges, and a mealy tomato slice, then topped it off with a heap of croutons. I slid into a booth with a plastic-covered bench that squeaked every time I moved. I knew I should eat: my stomach had gotten better and I was starving, yet all of the food on my plate seemed like the most depressing version of itself.

As I poked at my lunch I thought about how, after my dad's funeral, the casino had sent a catered meal to my mother's house, but the timing was off and by then anyone who had been stay-ing with us—my grandparents from Ohio, my aunt and uncle from Arizona—had already gone. Huge silver chafing dishes full of roast beef, pasta in a vodka cream sauce, shrimp fra diavolo, scalloped potatoes, Caesar salad, chocolate mousse, two kinds of cheesecake, and a greasy paper sack of garlic bread for just the two of us. We ate in the living room, so we didn't have to sit at the table with his empty chair, the rich sauces roiling in our guts.

I studied the rest of the room. Everyone grouped together, ac-cording to their jobs. The servers who worked at the steak house. The craps dealers, the blackjack dealers, the poker dealers. The cocktail waitresses, the front desk associates. The pit bosses, the junket reps, the security guys, the fussy cluster of secretaries who brought their own silverware from home. The only other person I saw from the spa was Luis, who brought his tray outside and scattered bits of bread for the birds. He must have clacked the tray down on the table loudly, because the three women smoking under the nearby awning started and gave him the eye, but he didn't seem to notice. Or maybe he did it on purpose. Maybe he liked the vibration of the impact in his fingers. Maybe it made him feel heard.

I felt a pang as I watched him, a reflexive desire to store away stories and facts to tell Matthew, to pocket and package everything I saw and present it to him later. I wanted to tell him about Luis, to talk about what it would be like to navigate the world in so much silence. Matthew loved stuff like that: stories of extremes. I wondered what it felt like with no noise to crowd his thoughts.

When I came back from lunch, I worked on memorizing the spa menu and its descriptions of services. We were trained to upsell whenever possible, but of course the company never called it that. *Enhancing relaxation* meant add-ons to services: an extra exfoliant, a foot scrub. *Pampering yourself at home* meant buying products. I had to hand it to the copywriters. They made everything sound like a gift, even when the guest was the one footing the bill.

"What's the difference between the Swedish Massage and the Premium Massage?" I asked Emily.

"Nothing but the price, I'm afraid."

"Well, then what do you say when people ask you?"

"I tell them that the Premium includes acupressure and reflexology."

"What are those?"

"Hell if I know. Most people will want to look like they know what you're talking about, like they do this all the time, so hardly anyone ever asks. People are always afraid of looking stupid. I suggest using that to your advantage as much as possible. Shame motivates almost every interaction."

"Okay, Freud," I teased, but I already felt like she might be right.

"Think about it. How many times do you do something, or don't do something, because you're afraid you're going to be embarrassed?"

"All the time."

"You and everyone else. If we're not being fat-shamed, slut-shamed, mommy-shamed, we're worried about being seen as deficient for not knowing a random term for a scalp massage or a foot rub. It's bullshit, but it's true."

"Emily, can I ask you a question? Why the hell do you work here?" I hoped she understood what I meant. She was clearly brilliant. I knew I only wanted to be here as long as it took to save up enough to get back to the city—three, four months. After all, I was *just pretending*. But what did Emily want? What mantra got her through her days?

She rolled her head in a circle, stretching her neck. As she did, a gold cross on a chain came untucked from the neckline of her shirt, and she reached for it without looking and tucked it back in. "Great question. I didn't go to college. So this, believe it or not, is the best I can do around here. There are hardly any jobs to begin with, now that everything on the other side of town is shutting down. Plus, it helps me keep up my acting skills. I have to pretend that the people who come here don't make me want to rip my fucking head off. Present company excluded."

"I'm flattered," I said.

"You'll see what I mean."

"Lily?" Deidre called. Her voice echoed from the hair salon. "Please come into my office."

"Time for you to get another lesson in Ass-Kissing 101."

"I think that'll make my hangover come back."

"She can make you feel the misery of every hangover you've ever felt, all at once."

As I walked back to Deidre's office, I pictured Emily on a stage or a film set. The way her face could shift from one mood to the next, the way she was conscious of how she moved through space, her gestures precise, her posture perfect, the way she so easily pretended to click through the books when someone asked her to schedule an appointment, so that they'd feel lucky and grateful when she managed to book them a space, like they'd received a special favor—all the while I was watching the empty slots scroll by and had to turn my face away so that I didn't give anything up. Was she like that with everyone? What secrets did she hide with her blunt humor, that quick wit? I wondered what aspects of her life, her personality, she wasn't letting me see.

ON THE boardwalk I stopped in front of a funnel cake stand, the air full of sugar and heat. I took Clara's card from my wallet, studied its little misshaped crescent moons, its off-center, faux-gothic text. Why was I feeling so nervous? After all, she was the one who had stolen from me, the one who had done wrong. I crossed the boardwalk to look at the ocean, hoping it would soothe me. There were birds diving out past where the waves broke—my father taught me that meant fish nearby. Sometimes I still tricked myself into thinking he was along the shore, casting a line out into the sea.

In the dunes, the feral cats hissed at one another, prowled through the sand for scraps like desert animals, their fur missing in patches and their whiskers bent from fighting with one another. If this whole town was blasted to bits, the feral cats would outlast us all. They'd go on pawing for scraps among the crackle of dying neon and broken bits of poker chips. The city had tried to spay them, put them in shelters, but it seemed that there were more of them than ever before, their mean, pale green eyes catching mine for a second before they slunk behind a patch of grass.

Clara's shop was wedged between a store offering cash for

gold, trays of pawned rings glinting dully in the window, and a soft pretzel shop, which smelled like starch and salt. There was a chalkboard sign out front of Clara's. *Summer Special, Readings $5.* Emily was right—at only five bucks a reading Clara and Des probably needed another hustle in order to eat.

A gold decal of the evil eye stared out at me from the window, which was draped with heavy damask curtains tied with tasseled ropes. The door was propped open, and another cat sat in front of it, licking its paws. I pushed through a tangle of beaded curtains and into the shop, which reeked of incense, the smoke sweet and thick. Along the closest wall, an old jewelry case held crystals and gems, pyrite and amethyst, hunks of quartz, and a pile of polished tourmaline. The glass shelves were grayed with dust. I looked up for cameras—a habit now—and didn't see any. A leak had spread a urine-colored stain along the ceiling.

"Ah. I knew you'd come." I turned and saw that Clara had stepped into a room through a door in the back of the shop.

"I just want my bracelet back."

"What bracelet?" Clara blinked at me.

"Oh, come on. The one you snatched the other day at the spa. Look, I really don't have time for this, I need to see this phone guy before he closes." I held out my cracked phone like evidence.

She yawned and stretched her arms above her head, arched her back. Her shirt rose and revealed a slice of skin, concave stomach, the twin bones of her hips.

"Why don't you sit down, let me give you a proper reading?"

"What, so you can steal from me again?" I tried to stand a little taller, but there was a flutter of nervousness in my voice. I was curious but terrified that she might see in me things I didn't want to see myself: My desperation. My fear.

"Here." She pulled out an old folding opera chair covered in gold velvet. The shop didn't seem to have air-conditioning and I knew it would be uncomfortable—to listen to her read my cards, to sit in that hot, dusty room—but I found myself taking off my blazer and sliding into the chair.

Up close, I could see that the tablecloth was a bolt of fabric that had come off a roll from a fabric store. No one had bothered to hem the raw, frayed ends where it had been cut away. Clara had her back to me, busy arranging something in the glass cabinet. She turned over her shoulder, smiled. I wasn't sure why. Her braid was coming a little loose, and for a second she looked almost like a girl her age should look, like she had just been laughing with friends over strawberry smoothies at the mall or running across a soccer field after school. I tried to imagine her face underneath the heavy foundation and the thick strokes of black eyeliner: earnest and sweet.

"How old are you? Sixteen?" Clara frowned and I knew I had guessed right. She sat at the table, tamped the cards in her hand the way people do with packs of cigarettes.

"Twenty-one."

"I don't believe you. Your mom just lets you do this?"

"Oh, God. Des isn't my mom. She's just my aunt."

"Your guardian, then."

She ignored me and shuffled the cards, turned one over on the tabletop. It showed a man in a tunic and tights suspended from a tree branch, dangling by a single foot.

"That's the Hanged Man."

"What's a Hanged Man?"

"He usually means that you need to go through discomfort or pain in order to grow or achieve change." She flipped another card. This one showed a hand extended from a cloud, holding a star-shaped symbol. She turned another one over: three women hoisting golden cups in the air.

Clara ran her fingers over the edges of the cards and nodded. "Three of Cups, Ace of Pentacles. Hmmm. Yes, this all makes sense."

"What all makes sense? It's just a bunch of pictures arranged in a random order. How does it make sense?"

"It means that you'll fall a little further before you can rise again." Her voice shifted into a deeper register, self-serious and solemn.

"What's that supposed to mean? Fall further than this?" I raised my arms at the sun-faded Oriental carpet, the rickety table, the plastic crystal ball. "And while we're at it, what did you mean, that thing you said at the spa?"

"Your pain over your father," she said. This time she looked straight at me. "You can't pretend not to feel anything. You can't hide from it. It'll only make things worse."

I was too stunned to say anything else, or even to nod. Clara turned her head to look out the window as though to give me a moment to sit alone with what she had said. I peeled away a strip of skin from the cuticle of my left pinkie until I felt a satisfying pain.

Four years ago, the casino was building a new garage as part of the expansion, but the engineers and the architects had orders to rush things along as quickly as they could. The construction team ended up completing one floor a week rather than one floor every three weeks. Then, on the morning before Thanksgiving, the supports collapsed and seven people were killed inside. Three times that many were injured. My father was one of them. It took hours to even find him in the rubble. He was brought to the hospital in the center of the city, where my mother and I sat by his bed and listened to his machines beep. The doctor was frank when he explained the swelling of his brain, the extent of the internal bleeding, that he was essentially already gone. But still we waited two more days before my mother signed the paperwork, agreeing to let him die. Even with all the charts and images, even with the IVs and the machine that was breathing on his behalf, it still seemed like he might wake up. There was a scrape on his left cheekbone and a cut near his hairline, but other than that, he was my father, with the same face, same expression even, he had when he was simply taking a nap on the sofa in the evening after an early start at work.

I understood that my mother had no choice, that there was no hope, that he was gone, as gone as the rest of the men whose pictures had appeared on the evening news. She lifted her pen, paused above the first space for her signature, and stared at me. She waited to sign until I nodded at her. I still think I will never forgive her for looking to me before signing that paper to remove him from life support, for making me be the one to say yes, go ahead. Take him away. I remember the sound of the pen on the page, the way her hand shook, and then we were left to listen to his body take its last rattling breath. How could we continue, how could we still squish through the grass barefoot to water the basil in the garden, how could we hug the same way, laugh over white wine at lunch, when we had colluded like that?

I jumped when a man pushed his way through the beaded curtains at the entrance of the shop.

"I'm here for a, uh, a private reading?" He seemed anxious, an apron of sweat on the front of his pale blue T-shirt. His skin was the tender-looking pink of a whole pig slow roasted over an open flame. He looked like he belonged in one of Brueghel's carnival scenes, a beery shopkeeper draped over a keg.

Clara looked at me as she spoke to him, as though she were trying to tell me something instead. "Ah, yes, please let me show you in." She rose from her chair and showed him through the door at the back of the shop, raising her finger behind his back to me to tell me to wait a minute.

I thought about what Emily had said to me back at the spa—that Des and Clara were up to something else, something secretive, illegal. I knew it was irrational, but I was angry at her for bringing him into the shop while I was there. I felt like it cheapened what she had just told me, the intimacy of it. The pain.

"What's a private reading entail?" My voice was mean, snide.

"Shh. Keep it down." When she'd spoken of my father she seemed open, unguarded, almost dreamy. But now her eyes were narrowed, her jaw clenched.

"How much does it cost?"

"More than you can afford."

"Do only men get them?"

She sighed. "It's not what you think. It's just a . . . it's just a date. "

"Jesus. I can't believe this. Emily was right. At least tell me you're still in school?" She looked away, and I knew I'd hit a nerve. It might have been a trick of the light, but her eyes shone. Though she turned back to me with venom in her voice.

"Why can't you believe? You hardly know me. What does it matter to you who I am or what I do?"

I had the feeling that this was some kind of test, that even as her tone grew angry, she wanted me to do something, step between her and whatever was going to happen with that man. She raked the tarot cards into a pile, but she was having trouble with the drawstring of the silk pouch—her hands had started to shake.

"You don't want to do this," I said.

"Do what?"

"Whatever you are about to do. With him."

"Just go, okay?" Nearly a whisper.

"Fine, do whatever you want." I slung my bag over my shoulder and made my way to the door.

"Hey Lily," she said, her voice stronger now. "Catch."

It was in my hands before I made sense of the shape—my bracelet. The pearls still held the warmth of Clara's skin. As I

stepped out of the shop I shivered to think of that man waiting
for her, what he might be asking her for, what she might give. He
must have been at least forty five. She certainly wasn't eighteen.
That pink, cooked-looking skin. The smell of his sweat. The
drum of his stomach. That twitch in Clara's hands. I wanted to
scream. Scream for help, for her, for me. For everyone I had met
since I came home: Beautiful, brilliant Emily stuck behind that
desk. Carrie and the bile on her breath. Luis, whose personality was buried deep within his layers of silence. My mother, who
had signed that paper in the hospital, saying yes to an impossible
question. My father, and this city's short memory: another stupid parking garage now stood in the same place where the first
one collapsed. And because right then, probably, Matthew was
watching the sunset slide behind the Manhattan skyline or in the
back of a cab on the way to a fabulous restaurant, and everything
I had worked for had dissolved in a single night.

Across the boardwalk, the roller coaster rumbled down its
tracks and people cried out as they plunged toward the ground.
Were we all like the people on the ride, even Clara, who claimed
to be able to see? Whipped around helplessly, our fates playing
out on a fixed course?

A man in tattered clothes approached me, shook a plastic cup
that jingled with loose change. Every sound seemed too loud,
garish. Everything was magnified, intense, too much of itself:
The tinny noise of his coins bouncing together. The rank smell
of his clothes. The squawk of the seagulls, the red of Clara's awning that had at first looked tawdry and now simply looked sad.
I moved past him, trying to escape the din.

"You stupid bitch!" he yelled. "Your hear me? Fuck you, you
stupid bitch!"

I leaned against the wall of the candy shop and tried to slow
my breathing, but my vision was getting hazy and everything

seemed so crushingly close. I was sweating through my shirt, could feel the dampness collecting and dripping along the backs of my knees. Taped to the glass was a poster of the missing girl, Julie Zale, her photo blanched by the sun.

The anxiety took over, blotted out my thoughts until everything was constricted, filtered through a physical, illogical terror: the heat that seared through my body, the certainty that a curtain of black would fall over my eyes, knowing that my heart was rushing rushing rushing, but there would soon be a pinch of pain in my chest and it would stop. *You will fall before you will rise.*

It felt like a curse.

LUIS

HE WATCHES HER AT WORK as much as he can without getting caught. A few times she's tried to speak to him, but someone must have told her that he's not like everyone else. She's awkward when she mimes things to him. Points at her watch, then at the mop, her cheeks and neck going red. He dunks the mop into the bucket. She smiles at him, and that's when he remembers where he has seen her before. He thinks of the man who used to come into the bakery in the mornings, his easy grin, the way Luis never had to wonder what he wanted: a single roll and a cup of coffee, nearly white with cream.

In the break room Luis reaches into his wallet, finds the $2 bill, turns it over, runs his finger along the squiggle on the back. The man always gave him an extra dollar, pressed the single bill into his hand, but that day he must have been out. He raised his eyebrows at Luis as Luis eyed the bill, its careful, intricate design. Then, the man didn't come the next morning and Luis had a bad feeling. The day before he had been sliding a tray of rolls from the oven when he felt the boom in his feet. His boss ran out the door to see what had happened, came back with his hand over his mouth, scrambled for the telephone. A few days later, the man's picture was in the newspaper, a grainy gray and white that flattened his smile.

Luis and the owner of the bakery had gone to the churches—so many of those pictures were of men who came in for breakfast, lunch, coffee—and it was in one of those churches where he'd seen her, the girl with the man's same eyes. She leaned against another woman with dark hair, both of them in black, as they followed the coffin out of the church. It was like seeing the man again, even as her eyes blurred with tears.

Now that he remembers, it hurts to look at her directly, and sometimes he even feels a jolt of anger when he sees her. He doesn't know what it is about this city, the way it swallows up anything kind and good. He still remembers the dust that coated the bakery windows after the accident, thick enough to choke on.

HE THINKS of ways he might tell her, might show her without making her afraid. He tried to come up with the combinations of words, but none of them could ever be enough to match what he feels. Every day he went to school and got hurt, teased. Boys stuffed him into the lockers, and once they locked him in the custodian's closet and no one found him for hours. When he was ten, his grandmother saw the bruises when he took a bath, and he never went back again. He waited for someone to come look for him, his teacher or someone from the offices, to come to their door, insist that he had to go back. He doesn't know if his grandmother spoke to the school, or if no one bothered to find out where he had gone. But no one ever came.

That was the year his grandparents needed his help more than ever. His grandfather's limp had gotten worse; his foot started dragging along the floor. His grandmother rubbed cream that made his nose tingle into his grandfather's knees. His grandfather kept a bullet in a tin box in his nightstand drawer, would hold it up to Luis, point to his knee. Luis would hold the bullet as his grandfather unfurled the map. *Europe*, with its small pastel shapes, most of them not even as long as his little finger. Then, they would go through the photographs. His grandfather in a green uniform, his helmet tucked under his arm. His grandfather, face smooth and the hair on his head full and dark, doing exercises on the deck of one of the old hotels, a row of men missing limbs, the ocean in the background, large boats hulking darkly near the horizon. Luis was never sure if the boats were bad or good. If they meant protection and safety or if they were something else to fear.

His grandmother taught him practical things: how to clean an oven, bake a pie, rewire a lamp, mend his clothes. He thinks of her when he goes to work now, the way she concentrated on these small tasks, in doing them well, her lips pursed until a pane of glass shone or a tear in a dress was mended. He tries to think of her when he gets angry—at the people who leave their plastic cups all over the place, who frown at the cleaning women in the halls, as though everything at the casino should clean itself magically in the night. As though the workers are the ones in the way. He is glad that she can't see the city now, how dark it has become, how unclean. Glass spangled over the sidewalks, used condoms left in the streets.

During his next shift they have him cleaning all day long, changing light bulbs, climbing stepladders to dust the tops of shelves and light fixtures. By the end of the day his hands ache from dusting and wiping and mopping everything until it shines, until the blonde girl nods at him to go home. His fingertips are swollen and his back is sore, but he feels that old pride that his grandmother taught him. He holds his head a little higher when he walks out the door.

He stops at a pizzeria for dinner on his way back to the boardinghouse, points to a slice dotted with circles of pepperoni, holds up two fingers. As he waits, he picks up one of the matchbooks on the counter, turns it in his hands, slips it into his pocket. He eyes the stretchy, gooey strings of cheese that hang off the end of each slice as the man behind the counter slides them on a paper plate. He snows them with shaved cheese and red pepper, his hunger rising up, roaring now.

He's standing outside, about to take his first bite, when he sees the dark car, the windows tinted black, the purple sticker with the silhouette of the busty woman on the back. The men. He starts to walk away, thinking he can slide from their view, slip loose. He feels them behind him but refuses to turn around. He walks faster, feels footsteps slapping, sees their shadows on the ground, and then a hand claps him on the shoulder.

They circle him. The dark-haired one elbows Gold Tooth in the ribs, motions to Luis's pizza, rubs his hands together. He tries to step around them, but Gold Tooth grabs his shirt, pulls him back. The paper plate wobbles in his grip. They make their eyes big, looking at the pizza, cartoonish and stupid and mocking, then the dark-haired man reaches for a slice, folds it, and takes a bite that makes a third of the slice disappear. Gold Tooth laughs and does the same, each of them returning the slices to Luis's plate, nodding at him in pretend thanks. Just when he thinks he's free, one of them trips him from behind. His chin scrapes the sidewalk and there is pizza smashed into the front of his shirt.

He knows he's done nothing wrong and still, he feels the shame, hot and bright, in his cheeks. It's the same as when he was a boy, at school. When the other kids beat on him, but he was the one left feeling as though he had done something bad. His shame expands when he feels the tears begin to well behind his eyes. The men look down at him, and their smiles get bigger. He wants to kick their shins, land punches to their guts, tear at them, rip those chains from their necks. Finally, Gold Tooth pats him on the arm—the greatest insult of all—as though they are friends, they're all in on the joke. They part to let him through, and though he thinks of the way his grandmother showed him to take deep breaths, to count to ten on his fingers, and sometimes that still works, this time he leaves behind the mess of plate and half eaten pizza and breaks into a run.

He doesn't stop until his chest is heaving and he's reached a barren part of town, where a single house stands in the shadow of the blue glass tower, the one built a few years ago that's already empty and locked up. He keeps picturing that gold tooth winking, the cruel gleam in their eyes. His hunger has now been replaced with a desire for revenge. A desire to make them sorry, to make them—the men, the cops, the city, everyone—hurt worse than they hurt him.

JANE 4

YOU ARE HAPPY, UNTIL YOU'RE not. It happens as quickly as someone throwing a bucket of cold water over your head, the way the team did that spring sophomore year when you took first place in the 400 at States. One night you are out with your friends at the diner, Amanda dragging the last nubs of her french fries through ketchup, making little zigzag tracks, Francesca picking at her fingernails and cutting her eyes across the room at the table of guys from Freemont Prep. A woman comes in, and you can tell by her walk, her posture, that she's high. As a girl, you learned to watch for the sway in your mother's footsteps when she was using. You can't see the woman's face from underneath her matted tangle of dark hair, but you break out into a sweat. *It's her*, you think. After all these years, she's come to take you back.

You realize you've been waiting for it, that sometime along the way your fear alchemized into something much more dangerous, something closer to hope. You wanted the pain to begin so it could be over with sooner. So that you wouldn't have to live looking over your shoulder at every cigarette-roughened laugh that tails off in a wheezing cough.

Deep down, you wanted to be reclaimed by the life you came from, the one where the electricity was always getting shut off and you could fit all of your belongings into a pillowcase when you inevitably got kicked out of wherever you were staying. A world where you heard the headboard banging against the wall all night, while you pretended to be asleep, but secretly you opened an eye and tried to understand what was happening, whether that slapping sound of flesh on flesh was injury or love or a little bit of both. And then there might be money on the nightstand, while she slept through the morning, and your stomach raged with hunger but you knew better than to take it, to even touch it. And forget about telling her you were hungry. *You're always complaining*, she'd say. *You're no fun.*

The woman in the diner who is not her, can't be her, leans on the counter, brings her palm onto the bell. *Please ring for service*, again and again, even though the waitress is still bustling behind the pie case. *Just a minute*, the waitress says sharply. The woman hasn't turned, and by now you know it's not really her, but the bell reminds you of the time she took you to the mall to have your picture taken with Santa. She had been high then, too, pulling your arm too hard, dragging you toward the cottony mounds of fake snow while Christmas carols warbled, tinny and too loud, through the speakers. She grabbed the bell out of the hands of the Salvation Army worker clanging for loose change. *Santa, santa, we're here*, she had yelled. She pushed through the line, and when you stood before the man in the suit, you looked up to see Santa frowning down at you. *Julie's here to see you, go ahead, tell 'im what you want.* She gave you a shove, too hard, and you landed in a sprawl in front of Santa's boots. A child behind you started to cry. Other children were always crying in response to you and your mom. You closed your eyes and waited for all of it to end. There was the crackle of the security guard's radio, a voice over your head. *Ma'am. Ma'am, there's a line. You can't just butt in. Ma'am, you have to go.*

That phrase has worked its way back into your brain, into your bloodstream. *Ma'am, you have to go, you have to go.* Go go go.

Back in the diner, Amanda snapped her fingers in front of your face to get your attention. *Earth to Julie. Helloooooo? You owe seven bucks for the bill?*

Amanda's mom picks you up. You are driven home in this clean car, this safe little capsule of steel and glass, and it strikes you as absurd. How protected you are, how completely sectioned off from the ugliness of the world. Is it even real, to live this way? To sleep through the night without hearing glass breaking, a car alarm going off, shouting in the streets? Has this all been one long dream?

At home, your bedroom is immaculate. You've never left so much as a sock on the floor. You know your aunt would never say this, but she wishes you would. Wishes you, for once, would put a cup down without using a coaster, would forget to take your dirty sneakers off at the door. But no matter how many nights you sleep in this bed, with its gingham coverlet that your aunt sewed by hand, or how many meals you eat that your uncle has cooked from his well-thumbed copy of the *Joy of Cooking*, or how many medals you earn and how many checks they write for your track uniforms and your Honors Society dues and your dresses for homecoming and prom, you will never believe that this life is yours, that there isn't a shadow version of yourself out there, picking through dumpsters for scraps and checking the slots of pay phones for change, a shadow self that you are going to have to join one day, because a person can't live split in two forever.

When you first came to live with them, your uncle wept when they said you had scabies, lice, a urinary tract infection, then looked at you with a face full of guilt. For crying in front of you? For not stepping in earlier? For waiting until you spent three nights in a home after your mom was arrested, simply waiting for someone to come? You were like a stray dog in from the street. This was a form of care, but why did it feel so much like punishment? The doctor studying you, examining you with his blood pressure cuff and his tongue depressor and the little light he shined in your nose and ears, asking questions that embarrassed you. The psychologist, who found different ways of asking you if anyone had ever touched you. Any of the strange men—dealers, one-night stands—who used to come by the apartment. She asked so insistently, reassured you, in so many different ways, that you could tell her anything, that you started to wonder if it was wrong that no one had. How were you supposed to tell her they were always too high to even know you were there?

You pick Atlantic City because the bus fare is cheap, and you remember a mug from your first apartment: red, with *Resorts Atlantic City* written on it in white letters. There was a single chip on the rim, but it was the thing from your childhood that was closest to whole. But you don't choose Atlantic City because you think she will be there. She's been dead for nearly a year by the time your bus from Baltimore pulls into the depot. In a way, you'd been waiting for her death your whole life, the question always in the back of your mind. Not *if* but *when when when*. A cellulitis infection took her. Your uncle and aunt hadn't needed to explain that she got it from shooting up.

And yet, she's here in Atlantic City. She's at the bus shelter, smoking a Pall Mall. She's waiting in line at Harrah's for a pots and pans giveaway. She's at the McDonald's near the bus depot, stirring six packets of sugar into her coffee, licking the pastry crumbs and grease from a cardboard apple pie container. But it's not your mother you're looking for, it's your shadow. With every potential fuckup, every misstep, you felt her step closer—the girl you've been fated to become all along. Now you've decided to just meet her, to reach out and shake her filthy hand. One night you are walking along the dark boardwalk and stop in front of a psychic's shop. The lights are out and you stare at the gold evil eye symbol on the glass. You let yourself feel held in its gaze for a moment, wondering what it sees. A feral cat winds its way around your ankles, its whiskers holding the light from the moon. Something lost recognizing one of its own.

YOUR FIRST night on the streets, you think of how you used to pee the bed every night when you originally came to live with your aunt and uncle. You slept on the damp sheets the first few times, the wetness chafing your skin. You wonder if even your aunt and uncle are thinking it: that you've turned out just like her, that something in you just soured, and you've started hitting the pipe, too. But you haven't—you've never even smoked pot. Never even had a drink. You know it looks like ingratitude, but to you it's the opposite. Lightening their burden, removing yourself from all the things you never could believe you deserved. The scholarship offer from University of Maryland. You'd gone online and looked up the tuition. Even with in-state rates you couldn't believe all the money it represented. You couldn't believe that you had earned it—it felt too much like a gift, and gifts scare you. Gifts always feel like they can be lost, reclaimed. You would rather get the loss over with, or else it will hang over you indefinitely, the good, beautiful things in your life just a debt you'll never be able to pay back.

CLARA

AFTER LINING UP TWO MORE dates for me, Des was already having trouble finding men. Apparently she'd thought it would be easier to attract the ones who weren't looking for more than dinner or drinks. Men who just wanted to look and spend. The man who had come in while Lily was in the shop took me to a steak house, where he talked at me as he sawed into a rare piece of meat. Speckles of blood on the white tablecloth, a pool of it on the white plate. The fat finger choked by a gold wedding ring. Still, I smiled at him, like he was some kind of prize, and asked him about his childhood dog, who I glimpsed in a vision before the bread was served. The second was a narrow, chain-smoking lawyer who only wanted me to sit next to him at the blackjack tables—the pit boss frowned at my ID, but he slid her a hundred bucks and I watched him lose $500 more. The vision I had when I was with him was more complicated: a classroom, a teacher bringing a ruler down on top of his desk, inches from his hands. He was terrified of being embarrassed, of being belittled, so I made sure to slip my arm into his, to lean close, ask him questions about how the game worked. And each one gave me a little extra on top of what he gave Des, so I was up to $450 pressed into the back of my book. Even so, I was relieved there wouldn't be any more dates. But I should have known that, like the cool wind from the ocean, relief was always short-lived.

When I went down to the shop on July 5, I found the eviction notice on the floor. My ears were still ringing from the sounds of the fireworks. I used to like watching them when I was younger, but now I wondered if all of that money turned into smoke and ash wasn't just a waste. It was close to ten in the morning and Des was still asleep, her shades drawn against the light. She groaned when I raised them. Her pillowcase was a mess of blue glitter and red lipstick. I thought of the way my hands shook on the first date with Tom, when I lifted the wineglass to my mouth. I thought of the way the man after him had pinched me on the ass, hard enough to leave marks. We had ten days to leave, or else Bill was going to call the cops.

"What the hell, Des? Shouldn't we be caught up on rent now? That's why I was going on those dates!" I waved the notice in front of her face. She rubbed her eyes, and one of her false eyelashes clung to the back of her hand like an insect. "Bill is evicting us, Des. We have ten days to pay the rent we owe, plus this month, or else we get kicked out. Where will we live? Where can we go?"

"Darling, it's not as bad as that."

"Don't *darling* me! I'm not one of those dupes from the club or a dumb tourist. I'm not just another person you can con."

"Let me see this." Des took the notice from my hands. The money I'd saved was enough to cover some of the back rent, but I didn't know where we'd get the rest. By my math, we needed almost two thousand bucks.

"How much do you have saved? Des? Tell me."

"Three hundred, maybe. Could be a little less than that." I figured she had $100, tops.

"Where did it go, Des? I thought that was the whole reason I was going out with those guys. So we could pay our bills."

Her voice rose to match mine. "So I bought some new clothes. So I went out a few nights. Poor little Clara had to eat fancy dinners with a few rich men, giggle a little bit. Boo hoo. Such suffering. Well, you know what? I'm sick of living here, where everything feels like half of what I used to have, then half of that, then half of that. So sue me if I want to find a little joy in the tiny little bit of my life that I have left."

Des had been unhappy for a long time, but she hadn't always been like this, with the drinking, the pills. I remembered her smiling more when I was a kid, when she was still slinging cocktails at the Showboat. Some nights before her shift she would dress me up, too, and we'd dance in the living room, singing into our hairbrushes. Then her shifts started getting cut. Then business at the shop started to falter. Then we started plucking wallets and billfolds from people as they bent over the craps tables or fed money into the slots. I had that $450 and was tempted to just pick up and leave, but I knew I wouldn't go. Not until things were a little steadier for Des. She was far from perfect, but she had never wanted a kid. She could have left me a long time ago. I felt the anger surge through me, an anger that I tried, most of the time, not to let myself feel. The way her need sucked up everything else. If I looked at that anger head-on, it would swallow me whole.

"You've found a lot of fucking joy in that money, by the looks of things. I hear that joy rattling around in your purse, you know. I'm not stupid, okay?"

If we hadn't heard the knocking, I think she would have slapped me. She wasn't used to me talking back, to me being outside her control. We looked at each other, then at the eviction notice, which I had dropped facedown onto the floor.

"It said ten days, didn't it?" I asked.

"Leave it to that bastard Bill to give us ten minutes." She pushed her hair away from her face and looked up at me. "You need to go answer it. He'll have more pity on you. He can't do anything to a minor. Tell him I'm out. Or better yet, try to butter him up a little." She ran her fingers through my hair, pinched my cheeks to give them color. "You know the drill."

I sighed and made my way down the stairs, into the shop. Des crept behind me so she could listen from the hall.

The beaded curtain at the front door divided the figure into strips, but right away I knew it wasn't Bill. I could see a woman's feet.

"False alarm," I called to Des. "Someone for a reading, I think." I hated that this surprised me, someone showing up at our door because they thought we had something to offer.

The woman had on a pair of those Chinese mesh slippers with the sequined flowers across the toe. I unlocked the door, pushed the curtain aside. She had long blonde hair, dark at the roots, and a small mouth that she tried to press into a smile, but it didn't really get there.

"Can I help you?"

"Hey. I'm here to see the psychic? Clara Voyant or whatever?"

"Hello, that's me." I was flustered. Where had she come from? Why did she need a reading so badly? "Please, have a seat. Sorry, we usually don't open until eleven on Saturdays." The crawling feeling started again, and I scratched my nails along my arms.

"Cool," she said, watching me itch. I dropped my hands to my sides.

Her eyes roved over the counter, which was crowded with statues of saints Des had bought from the dollar store a few blocks down, plus a single jade Buddha she stole from the Eastern Delights Massage Parlor—payment, she explained, for them giving her a mediocre foot rub.

"Just give me a minute." I pulled the curtains open, tied them back, and the shop flooded with sunlight so suddenly that the woman winced. I made my way over to the shelf, took the satin bag of tarot cards down, and wondered if I should choose a crystal. Sometimes I brought one over just for show, but she didn't seem like the kind of person who would go for that kind of thing. She seemed a little embarrassed to be here at all, which didn't make sense to me yet, given the way she had pounded on our door. I carried the tarot cards back to the table and started to shuffle. She kept her eyes on my hands.

"I usually start readings with a question. Is there something you came here to find out?"

She stared down at her fingernails, picked at her cuticle.

"You don't just . . . see shit and tell me about it?"

"Not exactly. It helps to have a focus. Something you care about."

She blew her bangs away from her forehead. "Something I care about. Ha."

"You can think about it for a minute. No rush."

She looked out at the boardwalk again. It seemed like she was watching for something, someone, but I couldn't tell what. The seconds beaded into minutes. I didn't mind the silence, unless it meant that she was going to change her mind about the reading entirely—like that other woman had. She shifted in her chair, continued to pick at her nails. Then, just as I was starting to get worried she might get up and leave, she spoke.

"I want to know what's going to happen to me . . . like, what's next? Like, is this just my life?" When she faced me again, I realized that she was younger than I had first thought. Probably only five or six years older than me. But her skin was bad underneath the makeup, and she had that hollow stare of someone who'd seen too much.

"Okay, so you want to know about money? Your job prospects?"

She snorted. "Job prospects. Christ, that's rich. Seriously? So many fucking questions. Aren't you the psychic?"

"It doesn't work that way."

"How does it work, then?" She switched the crossing of her legs and her sweatshirt fell off her shoulder, revealing a tattoo on her chest: a peach, with a bright green leaf hanging from its stem, *Peaches* written in complicated, scrolling cursive above it. She noticed me staring. "A nickname," she said. "No one's used my real name for years." I waited for her to say more. She sighed. "Fine, you wanna know about me? I left home three years ago," she said, huffing at her bangs again. "I never thought it would be permanent. I told myself I was in love. So much for that. Or *I* was in love, him . . . well. If he was, he had a weird way of showing it. Like leaving me on the side of a highway after we got in a fight. Didn't even have my shoes on." I let her talk. The more she told me, the more I'd have to work with when I read her cards, in case a vision didn't come through clearly, and I didn't trust that one would. All of those other images and sounds were still spilling into my brain, interfering like radio static. Another fly tickled down my spine.

"I guess I never really thought about the future before at all. I don't even know what I want to know. I've never really believed in anything before . . . but now . . . now I think about the future keeping up like this and I can't picture it. Can't stand it—is more like it. I want to know if things will change. When. How."

I thought of telling her that I felt the same way. That if I didn't have my dreams of California, the thought of staying here, with Des, stealing, doing readings, meeting men, would kill me.

I turned the first card over: the Fool. The next was the Five of Wands, and the third was the Tower. My breath caught in my chest. All of the readings I had done lately—this one, Julie Zale's uncle with the bandana, the woman with the locket, the one I had given Lily—were full of darkness, warnings, bad omens. But this was the worst one yet.

"What?" she said. "What does it mean?" I took a breath and tried to think about how I could spin things, how I could approach the cards and not feel afraid.

"This is the Fool."

"What, is that me? Shit, man."

"People make that mistake a lot. The cards aren't you—they represent elements of your life. There's a difference." She raised her eyebrows, which were over-plucked, and the skin around them was still pale where the hair used to be. "The Fool represents a journey. Maybe you are about to go on a trip, about to leave town. It can be a real journey or a metaphorical one. That you'll start something new, a project, or start thinking in a new way."

"I like the literal journey. Wanna get outta this dried-up town as soon as I can."

"Me too," I said, before I could help myself.

"All right, babes. We'll carpool, then." She smiled. At first, I thought she might be mocking me, but then I realized she was just being nice.

"And this one, the Five of Wands, represents conflict—a lack of connection or failure to communicate. Stubbornness or resistance to change."

"And what about that one?"

I paused. There was no way not to talk about it. I wished like anything I could tell her it was something good. Especially now that she had just started to like me. "That's the Tower."

"Jesus. There's people jumping away from a fire inside of it. That can't be good."

She was waiting for me to offer an explanation, to say something comforting. But there was no getting around the Tower when it showed up. You could try to soften it, to say that something was about to be ruined, in order for growth to take place. But it was a brutal card. No spin would change its essential meaning: the recipient's life was about to be torn apart.

"It usually means destruction. Turmoil. Upheaval. Change that will force you out of your own ways. For some people it's divorce or the loss of a loved one."

She looked at me pleadingly. She wanted me to offer her any kind of consolation, deliver a caveat.

"The cards don't predict the future, necessarily. They offer guidance. I like to think that their meanings can shift, depending on how you act, the choices you make. It's up to you to put yourself on a path where the Tower takes on a different meaning, something that's potentially good."

"Ha. You've been talking to my mom, huh? She wants me in rehab. Twelve-stepping it with all those fake-ass losers. Avoiding trouble isn't my strong suit. There's something bad—well, I pretty much run smack into it." Her eyes started to water, and I looked down at the floor. There was a pair of shoes in her bag, stilettos with laces that must have climbed up her calf like vines. It was only then that I remembered where I had seen her before, her face contoured differently in the shadows, her mouth traced with red lipstick. Waiting in the dark corner of a casino bar until a man came and sat down next to her, angling herself toward him, arranging her legs so her ankle pressed against his.

I tried again. "These cards are a warning. I can't see what they are warning you about, exactly. But you should be careful, I think. Take care of yourself. Maybe the journey you need to take is back home. Back to your mom."

"Maybe. Maybe you're right." Her voice had changed, and the hardness in her face seemed to break apart. A few tears rolled down her cheeks. When she wiped them away, I noticed one of her fake nails had come off, and the real nail underneath it looked tender and pink.

"Sorry," she said. "It's just that everything feels so . . . fucked."

I didn't need to pretend to know what she meant. The eviction notice. The memory of Tom's tongue in my mouth. I understood.

"How much do I owe?"

It felt wrong to charge her for such a harsh reading. But then I pictured the yellow notice again. I knew I would need to use my California fund to save the shop. That I would have to start over. "Twenty."

She reached into that big bag, underneath the high heels, and pulled on a strap, produced her purse. It felt like déjà vu, at first, my brain jumping and skipping through time, but it was the same bag that the other woman, the one with the locket, had. A tooled leather purse with an oval of a turquoise stone at the center, right above the clasp. She took out a fat roll of bills and held out a twenty. I hadn't noticed before that she had small, almost childish hands.

"Where did you get that?" I said.

"The cash? Ha. You don't wanna know, sweetie."

"No . . . no. I mean the bag."

"What? You like it? To be honest, I found it on the side of the road. No wallet in it, unfortunately. Here. It's yours. Easy come, easy go, and all that shit, right?" She shook the bag upside down, sending a collection of lipsticks and lighters and mints, matchbooks, loose change, and compacts clattering across the table. One of the eye shadows popped open and left a sprinkling of green dust on the tablecloth. She raked them all into her big bag and tossed the purse into my lap. I thumbed the clasp. Just like I thought—it would have slid out easily, without a sound. "Actually, that's how I found you. Your card was in that little pocket on the inside. Whoever got to all the goods left that behind, I guess. I took it as some kind of sign. Stupid, right?"

"No, I'm glad you came." I meant it. I liked her, this woman with her sarcastic smile, her sad eyes. And I didn't want to tell her, but it felt like I was meant to know about the bag, about her.

"Well, catch ya later. Thanks for . . . well. Thanks."

She slipped her feet out of the slippers and pulled the heels from her bag. She wrapped the straps around her calf with an expert quickness, and by the time she tied them into a bow her face was hard again. Before she left, she stood in front of the statues at the counter, their pious eyes all glancing upward like they could see God hovering just above their heads. Maybe she was thinking what I always thought—that for saints, their mouths had been painted such bright, voluptuous reds.

DES CAME down the stairs after she left. "What was that about?"

"Just a reading." I wondered if the woman really went by Peaches, or if she sometimes used her real name. We were alike that way. Another person with two names, one for each version of our lives. Clara Voyant and Ava. Peaches and whoever she had been.

Des pinched the twenty from the table. She still looked tired, and the lines between her eyebrows seemed like they were painted on. "Well, at least it's a start."

I took a breath, pictured the wad of bills that Peaches had pulled from her purse. The shoes, the tight dress. "Look Des, I've saved a little bit, pawning stuff at Zeg's and all. It won't cover everything. But I know what we need to do. I think we'll be okay."

Before I could change my mind, I told her about Tom slipping me his number, about the offer he had made. I knew it was our only chance, but still I waited for her to put her hand out, to say no. To tell me I was too young. That she'd handle it. That I should go back to school in the fall. I was always waiting for her to show me something that looked even a little bit like protectiveness.

Instead, she squeezed my arm, excited. "Well, what are you waiting for, Miss Clara Voyant? We don't have any time to lose." I felt another one of the phantom flies creep along my shoulder. I rubbed at my skin, shook my hair off of my neck, and still I felt it. My ankle. My earlobe. My left eye.

"What's the matter with you?" Des asked. "You keep twitching."

"I don't know. Nervous, I guess." It took all my willpower not to rub at my chest as the sensation crawled across my collarbone.

I found the paper with Tom's phone number on it in the back of my dresser drawer. I wondered what it had meant, that I saved it at all. Surely another girl would have thrown it away—had I sensed this coming? That one day, sooner than I could have thought, I'd be desperate enough to call? Des handed me her phone, and while it rang I prayed he wouldn't answer. For a moment, I let myself think I was safe, but he picked up on the fourth ring.

"It's Clara," I said. "From Atlantic City?" My voice was a pitch too high. Des shook her head. I tried again, swallowed the lump in my throat. "Remember me?" *Better*, Des mouthed.

"Hold on a minute," he said, and I listened as he muffled the receiver. I tried not to picture who he was stepping away from.

"Well, this is a nice surprise. How are you, my dear?"

"I've been thinking about our date," I said. "About what you said. I'd like to . . . to stay over with you."

"I'd like that, too. I suppose I might be able to slip out of town, for a last-minute business trip, if you know what I mean."

"Great," I said. Des nodded at me, encouraging me to go on. "I need to make one thing clear first. This is going to be . . . an investment." That was the word Des told me to use. "After all, there's only one first time for everything. If you know what I mean."

He let out a small groan, like he had just had a taste of something delicious, and I felt the goose bumps rise on the skin of my arms. "Oh my goodness. Well. Whatever you need. I'll let you know where, what room, as soon as I book."

An hour later the text came through: a hotel name, and a room number with a winking face. We would meet on Tuesday—three days away—at 9:00. Des lifted the screen for me to see, threw her arms around me, and whooped. I wasn't happy or afraid. Instead, an eerie calm slid into my gut, where the anger had been.

That night I put the purse on my nightstand. I would have liked it, if I hadn't known where it had come from. If it didn't make me feel nauseated to picture it on the side of the road—what road? God, why hadn't I asked?—and what it meant that it had been abandoned. *Maybe she got mugged*, I told myself. It happened often enough. Des said the girls at the club all carried mace or pepper spray, because thieves targeted strippers, waitresses, bartenders. The ones they knew would have cash. After all this with Tom was over, I would try to find Peaches again. Ask her where the bag had come from, how many days it had been since she found it. Maybe whatever Peaches had to say wouldn't lead me anywhere. Maybe whatever had happened to the bag was the betrayal the cards had said to watch out for. But something told me it was deeper than that. Me, Peaches, Lily, Julie Zale. And that it wasn't over yet.

I KNEW that girls bled the first time, but it hurt so much that it felt like something must have gone wrong. That kind of pain could not be normal. But when he asked if I was okay, I told him I was fine, tried to shape my grimace into a smile. I wouldn't have believed me if I were him, but that was the thing about people—they wanted to believe whatever was easiest to accept.

Afterward, I was surprised at how small the bloodstain was, on the sheets. The pain—and what had caused it—had seemed so much bigger than that. I knew it was strange to feel disappointed, but a part of me wanted to see those sheets soaked in blood, something I could point to and say *that's what they did to me.* Tom and Des and my mother and the clerk at the desk who had handed me the key to the room, the woman who asked what floor when I got on the elevator, and pressed the button for me on the way up. Zeg, when he bartered with me for some stupid trinket I had lifted and made me take less than half of what he would sell it for. The bartenders and waiters who never even asked for my fake ID. The man who only had twenty bucks left in the wallet I stole. The girls at the spa who wouldn't let me in to read people's cards. This whole failing town and its closed casinos, its empty parking garages, the ocean and bay that hemmed us all in. I wanted a sheet bloodied enough to make everyone see how wrong it had all gone.

I slipped out of the room when the first hint of sunlight came through the blinds, my purse filled with the bills Des had told me to ask for up front. I hadn't slept at all and my body felt light and drifty, like I was moving through a dream, but the bones of my face ached. A housekeeper trundled her cart down the hall and looked at the ground as I passed. In the elevator down, I saw myself reflected in the gold panel of buttons—my eyes dark with smeared makeup, my face pale, my hair too bright against my skin. I was wearing my dress and heels from the night before—I hadn't thought to bring anything else. I thought of Peaches and her little mesh slippers, and the way her face changed when she took them off and tied those straps around her legs. As I cut through the floor, a woman eating a Danish at a slot machine looked up at me and sneered as I passed. *Whore*, she was thinking. *Hooker, slut*. A dull throbbing had replaced the pain between my legs, and I tried to tell myself that when it went away, I would be able to forget everything that had happened the night before, the way you come back into yourself once a headache releases its grip. But I knew it wasn't true. I would never be able to forget how he looked at me. Not with hatred or horror or desire, but like I wasn't even there at all.

I waited for a jitney underneath a banner advertising a poker tournament—*It's July, Summer is just heating up*—and was relieved when I got on that it was empty. My skin felt feverish, and I leaned my face against the window's cool glass until we arrived at the Tropicana and I could walk back to the shop.

On my walk, I passed a telephone pole with Julie Zale's picture stapled to it. The photograph had become faded, the ink ran in the rain, like mascara tears sliding down a face. The paper was tattered and peeling away from the staples. I wondered about her uncle, back in Baltimore now, probably. Jumping at the sound of the telephone. Peeking in Julie's old room to admire her trophies on the wall, the track medals hanging from nails above her bed. I was sick of thinking about the girls I would never be: treasured, adored. The girls from middle school, sipping their vodka and lemonade, flipping their hair. That was how their wholes lives tasted—a combination of pink lemonade, vodka, and strawberry-flavored lip gloss—everything for them was sweet and exciting. Julie still smiled out from her photograph. I reached out and ripped the poster, shredded it until the paper was confetti in my hands. I watched the pieces blow down the street, and a coldness moved into my body. How stupid I had been to think that my visions and my tarot cards could get me anything. The world wanted things from me, but they weren't insights or answers. It didn't matter who I was, or what I might be able to see. Look at how it happened with Tom—I had a glimpse of who he was, and still, I ended up underneath him while he drove himself into me, biting my lip to keep from crying out.

I had given my savings to Des for the back rent, and now with the money she had and the cash from Tom, we nearly had enough to cover what we owed. But in another month another rent check would be due. In three, four months, another eviction notice on the floor.

When I got home, Des was sitting in the kitchen. She must have been thinking the same thing—how the bills would continue to come, the demanding envelopes stamped in big, bold lettering. I already knew what she was going to propose. I had opened up a door that I couldn't walk back through.

LILY

WHAT DID I DO, WHEN I wasn't working? My days off were lazy and without purpose. I couldn't remember when I had ever had so much free time. In high school, I'd loved dragging a chair down to the beach and setting it up at the water's edge so that the waves washed over my feet, but I had done that once so far since I'd been home and it felt like a mistake. I remembered why I'd avoided visiting my mother the past four years: everywhere I could see my father. I looked out to the jetty and saw him there, standing barefoot on the cold rocks and casting his line out into the ocean. He'd taught me how to hold the other end of a drag net, the two of us stepping in time in the shallows. We picked the flopping minnows from the black netting and plopped them into our bait bucket, and I felt the pulse of the little fish in my hand.

One good thing came out of my boredom: I had taken up drawing again. I found myself sketching these images from my girlhood—the minnows gasping on the shoreline, bright shocks of seaweed that washed in on the tide. I liked making the loose scribbles, the meditative act of slowly, through line and shape and shading, distinguishing what something was versus what it was not.

Across the street from our porch, where I was sitting with a pencil and notebook in hand, an older woman backed her long silver Cadillac into the driveway. I'd seen her before, in passing—gathering the morning paper in her giant sunglasses, swaddled in a navy bathrobe—but we hadn't spoken.

"Yoo-hoo! Yoo-hoo?" she called. "Could you help me lift this?" I crossed the street, blood rushing to my head from laying still for too long. "Thank you so much! I just bought all of these plants and someone at the nursery helped me lift the bag of potting soil into the car, but I didn't even think about what it would be like to lift it out again. I don't know why they only sell this stuff in fifty-pound bags."

I didn't want to admit it, but even I had trouble heaving the bag out of the trunk. I used to go to exercise classes almost every morning in the city, but I had fallen out of shape quicker than I wanted to admit. "Where should I put this?"

"Oh, inside the garage, please, dear."

I dropped the bag and shook my arms to relieve the strain.

"That's perfect, thanks again. Can I offer you a glass of iced tea? I just brewed it."

"Oh, I'm okay, thank you."

"No, really. Come in, I insist. Just one glass." She put a perfectly manicured hand on my arm. "Now, your mother tells me you are here for a little while? From the city?"

My mother rarely mentioned the neighbors, but I supposed she and this woman might have chatted now and again.

"For now. Just the summer." Walking through her garage door and into the kitchen, I was struck by the smell of her house. A combination of Windex, cigarettes, and kitty litter. "I'm sorry—I don't know if we've met before. What's your name again?"

"I'm Mildred. But you can call me Mil. Mildred is such a miserable name. You're Lily, right? Your mother has told me all about you."

"Yes." I blushed. I wondered what my mother had told her. Chances were that any achievements my mother had bragged about were now out of date.

"Now sit there, and I'll be right over with something to drink. I bet you miss the city. I used to go up there every fall and spring for the fashion shows."

"You did?" I didn't mean to sound so surprised.

"For a long time I owned a boutique on Pacific Avenue, back in the fifties and sixties. Oh, I carried the best stuff. Furs, beaded handbags from Belgium, Ceil Chapman dresses, the most drop-dead gorgeous shoes. Marilyn Monroe once bought a sweater from me when she was in town. Poor thing didn't know it was still pretty cold here in May." She eyed me up and down, a wry little smile coming into her face. "I still have a ton of the stuff upstairs, if you ever want to look. My grandkids all live in Washington so they'll never get to see it." I could picture the closets packed with thick velvet dresses. Beaded cashmere cardigans. Tweed suits in pastel colors. "Had to sell the store off, though, in the seventies. They were saying things were bad then, that the casinos would turn it all around. And get a load of them these days. Now there's no one to turn them around. Anyway, while you're here, you should come upstairs and have a look at some of these things. Follow me."

"Oh, really, thank you, but I couldn't."

"Oh, come on. You'd make an old lady's day." She got up and left the room, and it seemed I had no choice but to comply. It made me nervous to watch Mil go up the stairs, though for a woman her age she was pretty quick on her feet. She opened the door to a room she must have used as a spare bedroom. It had a green chenille bedspread and a large art deco dresser, the top crammed with old perfume bottles, and I suspected no one had visited in a while. The vanity mirror was furred with dust.

She opened the door to the closet, and I was shocked to see that it was almost as big as the bedroom itself. She yanked the chain, and a light bulb mounted to the bare wood of a rafter cast a yellow glow over rows of garment bags. She started to unzip them and clacked through the hangers, pausing every minute or so to wrestle a piece from the bag and hold it to the light.

"Cute, but not right for you, perhaps. Let's see . . . I think there's another one like it but without the pleats." She mostly seemed to want to talk to herself, hold her own council. I could picture what she had been like as a shop owner. Authoritative without being bossy. Never afraid to step in with a recommendation, but not too pushy either. I was scanning the rest of the closet, trying to add up how long it would take her to sort through all of the bags, when I saw that there were frames propped against the wall. I could only make out their bottom edges—someone had draped white sheets over the tops. I hesitated, pinched a corner of the sheet between my fingers. She had been so insistent on showing me upstairs that I figured she wouldn't mind—just a look.

While Mil unzipped more garment bags, I lifted the fabric and took a small, almost involuntary sip of breath. I had expected some horrible 1970s paint-by-numbers, a velvet painting depicting a Playboy-esque nude, a tacky crewel made from fuzzy, fraying yarn.

I'd found instead a painting of a man with a bandage over his eye. He was seated, and it took me a moment to realize that he was in a wheelchair, but then I noticed the arms of his chair at the bottom of the frame, the handles jutting out behind him. His gaze was turned away from the viewer, and his expression gave me the feeling that he hadn't wanted to be seen, that he felt ashamed, even. I crouched to look at the brushwork: precise and delicate on the face, while the broad strokes of his shirt gave the impression of haste. The discrepancy made his expression all the more intense, the evasion in his eyes all the more legible. Behind me, Mil was saying something about box pleats versus kick pleats. I lifted the rest of the sheet: another portrait, of a woman, in what looked like an old nurse's uniform. Her hair fell in limp curls around her chin, and even though, unlike the man, she stared straight out of the painting, there was something withholding about her, something crimped about her expression. As though she were pinching herself outside the frame. Mildred turned, holding out a belted navy dress.

"Oh, you found the pictures, I see. My husband collected them."

"What are they? Who did them?"

"Someone around here, I think. The ones you're looking at are portraits of patients from the Thomas England Hospital, but there are others, too. My husband used to buy them from a friend of his. I don't know who the artist is, though. Wonder if they're still around. Not much left to paint, I guess."

I didn't know where to begin with the questions. "Wait. The *what* hospital?"

"Oh, it's been torn down for decades. It's where Resorts is now. But it was the largest hospital in the country during World War II. My husband was a vet, so he was most interested in the history of the hospital. Those were the first ones he bought, and then it just expanded from there. He kept bringing them home. Didn't bother me, because I don't think he paid much, and they made him happy. You like them? Those hospital pictures are so depressing."

The portraits made me feel melancholy, wistful, even a little bit angry. I was looking at a third that showed a man—no, a boy, he had a boy's apple cheeks and dense, sun-bleached eyelashes— with a line of stitches along his cheekbone, holding his hand to his chest. The tips of his fingers were missing. I lifted another sheet. This one showed a woman in a bathing cap, with a smile that edged toward a grimace. She was turned to the side with a slice of crowd behind her, and she had reins gathered in her hands, beads of water running down her face like tears. One of the girls who used to ride horses off of diving platforms on the boardwalk and land in those shallow pools. The thought of the impact made my teeth ache. Boardwalk and street scenes, façades of shops and billboards that had been torn down for years. Woolworth's. Planters Peanuts, Irene's Jewelry, the Schmidt's Beer clock. A woman with her mouth painted into a perfect cupid's bow and a Miss America sash draped across her chest as she looked out across a stage, wringing her hands.

"I love them. I mean, they *are* sort of depressing. But they're so . . . human. Vulnerable." I thought of the artists Philip Louis had been signing at the gallery the past few years. The postmodern, post-beauty, post-meaning types. Everything they did was ironic, arch. I had almost forgotten that painting could make you feel like this. That the right work brought you into it, then sent you back out into the world, ready to reinvest in the details of your surroundings. They were so different from so much of the work I was seeing in the city: These paintings were simpler, unafraid of approaching sentiment, of asking people to feel something. They didn't give me the sense that I'd had when looking at a lot of contemporary stuff, like I wasn't in on the joke. After everything with Matthew, I craved that kind of earnestness.

"No argument there. A little too human, if you ask me. I prefer landscapes and still lives, myself. Snowy woods and fruit arranged nicely in a bowl, all that, thank you very much. But you can come look at them some time, if you'd like. There's more in the other bedroom."

There was a signature on the bottom right corner of each canvas, but I couldn't make it out, just the swoop of an S at the beginning of the last name. Most of them had dates, too, ranging from the eighties to the late nineties, but nothing since. "Have you ever showed them to anyone?"

"Other than you?"

"Like a professional? They're really interesting, Mil. Someone might want to buy these. Maybe even a museum. Or the Atlantic City Historical Society?"

"Oh, I doubt that. He bought them for nothing, a few dollars each, I think. They don't have any *value*. God, I wish this was one of those *Antiques Roadshow* situations. I'd get myself a nice little condo in Palm Beach in a second." She turned and rustled through another garment bag. "Aha! Here's what I was looking for."

She held up a red gingham sundress with a halter neck. It looked, I thought, more like a tablecloth than something to wear.

"Take this. It will look adorable on you. Perfect for this time of year. Now all you need is some handsome boy to take you on a beach picnic."

"Thanks," I said, taking the dress, the old cotton supple and soft. I didn't bother to tell her that I was planning on staying away from handsome boys for a while. "It's been really nice talking to you, Mil. I hope . . . Would it be okay if I came back later this week? I'd love to talk more, and maybe look at the paintings again."

"I would love that," she said.

As I crossed the street back home, I felt a familiar hum in my nerves—one that reminded me of sitting in my first art history course freshman year, watching slides of paintings click by, color-struck, nearly twitching with excitement. I tried to recall all of the portraits one by one. The man with the tattered ears and slack jaw who operated the roller coaster out on Steel Pier, a cigarette pinched in his fingers. The woman with a flower pinned to her lapel and a piece of yellow carbon paper crumpled tight in her hand. The man with a prosthetic arm from the elbow down, the way the artist had emphasized the mechanical gleam of it in the light.

This painter wanted people at their weakest or their greediest or their most pandering selves. I wondered how I could find out more, if that swooping S in the signature gave me enough information to start with. *Here*, I thought. *Here is where everything changes, the upswing. This is when I start inching my way back to who I'm supposed to be.*

IN CONTRAST to the buzz of excitement about the paintings, my shifts at the spa had been brutally dull. I had forgotten the reality of service jobs: the stretches of hours spent both waiting for something to happen, for customers to serve, and also hoping that you wouldn't have to do anything at all. Or the exhaustion of having to be subservient to the customers who did come in, the brutal self-effacement it involved. *Yes ma'am, of course, sir, please, allow me. My pleasure my pleasure oh no it's really my pleasure.*

By the end of every shift, I felt numb and empty. On my way out I often stopped at the bar, exhausted, ordering a drink or two because it felt like something to do, because it felt good to be the one who was waited on, who got to make requests. Then, walking lazily through the rows of slot machines while I waited for the drifty, buzzed feeling to wear off, I watched men in VFW hats and women wearing fanny packs that bulged like exterior organs smoke Marlboro reds and sigh at their bad luck.

I saw the prostitute with the peach tattoo every now and then: sucking on an ice cube at the bar, crossing and recrossing her legs every time a man walked by, then relaxing into a slouch when he looked away. Rubbing her eyes as she sat on the curb waiting for the jitney, her stilettos in her hands. Once I walked past her in the hallway near the Guest Rewards lobby. I braced myself for her to mock me again, but when she saw me staring she just frowned, then reached into her pocket for a packet of Sweet'N Low, tipped her head back, and shook it into her mouth. She always wore the same style dress, and I could usually see the stem and the leaf of the tattoo peeking above the fabric. Once she had styled her hair in a dramatic swoop over her face, but when she turned I could see that underneath it she had a black eye.

Clara didn't come back to the spa until my sixth week there, early in the morning, while I was alone at the desk. She wore a purple bandana tied around her head and a matching purple halter top, a belly button ring with a dangling charm in the shape of a flower that glinted and jiggled as she walked.

"Good morning, lovely." No sign of the worried girl I had left behind in the shop. She made it look so easy—smoothing over the rough parts of her life. "How have you been lately?" There was a bemused curl to her lips that suggested she knew the way I had fallen apart on the boardwalk as soon as I'd walked out of her door.

"What did you do to me?" I asked, leaning toward her so that I could whisper. Speaking with her about her gift, as she had called it, made me feel insane.

"I don't know what you're talking about, but you sound crazy. Do you mean the reading?"

"Shh! Yes . . . you . . . you did something to me." Maybe she had been angry about what I had seen. I understood that—the desire to punish anyone who witnessed your pain. Hadn't I done the same to people who had known me here, after Steffanie died? If only for a moment, to make yourself feel as though you weren't so weak.

"Like what?" She smirked. "A hex? A curse? You broke a nail?"

"No, I . . ." I thought about trying to explain to Clara what I'd felt on the boardwalk. Like I was in the grip of a vise, the light-headedness, the breathlessness, the wild, jostling thing that was my heart. Eventually a woman had come out of one of the nearby souvenir shops and offered me a cup of water. It had helped, not so much the water, but feeling seen, her hand tentative and gentle on my back. "Never mind, okay. Why are you here?"

"I want to use the spa."

"Clara, you know I've been warned not to let you back there."

"I'm a paying customer." She wiggled her fingers into the pockets of her shorts and produced a crumpled fifty-dollar bill.

"Doesn't matter. Number one, I don't think you're even eighteen years old yet. Number two, even if you pay, I'm not supposed to let you in. Emily said you stole the hair dryer the last time you got back there."

"How would I do that? They are screwed into the wall."

"She said your nails were bleeding when you left."

She shrugged.

"Would you please stop doing that?" I asked.

"What?"

"Shrugging like that. Like you have no idea what's going on, what anyone is talking about. What you're doing . . . you know everything. I don't know how, but you do."

Out of the corner of my eye I could see a trio of women coming down the hall, Swarovski shopping bags slung over their arms. I guessed that they were a 10:00 appointment, and Emily would be in any minute. I believed in Clara, but I didn't want Emily to see that I did—Emily, who found it so easy to shoo her away like a fly. She would think I was stupid, weak.

"Please go, Clara."

She sighed. "You should let your hair down. Literally. You look like a librarian." I winced. Matthew had always liked when I looked a little stern. Or rather he liked undoing it—pulling my hair out of a bun, stripping me out of my pencil skirts. With Matthew, my seriousness had made me feel important, like I could anchor his more impulsive, erratic qualities. The unpredictable schedule. The disregard for paperwork, his lack of interest in grocery shopping, of simply making sure there was milk for the coffee and bread for the toast and soap for the shower. There were times when I resented it, a little bit, but he could always sense that. He had a habit of naming my poses as though I were a sculpture he had made: *Lily Chopping Onions. Lily Scrubbing. Lily, Arms Crossed*. Some of my anger would unravel then, but I wished now that it hadn't. Maybe that anger would have protected me.

"Thanks for the fashion advice. Now, please go." But she didn't budge. She seemed to be weighing something in me, measuring me, and it made me uneasy.

"Okay, I'll leave you alone, but I want to talk to you about something first."

"Me? About what?" I had the feeling she was going to ask me for money or for a favor that could make me lose this stupid job.

"I don't want to talk about it here. Meet me somewhere?"

"I don't know, Clara, Emily warned me about you. And that thing after the reading, how I felt . . ."

"Emily's a hypocrite!"

"Shhh! Keep your voice down. Okay, okay, fine. If you leave right now, how about I come by after work? I get off at six." I glanced up at the women again, now just a few feet from our door; I felt flustered and annoyed that Clara had manipulated me. But then I reconsidered. How different my life at sixteen had been compared to hers. Maybe she needed help: Going to the cops. Finding a way to get away from Des.

"Meet me at the shop," she said. "Des will already be gone for work by then." She sauntered away, and I watched the trio of women sneer at her as she left. I sighed. I had planned on doing more research on the paintings when I got off work—whatever research meant, when I only had a single legible initial, a broad range of dates.

But after I checked the women in and walked them to their lockers, I wondered if Clara might be able to help me there, too. It was a ridiculous, almost feverish thought, and yet—she knew things she shouldn't know. She saw things she shouldn't have been able to see. Would she be able to tell me something about the paintings? Maybe not. But I had next to nothing to go on. If she was going to rope me into meeting her anyway, it was worth a try. I felt a flush of shame at my selfishness, how quickly my motivations had flipped from altruistic to self-serving. Maybe Matthew and Ramona had rubbed off on me more than I had thought.

I WAS hungry from another depressing lunch break in the cafeteria, and the smells of fries and soft pretzels and fudge on the boardwalk made me ravenous. I approached Clara's shop and saw a new message on the chalkboard sign out front. A picture of a crystal ball in the center, and in the corner, a tiny star. I looked in and saw she was alone, sitting on the floor in front of an oscillating fan with streamers tied to the grate, turning the pages of a *People* magazine. I pushed through the curtain, the beads tangling in my hair.

"Ah, good. You're here."

I picked a jade Buddha statue off the counter and turned it over in my palm. Embarrassingly, I was nervous again. In the spa, I had authority, I could enforce the rules. But not here.

She flipped the magazine closed. I noticed that the mailing label on the cover was addressed to the spa, under Deidre's name. Of course.

"Have you seen these posters around?" She rustled behind the counter where the old register sat and handed me a piece of paper. It was the poster about the missing teenager, Julie Zale.

"Yeah, I've seen them."

"What do you make of it?"

"What do I make of it?" If I were being honest, I would have to say that I hadn't thought about it much. But it was different, looking at the girl's photograph up close. According to the date of birth on the poster, she was eighteen. I remembered what it was like to be eighteen. The year before was when Steffanie and I had started sneaking into clubs. A girl that age was hungry for all kinds of experiences, even ones she knew might hurt her. I'd done a lot when I was eighteen that I had told myself I would laugh about one day. The night I let a stranger finger me in the mosh pit of a concert. The time a couple of guys Steffanie and I had crushes on convinced us to kiss and feel each other up in the middle of a crowded party after too many hard lemonades. The pill I took with a boy I hardly knew, thinking it made me look brave and bold and carefree not to ask what it was before I washed it down with a mouthful of Bacardi Razz. Julie Zale was any of us. But one of the mistakes that she told herself would build her character, make her into a woman, had destroyed her somehow.

"I feel sorry for her. Whatever happened to her—whether she chose it or not—probably happened faster and more easily than she ever could have thought. Why? Do you know her or something?" I thought about finding Steffanie on the bathroom floor that night, her face pale, pressed against the tile. By the time she died, it had been four years since we talked. I had heard rumors, though, about her drug use. From New York it was easy enough to dismiss, pretend that it was just hearsay. But at the funeral I couldn't avoid seeing how gaunt her face had become. I knew that whatever had happened to Steffanie since we left high school had everything to do with that night at the club. I knew, even though we had never talked about it, that she spent the rest of her life feeling like she'd been used up and thrown away.

"Her uncle came to me, asked me if there was any way I could help him find her. But things don't really work that way for me. I can't just solve mysteries. Or else I'd be a cop, or detective. Famous, probably. Rich." She smiled at the idea. Selfishly, I felt disappointed: it didn't sound likely that Clara would be able to help with the paintings after all. "But things have been weird ever since he came by."

"Weird how?"

She rubbed her eyes with her palms. "Ever since, I've been having weird visions. Not the usual stuff. Normally I get a glimpse of something, of someone, but they have to be . . . available to me. They have to be near me, close enough for me to see them, to get a sense of them, the way they move in the world. But this . . . I don't know. I've been having visions that don't have any context."

"What kinds of things are you seeing?"

She hesitated. "A few days after he showed up, I started seeing things and hearing things, but I couldn't tell why, where they were coming from. Music, mostly, but also this weird vision of a bloody tooth that was like . . . knocked loose." I couldn't help but wince and touch the tips of my fingers to my mouth. "Then another woman came to me and she was acting really weird. She ended up leaving before I even read her cards. A few days later, I started hearing a baby, crying, screaming."

"Okay . . . " What was she getting at? Was I falling for a ruse?

"Like I said, that's not how things work. But for days, I was hearing this crying sound. When I was on the boardwalk, when I was in the casinos, at night when I was trying to sleep." She smoothed her hand over her upper arm. "And I keep getting this feeling, like something is crawling over my skin."

"You're not on drugs, are you?"

"No! Come on, be serious. I never ask anyone for anything. But I feel like I'm going crazy. And I need help."

"Okay, okay, I'm sorry. Can't all of those . . . visions . . . just be some kind of . . . I don't know, fluke? Like you've got a signal crossed or something?" The absurdity of the situation wasn't wasted on me, sitting there parsing out problems with a psychic's sixth sense. I didn't even have the vocabulary for a conversation like that. But Clara seemed genuinely upset. The detached, composed girl I had met on my first day of work was gone. She was asking for help.

"Yeah but then, a week later, another woman comes and she has this first woman's purse. Said she found it on the side of the road, which makes me think something happened to the first woman. Maybe the crying was, like, a warning. Maybe there was something I was supposed to do. Or that I'm still supposed to do. A few days ago, I started having visions of blurred streetlights. Like I was in a car. And I felt sick, like I was going to throw up. There were other things, too, sort of random. Someone's hands, with lots of little cuts around the knuckles. The floor underneath a bed."

"But those things have nothing to do with one another."

"I know. But I can't get over the feeling that this might also have something to do with her." She nodded to the poster of Julie Zale.

I couldn't help but sigh. "I thought you said you weren't in the business of solving mysteries."

"I know, and I probably wouldn't be thinking about it so much if Peaches hadn't just shown up with the other woman's bag." She reached under the tablecloth and produced a little tooled leather purse. A prop, a ploy?

"Peaches?"

"I don't know if that's her real name. I guess it's not, but she's got this tattoo on her chest of a peach and it says *Peaches* in big cursive letters on top."

The woman from the valet. The prostitute who mocked me. "Her. Yeah, I've seen her around."

"Wait—where? I need to find her. I was too surprised to even ask her any questions. Like when she found the bag, and what road she was on, and maybe if she saw anything else nearby."

"She hangs around at the casino. Sometimes she's at one of the bars at the end of the day when I'm there. I saw her once early in the morning. I guess she had spent the night. She gave me the finger."

That got a smile from Clara. "She doesn't come into the spa, does she?"

"No. Or at least she hasn't since I've been there." She stared at the poster, tracing her fingers over the phone number at the bottom. "Clara. Why did you ask me to come here?"

She blew a puff of air out of her cheeks. "I guess I didn't want to carry all this around by myself anymore. I wanted someone else to know what I see."

"But why me? Why not Des?"

"Des doesn't give a shit about anything as long as there's money coming in. She believes in my gift and all, but if I tell her that I'm seeing things that don't make sense, the first thing she's going to worry about is whether I can still work. You know when you came in earlier this month? After I took your bracelet? I could tell, when I first met you, that you believed me. That you would listen to me. And I felt that way even though you were mad at me. Some people, even when I tell them things, about what I see, they don't believe it. They think I've cheated. That I've looked them up online or something, I don't know what. You're not like that. I think you want to tell yourself that I'm crazy because what I do is weird and scary to people. It's weird and scary to me sometimes, too. But you're still sitting here, right?"

I wondered if it was my father's superstition that let me believe in what Clara said. When you grow up believing in lucky dollar bills, maybe you're agreeing that there are things about the universe that you can't know or control. Maybe, maybe that's what Clara's gift was, too. Something I couldn't rationalize or explain, but that existed. And whether or not I believed her story, I believed in her distress. "So, what do we do?"

"Well, that's what I thought you could help with. Can't you see things at the spa? You have all of those cameras Emily is always threatening me with. And so does the casino. Can't you see the videos? Maybe you could watch the footage, see if Peaches has been hanging around. Or you can at least see who has stayed in the hotel, right? Can you check to see if she's come in lately? Maybe we can find her and warn her . . . just tell her to leave town. She might not believe me, but she will probably believe you. If you tell her you agree . . ."

I cut her off. "You have to be a supervisor to access the security system. Emily might be able to, but I can't." I didn't want to tell Clara that it would probably be impossible to find Peaches that way, that the sheer number of hours and angles that the security cameras represented created an insurmountable amount of footage. Because, of course, I had had the same thought already, about finding my father somewhere in all that tape.

"Well . . . can you get her password? Figure out how to get in there?"

It was strangely revealing what glimmers you could see of someone's life in seven to ten characters. I would have loved to know what little scrap of herself Emily used for hers. "I don't know about that either."

"Please, Lily. At least try? I'm worried about Peaches. I gave her a reading, and it was dark."

"That seems to be your specialty. But sure. Fine. I'll see what I can do, but I'm definitely not making any promises."

"Whoever sees her first can ask her about the purse, what day it was that she found it, and where it was. Maybe that will clarify what happened to the other woman, the first one. I wish I knew her name."

"What about Julie?"

"I don't know what to do about her yet. Let's just start with Peaches and see where we get." She pulled out one of her business cards and scribbled a number on the back. "I just added minutes to my phone, so you can text me if you find out anything. Here, give me yours. Oh, and what do you think about that guy you work with? The janitor?"

"You mean Luis?"

"Yeah. I see him around a lot. He gives me a bad feeling. Something's up with him."

"I mean, he's mute and deaf, so I guess I don't really know him well? He's a little strange but no more than you'd expect." Luis? What did Luis have to do with any of this?

"Well, that at least explains why he didn't rat me out, I guess."

I was about to ask her what she meant when a shadow crossed the shop and we both turned: a man stood in front of the window. Clara's posture sagged. "Shit. You should probably go."

"What's that about, Clara? Another *date*?"

"It's complicated. Let's just say fortune-telling doesn't pay the rent anymore."

"How do you find them?"

"Can we talk about this another time?"

"I mean, you're worried about Peaches, but look at you. Also, how do you know that these guys aren't cops?"

She laughed, a cynical chortle. "Some of them *are* cops. But most cops prefer the Asian massage parlors." I knew the kinds of places she meant. The ones decorated with cheap bamboo screens and thwarted-looking bonsai trees. "We're not the only ones. Take a look next time you go for a walk around here—every single one of them has the same door in the back. I'm sorry. I'll tell you whatever you want to know. But right now I really do need you to go." Every nerve along my body tightened when I stood to leave, but what else could I do?

Instead of walking to my car right away, I stood across the boardwalk and waited. I remembered what it was like, to be thirteen, fourteen, and notice that men started looking at me in a new way. Like they understood something about me that I didn't know yet. But I wanted to see what kind of man would walk into that shop and arrange to buy someone that young. Who had no qualms about doing it so openly. A man who felt like he had nothing to fear.

A man in a suit who had been standing against a light pole looked at his watch, glanced over his shoulder, and went into the store. Clara came out a moment later, picked up the chalkboard sign, carried it inside. I watched as she switched the hanging sign on the door from *Open* to *Closed* and drew the curtains across the window.

I listened to the *tick-tick-tick* of the Crazy Mouse crank up the tracks. I wondered if she was making up everything else. Was all this about the missing girl and the inexplicable visions, the strange sensations, the bad dreams, a way to ask for help without having to talk about the other things that were really going on? I could tell her fear was genuine, even if she was masking it behind this search for these women. And I even believed that she saw things sometimes. But this, with the women, could it be true? I sat on a bench, rubbed my temples. My life here was supposed to be simple, even dull. And now here was this girl—a thief, a con, a prostitute, and maybe a psychic—insisting she needed my help. I didn't know what Clara could actually see or not, but either way, I didn't want to fail anyone the way I had failed Steffanie.

I stayed like that until I had the sense that I wasn't alone—that I was being watched. I looked up and scanned the boardwalk, and the loose, loping gait, the narrow shoulders. Luis. He had already turned his back on me, but I was sure it had been him. What was he doing here? It wasn't strange that he might come to the boardwalk, but why, when I lifted my face to look at him, had he turned away? Was there something off about him, something I should be worried about? A sense of dread bloomed in my gut, souring the evening's beauty: the light on the ocean, the creamy-looking sand. Across the boardwalk, the sign on Clara's door still said *Closed*. The curtains remained shut. I lingered for another twenty minutes, but nothing changed, except the steady sense of worry that crimped my shoulders and my neck.

JANE 4

YOU DON'T KNOW HOW HE'S tracked you down. You left no trace, no clues. And then one day you see your own face on a poster at the boardwalk, on telephone poles, in the windows of stores. It's your old face, the face of a girl who still believed she could live a different life, who believed she could hide from her shadow-self forever. At the bottom, the phone number your uncle had you memorize when you first moved in. You've still got the rhythm of the numbers in you—you could call that number from the middle of a dream.

How did he know you were here? You've been so careful. You don't like this, the inversion of things, your second, better life reaching to haul you back. You'd made up your mind about who you are and what you deserved.

Who you are: a girl who sleeps at the shelter, listening to the others cry in their sleep.

Who you are: a girl whose mother wrote to her from prison, only to ask for money in her commissary account.

Who you are: someone who is running out of money to wash her clothes at the Laundromat on Kentucky Avenue.

Who you are: not too numb yet, to not feel afraid.

YOU REMEMBER, moments after you see the first poster, the time you left your wallet next to the sink in the bathroom. You had no plan to use the cards, so you only checked that the cash was missing. Two hundred dollars, gone. You had been so worried about that that you hadn't thought about the Amex for days. The one your aunt signed you up for in case of emergencies. Chances are, she would call everything since you've left an emergency. You realized eventually that if someone had used it here, you could be traced. You hoped whoever stole it would wait until they got to another state. You would have canceled it, but you liked the idea of throwing everyone off. It's not that you wanted anyone to look for you. (Or . . . or did you? Do you?)

And then, Jesus, the day you saw him. Your uncle. Sitting there at the cheap little restaurant on the boardwalk, the one with all the yellow plastic tables and chairs, the only person without a Bloody Mary or a mimosa next to his plate. Was this what you wanted? To see your uncle slumped over his phone, probably texting your aunt that he was hopeful the posters would help, even though you saw his posture was broken by exhaustion. And it was all your fault.

You couldn't help it. You followed him a few blocks after he paid his bill. You thought how easy it would be to catch up with him. Seven, eight strides? Even now that you are no longer in race shape. You could tap him on the arm, say you were sorry. But none of that would change the chemistry of your personality.

How to tell your uncle about that? He and your mother grew up in the same tidy little split-level, on a cul-du-sac, where the streetlights weren't shot out once and never repaired, where whatever was in your mother must have been wrong since then, and it's wrong in you. You are different from your friends, your coaches, your aunt and uncle. They cared so much about you winning those meets, they screamed your name—your friends even painted it on their cheeks. It had been easy to run that fast, but the attention embarrassed you, made you feel guilty. They couldn't see that you were slowly souring from the inside out.

You decide you'll scrounge up enough for a bus ticket somewhere else, somewhere farther away. You've heard the other women in the shelter talking, talking about sleeping with men for cash as though it were as easy and impersonal as working a shift at Burger King. And isn't it your right? Your body, at least you get to sell it or rent it out as you see fit. And besides, you would only need to do it once, just to get enough to get out of here, to go somewhere you can breathe.

It's not that you think there is anything elegant or noble about suffering—pain is just pain, too abundant and easy to come by to mean anything, other than itself. It does not mean redemption, or absolution, and it doesn't make you stronger. But happiness can be a burden, too. When it comes down to it, you don't know how to be a human, how to bear either pain or joy.

WITH YOUR mother, you didn't think of it as prostitution because it was rooted so strongly in need. Cause and effect, no frills or pretenses about it. Prostitutes were women in red dresses and heels, women with too much makeup on, women who marked themselves in obvious ways as available for sex. Women who liked it too much—when you still thought that women weren't allowed to want sex like men did. You've seen those kinds of women around here, too. Like the one with the peach tattoo who got in your face the first time you tried to pick someone up, so you left the bar and were stuck in AC for one more day.

So now you go down to the parking lot of the Sunset Motel. You heard that's where some of the other girls hang out, that it would be easy—though you couldn't expect to get paid as much. You spend twenty minutes toeing bottle caps in the parking lot before a man approaches you.

In the room the light comes through the cheap curtains and you let the man touch you. You feel the shadow Julie stepping closer, the gap between your selves growing smaller than it's ever been, an arm's length, then a few inches as you take off your clothes, then a sliver as thin as a slice of paper when he pushes you onto the bed. You're scared and a little bit embarrassed by his want. It's not your first time—Kevin Luther, last spring—but it's already so different that it might as well be. Kevin pausing after he entered you to tuck a strand of hair behind your ear, like you were something delicate, something that could break.

This could be one of the last ways you might understand her. You're still scared to go all the way, to open the gates of your brain to the drugs, but this . . . this is something you could point to and, if you were to meet her again (impossible, impossible, but how little all that seems to matter now), you could say that you understood her desperation, understood the sadness and the strangeness and the loneliness of some man on top of you, groaning a name you gave him that wasn't yours.

Afterward, you weep to yourself on the long walk back into town, the marsh grass wavering, rippling like a prairie.

You wait a day and tell yourself you'll do it just once more—you want a cushion, after all, just a little bit more cash. You wait until it's dark, moths weaving in and out under the streetlights. Cars blare their horns at you as you make your way down the shoulder of the road, warning or greeting. Your uncle could drive by at any minute, if he hasn't already gone home. But still, a part of you wants to rescue yourself, the *you* of the gingham coverlet, the *you* of the track medals hanging above your bed.

When you get to the Sunset Motel, you're not the only girl there, but you're the newest, so you sit on the edge of an old planter box until the three other women pick someone up. The parking lot is empty, and all you can hear is the feeble buzz and crackle of the neon sign above your head. The name of the motel, and then a sun, a half circle with sticks of neon that light up one at a time, like rays, and then go dark. A man comes out of a room and you hold his gaze. You can't tell if he's checking you out or is about to call the cops. Just in case, you look down at your feet as he comes near.

He introduces himself as John, and you introduce yourself as Suzanna. Your mother's name. It carries a current on your tongue and makes everything afterward both more real and less real. He asks you if you're looking to party, which you guess is one of the ways people talk about what you're about to do. *Maybe*, you say. You feel stupid, that you don't entirely know what you're signing on for if you say yes.

He tells you he's got some stuff in his room. He's still looking at you in a way you wouldn't quite describe as sexual. Hungry, maybe.

He pulls out a chair, motions for you to sit. He offers you a pill, and you hesitate a second before you pinch it from his palm. He watches you place it in your mouth, mime a swallow, and slide it under your tongue. You want to please him but not obey him. What you've given up so far has been things or parts of yourself that you were already willing to lose. You wait for him to take a pill, too, and when he doesn't, when he turns around, you slide the pill into the pocket of your jean shorts, the white surface puckered and cratered where it had started to dissolve. You catch the brassy glint of a ring on the bedside table, the kind of weighty championship ring the football players wear at school. You stifle the impulse to smirk. A man that age still hanging on to a scrap of old glory. You are only eighteen, and yet all of those victories feel like they happened so long ago.

You wait for him to touch you, to ask for something or demand it, but he only sits on the bed, watching you. Once, you and your friends found a list of strange fetishes online, read them off to one another at school, and laughed so hard that your abs were sore the next day. Foot fetishes and men who wanted to be peed on, men who wanted women to talk to them like babies, people who dressed up as fuzzy animals and had sex, men who wanted to be kicked in the balls. You wonder if there is a fetish for watching to the point of awkwardness, for making women uncomfortable.

Minutes pass. How many? Three? Ten? Forty? You can't tell anymore. The room feels small and the minutes feel long and you start to feel hot, then cold, then hot again.

"Where'd you put it?" he says. He looks mildly amused.

"What?" you say, but you know he means the pill.

He sighs. "You've gone and made this difficult, haven't you?"

It's like your body knows something before your brain can put it into words. Your jeans go damp. You are nine years old again, still pissing the bed in your aunt's house every night. He rises from his chair, and the next thing you know there is a cracking noise that splits the air and you cry out, but then something covers your face and you can't breathe right, then you can't breathe at all, and your lungs are burning, burning in a way that reminds you of running. In your mind you are running, running out of the parking lot, back down the dark road, down the boardwalk, which stretches on and on, somehow carries you all the way back home.

Home, which has nothing to do with Suzanna, or with this version of yourself you've been experimenting with. Home, where you climb underneath the gingham coverlet and sleep.

JANES 1, 2, 3, AND 4

IT IS NEARING THE END of July and there has been no break in the heat. The women remember a time when heat like this was related to desire, a ripening of hunger, of want. The kind of heat that made you crave wet, juicy foods. Peaches whose juices dribbled down your forearms; cool, crisp watermelon; cherries that turned your mouth a sultry purple. Desire for feeling, too, to wear tank tops without a bra so that the fabric skimmed your nipples. For the cool water of the ocean sluiced between your legs, the shimmer of sweat collecting between the jut of your hip bones, the reassuring weight of a damp towel over your shoulders, like an embrace.

There is a sisterhood among them, these women in the marsh. Each time he brings another one, they understand what she has seen. His hatred of them, which he had once masked to look like love, or desire, or sometimes something they interpreted as fear. The way the pill he gave them made the edges of their vision go blurry and a strange halo of light appear around his head, so that he looked like an angel or a saint cast in stained glass. How they only saw him grit his teeth with the effort of it at the end, glance at the blocky sports watch on his wrist as though to count the seconds they had left, as their lungs burned and their limbs became so heavy and their thoughts were reduced to single words that filled their whole bodies: NO or OH or PLEASE. And then the blind, mute pain, the state beyond language, and after that there was only darkness left.

Fireworks have exploded over them, trails of sparks streaking through the sky. Then there was a memorial service for a young man who drowned in a boating accident, and his family carried candles and white carnations in the sea. For a moment the white heads of the flowers bobbed on the surface of the water. The next morning many of them washed up, a mess of wrecked petals or woody green stems stripped bare. The women shivered with jealousy. All of those footprints in the sand, those hands cupped protectively around flames.

The indifferent orange neon *VACANCY* sign of the Sunset Motel blinks weakly through the dark. The building is one of seven squat structures still standing along the Black Horse Pike. They were erected in a strip in the 1950s to accommodate the overflow of tourists pouring into the city on Eisenhower's new highways, cheap and cheerful alternatives to the big hotels along the boardwalk. Pictures of these motels looking bright and sweet were stamped on postcards, sent to Grandma back in Allentown or Binghamton or Rego Park. *Greetings from the Gateway to Atlantic City.*

Families used to stay here: mothers who packed picnic baskets lined with cloth, fathers who taught their boys to throw footballs in perfect spirals, children who ran around with a thick paste of zinc on their noses, grandfathers who showed kids how to catch crabs in the inlet. But the motels' doo-wop cheer has long faded—the aqua and coral awnings blanched by the sun or torn away by storms, so that their metal skeletons are exposed. Their stucco façades are spotted with gray mold. In the 1990s, they were used to house people on welfare, until county officials raised concerns. Now there are oil stains in the parking lots, syringes in the gutters, condom wrappers and chewed gum and mashed cigarette filters collected in the empty planters. It's a place for hard drugs only, where dealers sell heroin, coke, crack, speed. Guests wake up with welts from the bugs and rashes from sheets—but if they're here in the first place, they're usually too far gone to care. Fifteen bucks a night for a place to sleep, you take what you can get. It's better than the street. Sometimes if a girl makes enough money here, she'll buy herself breakfast at the Quality Inn across the road—seven bucks, all you can eat.

The motel manager will grumble to anyone who will listen that he has to replace light bulbs all the time—crack addicts make off with them, scrounging for anything they can sell. Sometimes you get a room with no lights at all and no one will come fix them, no matter how many times you call. Men beat women out in the parking lot, and everyone pretends it's not their business, even as the screams get louder and louder and they can hear the fleshy *crack-crack-crack* of the blows—who can risk the cops showing up, shining flashlights into cars and knocking on doors?

The women see, too late, the symbolism behind the name, why he drove them here on that last night: He told them that the sun had set on Atlantic City. There is something bad in the air and in the water now, something rotten and wrong. A moral disease. The city needs a warning, a biblical punishment. It needs to change, to repent, before the sun can rise again. He wants to bring them all to their knees. God has clearly brought a few misfortunes to the town: The storm that tore away a stretch of boardwalk and filled the streets with water. The way so many of the casinos have shut down. But bad luck and floods are not enough. That's where he comes in.

There is a fourth woman with them now, a young woman with blue toenail polish and long, dark hair. Their bodies hummed like tuning forks as he carried her through the tall grass, arranged her like the rest with gloved hands. The rhinestone in her nose sparkles in the sun.

The marsh is supposed to be protective, a buffer between the land and the sea. It's where things transition, where water and land slide together into one. Blue claw crabs scuttle through the murky water, sometimes finding their way back to the ocean. Birds raise their young here, where there are fewer predators and plenty for them to eat. Egrets pick their way through the mud with elegant care. But for the women, it's purgatory. Nothing in the marsh is either/or, water or land, lost or found. Their bodies are starting to become something else as their tissue softens and the blood pools in their limbs, something not bound by muscle and skin. They're not women anymore, and yet they aren't free and light like spirits. Free to float away, to rise above the marsh like ghosts.

They sense the shift in the wind during the final stretches of July. They know that this new month will bring warmer water, longer nights, cooler breezes. Then, the ocean will brew storms, hurricanes that surge their way up the coast. Wind that tears at the grass, tides that could scatter them, wash away what's left. They think this means they're running out of time. Time to tell their stories, time to be heard. They plead again for someone to see before it's too late.

CLARA

IT DIDN'T TAKE ME LONG to see how quickly a person's code could crumble, how easily the world would wear away at your rules. Des had told me I wasn't supposed to meet anyone she hadn't found. At first I listened, content to scrounge money from the ones she approved of with an extra sticky-sweet smile, an extra kiss. But then, one afternoon I lifted a porcelain doll from the gift shop at the Borgata and was walking to Zeg's to see what he'd give me for it, when a car pulled up, the window cracked. The driver asked me if I felt like going for a ride. I could only see his sunglasses, which made me nervous. But the math won out. After paying Bill, I was back to $250 again.

I knew I was being reckless. For a moment I thought of Des pointing out a woman on the street once, when she saw me staring at the strange scars on her face. "Acid," she said. "She got together with the wrong man and now look at her. She'll have his marks on her until the day she dies." Her skin looked like it had melted into itself, the glazed-looking scars, the tragic air that hovered around her because she still carried herself as though nothing about her had changed. And then I thought, *So what*, and reached for the handle of the passenger's side door. I had been dreaming of oranges that week, oranges heavy with juice, on the knife's edge between ripeness and rot like the ones that my mother said splashed into the swimming pool outside of her guesthouse. It felt like a sign—I would rot if I stayed in town any longer. My life would have to get uglier, messier, before it would be clean and bright—I would need to do whatever it took to be free.

"Sure," I told him, making my voice husky and low. But I couldn't help but look over my shoulder before I got in, and now I really knew what those girls felt, the ones I had watched all my life. How they probably wanted one last fresh breath of air, one more moment to arrange their face before surrendering themselves to someone else.

HIS CAR smelled like cologne and peppermint candy. He tried to act calm but he was nervous   he gave it away in the way he kept scratching at the side of his nose.

"What do you have there?" he asked. I held up the doll. He laughed so hard he sprayed spit all over my arm. "A whore with a fucking doll. This place is too damn much." *Yeah*, I thought. *I feel the same way.*

He drove to the parking garage at Bally's, a shady spot on the upper level. He reclined his seat, unzipped his pants, closed his eyes. When I hesitated, he took me by the hair and pushed my mouth toward his crotch.

When it was over, he gave me a hundred bucks. Up to $350—$1,650 and then I'd never have to do any of this again. He didn't offer to drive me anywhere, so I got out in the parking garage. I was studying the constellation of old chewing gum at my feet when he called to me.

"Hey," he said. He hadn't asked my name. "You forgot this." He handed the doll out the window. I could hear him laughing as he drove off. Once his taillights disappeared, I threw the doll as hard as I could against a concrete pillar. Her face broke into pieces: a sliver of cheek, a blue long-lashed eye. Outside, lightning crackled in the distance, the clouds dense and greenish, otherworldly. The wind whipped through the city, and finally the clouds deepened in color before they broke apart and released rain. Huge drops fell, splashes as big as poker chips, and the thunder boomed through the garage, loud enough to trigger a few car alarms. I sat and watched the city get drenched, listened to the blare of the alarms, and savored the feeling that no one knew where I was. For the first time I could understand what would make a girl want to disappear. No one else to see the bad things you had done.

I HOPED that Peaches would come back—some people did, after a tough reading. They wanted it to be like the casinos, when a new deal, another shuffle, might refresh their luck. When she didn't, I decided to search for her: in the dim little casino bars on the floor, at the nightclubs, where I sat at the bar and drank an orange soda until the strobe lights gave me a headache. Every time I heard the *click click click* of high heels on marble, I turned to make sure it wasn't her, strutting in those heels with the ties. I didn't hear the crying anymore, but I was still having visions, a baby's hand uncurling then clenching into a fist. Little legs kicking in the air. Another, of moths fluttering in and out of a streetlight, the blare of horns. But what I didn't know, couldn't understand, was why the visions lingered, repeated on a loop. They interfered with anything else I might see. For the first time in years, I couldn't use my intuition, those little bread crumbs of knowledge that had been helping me get through the world. Like when I was younger and a bad storm rolled in off of the ocean, and the TV went fuzzy, then dim. I hadn't thought of how vulnerable I might feel without my visions. One more reason to go to my mother—to ask her what was happening, to see if she could help.

I had been looking for Peaches at the Borgata when I met the next man. At the other end of the bar three drunk girls screeched along with a karaoke machine and spilled their drinks over the rims of their glasses when they danced. We sat one stool apart, but he ignored me at first, simply sipped a beer and frowned at the women in small denim skirts helping one another climb up and straddle the mechanical bull, cackling when they toppled to the ground, their leopard-print underwear exposed for everyone to see. Then I felt his eyes fall on the skin of my forearms, where I'd scratched a few jagged tally marks—one for each man who touched me. He slid over a stool and bought me a drink, something cloudy with sugar that held a bright sprig of mint crushed under cubes of ice. I knew I was being stupid, getting in over my head, but I'd make my money fast, get to California, and learn how to forget.

As we talked, I kept one eye on the hallway, the slow trickle of people passing by. I watched for the other woman, too, the one who'd run away from her reading. If I saw her, it would feel like proof that whatever trapdoor was supposed to open in the universe and swallow her up had been faulty. Maybe she had already gone home, back to whoever was waiting for her. But that didn't make sense. If the first woman had left, why had Peaches found her purse on the side of the road? And even if I found Peaches, would the answers help? Still, I carried that purse wherever I went, hoping it might bring one of them around, like bait.

In the man's room, the chill from the shuddering air conditioner sent a prickle of goose bumps up my arms. He pulled my hair so hard I pictured a fistful of it coming out in his hands. I didn't cry out, even though he probably wanted me to. I bit my lip and waited for the sharpness of the pain to ease into a dull throb.

He kept a length of rope coiled in his dresser drawer, like a snake. He tied me to a chair, knotting it tight enough so that my head jerked on my neck with the force, and the rope rubbed and scratched against my arms. Then he sat across the room, lit a cigarette, and watched the smoke curl toward the ceiling. I watched him, both knowing what was coming and hoping I was wrong. He looked at the cigarette and tilted his head, playacting like the idea had just come to him. I shut my eyes and listened to his footfall cross the room. He stood over me until I opened them again, and that's when he pinned my hand down and pressed the coal of the cigarette into my middle finger.

I screamed at the first hint of pain, my voice high and childish. I imagined the burn boring into the bone. I could smell the singed skin. He lit another cigarette and held my left hand. This time the pain felt brighter. I couldn't think of anything besides how much it hurt—it was as though I had never lived a single moment without this sensation, that burning, white-hot scald, that awful smell.

When he was done I forced myself to look down at the marks. The wounds were an angry red, perfect circles dug out of my skin. The tears fell in a thick patter, rolling off of my chin and into my lap. He watched me cry, then reached for the buckle of his pants. I listened to him come, the strangled cry escaping through his gritted teeth, like any pleasure was something he was trying to keep in. He washed his hands before he untied me, the wounds throbbing. He left three hundred dollars on the table. I could hardly pick it up. I couldn't decide if it was a lot—after all, I hadn't had to touch him—or not nearly enough.

Back in the apartment, I smeared the wounds with ointment and wrapped Band-Aids around them. It took me longer than it should have, but my hands wouldn't stop shaking. The dread I had felt all summer was like a knot in my throat. I took the cash from my pocket and smoothed it into the back pages of my book. I counted again: $650. Enough for the bus, for the taxi ride to my mother's place. It should have soothed me a little, made it feel worth it. But I could feel my pulse in each wound, and the thudding of it in my ears when I tried to go to sleep.

WITH EVERYTHING else that was going on, finding Peaches, and the woman who had run away, gave me purpose, though the strangeness, the pressure of it all, was getting to me—I had started to jump at even the smallest of noises when I was alone, or suffer crying jags that swelled up suddenly, full-body sobs that left me feeling used up. The day after the man burned me, I forced myself to leave the apartment, even though all I wanted to do was curl up and sleep.

Out on the street, a jitney swerved around a taxi, both drivers leaning on their horns. A few drunk college students swayed down the street, bickering about where to go next. *This place is a fucking joke,* one of them complained. *The chicks here are fucking busted.*

I walked toward Zeg's pawnshop. I hadn't been there for a while and for once had nothing to sell, but I was lonely enough that I was willing to listen to his scolding for the afternoon, just to talk to another person, to hear my own voice out loud. I once had a vision of Zeg helping a man who must have been his father at a shoe store: his father would hold out a shoe to a customer, and Zeg would hurry into the back room to look for the proper size among the stacks of white shoeboxes. In the vision I could see out the front window to what must have been Atlantic Avenue, the marquee of the old movie house. The theater was closed now and the store across the way, where Zeg's father's shop would have been, was now a fried chicken restaurant. So that explained Zeg, I guessed. He was just like the rest of us. He couldn't let go of what he had lost and would spend the rest of his days hoarding the wrong things trying to make up for it. Maybe his father had gone out of business when the casinos were built. Maybe his pawnshop was his small way of getting back: collecting gamblers' wedding rings and lucky coins when they came to him pleading, liquor wafting out of their pores, eyes bloodshot, hands shaking, giving them a tenth of what their most prized possessions were worth. Maybe he felt like he was getting his revenge by being exacting, cheap.

A strip of bells attached to a leather strap jingled when I pushed through the door. Zeg was bent over a copy of the *Press of Atlantic City*, and I could see the thinning hair at the top of his head. His store was a mess, but he knew where everything was, as though at the end of the day he brought home a map of his inventory and studied it before he slept.

Below him, a glass case gleamed with rhinestone necklaces, tarnished silver spoons, gold bracelets and earrings, old watches, all stopped at different times, and a few newer ones that told the times in other cities, too: London, Tokyo. I loved looking at the things in his case, but he was as indifferent to all of it as though they were tabs from soda cans, bits of penny candy, tokens from the arcade. They were like the visions in a way. Scraps of a life, clues. And then I had an idea.

"Good morning," I called. Flirting didn't work for Zeg, and stealing from him was out of the question—he was way too vigilant for that, one of the few people I knew who actually paid attention to how other people moved through space. I always wondered, what did he want, other than to read his paper and exact his revenge, piece by piece, pawn by pawn? I couldn't tell.

"If you're bringing me some old movie poster or a porcelain doll, you can forget it. I'm up to my neck in goddamned porcelain dolls. And I don't want to deal with paper goods. They don't hold up, too much salt and water in the air."

"No dolls. I'm here as a customer today."

"A customer? That's rich."

I didn't say anything, but crouched to look at the sleeves in a box of old records.

"Where's Des been? Haven't seen either of you around much lately."

"Des? Your guess is as good as mine."

"So, what are you looking for, anyway?" He must have felt sorry for me—his voice had softened.

I glanced at the trays of rings. The blonde woman had that pale band of skin on her finger. She had rubbed it as she spoke. "Hey. Has anyone pawned any wedding rings here lately?"

"By lately you mean what, today?"

"Like three weeks ago. A woman. Sandy-blonde hair. About as long as mine. Locket around her neck."

"How do you know that? She steal something that you stole first? She was real shifty when she came in. I would have rather had that necklace, to be honest. You have no idea how many wedding rings walk in here each week. Lockets, not so much."

"Which ring was it?"

"Christ, you think I remember?"

"Zeg, I know you remember."

He sighed, produced another tray from the case, scanned the rows of rings. I thought of the reading I gave her: the Four of Wands, the happy home life. That ring had meant something to her, once. Zeg plucked a gold band from the tray and handed it to me. It had a pattern of tiny flowers engraved on the outside. I tilted it to get a look at the inside. In scrolling cursive: *Victoria and Zachary, 7-13-14*. I felt gratified that the reading had been accurate, until I realized that also meant there was something bad waiting for her.

"Victoria," I said out loud. I don't know why it felt so good to have a name—a name didn't tell me anything else about her, didn't help explain where she had come from, why she had been so nervous around me, or where she had gone. It didn't explain why, after she came to me, I saw images of her baby, heard its cries rip through my brain. But it was some sort of comfort, one more thing that helped make her feel real.

"You done with that?" Zeg asked.

I held the ring in my palm, traced it with my fingertip, then clicked it onto the counter. "Yeah. But what can I get for twenty bucks?"

"Nothing."

"Oh, come on. Not true." Zeg rolled his eyes and crouched to pull a few trays from the case. A row of vintage buttons with rhinestone centers, still sewn into the card. A single shoe buckle. A glass marble. A thimble. I lifted each item, weighed it in my hand. I was stalling, because it had felt good to come see Zeg, like when things were simpler. When I was just busy plucking bracelets from drunk ladies' wrists, stealing wallets from senior citizens.

"What are you smiling about?" he asked.

"Nothing," I said. "Hey, show me those?" I tapped on the glass to indicate a tray of pocketknives. The one that caught my eye had a pearly handle decorated with silver swirls. It gleamed in the light.

"Out of your budget."

"Can I at least see?"

Another grunt, and Zeg crouched again.

He pushed the knives toward me. "You are wasting my time." Some of them had handles that looked like bone; others were carved with marks and symbols that I didn't recognize. I touched my finger to the one with the silver swirls.

"Don't even think about it."

I touched another, a longer one that looked less ornate. "Uh-uh."

I picked up a third, and when Zeg didn't say anything, I flicked the blade open. It was freckled with a few rust spots but otherwise it seemed okay. It was simple, silver, and a little shiver of feeling moved through me when I looked at it, felt the cool metal against the skin of my palm.

"How about this one?"

"What do you even want that for?" I didn't really know, other than it made me feel good to hold it. A little less small, a little less afraid.

"Forty-five dollars for that one."

"Twenty dollars is all I've got." I pushed the bill toward him and his eyes caught on my fingers, the matching Band-Aids, and something like surprise crossed his face. Just for a second, and then it was gone. Sometimes I thought Zeg might have a little bit of the gift, too.

"You're robbing me blind, kid."

I handed the ring back to Zeg, pushed my twenty in his direction, and slipped the knife into my bag. Down to $630, but the knife had called to me, and I knew better than to resist a feeling like that.

I was a block away from home when the tingle came back and a vision moved through me, like a kaleidoscope turned too fast. Highways, roads stretching endlessly. A woman baking bread in a sunlight-filled kitchen. A hotel room, the sense of being hit hard across the face. Something soft and pale, something bright— shining discs, hanging above a bed.

I came to exhausted. My limbs ached, the way they had when I'd had the flu last year. The throbbing in my head from the blow lingered, and I had to blink a few times before the street around me came back into focus. Each step toward home felt heavy, full of effort. Her name was in the back of my throat, but I didn't want to say it, to match up what I knew with the thing I had been afraid of.

The vision was about Julie. Julie Zale. The tooth, Victoria's crying child. I couldn't deny it anymore. There was something evil and ugly at work behind these visions. And now someone had gotten to Julie Zale, too. I texted Lily. *Please, can we meet?*

LUIS

ON HIS DAY OFF, HE buys food for the cats, and in the afternoon he carries three plastic bags of cans to the bulkhead. When he slips beneath the boardwalk, he takes a moment to relish the shade, the sand that has cooled underneath the planks. To his left, the pier juts out into the sea and a pair of men are talking, one of them leaning against a piling. Luis pays them no mind and stoops to open the first can. The cats crowd around him, curl around his feet. He's only opened six of the twenty cans when he feels a tap on the shoulder. One of the men from the pier, who jerks his thumb over his shoulder. *Get out of here.*

Luis points to the bag of cans, to the cats that have only just crept across the beach and who are still hungry. The man shakes his head, and when Luis turns to open another can, the man grips his shoulder and spins him around. This time, he's raised his shirt to reveal a black gun nestled against his skin. The second man joins him and Luis knows to raise his hands in the air and surrender—all he ever does anymore. On his way back he passes the shop with the golden eye in the window, and when the girl with the red hair looks up at him he scurries away.

Instead of going back to the boardinghouse—its musty carpets, the dim rooms—he makes his way to the lot where his old house was. Now it's just another gap where weeds have grown up through the dust and people have tossed their empty beer cans. He's furious that people are so cruel, so indifferent, that they permit the rot he notices at every corner. He stalks away, grinding his teeth, stopping to kick signposts, throwing loose cans and making them bounce off fences and walls. He shoves his hands in his pockets and feels the jingle of his change from the pizza joint, the matchbook he slid from the counter as the man warmed his slices in the oven.

The matchbook. It's nothing more than a scrap of cardboard, a red-and-white drawing of a pizza on the back, a few sticks inside, and yet, it feels special, important. He stops to study the row of abandoned homes before him: a hint of blue paint on one of the windowsills, a molding doormat on the porch. A sign on the door looks like a warning, but it's faded enough that he figures if it mattered, it doesn't anymore. Maybe this house had been cheerful, beautiful even. Happy. And now lifeless, unused.

Inside, the air is thick with mildew and a smell that he recognizes as cat piss, which makes his nose and eyes burn. In the living room there's a folding table, an armchair covered in shredded, rose-printed fabric, a lumpy old sofa with stuffing poking through the seat. He strikes the first match and holds it to the stuffing, part of him hoping it won't catch, the rest of him egging it on, coaxing, waiting. He feels a strange pull inside of him, between terror and excitement, fear and hope. It smokes for a moment before the flame starts to grow. Already he is picturing the swarm of police standing in front of the charred ruins, their mouths agape. It pleases him, too, to release the house from its sadness, to hide some of the city's shame. If it can't be beautiful, the way it once was, then let it not exist at all. And it will give the cops something to do other than ignore his pain.

He closes his eyes and pictures the candles his grandmother used to light, the tall glass jars with saints' faces painted on the fronts. He opens his eyes and watches the fire get bolder, bigger. Flames rip from one end of the sofa to the other. He stands in front of it, holding his hands to the heat like it's a hearth. He feels some of his anger burning up, too, like it has been used up by the flame, turned to smoke. It clouds the air, low and gray, until it makes him cough and his lungs burn. A feeling he's never been able to forget. For many years after his grandparents died, he would still wake with a start most nights, thinking he smelled smoke wafting down the hall.

The flames catch the end of a pale panel of curtains above the sofa's left arm, licking their way up the fabric. He would do anything to capture the colors, bottle them: the bluish bud at the center, the yellows and oranges that change to red. He coughs again, gasping now, knowing he should leave but unable to look away. He takes one last look at the fire, admiring what he's created, then finds the back door, draws the fresh air into his lungs. He vaults himself over the sagging chain-link fence, and runs, flinging open his arms, feeling a little lighter, free.

LILY

ON MY NEXT SHIFT I waited until Emily was on her lunch break, then clicked around on the security system to see if there was any chance of looking at the archived footage—the system let me access the past twenty-four hours, but nothing beyond that without a supervisor's password. We were able to access the hotel's records to help with our scheduling and billing, but we could only see who was in the hotel at that moment—not who had stayed in the past or when. Just in case, I searched the name "Peaches," but as I suspected would happen, the system didn't turn up any results. Clara had wanted me to text her, though I found myself holding out. I was worried that once I told her I didn't have news she could use, she would bail. And I wanted to keep her close, watch over her. I couldn't stop picturing that man who had come into her shop. Couldn't stop picturing Steffanie, the way that, before that night at the club, she used to snort when she laughed.

I was struggling, too, to find anything else about the artist and the paintings from Mil's. I had gone back to her house to take photos on my phone. As I crossed the street, I'd worried that they wouldn't be as striking as I remembered, that I had only been impressed by them because they'd been so unexpected.

Mil surprised me by greeting me with a hug. She was wearing a stack of bangles that clacked against my spine.

"Sorry, I've got my armor on today."

"Oh, do you have plans? I can come back another time."

"Not at all. But you know how it is. Some days you just need a little . . . fortification. I'm so glad you like those paintings, but it makes me miss my husband is all."

"Oh Mil, I'm so sorry. We don't have to do this if you don't want to."

"Don't be silly. He would love this, a professional like you taking an interest in his stuff."

I winced. In New York, I was still best known as a hysteric or a pawn or, maybe the worst, a co-conspirator—someone just as cynical as Matthew who had accepted her role in the whole mess. "Mil, I work at a spa. Not sure how much of a professional I am anymore."

"Nonsense. You're brilliant and you know it. You head on up, and I'll get us some iced tea."

As I made my way through her house, I braced myself for disappointment. Back up that narrow, creaking stairway, wallpapered in a faded blue floral, into the little square of a bedroom with its chenille spread. I stood in front of the closet and held my breath.

But as I brought the paintings out of the closet, propped them up along the wall of the bedroom to look at them in the light, I felt the same thrill, the same hum of purpose in my chest. The artist's use of color was extraordinary, vivid and unexpected and strange. The painting Mil had mentioned, the demolition of the Traymore, showed clouds of gray dust lined in neon pink. It seemed to hint at the garishness to come, the blaring neons and gaudy mirrors, the pandering, hypersexed billboards. One of the paintings of the diving girl was done exclusively in shades of blue, invoking a somber, melancholy impression. Even her

perfect smile was shaded a lovely, sad periwinkle. A smile full
of secrets.

After several failed attempts to dredge up anything remotely
relevant via Google, I decided to go to the Atlantic City public
library before my next shift at the spa. Someone had to know
something about this painter—Atlantic City is too small a town
to hold that kind of a secret. Someone would recognize the signature or point me to a tiny vanity-press book about local artists.
I asked the librarian on duty who I could talk to about the paintings. I told her I thought that the painter might be working from
photographs, at least for some of the paintings, given the time
span they covered.

"Well, I'm afraid that due to the latest round of budget cuts,
the woman who maintains our archives is now only here on Mondays and Fridays. She's the expert, but maybe I can help?"

I scrolled through the images on my phone: the Victorian ladies on the promenade, the portraits of the soldiers and nurses,
the sleek chrome-accented cars of the 1920s, the first Miss America contestants in home-sewn costumes—until I found several
shots of the signature. The woman squinted at the screen, then
frowned.

"I've never seen anything like these before. Where did you say
you came across them?"

"In my neighbor's house. Her husband used to collect them.
She said he bought them from a man who sold used furniture and
odds and ends on a street corner, but she has no idea who the man
was or where he set up shop. Her husband passed away years
ago. She's going to dig through his papers, but my impression is
he was something of a pack rat so it might take a while to find
anything like notes or a receipt. I figured I would try you here."

She shook her head. "Sue might know. I would let you look
at the archives, but I'm the only one here today and I can't leave
the desk. Unfortunately only a small fraction of our collection

is digitized. We just don't have the manpower to get most of it online. But she's in, let me see, Friday at eleven. Can you try to stop by then?"

My first bit of luck so far: I had a closing shift that day and would be able to pop in again before I headed over to the spa. "Sure, that works for me."

"You can try to research in our databases, too, but so many of our subscriptions have been slashed."

"Friday sounds great, thank you so much. I'll come back."

"A few years ago, we would have been able to do so much more, but . . ." She shrugged and looked up. I became aware of how warm the library was, the muggy air pressing on my arms, and wondered if their air-conditioning had been cut, too.

I left unsure as to whether I should be hopeful or depressed. Maybe Mil would find something useful. At least the name of the person who sold the paintings to her husband, any scrap of information I could grab on to. Though a part of me also felt apprehensive about finding out who the artist was. After New York—where everyone was climbing over one another to get their name out, to trade in on favors and name drops to get laid, to get money, to get attention—there was something so appealing about the anonymity of this painter. The way he or she had continued to document and interpret the shifts and moods of the city, whether ever recognized for it or not, had integrity. It was humbling to see the care the artist had put into these paintings, and I loved the way they opened up the city, the layers of the past that were invisible otherwise. Like the city's memory of my father—lost.

I MOVED through the casino with the paintings still on my mind, seeing the casino and the people in it as the painter might have seen them. The senior citizens squinting at the slots. The rumpled-looking dealers at the empty blackjack tables. The hotel clerks bent toward their computer monitors. The exercise lent a strange dignity to everyone, made them seem worthy of being memorialized. That's what I loved about portraiture—how it captured the way a person's personality, their past, their secrets, their desires or disappointments, settled into their body, their face. Good portraits, like the ones Mil had, did that—they raised a single life, even an ordinary one, to the light.

When I got to the spa, I stood in front of the door and stared through the glass, studied Emily standing at the desk. I wondered how the painter would have captured her. I knew she wasn't religious anymore, and she would have hated to hear it, but there was a holy aspect to her face and hair. It had to do with the way the light came down from overhead. But that wouldn't be the right way to paint her—there would need to be a hint of her slyness, her humor. That sneaky smile, the knowing, witty shine of her eyes. She looked up and saw me standing there, pulled a grimace, waved at me to hurry inside. Behind her, Luis was working a mop back and forth through the boutique, leaving wet zigzags on the floor.

"I'm glad you're here. There's so much to do. We have a visit from corporate next week. Monday. Even Whitney will be here. Just got word from Deidre down in Charlotte. Carrie knows, too, of course, but naturally she doesn't give a shit so it's all on me— us—to make sure everything goes smoothly."

"Who's Whitney?"

"Christ, someone didn't pay attention during training!" That was true. "Whitney is our COO."

"Okay, and what is she going to be doing here?"

"Each spa location is rated on a points system across six different categories. Service, retail, facility, customer engagement, teamwork, and operations."

"Oh God," I said.

"Exactly. Poor Luis here is getting worked to the bone getting this place in shape. I'm coordinating with each department head—skin, nail, hair, and massage—to make sure we ace the service aspect. Mostly everything else is up to us. It's going to be a nightmare. Anyway, we can talk more about that throughout the day—I'll probably need to lean on you a lot." Luis looked up and I saw that he had a cut on his left cheek, a bruise on the underside of his arm. I wondered if he had gotten into a scuffle. His mood seemed sour and he frowned as he worked. I would have to ask Clara more about him—why he seemed to make her nervous, what secrets she thought he kept.

"Sure, let me know what I can do." She studied me for a minute, a little smile coming into her face. "What?" I asked.

"You've got some bounce in your step. You get laid or something?"

"Definitely not. I'm working on a project."

"What kind of project?"

"My mom's neighbor has this stash of portraits in her house, just sitting there. Of Atlantic City throughout history."

"Sounds depressing."

"No, they're amazing. A bunch of them are soldiers and staff from this old hospital—apparently the biggest World War II hospital in the country was here?"

"*Here* here?"

"Right on the boardwalk. It was one of the old hotels, and then a hospital, and now the original building is part of Resorts. I can't make out the signature, but I want to see if I can find out who did them. Let me show you photos of it," I said, clicking on the browser window. Emily hadn't closed her last tab, and it was open to her homepage on her Sallie Mae account. *Account Balance: $57,433*, it announced, in a strangely cheerful yellow typeface.

"Oh, uh. Sorry." I pulled my hand away from the mouse, and she reached over to close the tab.

"No, I'm an idiot for leaving that up." She flushed. I made $11 an hour at the spa, and maybe she earned a little bit more, but probably not much. I would have been one of those people, too, buried under student loans, if we hadn't received a settlement from the accident. It made me queasy to think about it. As though what had happened to my father had a price. I knew he was thrilled that I had ended up at Vassar, that he and my mom had planned to help as much as they could. And then, my senior year, when that check finally came in, and that balance shrunk to zero, I could only feel the kind of guilt that made it impossible to eat anything for the rest of the week.

I was eager to change the subject. "Here, look at this." I googled the Thomas England Hospital, scrolled through some of the images, enlarged the ones of the soldiers, the men who returned home missing limbs, doing stretches on a sundeck.

"That's the hospital?" She stepped closer to the monitor.

I nodded. "There are people who say that Resorts is haunted by the souls of soldiers who died there. Noises, voices." I had read reports online of guests waking to see the hems of hospital gowns trailing around corners, to hear moans in the middle of the night. I didn't believe it, but there was something affecting about the idea that this hospital had loomed over our beaches, all those souls that circulated through its halls. Other photos showed platoons of soldiers in dark uniforms and heavy boots thrusting their bodies through drills on the beach. Camp Boardwalk, it was called.

"Well, that would explain a lot. Maybe they're the ones setting fires around here. There was another one last night," Emily said.

"Another one? Wait, how many is this now?"

"Three, I think. Things are getting biblical-level bad around here." She made her voice deep and somber. "*By water also the world of that time was deluged and destroyed. By the same word the present heavens and earth are reserved for fire, being kept for the day of judgment and destruction of ungodly men."*

"Uh. Yikes."

"You wouldn't believe how much of that shit is still rattling around in my brain."

"I guess so."

There had been a series of blazes in the city—empty houses, mostly. A boathouse that had been abandoned on one of the creeks after Hurricane Sandy. A stretch of dry brush near the entrance to the Revel. The police and the fire department suspected it was arson, but they didn't have any leads yet. I'd driven past one of the sites on my way home from work: a two-story house near the bus depot, its façade charred black, its roof collapsed. I thought of the wildfires in California, the way that sometimes they would burn to reset the soil, to restore nutrients to the forest. I knew it wasn't the same, but I wondered if these fires might have been like that—the city's way of restoring itself, of regenerating through destruction. It was a nice alternative to the reality—that someone was setting fires just because they liked having something to ruin.

The plant guy came in, rustling his garbage bags, ready to take away the month's orchids and swap them out for new ones. I watched him lift the flower from the pot on the desk and drop it into the mouth of the bag, the delicate white petals swallowed in darkness, though when he saw Luis he straightened, gestured to the bag. Luis smiled at him and crouched at the man's feet, removed the orchid, and placed it into an empty Windex bottle that he had cut in half.

"Luis does that sometimes," Emily said. "If he's on shift when it's plant day. He likes to rescue them. Otherwise they just get thrown away."

Luis retreated, cradling his orchid in the crook of his arm, and the man bent to his little wagon for another plant, dropped a new orchid, identical to the last, in the other one's place. He left a small crumble of soil on the counter, and the earthy, damp smell of it briefly filled the air. Wild and dirty but real.

After he left, Emily and I restocked lipsticks and pans of blush from the late summer color collection, Indian Summer Dreams. As I emptied my second box, I looked up at the photo of the spa's founder, Geraldine Austin, that was mounted above the vanity mirrors in the boutique. That severe sheen on her leather riding boots, the gloss on the horse's coat. The grim set of her mouth, as though she knew that, in sixty years, two young women would sit on the floor of an establishment bearing her name and we would let her down in a way too beneath her to even articulate.

"Do you think that we are doing any good here?" I asked Emily.

"What's that supposed to mean? Are we good at our jobs? Customer service jobs are practically designed for failure. We have to depend on other people being patient, reasonable, *sane*, in order to serve them well. Or do you mean *good* good. Like morally? Because for starters, I'm pretty sure these lipsticks aren't cruelty-free."

"I don't know. Do we ever have the opportunity to help people? Do people really come here thinking that we can make them the better versions of themselves? Do we give them that in any way? Or are we just trading on their insecurities?"

Emily lifted a stack of eye shadow palettes out of the box. "I don't know. People confuse better and better *looking* all the time. I read that humans ascribe morality to people who are attractive, and they are suspicious of people who aren't. Even from the time you're a baby. We are preprogrammed to. Pretty equals good. Ugly equals bad."

"Great. So basically we're helping perpetuate that bias?" If all beautiful people were good, Matthew would have been a saint. The high forehead and the hair that was always falling into his eyes. The arcs of his shoulder blades. The dainty divot in the middle of his bottom lip that I stared at while he slept. In a strange way, to think that my trust in him had been hardwired comforted me. But what a mistake. So much cruelty was committed in the name of beauty. And in the name of art.

"Maybe. But I guess there are opportunities to do good. Last week, this woman called to schedule services for her sister to celebrate the fact that the sister's cancer had been in remission for three years. It's kind of cool to be a part of that. Even though most of the people who come in here are raging lunatics. Or perverts. Or petty thieves." Emily leaned back into a box of packing peanuts, rubbed her hands over her eyes. I still didn't know much about her. I knew she rented a room from a family in Brigantine. That she took college classes at night. But I didn't know what she did for fun, or even what she wore when she wasn't at work, when she was finally able to shed the impersonal black blazer and pencil skirt. Once I asked her whether she had brothers and sisters, but the look on her face made me wish I hadn't. When she was nervous, or anxious, she fiddled with the cross on the chain around her neck.

"Why do you ask, anyway? I thought this was just your 'get back on your feet' gig."

I didn't really know the answer. I had never asked myself at the gallery if it was good, or fair. I was getting what I wanted. "Just something I've been thinking about, I guess."

"One good thing about this company is that it's almost entirely run by women. It could be a good place to start a career, in that sense. Even if they are as crazy as the guests most of the time."

"How are your classes going?" I felt self-conscious asking— as though I were creeping back toward the discussion we didn't have about me seeing her loan balance, but I was curious, and besides talking shit on everyone else at the spa, school was the only other thing she'd open up about.

She sat up, and I picked a Styrofoam packing peanut from her hair. "Okay—I'm taking exams next week, and then I start a new session. At this rate, I'll be done in, oh, two, two and a half years."

"That's great."

"It seems like such a long time to me. Sometimes I wonder if it's even going to be worth it. Who will respect me for having a degree from a small local college? Working as a receptionist when other people are out interning with banks or learning about real estate or management psychology."

"What, you're not learning about management here? You practically run this place."

"Yeah. I don't know. I think, as a woman, I have to anticipate the one thousand ways people will find to dismiss me and how I can make up for it, or prove them wrong, before I can let myself think about what kind of credit they'll give me for anything I've done. As I get older, I keep waiting to step into a world that's different, where I don't have to think like that, and you know what? I'm still fucking waiting."

I wanted to say something reassuring, but what Emily had said was true. I thought of the way men like Matthew went striding through the world, assured that they deserved pleasure, success, money, and happiness, and that they would get it. Even the most talented, intelligent women I knew—Emily included—didn't think that way. We tiptoed, fingers crossed, making Plan A, Plan B, Plan C, always anticipating the way the world would push us aside.

Emily sighed, nodded at the display. "Does that look even to you?" She held out the instructions that had been sent by our corporate merchandising director. They were overfull of exclamation points and capitals. "PYRAMID SHAPES ARE EASY TO SHOP!!! AND REMEMBER, EVERY SALE IS A CHANCE TO UPSELL!!! AN ATTRACTIVE RETAIL SPACE EQUALS ATTRACTIVE PROFITS!!!"

I studied the display, the backdrop of which was a picture of a woman who was clearly white but wearing a lot of bronzer, dressed in a fringed suede halter top and skirt, sitting on a hillside, surrounded by flowers. "Looks even to me. Fucked up in other ways. But yes. Even."

"Okay, then. I'm going on my break. Don't forget . . ."

"Every sale is a chance to upsell?"

She rolled her eyes. "I'll see you in an hour."

Clara must have been watching us through the glass, lurking just outside the door, until Emily retreated to the break room. As soon as Emily was gone, she shuffled in. I was struck by how terrible she looked: pale, dark circles under her eyes, lanky hair.

"Clara, what are you doing here? This wasn't our plan. I'm not off till seven, remember?"

"I know, I know. I'm sorry. But this is important."

"Are you okay? What happened there?" She had Band-Aids over each of her middle fingers.

She glanced at her hands and shook her head. "I think it's bad, Lily. I've been thinking, and it seems like they must be . . . they're hurt . . . or . . . or even . . ."

"Hold on. Clara. Who? Who do you mean? Actually, wait a second. We shouldn't be talking about this here. Let's go out into the hall." I wasn't supposed to leave the desk, but there was a spot just outside the glass windows where a potted palm could obscure a person, maybe two. If Emily saw me talking to Clara, how would I explain?

Clara reached for one of the plant leaves, started tearing it into strips. "I think each of these weird visions I'm having are visions of like . . . something they thought about before they died. I know. Okay, before you say anything. I know what that sounds like. It sounds insane. I feel insane. But the woman who left her bag—her name, by the way, is Victoria, and Julie Zale . . . I'm seeing things about them that I couldn't possibly know. Intimate things. Things that would matter in the end. I don't know what to do." She had shredded the leaf into bits. Her voice kept breaking, as though she was going to cry.

"Okay. So tell me how I can help you. I don't know what my role is supposed to be in all of this. I haven't seen Peaches at all. Just tell me what you want me to do."

"I'm worried about her, too. That she's in trouble, too. I just wish there was a way to test the visions, to know if I could trust them, if they're even real."

"How would you do that?"

She took a big breath, sucking it in between her teeth. "I have an idea. You're not going to like it, but I think it might work. So Julie Zale had a bad childhood when she was really young, before she came to live with her uncle, he told me. Both of her parents were all messed up. I keep seeing a bedroom, a really pretty room with a checked bedspread, pink and white, and all these white pillows at the top. If I were Julie Zale, and I had grown up in a really shitty home"—she paused to issue a sardonic little laugh—"all I would think about, all I would dream about, was being somewhere that felt safe, like that bedroom. Where you felt cared for and where you could count on everything always being the same."

"That makes sense."

"So the vision I'm having . . . we just need to talk to someone who can confirm it."

"Someone like who?"

"Her aunt and uncle's phone number is on that poster."

The thought clicked into place, and I felt the resistance everywhere, in my hands, my feet, my spine. "Clara, no. My god. Absolutely not."

"Listen, I know it's weird, but it's the only sure way to know."

"Weird? It's downright insane. Cruel. What about . . . like . . . contacting one of her friends? Someone she knows on Facebook?"

"And saying what? I'm a stranger, but please tell me what Julie's room looked like?"

"No, not exactly. We could explain that we were trying to help."

"What? *Oh, hey, I'm a psychic and I think I can see your missing friend's room but I just want to double-check?*"

She was right about that. "Okay, so you want to call her old house and say . . . what, exactly?"

"Well, you can pretend to be like, one of her friends or something."

"*I* can pretend? Clara . . ."

"Please, Lily. I can't do this all on my own. It was bad enough talking to him the first time around and seeing how upset he was. Plus, what if he's the one who picks up the phone, and he recognizes my voice? Please help me with this. I've got a lot . . . a lot on my mind. I can't sleep."

I wondered if she was asking for help with other things, too, besides the call, and maybe she didn't know how to say it. "Are you still seeing strange men?"

"It's under control, okay?" Her eyes shined, and I realized how afraid she must be. How all of that defiance, when she first marched into the spa, must have been hiding so much. I believed that she wanted help finding out what happened to Julie, to Victoria, to Peaches, but I also thought that maybe she wanted help for herself, too. I had told myself I would help this time around, hadn't I? This time, I wouldn't sense trouble—watching Steffanie stumbling into the man's shoulder—and tell myself that everything would be okay.

"Okay," I relented. "So tonight we'll call . . ."

"Tonight? Why not now?" Clara was all raw nerves, desperation; so different from when I had met her a few weeks ago. A girl who shook with fear, who could hardly raise her eyes to meet mine.

"Here?" I looked around. I knew we didn't have any appointments coming in for two more hours, but still it made me apprehensive. If someone else, one of my coworkers, Emily, even Carrie, overheard, I would probably be fired on the spot.

"I can't spend another minute wondering. And then, at least if my visions are right . . . well. I don't know which to hope for. Whether I'm seeing something real, or whether I'm totally insane. And I don't know what it means, seeing her room like that. I'm worried that it means she's in trouble, or she's scared, or hurt. Sometimes . . . when things are uncomfortable, I think of something that makes me feel safe. I think of my mother, of the way she talked about her house in California. I just wonder if Julie is doing the same thing, only I can see it, too."

I looked up to the ceiling. "You have the number?"

She took a folded poster of Julie Zale out of her pocket.

"Tell me again what it looks like, everything you can see . . . or saw."

"A pink-and-white checked bedspread. White carpet. Green walls. Lots of white pillows on the bed. Oh, and a brown stuffed rabbit with a black nose."

I took a deep breath. I'd never been a very good liar, and I didn't know if I could do what Clara was asking me. But the pleading look in her eyes made me feel like I had to try.

I keyed in the number and hit send on the call, my hands shaking. I held my breath between each ring, hoping it would go to voicemail. Clara stared at me with such pleading intensity that I had to turn away.

On the fourth ring, a woman answered. "Zale residence." My voice was caught in my throat. "Hello? Hello?"

"Oh, uh, hi. Mrs. Zale?" Clara reached out and put her hand on my arm.

"Yes? May I ask who is calling, please?" She was formal, but polite. Almost warm.

"Hi, uh, you might not remember me, but I'm a friend of Julie's. I'm Lauren. I, uh, was in history with Julie freshman year."

"Oh . . . hello, Lauren. How . . . how are you?" She paused, and I knew that whatever I said next would have to be a leap. Clara looked at me beseechingly. I wanted so badly to hang up.

"I'm sorry. I hope it's okay that I called. I was just thinking about Julie today."

"Oh, sweetheart," she cooed. "Yes, well. I think of her all day, too. Not a minute goes by. Even if I'm not thinking of her, I feel it. I feel it in my bones." I felt hot, sweat collecting under the neck of my blazer. I was no better than them, was I? Matthew and Ramona. All three of us were liars, fakes, even if the lies were supposed to be in service of something good. I took another deep breath.

"I was just thinking of the time I was over at your house that spring. I don't know if you were home."

"Yes, sweetie? Maybe I wasn't. I volunteer at the library, or I could have been down at the store."

She must have heard the shakiness in my voice. But I had gone this far. There was no backing out of it now without hurting Mrs. Zale, leaving her confused or forlorn. "I was thinking of how much I liked Julie's room. How cozy it felt. How it felt like her, all of the decorations and colors."

"Oh, yes. Well, she hated those pink walls. Ha."

I looked at Clara. She had said that Julie's walls were painted green. I started to shake my head. "Her uncle took one look at it when I was done and just said *no way*. Said it was all wrong for her. He painted that green right over himself. Tracked it on the white carpet we just had put in. Julie got home from camp and she was never the wiser, said she adored the green. Of course, I should have guessed. And she never wanted to replace that coverlet I made her a million years ago. I asked her so many times if she wanted a new one, that old plaid one was what I put together for her when she first got to the house, as a little thing. Sometimes . . . oh, sometimes I wonder if I smothered her. If she felt overwhelmed here."

"She seemed happy to me, Mrs. Zale."

"To me, too, dear."

"Well, I should let you go, I think. I'm sorry to have bothered you. I just wanted . . . wanted to talk about her."

"Call anytime, sweetheart. Okay? And you keep praying. We'll get our girl back. I know we will."

I knew if I said another word, I'd cry, so I simply ended the call. Clara gripped my arm. I had crumpled the poster in my hand.

"You're right, Clara. That was terrible. I— I think I need to sit down." I was so overwhelmed that for a few seconds I didn't register Clara's silence.

"Did you hear me, Clara? I said you were right. At first she said pink walls, but the uncle painted them green before Julie came back from camp, or something. He knew she wouldn't like the pink. White carpet. She sewed the plaid blanket herself."

She put her head in her hands. I looked up and started: there was a man leaning against the opposite wall, his baseball cap pulled low, a pair of sunglasses masking his eyes, a windbreaker with the Harrah's logo emblazoned across the chest. The poker players always skulked around like that, like B-list celebrities in exile. He was already walking away. How much had he heard? It wasn't so much that I thought he would do something about it: call the Zales, and what, report us? But it was deeply shameful, the idea that we'd been overheard.

"Clara, that guy . . . I think he heard us."

She mumbled something, her fingers still over her eyes and mouth. It sounded like *I don't care.* One of the Band-Aids had come unraveled. It had covered a perfect circle of a wound, one that wept with infection. The skin around it was bright red. A cigarette burn.

"Clara, let me see that." I reached for her wrist, but she was quicker, pulled it away and hid her hand behind her back.

"What are you doing here?" Emily, returning from break early. I pushed Clara's phone back into her hands.

"She's just leaving. Aren't you? I escorted her out here in the hall, so she wouldn't bother guests." I tried to stand straighter, hold Emily's eye. Emily studied me, and I was sure she knew I was being untruthful, and I couldn't explain why I'd had Clara's phone. I simply had to hope that she wouldn't ask.

"Sure, I am. *Hypocrite*." Her eyes were narrowed on Emily. She glowered at me, too, which I assumed was just for show, and left us without another word.

"God, can't keep the grifters out, huh? Lily, I'm assuming you're ready to go back to doing your job?"

"Yeah. Why'd she call you a hypocrite?"

"Who knows? Maybe she thinks we're all on the same page. Just some gals stuck here in Atlantic City, peddling our services for a buck until something better comes along. But with those two, everything is just a setup for one of their cons." Now Emily's hostility toward Clara made me wince, and for a second I considered telling her about the burns.

A few minutes later, my phone lit up with a new text. I figured it was Clara, asking me when we could meet up again. *See a doctor first*, I would tell her. But I almost dropped the phone when I saw who it was.

Hey, Lil. Are you over your slumming at the shore phase yet? We should talk.

Matthew.

I had wanted this for most of the summer, hadn't I? Some kind of acknowledgment from him? But the text only made me furious. I didn't have time to puzzle out what Matthew wanted, what he could possibly be up to. I was spent. Cold, where the sweat on my back was now drying in the chill of the air-conditioning. I couldn't get Mrs. Zale's voice out of my head. I kept picturing her walking upstairs, creaking open the door to Julie's room, sitting on the bed. Taking the velvet of that stuffed rabbit's ear between her fingers, waiting and waiting and waiting for her girl to come home.

JANE 5

PEACHES SPENT THE TWO DAYS after the tarot reading at the library, leaving only when the librarian rang a bell and announced that they needed to close. All of the homeless men, wearing their puffy parkas in the full heat of summer, the old ladies whose palsied hands made papers rattle in their grip, the mothers scrolling through their phones while their kids tugged on their sleeves and held up picture books. Once, she slipped into the business center at Caesars, using a john's room key to access the tiny closet on the third floor where the casino kept two old Dells and a creaking, dusty printer. She added her name to lists, researched payment plans and Medicaid coverage. It had been one full day since she last used, and her head was already throbbing, her gut starting to churn.

It took nine calls and three waitlists before she got a bed at a detox center in Hammonton, and she used most of her cash on the cab ride there. She remembers these small farm towns from when she first came to Atlantic City, three years ago with Josh. They remind her of home—all those blueberry trees, the rows of stout bushes, their branches tipped with fruit. *Welcome to the Blueberry Capital of the World!* a sign announces cheerfully. The cabbie frowns at her in the rearview when she laughs.

The cab cuts through the town's main street, and she watches other people moving through their tidy lives. A man raises the grate on the front of the hardware store, a paper cup of coffee in one hand. A woman lifts a pastry from a waxed paper bag, closing her eyes as she takes a bite, releasing a puff of confectioners' sugar into the air. Already, Peaches is sweating so much that her hair is soaked, her stomach lurching. The cab stops at a squat building that looks too ugly to be a place where anyone might get better, might heal. She wants to ask him how much to go back, to turn around and head to AC again. She closes her eyes and thinks of that card, the Tower: the leaping bodies, the creeping flames.

At check-in, she clicks her license down on the counter. In the photo her hair is purple. She fought with her mother about that, her palms still stained with dye.

"Why's your name Georgia if you're from Pennsylvania?" the receptionist asks. She pictures the photograph on her mother's mantel. The stern-lipped great-grandmother in the black velvet dress, a starched white collar tight around her neck. Georgia Maxine Standish, in little black leather shoes peeking out from under her hem, the ones that looked like they pinched her feet into hooves. The original Georgia's disapproval filled the room, even when she was a little girl. By the time she met Josh, Georgia asked him to call her Peaches. The only way she knew how to free herself from her great-grandmother's legacy was to make herself into a joke.

A nurse takes her to her room, starts to explain how things will work. Dizzy already, Peaches tries to think of a mantra, a phrase she can cling to when the sweats get worse and her muscles start to seize and her heart feels like it's trying to punch its way out of her chest.

The first time she shot up was with Josh. She went first, as he helped her tighten the strap, find the vein. When she pushed the plunger she felt her nerves sing. Josh, though, for no reason she knew, decided not to get high that day. Looking back now, it's like he led her to a cliff, wanting her to see the view, then shoved her off the edge. Last time she heard from him, he was living down in Tampa, working at some marina where rich people spilled champagne all over the decks of their boats. The nurse is still talking, but Peaches only catches every other word. Doctors, therapy, seizures. The blinds are half-open, making stripes of sunlight on her bed. In the photograph on the opposite wall, a sunrise's beams of light reaches toward the earth like fingers. She knows it is supposed to be inspirational, but she finds it insulting. Even after she detoxed, after she wrung her guts of the drugs and talked her mouth dry in therapy, her future was not a fucking sunrise. Every day, she'd grit her teeth against the desire to use herself up. To fail just like her namesake great-grandmother had known she would.

THOSE FIRST days' shakes rattle her teeth; the hot cramps sear through her guts. She becomes so dizzy that the stupid sunset photograph turns on its side. But the nightmares are worse than the physical symptoms. Her dreams humiliate and terrify her. She moves through the underbellies of dark, unrecognizable cities, where she's chased, attacked, beaten. In one, she is swallowed whole by a creature that looks human but can unhinge its jaw and consume her in a single gulp. She's in the wet insides of its body, screaming and using her fingernails to claw her way out. She dreams of children she went to elementary school with, who lay her out on the teacher's desk, tell her that her stomach is filled with worms and cut her open while she's awake. They pluck the worms out, pink and thick, dangle them over her eyes. She tries to scream but finds that her mouth is stitched shut, even though she can feel them writhing under her skin.

Over the next seven days she sweats through her sheets until they smell sour and ammoniac, like pure animal fear. She pictures that tower again, the people free-falling away from the flames, reminds herself that this is her way of answering that card's demand. And it is more terrible and torturous than anyone tells you. Even sleeping is full of effort. Her jaw aches from grinding her teeth in her dreams.

And then one day she wakes, and the room is clean and bright. She recalls snippets of troubled dreams, but in the morning they yield to something like peace. She realizes that's her problem, has always been her problem. Peace feels too much like emptiness. She wonders if chemically, neurologically, she's missing something that would help her differentiate between the two.

The doctor confirms that the worst is over, and talks to her about therapy, about group meetings, about methadone, but she stares past him, at the sunrise photograph on the wall. The metaphor well worn, clichéd, but maybe, just maybe, true.

THEY NEED to give her bed to a new patient that night, so she stands outside of the facility, her bag at her feet. She counts her money and almost laughs when she realizes that her fifty is gone, all she's got is a ten crumpled at the bottom of her change purse. She only left the bag unattended for a minute, while she signed her discharge paperwork at the front desk. She should know— that's all it takes, a second or two; never trust a junkie. A group therapy session went on break, four or five people stepping outside for cigarettes. One of them knew to dip their hand into her purse, find the wallet, shuck the cash out. One of those people would go back to their circle, speak about how getting high wrecked their life, made them desperate and mean, then would go out and score later. The thought made her too jealous to be mad about the money.

When she hangs up the phone, the nurse offers to let her wait, try again, but she shakes her head no. A counselor drops her off at the bus stop, shakes her hand, and wishes her luck. She can't remember the last person who shook her hand before that.

Back to AC, it is, she thinks. She wonders if they would let her back into the shelter, even though last time she got kicked out for stealing. It was only a half-empty pack of cigarettes, but rules are rules, or so they told her when they asked her to pack her things. She could pick up a john, though she hates the idea of sleeping with a stranger without the treat at the end, the relief of a needle in her hand—that was always the whole point of it all. But she just needs enough for a place to stay, for a bus ticket back to Pennsylvania. A hundred bucks. It seems both cheap and dear, the price of freedom—twenty minutes with a man.

Does she trust herself to fuck a stranger and not use afterward? Maybe. She's not sure she believes in triggers. But she's always moved through life throbbing with want. She tells herself she's defeated the Tower. She chides herself for letting it bother her so much—that girl, that kid, in the shop, playing around with palm reading and cards—but there was something real in the girl's face when she turned that card over, a combination of worry and sympathy that Peaches couldn't ignore.

She arrives amid the white light of the afternoon. An ugly, revealing time. For AC, for herself. She imagined that after detoxing she would look like herself again, whoever that was. But her face is puffy and pale, and for some reason the whites of her eyes are jarringly bright, like a child's.

She doesn't know what she'll do about the night, about getting back to her mom's. Whether her mom will even let her stay. She decides that when the bus gets into the depot, she'll go to the old parking garage at the Taj Mahal. Whenever she needed to be alone she would slip past the broken pieces of plywood at the entrance, the spray paint warning *Keep Out*, walk up the sloping ramps until she was at the top. She liked to press herself into the concrete barrier and look out over the city. An ocean view to the east, the hospital to the west, the ambulances pulling in and out all day long. She'd watch EMTs hustle in with their gurneys. From that height, the human drama was shrunk to the size of a diorama like the ones her mother's students built out of shoeboxes and filled with miniature cars and trees. Easy to watch and think she was not a part of it all.

Her mood gets more resigned, grimmer, as the bus speeds down the Black Horse Pike. Past the Ramada Inn, the Sunset, and all of the other little aqua and pink and coral stucco motels just rotting into the side of the road. She tastes the scatological stink of the marsh, which she's learned is the sulfurous smell of the mud exposed at low tide. Other people cover their noses with their hands or their shirts. She starts to feel paranoid—that the smell is coming from her, that everyone knows it. Without the drugs to cover it up, the thing that makes her wrong inside is seeping out, filling the air like poison. *No*, she thinks. Paranoia: the brochures warned about that. It's a symptom, real but not.

But even after she gets off the bus, she feels the smell of the marsh on her, in her. She wants to shower. Drink a glass of water so cold she can feel the chill sliding down her throat. She uses the pay phone at the bus terminal—before she can decide anything about how and where she'll spend the night, she needs to know about all the nights after that. This time the phone rings twice before her mother answers, the brisk *hello* she reserves for strangers.

The word feels unpracticed, underused, and it takes her a second to say it. She can feel the pressure of all the questions she wants to ask. *Do you still love me? Do you know that I really am sorry, so sorry? Will you tell me all of the bad dreams weren't real?*

It's another question, and an answer, at once.

"Mom?"

LILY

I KNEW CLARA WAS WAITING for me in the casino lobby at the end
of my shift, but I needed a drink first, some cold blunting gin, the
familiar rattle of ice cubes in my glass. I made my way to the bar
on the casino floor, the one near the penny slots. I was still rattled
from making the phone call earlier that afternoon and kept re-
playing the conversation with Julie Zale's aunt in my head. What
did it mean that Clara was right? I told myself that all she really
knew was the colors of Julie's room. A few details. Maybe Clara
hadn't even really intuited them. I found the website that Julie's
family had made, asking for tips, and scrolled through to see if
any of them showed a shot of her bedroom—maybe Clara had
already seen it subconsciously, and what she was calling a vision
was really just submerged memory, something sifted from the
millions of images and impressions we're bombarded with every
day. I squinted at the background of every shot, but nothing
seemed to match what she and Julie's aunt had described.

I finished my gin and tonic too quickly, ordered a second anyway. I couldn't bring myself to meet with Clara, to face what she
thought her visions meant or to confront her about those burns.
Was it worse if she'd done it to herself? Or if it had been someone
else? I was so tired of living in a world that abused women. I kept

picturing Steffanie's face, the bruise already tender around her eye, when I found her in that bathroom, rag dolled around the base of the toilet. Didn't anything ever change?

Someone put their hand on my shoulder, and I nearly dropped my drink. But it was only Clara.

"What are you doing here?" I asked.

"What are *you* doing here? This isn't where we were supposed to meet."

"I just needed a second to . . . think . . ." Clara pulled out the stool next to mine. "Maybe we should go somewhere else. You could get in trouble here."

"Don't worry about that," she said. Sure enough, the bartender came over without a word and poured her a rum and coke.

"You a regular?" I asked.

"I come here from time to time."

I sighed. "I don't think I want to know any more about that." I had a chance to study her fingers. She had put on fresh bandages. She noticed me looking at them and dropped her hands into her lap. "So. What are we doing? You really think that something has happened to Julie, and to the woman who came to your shop?"

"I do."

"Why?"

"I don't know. I only know that these visions . . . they break the rules. This isn't how things work for me. And I think it has to mean something. It's not random."

"I mean, why do you think you're receiving this information? If these women are sending out . . . I don't know, signals? Why are you getting them? What are you supposed to do?" I could feel the heat rising in my face. Talking that way, about signs and symbols and visions, still made me anxious, made me feel like I was on the wrong end of a prank. There was a part of me, too, that didn't want to trust Clara. I couldn't imagine what she might be after. I was wary, on edge. But every time I thought about telling her it was too much, too strange, I saw Steffanie again.

"I don't know that either. Trust me, this sounds crazy even in my world. But I feel like I have information, whether I like it or not, and now I have to figure out what to do with it. Some things just *are*. I don't know why so many people refuse to believe that we live in a world where not everything can be explained. Just because something is hard to explain, that doesn't mean it's not true or real. And maybe if other people around here were open to listening, to feeling things, they'd know it was off, too."

I thought again of New York. Of all the signs I'd missed. The creeping sense that something was off-kilter, but being unwilling to say it, because I couldn't point to it, couldn't say exactly what it was. Like trying to describe a color in the dark. "So now what? What about going to the cops?"

"With what? I believe what I see, but I still don't know exactly what happened. Or how the visions are tied together. But they're getting more violent, more detailed, and I think if we can find Peaches, we'll have time to warn her. Were you able to look at the cameras?"

"No luck," I said. "My security clearance won't work, and I couldn't get into Emily's account." My attempt at guessing her password had been nearly comical. I didn't know her middle name, or which state she came from.

"Maybe we need to be more organized. Go to other casinos— maybe Peaches got in trouble with security here and can't come back. Happens to Des and me all the time."

"Clara, can I ask you another question? Aren't you worried? About yourself?"

"What do you mean?" she said slowly. Something hardened in her face.

"I mean, you're meeting with strange men. Men who clearly think they can get away with abusing you because you're young, or because you're vulnerable, or because they're paying for it. I saw that mark on your hand; it looks really bad. If you think something bad is happening to women here—women who . . . see men, don't you think you should take it easy? Lay low?"

"I can take care of myself," she said. But she wouldn't look at me; she only ran her finger around the rim of her glass.

"I know that. But I just think you should be careful, okay?"

I was surprised by how quickly the anger clouded her face. "What do you know about it? You go home to your nice house with your nice mom and live your nice life, and you're not even grateful for it. All you want is to leave. Well, guess what? So do I. But you know it as well as I do—leaving takes cash. There are no jobs here for someone like me, even if I wanted one. This is how things are."

"Fine, I just think . . ."

"Leave it, Lily. Okay? I didn't come here for a lecture. We just need to make a plan."

My phone, faceup on the bar, lit up. Matthew again.

Okay, I know you might not want to talk to me yet. But I just wanted to say that I miss you.

Clara snorted. "See? You're just going to bail again, as soon as you can. Go back to this Matthew guy, forget this whole summer ever happened."

She sounded so jilted. It made her seem both older and younger at once.

"I'm *not* getting back together with him. I haven't even responded to his texts."

"You're thinking about it. I can tell."

I opened my mouth to argue, but she was right. Despite everything that had happened, this afternoon I'd allowed myself to imagine what it would be like to go back. To pretend things could return to how they had been. Parties that lasted until dawn, rooftop views, waking up with my tongue furred from champagne. That hollow, easy life.

"What even happened? What did he do?"

"It's complicated."

"So tell me. I'm not stupid."

"No, that's not what I mean. It's just that I'm still figuring a lot of that out." I took a long sip of my drink. "It wasn't all his fault. Matthew is brilliant, but he's not conniving. He never would have thought of all of that himself. There was another artist, a painter, named Ramona. She helped him stage the whole thing. I introduced the two of them. I was hoping to represent her work. I thought I could launch her career. I guess I did, in a way. Now she's famous, getting coverage in magazines, making a ton of cash."

"Wait, what did they do?" Clara was leaning toward me, eyes wide. I hadn't told anyone the full story. My friends in New York only knew what they'd heard passed along the gossip lines, or whatever they read in the blogs, but I had ignored the concerned texts, the querying emails disguised as support. Like my old clothes, the people I used to spend time with—other artists, other gallery girls—seemed to belong to a staged, unfamiliar version of my life.

I grasped for a starting point, an origin, but I really didn't know where everything had begun. I had tried to patch together the story all summer, but there was so much I had refused to see.

I described for Clara the time Ramona met me for lunch at Union Square Cafe, me brandishing my corporate card like a proud child. The night she invited me to her apartment to look at her work in progress, how sorry I felt for her, in the cramped little Lower East Side tenement apartment she shared with three other girls. Before I knew it, I was telling her she should use a spare room in Matthew's studio. I knew Matthew would be angry that I'd extended the use of his space, but he never worked in the mornings, and that's when Ramona liked the light the best. In my mind, they would never cross paths, never even meet.

"So wait, why did they?" The gin and tonics I was drinking seemed to have materialized from nowhere, and before I knew it I was rattling the ice cubes at the bottom of my empty glass again. I hadn't eaten much at the caf, and I had quickly reached the open, hyper-confessional stage of drunkenness, when the person across from you morphs into some idealized receptacle for your stories: the most sympathetic person you know, the most genuine, the most worthy of your secrets, your trust. All of a sudden I was burning to tell.

"That's what I don't know!" I slammed my hand on the bar, and the man next to me turned to look at us. I lowered my voice. "I knew something weird was going on. Ramona and I had met up again to talk about her work, and I was talking about Matthew and she just had this look on her face, like she couldn't even keep back how much she disliked him. So I asked her, and she said he seemed entitled. Arrogant. Which, yeah, he was. Is. He is."

"I don't understand," Clara said.

"Neither do I. That's part of it. All I know is that the next thing is my boss, who represents Matthew's work, tells me that he doesn't want me working on Matthew's show because of our personal relationship. Fine—fair enough, Philip Louis dated clients and it always fucked things up, but he ran the gallery so it was different for him. So I don't know anything about the show and Matthew was always really secretive about his work, especially when it was going well. Superstition or whatever, and for a long time I found that really charming, so I respected it, gave him space. The night the show opens, I get to his studio, which is in this giant warehouse in Bushwick—that's this sort of gritty

neighborhood in Brooklyn, so ugly that people think it's cool—
and there's a crowd of people there, and this energy, a tingle of
something, about the way people are looking at me. And I feel
like I'm being paranoid or wonder if it's sort of, you know, nice
attention. Like, oh, there's his girlfriend, she's so lovely, rising
star, blah blah blah." Even in this open, unfiltered mode I felt
embarrassed to admit that—that I had wanted to be admired.
Craved it enough that I was willing to ignore the feeling of low-
grade dread tugging at me, telegraphing that I should be wary.
That something was off.

"You needed to listen to your intuition." Clara tapped her
forehead to indicate her third eye. "Seriously. I don't even believe
in all of that psychobabble stuff and I'm a psychic, but I'm telling
you. Trust yourself more. Anyway, keep going."

"So the show, I find out, is comprised of two artists' works.
And the other artist is . . ."

Clara leaned in even closer, her knee touching mine, her hand
on my wrist. "That bitch Ramona!" For a second I remembered
just how young she was. How, when I was her age, my friends
and I were riding our bikes to the Wawa and pooling our money
to buy a milkshake to split.

I gave her the rest of the story in the most straightforward
way I could muster, and it still felt muddled and strange. The
first piece I saw at the show was a single canvas tacked to the
wall, unframed, ragged at the edges. There was a streak of green
paint at the top and several more below it, seven in total. The
first six streaks were various greens: pine, emerald, bottle-green,
seafoam. Someone had penciled letters next to each stripe. R, R,
R, R, R, R, and M. The last streak, marked with the M, had much
more yellow than the others, more of a chartreuse. In the next
room, I saw a painting on the wall: a girl curled up in a wing
chair, wearing a dress that was the same color as the last slash of

green on the canvas. She was looking across the room at something, unaware of the viewer. It was a well-executed painting but
restrained compared to Ramona's newer work, mannered and
too careful. Not good enough to be shown with Matthew's sculptures, and not what I had expected from her at all.

In the next room: one of Matthew's sculptures, small for him,
delicate even. *Oh no*, I had thought. What had happened? He
always called that kind of work timid. More like toymaking than
art. A placard on the wall said *The Flame*. As far as I could tell it
was abstract, made from peels of metal welded into a fan shape. I
tried to read the negative space but nothing emerged for me. People around me were nodding. *What?* I wanted to ask. What did
they see that I couldn't? Around the corner, another small sculpture. It had the fluidity of Matthew's larger works—it was called
The Idea, and it looked to me like smoke—but again, the scale
was disappointing. A photographer came around the corner and
took my photo, and for a moment the brightness of his flashbulb
left stars in my eyes. I saw that photo run somewhere else later, I
couldn't remember where, but my eyebrows were knit together,
like a disapproving schoolmarm's.

Temporary walls sectioned off the warehouse space. They
were genius for building tension, having the viewer wind through
that maze; meaning, wholeness felt just around the corner, but all
I could feel was frustration. Matthew told me once that I was his
muse, but I had yet to see myself in any of his pieces. I wondered
what Ramona was up to, too, going behind my back to Philip
Louis, or to Matthew, or however it had happened. I pulled out
my phone and texted her.

Why didn't you talk to me about this???

I rounded the next corner and was shocked to see, mounted
on the brick wall, a photograph of Ramona and me, blown up
very large, five by four feet.

I realized quickly that it had to have been taken through the window of the wine bar where I had met her in Alphabet City—I remembered Ramona's outfit. We were both reaching for the check, but you couldn't see our tabletop, so in the picture it looked like we were holding hands. But who would have taken it? And why? Neither Matthew nor Ramona even worked in photographs. I looked closer but didn't understand until I backed away. There was Matthew's face, reflected in the glass, imposed over us both.

Matthew, answer me! What is this?

I nearly tripped rounding the next corner, pushing past people, even stepping on someone's toes. A painter and his wife were looking at a series of Matthew's sculptures, six in total. They seemed to be in pairs. The first was called *Lily I*, the second, *Ramona I*. *Lily I* was tall, nearly nine feet if I had to guess. Ramona I was three feet. You hardly noticed her at all. In the next sculptures, *Lily II* and *Ramona II*, Lily was perhaps a little shorter, Ramona about the size she was in real life—five and a half feet tall. And by the third, the sequence had established a victor: *Lily III* was six feet tall, and *Ramona III* had grown to seven. My hands were shaking as I typed out another message to Matthew.

Where are you? Is this a joke?

We need to talk. NOW.

Someone looked at their phone and laughed. And yet I still didn't understand the extent of the show, its depth, its scope.

Then the sound of static crackled through speakers—had they installed a PA system for this?—followed by a rustling noise. Then, a moan. A man's. A woman's. Mine. Matthew's. He had recorded us in bed. And then, a third voice. Lower pitched, sort of a growl. Matthew groaning. *You like that?* Ramona. And there we were, the three of us, dubbed together, becoming louder, orgasms harmonizing. I covered my ears, but I could still hear everything. When it was over, reduced to a series of breathy pants, a giggle, the smack of a kiss, the track started over again. I thought I was going to throw up.

The walls finally opened into a large space at the back of the studio, where a screen showed the feed, in real time, of all the messages I had sent to Matthew that night. Next to it was another screen that showed the photos that had been taken since my arrival: me wringing my hands, me frowning at the young girl who had been assigned to stand with me in the lobby, Ramona and me—she looking completely composed while I looked angry, drunk, my eyeliner smeared, my eyes shining. There was another framed piece full of letters—letters!—that Ramona had sent to Matthew. The painting Ramona had done of Matthew, her first male subject as far as I knew, was large enough to fill ten feet of the west wall. He was naked except for a necklace I had seen Ramona wear a few times, a Saint Agatha medal on a piece of leather cord. I felt my knees give, and I threatened to fold in on myself right there, like an injured deer.

Then, I heard a laugh. Matthew's laugh.

They were standing together at the end of the room, Ramona and Matthew, their backs turned to me, talking to someone I couldn't see. Ramona was the first one to feel my stare, and she turned, the corners of her mouth ticking up in a smile.

"What the hell!" I shouted at them, slipping again in my shoes. I was vaguely aware of a photographer's bulb flashing at the corner of my eyes, but I couldn't think about him, about anything else other than my need to scream, to demand an explanation, to feel someone seize my shoulders and find myself home in our bed, waking up from a dream. The man they were speaking with edged away when he saw me approach, touching Matthew on the elbow, mouthing that he would call.

"Lil."

"Don't 'Lil' me." He held out his hands like I might charge him. His hair fell in his eyes like it had the first night we met. I loved him, I hated him. I wanted to ruin him, but I would have let him put me in a cab and take me home if he put his arm around me in the right way.

"This is disgusting, Matthew. How did this even happen?" I was spitting the words between gritted teeth. "You two weren't supposed to see each other. You were never supposed to meet. That recording? When the fuck did you record us having sex?"

"Lily." He braced me by the shoulders, turned me away from where a circle of people had gathered to watch us. "Listen to me, would you? Before anything else happens. We did this for you. Ramona and I. For all of us."

"For me? What part of this is for me? Please, tell me how that works. I'd love to hear you rationalize that."

He lowered his voice, and now he was whispering. "Everyone in the city is going to be talking about this show, writing about it. And who represents Ramona Avalon?"

"Hell if I know."

"No, Lily. She's your client. She wants to work with you."

"Well, she probably shouldn't have fucked my boyfriend then."

"I'm telling you, Lily." He picked up my hand, pressed his fingers into my palm. "First of all—it's fake, okay?"

"Doesn't sound so fake to me. You moaning her goddamned name sounds pretty real."

"Lily. The sex, it happened, okay? But it's just a means to an end. I'm telling you. This will make your career. You didn't want to be a gallery girl anymore? Guess what? You've got the attention of everyone in town. You've got more control than you think."

"Control? I'm a pawn! You turned me into a spectacle? Cheated on me? You're broadcasting what I sound like in bed? If you think anyone can respect me after this, you're absolutely insane. And if this is supposed to help me, why couldn't I be in on it?"

"You know that wouldn't work—it needed to be authentic, raw! Lily, you of all people should appreciate this. We made art out of normal life. This stuff happens all of the time—people messing around on one another. It's just acting. Really. No genuine feelings exchanged."

Ramona had broken away from a group of buyers and edged against my side, between Matthew and me, whispering in my ear. "We talk about this stuff all the time, Lil. How people crave stories more than anything else. We just gave them that."

There was one brief moment when I stopped to consider whether they might be right. Whether I could intellectualize this away. How much easier everything would be if I accepted their reasoning. It was so tempting, to pretend it might actually be okay.

"I was trying to help you," I said to Ramona. My voice had dipped into another register, one below the anger. I sounded sad and shaky and small. "I cared about your work."

Philip Louis pulled Matthew away and the two of them leaned together, whispering and looking in my direction.

"You're angry. I know. But Lily," she said, "he will tell you one thing about all this, and let me tell you another. You need to be free of him. His name. What about you? What about *your* name?"

"What are you talking about?" I spat.

"It will feel good, to take something from him. Admit it. To take some of that success for us, to use it to our advantage. Whatever he says, the way I look at it, this show was about you and me, about the conversations we had about *our* work, *our* goals. We will be unstoppable after this. We will leave him in the dust." Her lips were so close that they brushed my ear. She looked down to where my hand was clamped around her wrist, looked back up at me. I didn't care that she might be right about Matthew. I let go.

I shouldered my way between them, slipping out of my shoes as I walked. One of the shoes slid off my foot. I kicked the other off with a grunt and stopped to pick them up. I could hear that awful tape still running: me and Matthew and Ramona orgasming together. I looked up to see that painting of Matthew, that smug smile on his face, like he could see me coming. Like he'd seen me falling apart, since the moment he posed.

I swung one of the shoes at the canvas, the heel catching in Matthew's painted neck. Behind me I heard the sounds of people gasping, some cheering. I got one more swing in, this time ripping Matthew straight through the chest, before two men grabbed my arms and led me away. "I left the next morning."

"Lily," Clara said. "That's insane."

"I know. I still don't know whose version of things to trust." It had felt good to tell someone the whole story, to unload. Clara, unlikely as it was, seemed like the right person for it. She didn't have Emily's ruthless, withering judgment. She wasn't going to weep with sympathy the way, say, my mother would. I had managed to hold it together as I spoke, but I could feel that familiar lump forming at the base of my throat. But I told myself it would be insane to cry in front of Clara. Clara, the teenager with cigarette marks on her fingers.

"How about neither of them? Those two both sound like psychos."

"You're probably right about that."

"So why do you still want him?"

"It's not even that I still want him, exactly. I know I can't go back to the way things were. But when we were together, I just kept thinking that my life would be better with him, more exciting, more interesting than it could ever be on my own." It was the most honest I had ever been about Matthew. I was always sure that his life would be better than mine, and that the best thing I could do was stick around for the ride.

"Yeah, you'll never know when he's about to cheat on you with one of your friends."

"It wasn't cheating, exactly."

"I don't care what you say or what they say. That's not art. What about your life? Why can't that be an adventure? Why can't you be that person to someone? Instead you're just going to attach yourself to this asshole like a . . . like a barnacle."

"I'm not a barnacle!" Though I might have been offended, it only made me laugh. Soon, mostly without reason, we were both laughing, tears at the corners of our eyes.

"Excuse me," a man's voice said from behind us. "But you ladies mind if I sit down with you?"

I watched Clara's face shift again, the oversweet smile, the shift in her posture, the crossing of her legs. "Well, it'll cost you," Clara said, changing her voice so that it was syrupy sweet. *That quickly*, I thought. She tipped her chin down so that she was staring up at him through her eyelashes. "One drink each."

"Clara," I said, my voice low, a warning. She gave me a look that I had seen before: regret for the way things were, and that I was too blind, too sheltered, to possibly understand.

LUIS

HE DIDN'T THINK IT WOULD go on, past the first one. That initial release, the thrill of color and heat, the pleasure of being the one who undoes. He used to get the same thrill from making things, but maybe now he's too far gone. Too angry. Too lonely and separate from everyone else. The girls at work still watch him like he's contagious, or else they ignore him. Even the one who has her father's kind eyes. He still thumbs the two-dollar bill, thinking he could show it to her, like proof. But he's worried she won't know what it means, that it will be one more reason for her to think he's broken or strange.

He's set three more fires since that night when he burned the house—one fire for each time the men left him with bruises and scratches, the cut above his eyebrow that might scar, and the cops hadn't stopped them, only watched from behind the shine of their sunglasses. Each house feels like relief or even revenge. Maybe if he keeps going, the cops will finally be sent out into the city with work, real work, to do something other than laugh at the people they're supposed to protect. With every fire, he feels a weight lift from his chest.

Of course his thrill comes with new worries. What would happen if the police knew it was him? How many years would he

spend behind bars? Swallowed up in a prison, disappeared from
the world. The nerves that keep him awake at night, staring at
the ceiling, are only calmed by more fires. Sometimes he will sit
in his room and strike a match, just for a little taste of heat, a hint
of power. A mere reminder of what he's capable of. He's seen the
pictures in the papers—the dark husks and charred frames, the
firefighters in their yellow helmets, the stern lines of their mouths.

He still follows the girl, too, though he doesn't know what
he wants from her. Maybe he wants to simply say he sees her. He
sees her pain, which must feel like his when he thinks about his
grandparents. The ache between his ribs. The sense that the city
stole them, too; stole something he'll never have back. He prac-
tices writing out the words, the ones that inch toward describing
what he means. He writes *I SEE* on a scrap of paper. He tries to
think of what else there is to say, but there aren't any words that
could protect him—he hopes *I SEE* will be enough. He folds it in
half, then in half again, until it's small, another secret he'll keep
close until the time is right.

He takes to carrying the scrap of paper in his pocket, and soon
it becomes as worn and soft as the two-dollar bill. He follows the
girl on her lunch break, sometimes through the parking lot. He
follows her to the boardwalk again, where she goes to the red-
haired girl. While she was inside, he told himself he'd give her
the note and the bill that afternoon, in the bright glare of the sun.
But he noticed another man standing just outside the door, waiting, listening, his eyes so pale they looked like glass. Something
about the man scared Luis—the way he stood or cocked his head
toward the doorway. As though he owned it all.

He goes for another one of his walks that night, a lighter in
his pocket, still thinking of that man's stare, the angle of his head,
the strange smile that looked a little like a grimace. The buildings
of the city are spread before him, like a buffet, but none of them
have the right feel. Nothing calls to him, summoning him in the

way he's come to expect. He walks farther, alongside the Black Horse Pike, underneath the spotlit billboards featuring bright blue drinks, platters of seafood, or big-breasted women in their underwear, blowing on a pair of dice. How beautiful it would be to set one aflame, to see one of those garish, ridiculous signs ablaze, an island of fire high above the grass.

The marsh. He won't do it, but he likes the fantasy of it— the picture it creates in his head. He steps off the shoulder of the road, into muck that swallows his shoes. He looks back toward the skyline, the places where it's gone dark, the hulking rectangles of concrete where the beautiful buildings were. If he lit the marsh, a straight line of lighter fluid drawing the fire across it, it would look as if the whole city was burning, about to be swallowed whole.

Of course, the marsh is actually quite peaceful. He used to come here to trap crabs with his grandfather when he was a boy. He thinks he could still find his way back to the creek where they used to find the blue claws, where they might find a nest of young birds, their feathers a wild fluff on their heads. He steps deeper into the grass, flies circling his head—he remembers that well, too, his grandfather taking aim and slapping them away.

Above him, the neon sign of the Sunset Motel casts a feeble yellow glow on the grass. He sees a hint of glitter that, for a moment, he takes to be water, a slice of the creek sparkling under the light. He steps closer, pushes through the grass, and what he sees makes him feel the way he did when Gold Tooth punched the air out of his lungs.

For the first few seconds his brain rejects what he sees, though the understanding seizes his limbs, his guts. His brain can only understand the scene before him in a series of shapes. The curve of a calf. The angle of an elbow. A parabola of hair. The arch of eyebrows. The thick lines of clotted blood that must be cuts. Then he processes colors. The white-blue of the skin, the rings of purple around their necks. The bruises. The glint of gold: an ankle bracelet dangling a dozen little charms. The smell hits him next, the smell he thought was a part of the marsh but must be them. He hits himself in the face, slaps himself hard a second time. He closes his eyes and waits to wake up from a dream. Flies land on his eyelids, his arms, the back of his neck. He steps closer, reels back. One of their faces looks collapsed. And their eyes are open. They see him, judge him. They know everything he's done.

He sprints back through the marsh, out toward the road, to retch into the gutter. His stomach convulses painfully, as though it is wringing itself out. He can only think about catching his breath, about wiping the tears from his cheeks, the vomit from his lips. Once he is sure he can breathe, he starts to run back into town on wobbling legs.

He can't stop thinking of their fingers. Like they were reaching for one another, trying to hold hands. Trying to hold on.

LILY

OUR SHIFT FROM SAFETY, LIGHTNESS, toward darkness was so quick, so subtle.

The man who approached us looked like he might have been a high school football coach. It took a good deal of maneuvering for him to sit on the barstool and shift so his stomach wasn't pressing up against the bar. But the redness in his face implied anger coiled in him, waiting to strike. Underneath his smile, he was the kind of man who smashed bottles at bars.

"What do you want, Long Island iced teas? Ladies seem to love those Long Island iced teas."

"You must buy a lot of girls drinks, huh?" Clara said. "And here I thought we were special."

"Well, then I'll buy you two, darling." He was already licking his lips. "If it'll make you feel special. If it'll make you feel good."

"I'm sure that will make me feel good," she said, laying her hand on his wrist. I felt a little jilted that she had seemed to care about my story and now her attention had been so easily redirected to someone else. The man murmured something near her ear, and she giggled in a way I hadn't heard before, giddy and girlish. I didn't think I could stand it, watching her hand fall again and again on this man's arm. His hand creeping from her knee up her thigh. I reached for my bag, waited for the bartender to turn around so I could close out my tab.

The man raised his eyes from Clara's mouth to look at me. "Hey, missy, you look a little lonely over there. I have a friend who I'm sure will want to keep you company."

"I'm about to go," I said.

"Oh, Lily, don't," Clara said. She inched closer to me, put her hand on mine. "Just for a little while?"

"Another round on me, until he gets here," the man said.

I didn't want to leave her with this guy. He was probably no worse than anyone else she'd met up with, but I still felt responsible. Like I could steer the situation, control it. Maybe eventually talk her into just going home. I would have to take a cab home anyway, and it could drop her off on my way back. My mood was turning sour; tomorrow would already be marred by a hangover. I was stuck, regret on either side: past and future. The only thing to do was wade through the oblivious, gin-soaked now. I stirred my drink and thought of Clara's prophecy again: If I were really going to fall before I would rise, it might be better to get the fall over with. Better to face it, collide into it head-on. Some other humiliation, some other way the world was going to use me. I already had a sense that these men would make us into something smaller, less human. They would want to make us into a story for when they retreated back to their lives—*these two young sluts we met down in AC, throwing back Long Island iced teas like you wouldn't believe*—the way Matthew had made me his story. If I had learned anything it was that if you were someone's story, they owned a part of you, took a piece of you away.

"Fine," I said. "What the hell."

"Yay!" Clara leaned over, kissed me on the cheek, close to the corner of my lips, lingering a second longer than she needed to. Her eyelashes brushed my cheek.

"Well, now, ain't nothing better than two sexy women showing each other a little affection. Or a lot of affection, if you know what I mean."

"We certainly do." Clara gave me a theatrical wink.

"Well, I like the sound of that. Girls who know how to have a little fun."

"You have no idea how much fun," she said. I tried to ignore how sad it made me to hear her like this. She was so good at being what he wanted, at hiding herself behind clichés. And he was so easily pleased, so willing to believe that this was all she was.

My jaw clenched tighter. Was it this easy? Did people really talk like this? In middle school, one of my friends and I would watch porn on Starz after her parents went to bed. We were curious about sex, how it worked, how two seemingly sane, rational people ended up clawing at one another like animals, moaning and grunting. We were interested in the act, sure, but we also wanted to know about what led to it: Were there code words? Did the innuendo just pile up until you knew when to touch each other? Clara and this man reminded me of the scripts of those movies. The woman approaching the auto mechanic in his shop, letting him know she wanted him to do more than service her car. A raised eyebrow, a turned foot, a bitten lip, and in minutes they were all over one another, the woman's body smeared with black grease.

"Here's my friend Rob now. Wait till he gets a look at you two; he'll wish he cashed in his chips half an hour ago."

The two men could have been brothers: Rob was a little taller than the first man, but with the same large stomach taut against his T-shirt. He wore a black visor and his frequent player's card was attached to his belt with a neon lanyard. He nodded at us, not asking our names.

He surveyed the empty glasses and water-ringed napkins spread in front of us. "Looks like I've got some catching up to do." I wondered if we weren't worth a handshake, if he only wanted to touch us the way men felt permitted to touch girls in bars: at the smalls of their backs when pushing through a crowd, a squeeze on the arm for emphasis.

"Why don't you sit on the other side of Lily? She's bored by herself," Clara said. I kicked the leg of her stool.

"Don't mind if I do." I wasn't so sure he was right about catching up. Up close he smelled like rum.

"What's a girl like you drinking? Let me guess, vodka soda? That's what women drink to keep their weight down and still have a good time. My guess from the looks of you is that you like to do both." He ordered one for me, and a mai tai for himself. I was already too far gone: The lights of the slot machines beyond the bar started to blur.

I thought about standing up, walking away, jostling him with my shoulder as I did so he would go toppling to the floor. Making my way out the front door, hailing a cab. Going home, where my mother would be asleep in front of the TV. But then I thought, in my drunken, imprecise way, about Matthew. Telling that story to Clara had dredged up the old desire to impress him, the man to whom stories were the highest form of currency— mostly because he already had everything else. What would it feel like to lean into this moment? To let these men use us. To see what Clara was talking about. Maybe there was only one way to really know.

"Thanks for this," I said when the fresh drinks came. This time, I angled my chest toward him, like Clara did, and let my fingers brush the top of his arm. *Why not?* I thought. Maybe recklessness wasn't reserved only for men.

"Aren't *you* friendly," he said, looking at my lips, then at my chest. I was still fighting the urge to wriggle away. His shirt needed washing and I could smell acrid smoke, the tang of body odor. I could also feel Clara's eyes on me, even as she giggled. I wanted her to watch.

"So where are you from?" I asked. It was a misstep, I realized as soon as I said it. These men came here to feel big: They didn't want to think about whatever was waiting for them back home. The sagging gutters, the faded paint, the bills, the soul-deadening jobs.

"Avondale, Pennsylvania."

"I hope you're having a fun trip." I tried to make my voice breathy. "Did you do well at the tables? What's your favorite game to play?"

"I like poker mostly. Blackjack here and there."

"I'm no good at any of those. Maybe you could teach me a thing or two."

"Probably could. It's harder than it looks."

I touched his leg. "Oh yeah?"

"Yes, indeed." He swallowed, looked at me as though trying to measure something.

"Hey, so uh, we've got a room upstairs." Rob leaned over me to Clara. "Isn't that right, Luke?" I stared down at Luke's forearm, braced on the bar for balance. Even his arm was flushed. "Plenty more to drink. Not quite so crowded. Keep the good times going." His pores were giant and there was sweat gathering at his temples, glistening under the bristle of his hair.

"You like coke?" Rob whispered to me, his breath hot on my ear. "We've got enough to share." I nodded, even though it was a lie. I had never liked it very much, the way it made my heart buzz, the too-sweet drip of it down my throat. "I'm assuming you'll also share some of your winnings, Mr. Big Shot." I could do it: be this stupid, this bold. That's what they wanted, all of them. Matthew ranting on about how stories matter more than money, more than success. Ramona nodding in agreement, that you become the story you tell.

"I see." He didn't sound surprised. I suppose I had wanted him to.

"What are you waiting for?" Clara was watching me again. I wanted her to feel the force of what she had provoked. I was young. I had a body that was firm and soft in the right proportions. I had good skin and long hair. Why couldn't I use these fleeting gifts to a particular end? Besides, Matthew had and without my permission. Now, at least, I was the one making the choice, offering myself up. I would get all of the benefits of whatever exchange we worked out.

Fuck off, I texted Matthew, as I climbed down from my barstool. But I was still thinking about what words I would use to tell him about this experience. The look of awe and disgust and finally respect coming into his face. And it would answer Clara's prophecy: I would hit rock bottom. I would fall again before I could rise. The bad fate would buy the good. I pictured all of my misery reversing suddenly and absolutely, like the tipping of a seesaw.

The men lay bills on the bar and led us back through the floor, toward the eastern tower.

Clara edged closer. "Are you sure about this?" she whispered.

"What? You do it. It's like you said, no big deal. Under control."

"That's not what I meant."

"So what did you mean?"

In front of us the men were talking, too—probably about money. Who could pay for us. How much we would cost them. Whether they should drop us and head to a strip joint instead. What was my value, to the dollar? I had wondered this, too, after Matthew's show, when I read that it had sold out. A piece of me had been in the offing then, too. I suddenly had so many questions for Clara. Would the money always feel paltry, the amount too low? What did she do if someone didn't want to pay? Did she ever sleep with anyone simply because she wanted to? Or was she ruined for anything like genuine lust?

"It's harder than that. It takes a piece of you away. And you don't need to do anything with these guys. You should go. Before we get into the elevator with them."

"I'm not leaving you alone."

"It's fine, Lily. I'll be okay."

I nodded at her fingers. "Let's both leave."

"I need the money, remember? If I'm going to stop doing this one day, I have to get out of here. It's a means to an end."

"Funny, I feel the same way."

"Stop trying to prove a point you don't need to prove!" Her voice was loud. The men heard and turned around.

"Everything okay, girls?" Luke asked. He was swaying.

"Yeah, or do you need to kiss and make up?" Rob stepped closer to me. "Bad girls get spanked, you know. Have you been a bad girl?" I tried to imagine what it would be like, a man I hated putting his hands on me. How much different would it feel from being touched by someone I cared about?

"We're fine, aren't we, Clara?"

"I thought you said your name was Amanda . . ." Rob slurred.

"You know what? We have to go. You two have a good time," Clara said.

"But I thought we were all having fun?" Luke put his hand on my arm. "Come on. It will be even more fun upstairs. We can keep the party going."

"Come on, Amanda," I said, imitating Clara when she flirted. "You're hurting my feelings." She bit the inside of her cheek, shook her head. I wished I could say I felt dread as we approached the bank of elevators, the gold doors throwing back our reflections, but I was empty, cold. I could watch as Luke extended a hand toward me, grabbed my ass, as though it were happening to another person. I tried to think of the title Matthew would give this version of me. *Lily Groped.* Then I thought of my painter—how the artist would have captured the queasy turn to my mouth, the pallor of my face—but I pushed the image away.

We got into the elevator and Luke pressed the button for the twelfth floor. We were quiet as it rose. The cables squeaked. The car groaned.

Inside the room, two duffel bags were open on the floor, and I saw the sleeve of a Hawaiian shirt peeking out of one of them: attire for tomorrow's trip to the Swim Club—these guys were walking clichés. I tried to get Clara to meet my eyes, but she wouldn't look at me anymore. Rob made his way to the bathroom. I hadn't really believed him about the coke until I heard him cutting it, the scrape of a credit card on the marble vanity and the wet sound of his greedy snorting.

Luke came toward me, stroked my back. Clara was standing with her arms crossed, out of his reach.

"Come on, sweetheart. Show your girlfriend here that you're friends again after your little fight. Kiss and make up."

Clara raised her eyes. She was glowering at me and I could feel the heat rising from her body. Luke stepped away from me and pulled her by her belt loop. I still had the feeling that none of it was actually happening, that there wouldn't really be consequences for what we had set into motion. This summer had long since canted into the surreal. With the liquor, it was easier to tell myself that it was all part of a dream, and when I woke everything would slowly be neutralized by the coming of the day, that I would try to remember the details—the meaty, warm hands on me, the rum breath, the almost melancholy look of the Hawaiian shirt peeking out of the suitcase—and they would already have faded away.

Rob returned from the bathroom, grabbed my wrist, and pulled. The effects of that last drink were coming on and I stumbled a little as he pulled me.

I thought about what it would be like to sleep with this man for money—surely I had been underneath enough bodies in col-

lege to know what it was like to be an absence, really, during sex.
A man sweating and thrusting but also oblivious to me. Oblivious to anything but his own pleasure. But I hadn't thought that
he would want to kiss me. That his tongue would jab at mine,
and how the force and the taste of it would make me feel sick.
Strangely cool. Rum-soaked. The only thoughts I had now were
stop, wait. I pulled away from him and looked behind me, to
Clara. Luke had already pulled her shorts off, and she was in his
lap in the chair against the wall. She looked so small against his
big body.

"You don't like that? Fine," Rob said. There was anger in his
voice. Was there anyone angrier than a man rejected? Than a
man who had seen repulsion on your face when he had expected
to find admiration, lust? Was there any limit to what that kind of
man could do to you, the ways he felt entitled to retaliate?

Rob moved his hand to my shoulder and pressed me toward
the ground while his other hand reached for his fly. Then his
fingers were in my hair. He wound them close to the scalp and
pulled. And for a moment, I tried to imagine it, to hover above
the scene and wonder, what would Matthew title this one? *Lily
Punished. Lily on Her Knees. Lily, Hair Pulled.*

He was drunk enough that he was having trouble with the
zipper on his jeans, grunting and swearing in one indistinguish-
able string of obscenities. I rubbed my scalp.

"What's a matter, didn't like that? Can talk the talk but can't
walk the walk, huh?"

"I don't want to do this," I said. But he was already lifting my
dress. I tried to scream but it came out in a strange trickle of sound.

"Hey, stop that!" Clara stood up from Luke's lap.

"You bitches tricked us." I tried to break free, but his hand
tightened on my arm.

"I said let her go." Luke rose from his chair, a ridiculous erec-
tion tenting his shorts.

"What the hell?" Rob said. "What kind of customer service is this, huh? We pay for what we want, you give it."

"Just go easy, man," Luke said. "This is supposed to be fun."

Clara reached for her shorts, stepped into them. I thought for a second she was going to put them on and leave. It would probably be what I deserved, I thought, after instigating this. Insisting, thinking of it all as an adventure, a kind of game, that I could make into something else—a wild story that I would tell at a bar in a few years. But then she fingered something in her pocket. I saw a flash and thought, ridiculously, that it was a piece of jewelry, that she was going to attempt a bribe. It wasn't until she had stepped closer to Rob with the blade extended that I understood that she had a knife.

"What do you think you're doing with that, little girl?" He reached for Clara.

"Get away from her. We're leaving."

Rob laughed like a man who had nothing to lose. "No, princess. I'd rather see you try something with that. I can play rougher than you think." Clara cut her eyes in my direction and a second later she was lunging.

"FUCK!" Rob screamed, and let go of me, moving his hands to his leg. "You stupid little bitch. Are you insane? You fucking crazy bitch!"

"Lily! Let's go!" The knife was still in her hand, shimmering with blood. I turned behind me to see Rob holding his calf, blood dripping into his socks. I grabbed my purse. Rob stood before us, his eyes glazed, his mouth hanging open. We ran out into the hallway, toward the elevator. I punched the down arrow over and over with my fist.

"Too slow," Clara said. "Stairs." I followed her around the corner to a metal door, pushed through it, and we plunged down, stumbling into the turns of the staircase, the acoustics of the stairwell magnifying everything so that the sound of our pounding feet boomed around us. We didn't stop running until we reached the bottom, both of our chests heaving.

"This way," she said. I could feel my heartbeat in my ears, my breath catching shallow in my chest. It was more than the running—I had the same shaky feeling in my hands as when I had an anxiety attack. *No*, I thought, *please not now*. My sense of proportion was off, and the hallway seemed to press in on us, constricting to a pinpoint far, far away. *No*, I told myself more firmly. *You are stronger than that. You don't have to let this happen.* My breathing stayed shallow, but the pounding in my temples eased up, and I followed Clara to the back door near the main lobby.

Then we were outside, near the harbor, and in the soft night air I felt like I could breathe again. A few boats bobbed lazily along the bay, in little halos of light. We walked around to the front of the casino in silence. In the dark, the topiaries loomed, their overgrown shapes looking threatening, wild. Or maybe that was just my mood that turned everything strange. I pulled my phone out of my purse to see I had three new texts from Matthew.

I understand if you're still mad but I'd really like to talk.

I miss you.

What are you doing right now? Can I call?

I slipped it back into my pocket.

Clara watched me. "Are you okay?" she asked.

"Yeah, I think so." Between the adrenaline and the night air, I felt sobered. Penitent. I looked up and tried to see the stars through the clouds but could only find a few.

"That was really stupid, Lily. You were too drunk to go anywhere with anyone."

"You were drinking, too."

"I had two drinks."

"Oh, come on. They definitely bought us way more than two."

"Sam knows to pour me soda water with lime after the second, or Coke with no rum, whatever. It's part of our deal. He's never going to serve me more than two drinks even if I beg."

"Well, how was I supposed to know that?"

"You're not, that's what I'm saying. You had no idea what you were getting into."

"I'm sorry. Are you okay?"

"Sure, Lily. I'm okay."

"What was that, with the knife? Aren't you worried they'll report you?"

"No. They would have to confess to picking up prostitutes first."

"Well, they didn't pay us anything so are we technically prostitutes?"

"Who says we didn't get paid?" Clara pulled a wad of cash from her pocket, counted it, handed half of the bills over to me. One hundred dollars, hardly worth being treated like a toy. I tried to think of a price that felt fair but couldn't. What I wanted most was the thing I wouldn't get: the ability to forget about them, to push their leering faces and grasping hands out of my mind.

"How did you pull that off?"

"This? Before we even left the bar. I'm telling you, these visions are scaring me. I'm taking every chance I get to pocket some cash."

I nodded. I had a new respect for Clara's stealing. It seemed like another form of magic, another power she had. "Where'd you get that knife?"

"Pawnshop." She held the blade to the light. There was still blood on it, blood that looked black in the dark.

"Do you want me to drive you home?" I felt sobered up, by everything, by our run through the stairs, the night air, the adrenaline. "Or you can drive us if you want."

"I can't drive." Another bitter little laugh. "Never learned. Des doesn't have a car."

"Well, then let me take you. It's way too late for you to wait for the bus." I had thought she would demur, slip away like she always did, slide out from under my attention.

"Sure, why not. After all, I did stab a man for you. A ride is the least you could do." We smiled at one another, tentative smiles, a little shy.

"Okay, I'm not too far. That's my truck over there."

"I pictured you as more of a sedan girl."

"It was my dad's." Already, again, a lump in my throat.

She sighed. "You must miss him a lot."

"Every day," I said, my voice weak, light. "He used to work here."

"What happened?"

"You didn't see that part?" I asked, surprised. "Your visions?"

"It doesn't work like that. I don't get to choose. Sometimes if a memory or image is really strong, still really present, it just sort of intrudes upon me. Yours did." We got in the truck, and I started the engine.

"What was it? What did you see?"

She took a deep breath. I drove to the exit ramp of the lot, stopped, and pressed my employee badge to the window before the booth attendant waved me on. "A woman. Your mother, I'd guess. Sitting on the edge of a bed. A hospital."

"Just sitting?"

"No. Sitting and—and screaming. Sort of, clawing at herself. A man's hand on a white sheet."

Without thinking, I hit the brakes. If there had been room for doubt, her words undid it. That memory played itself in a loop on my worst days. How it had taken me a few minutes to reach for my mother, how we struggled against each other for a moment when I held down her hands.

"I'm sorry."

"Don't be sorry. I asked you to tell me." But I had only said that because a part of me refused to let myself believe, in what she said she could do and see. I hadn't been ready, truly ready, to look straight at either of these things: that memory of the hospital room, or the feeling like I had just been shoved into a new reality. That Clara had a talent that defied logic, a talent I couldn't understand.

"I can't imagine what it's like. Loving someone that much."

"Me neither. I wonder if I ever will."

"What about whatshisface?" That she pretended not to remember Matthew's name gave me a small jolt of pleasure, and I felt lighter as I watched the casino recede in the rearview.

"It was never . . . never like that. I think in a way, that's what I liked about being with Matthew. I felt safe from that kind of loss. I mean, it still hurt a lot when we broke up. It was humiliating. But I didn't feel"—I searched for the right word—"despair. I felt like a version of my life was over. But not like, my entire life. My mom? My dad was her entire life."

"She has you."

"It didn't matter. Not in those first few months. She kept threatening to take a bunch of pills. Or to leave the car running in the garage. Drop the hair dryer in the bath. It was like I wasn't enough to keep her here. I guess that's why I felt like I could leave. Like there was no real difference."

"I'm sure there was. I mean, she didn't do any of those things."

"I guess so." The clock on the dash said that it was 2:03 in the morning. The streets were mostly empty, save for a homeless man rummaging through one of the metal trash cans on the corner. I rolled the windows down and felt the stillness, the heaviness of the humid air. We were just a few blocks away from Clara's shop, but the night still felt incomplete. After all the tumult, it needed some sort of closure. We needed a salve.

"I have an idea. Let's go down to the beach."

"Why?"

"Why not? We've got the whole town to ourselves."

"You're sort of a weirdo sometimes, Lily."

"We can go for a swim. My dad used to say that nothing helped change your mood like swimming in the ocean. Like it could rinse everything bad away. I don't think I've gone for a swim since I've been back."

"I can't swim."

"Now you're screwing with me. You live right on the beach."

"No, really. Can you picture Des teaching me? I actually don't think she can either. I mean, she grew up in Newark. Where was she going to learn?"

"Well, if it's calm you should at least wade in. Get your feet wet. It'll be symbolic." I guided the truck up to the curb and cut the engine. "Let's go."

Clara sat for a moment, but as I crossed the boardwalk toward the bulkhead I heard her door open and slam shut again. The clouds had shifted, and the sand was washed with red, purple, green from the changing, blinking lights of the casinos behind us.

"This is sort of creepy," Clara called behind me. I pretended not to hear, but I knew what she meant. It was a little unsettling but also very beautiful—or maybe the eeriness was what made it beautiful. It reminded me of Mil's portraits. How the most absorbing aspect was their suggestion of something sinister, something unsettling, underneath the fabric of our days. There was a challenge underneath it all. You wanted both to look and to look away, break contact. Ahead, I could see the mound of a ruined sandcastle, a forgotten plastic shovel. A sudden sadness gripped me in the ribs, a physical ache for my childhood that nearly made me double over.

When I was out of my shoes, the sand felt soft and cool beneath my feet. The greenish glow of a pair of cat eyes beamed my way from the dunes and disappeared. The waves lapped at the sand in little ruffles of foam, and the ocean was silvered with moon. A few blocks away the Pier, the once-high-end shopping mall, jutted out over the sea like an accusatory finger, its billboards lit with spotlights that glinted off the water. I crunched over the litter of shell fragments that had been pushed into a pile by the tide.

The thrill of the cold water on my feet rushed up my legs. I waded out farther, until I was up to my knees, Clara behind me, tiptoeing into the waves. When the water was at my waist I kicked my feet out and let my body sink under the surface. The tingle of the cold was intimate and intense, cold on my scalp, cold on the back of my neck, cold over my hips, across my stomach. Water in my ears, dulling everything but the steady wash of the waves, I held my breath until I felt it burn in my chest.

When I came up, I heard Clara's voice, garbled a little by the water in my ears. "Didn't you hear me calling you?"

"Don't worry. It feels good, that's all. You should try it."

She crossed her arms close to her chest. "I'm going back."

"Don't be such a baby." I cupped my hand, splashed water in her direction.

"Cut it out!"

"Come on, it's as calm as can be. Just go under."

"I don't want to. This water is freezing."

"That's the point. It's refreshing. What are you so worried about?"

"Drowning. Dying. Getting eaten by sharks."

I smiled, though the last thing I wanted was Clara to think I was laughing at her.

"What?" she said.

"Nothing." How could I tell her, without offending her—that it was nice to see her talk and act like a kid. Clara inched her way toward me, grimacing. Then I understood. A wave splashed her hands, and it must have stung the burns.

"You need to go see someone about those."

"I'm fine. It's just cold." She pinched her nose and slipped under the surface. I plunged below, too. It was a relief, to shut out the rest of the world, to silence it, to rinse everything I had done from my hair, my eyelashes, every inch of my skin.

We surfaced around the same time. Clara pushed the wet hair from her face. Underneath it she was smiling.

"Nice, right?"

"Not terrible." The water was like ink. Each time I brought my hands above the surface, a part of me expected them to be stained. I thought of Winslow Homer's paintings, his seascapes tense with awe and threat. I remembered one of his paintings that I had seen at the Clark. *Undertow*. Based on a rescue Homer witnessed in Atlantic City, the picture showed a man hauling drowning women from the water, the men looking mighty and muscular and the women looking helpless, spent, pale. A beautiful picture, but a story I was tired of.

Behind Clara, back on the beach, I thought I saw something. A shadow outlined in neon. I tried to tell myself it was just a trick of the light, but already the moment had taken on a different feeling. The calm of the water became menacing. Our isolation became a vulnerability. I spun in a circle, making sure no one had snuck up behind us.

"What?"

"Nothing. I just thought I saw someone. On the shore."

"It might just be a homeless person. A lot of them sleep under the pier." But I knew we were thinking the same thing when I saw Clara standing a little straighter, her shoulders high: the men had followed us. To think we had gotten away had been silly, stupid, or that because we had cleared one danger we were protected from others, like the night's quota had been filled.

"What should we do?"

"Well, we can't stay out here forever." Clara's teeth had started to chatter. I felt goose bumps rise on my arms.

"Let's head in then. I'm sure we're fine." *Fine.* Was that true? How often had I hid behind that word when I meant its opposite? It was what Steffanie had said when I was able to see her after the attack. *Really, Lily, I'm totally fine.* We waded back, our wet clothes stuck to our skin. I scanned the beach for the person I thought I'd seen, but I didn't make out any shapes except for the lifeguard stand, ghostly in the moonlight. Clara and I made our way up the beach slowly, in silence.

At the boardwalk, Clara jerked her head in the direction of her shop. "I'm this way."

"You sure you're okay walking by yourself?"

"Do it all the time."

"Right." It had been, along with the night of Matthew's last show, one of the strangest, most disorienting nights of my life. But for Clara, was this normal? The danger? The ugliness? Maybe the only strange thing about it for her had been that I was there to witness, to screw it up. "What are you doing this week?" I asked. "I could teach you to swim. Properly. In daylight, I mean."

"Sure." I could tell she thought it was an empty offer, something to patch up the silence. Even I was surprised that I meant it. That something like trust had passed between us, solidified.

"I'm off on Saturday. Want to meet at three o'clock, three-thirty?"

"You can text me if you want. I just added more minutes to my phone." I wondered if she didn't have a real phone because she couldn't afford one, or if that was one more way Des kept Clara cut off, kept her under her thumb.

"Sounds good to me. I'll see you then." We stopped in front of the candy shop, where Julie Zale smiled out from a poster on the window. It was hard to look at her face.

"I keep wondering why she left home," Clara said. "Why she thought she might be happier somewhere else."

"Maybe everyone thinks they'll be happier somewhere else." Had I been happier in New York than I'd been here? Busier, maybe. More distracted. But happier? No.

"Some of us are right."

"You sure you're okay?" I asked.

She smiled. "I'm more worried about you."

"Don't worry. My car is right there. Get back safe."

"I will."

I watched her walk down the boardwalk huddled into herself, looking like a skinny kid, like girls I remembered from elementary school, the ones whose slight size meant they could jump the farthest off of the swings. I wished I had a blanket, a towel—I would run after her and throw it over her shoulders. As I turned away, another cat crossed my path, a brief streak of white-and-gray tail, and my exhaustion caught up with me, weighed on all my limbs. I was so tired of being afraid. And yet, it seemed that was all this summer was: learning all of the ways that dread could creep into my days.

DEBORAH

ON A THURSDAY AFTERNOON IN Eagles Mere, Pennsylvania, Deborah Willis's phone rings. She is in the middle of canning the strawberries she's grown in her garden, stewing jam on the stove. The air in the kitchen is humid, thick with the sweetness of strawberries and sugar. Deborah has pink stains across the front of her shirt. A mound of stems sits on the counter, and it is their peppery, woody smell that she will come to associate with this day, this call. The way it filled her lungs with something like dirt.

"Hello," she says, licking strawberry pulp from her thumb. "Hello?" She's surprised. No one ever calls on the house line anymore. She can smell the jam starting to burn and stretches the cord so she can reach over to the stove and turn the heat down, just a notch. Maybe she was too late to answer. Maybe the caller had hung up already.

She is about to hang the phone back on the hook when a voice says, "Mom?"

She sets her spoon down on the stove, wonders if she conjured the voice: she associates the house phone with Georgia, the vintage blue rotary dial Georgia loved as a girl. "Mom?" the voice asks again. She can't say anything yet—she knows that she is about to cry and the words will come out wrong, crimped by emotion: anger, gratitude, joy, sorrow, all rolled together. "Mom, are you there?"

"I'm here," she stammers. *I'm always here*, she thinks.

"Mom, I . . . I was wondering if I could come home."

Deborah grips the curly cord of the phone, as though she could use it to hang on to her daughter, to pull her closer that way. "Of course you can. Are you in trouble? Do you need money? Where are you?"

"Atlantic City," she says. "I can take a bus tomorrow. I have enough money for the ticket."

"What time?" Deborah says. She thinks of the last time she saw Georgia, three years ago. The scabs on her cheeks. Her bleeding, bitten-down nails.

"I would get into Scranton at seven."

"I'll be there to pick you up. You need anything? You sure you're not in trouble?" She thinks of Georgia at fifteen, the DUI, the stolen truck. Thinking it was a good idea to let her spend the night in jail. The next morning, the look on her daughter's face: the betrayal, the rage, the fear. Deborah knew she had made a terrible mistake. But she was a single mother trying to raise a daughter the only way she knew how. Never as straightforward as planting seeds, coaxing fruit from the garden. There was a whole alchemy of love and discipline that she must not have gotten right.

"I'm okay. I'll be okay. I just need to get out of town."

"Are you still with Josh? He hit you again?"

"No, not Josh. I've just got a bad feeling." She wonders if her daughter isn't alone. If she's afraid to say what she is afraid of.

"Will you be safe, until you can get on a bus?"

A pause. "I'll see you tomorrow, seven o'clock." Deborah doesn't know a lot of things about her daughter's life. But she can tell when she's scared. The small voice in the hallway. The sound of feet in footed pajamas padding down the stairs.

"I'll pick you up. Tonight. Tell me where."

"No, Ma, the bus is fine. That's too long to drive."

"At least tell me where to call you."

"The Sunset Motel."

"That's where you're staying tonight?"

"No, but you can leave a message for me there. Tell them it's for Peaches."

She doesn't want to know what this means, that her daughter is going by another name. Georgia, Peaches. It would be a little funny, if it didn't make her worry more. Despite herself, she can already hear the innuendo: *Have a taste. Shake my tree.* A shiver works its way up her spine.

DEBORAH DOESN'T sleep that night. Around 3 a.m., she heaves herself out of bed, goes to the kitchen for tea, tries to read. Her jam is lined up on the counter, the mess of the afternoon long since tidied away. When the first light comes into the kitchen, it makes the jars glow, a pinky red. The sight used to be comforting, but today it is unsettling. Maybe it's her sleepless brain, but she can only look at the jam and see blood. She thinks of her daughter coming home four, four and a half years ago after a night out with Josh, her lip split.

She keeps looking at herself in the rearview on the drive to Scranton. The lipstick perks up her face, but not enough to make up for the circles under her eyes. She's early. She watches the clock on the dash. 6:03, 6:27, 6:44, 6:58, 7:05.

The Atlantic City bus pulls in, hisses, sighs out a trickle of passengers. She waits to see her daughter among them, squints hard at a brunette girl—Georgia might have changed her hair— but no. None of them is her daughter. She waits until the driver is done heaving suitcases from the guts of the bus, slides Gee's picture from her wallet.

"Was this girl on your bus?"

The driver hardly glances at the photo, shakes her head no. All the passengers already gone, she says.

"No one in the bathroom?" She has a memory of walking in on Georgia taking a photo of herself in the bathroom mirror with her first cell phone. She had drawn a lipstick heart on her cheek, on each of her breasts, around the nipple. Who was it for? Deborah wanted to know. For a man online? To text to a boy? Or just for herself? She hoped it was the latter, just a celebration of being beautiful, of being young, a private, exuberant joy.

At half past seven, she walks up to the ticket window, taps on the glass. "Any other buses coming in from Atlantic City tonight?"

The woman shakes her head, pulls a sliver of onion from her burger, coils it onto the paper wrapper, licks a spot of ketchup from her thumb. Deborah fumbles her phone out of her bag and dials the number for the motel Georgia told her about. It rings and rings and rings, but no one picks up.

Deborah sits in the parking lot until after midnight, thinking of the sound of her daughter's voice on the phone, the light coming through the jars of jam. At 12:03, she turns the engine on. It's a three-hour drive to Atlantic City. She hasn't been there since a trip she took with a few other schoolteachers, back in '99. She was shocked at the dinginess of it back then. It can only be worse now. She's seen stories on the news: the opioid epidemic, the casinos shutting down, the gang violence, Hurricane Sandy battering the coast. It's a wonder there's anything left.

She stops for a coffee, even though she doesn't need it. Her body is humming with purpose; her heart feels like it's gotten loose, untethered, tumbling around in her chest. She'll bring her girl back. This time, Georgia will come home.

CLARA

AFTER I GOT HOME FROM the beach, I slept soundly for the first night in a long time. I woke up with sunlight bright at the edges of my blinds, and as I opened my eyes I could hear the pushcart men on the boardwalk calling *ride ride ride*. Seagulls screeched, the waves thumped against the shore. But otherwise, silence. No screaming babies. No visions of strange rooms. There was a new clarity and stillness to everything around me. I felt like I could breathe again.

I knew Lily was right, even before we got into trouble with those men. My life had to change. I had $630 saved. It might have to be enough. Enough to get to California, at least, and figure things out from there. But now when I thought about leaving, for the first time I couldn't picture doing it. Not until I found Peaches. Until I learned what she knew, and maybe, maybe, figured out what these visions meant. It seemed wrong, unfair to all of the women, to take off like they didn't matter. Like I wasn't carrying around pieces of their lives.

I got dressed and slung Victoria's purse over my shoulder. Des wasn't home—another one of her nights out that bled into morning. I was worried about her, too, but also relieved. I didn't know what was going on with the rent, but with her gone I wouldn't have to deal with meeting anyone else in the back room.

Outside, the heat had finally broken, which created a lulling sense of calm that I almost let myself believe in. The ocean looked glassy and smooth. But I remembered the bloodstained knife in my purse, and the way Lily had thought she saw someone on the beach when we swam. I looked down at my fingers. The saltwater seemed to have helped the infection, but I wondered if they would scar. If I would walk around with a reminder of that man's anger for the rest of my life.

It was early, but Tropicana already jangled with arcade noises. Fake trumpets and prerecorded applause warbled out of the slot machines, mingled with the phlegmy coughs of senior citizens and people carrying on loud cell phone conversations as they wrestled quarters from Ziploc bags heavy with loose change. The cigar bar near the poker lounge was already muggy with thick, sweet smoke. A man with wide shoulders and a broad, stout build stood as I passed, and I jumped because he reminded me of the two men from the night before. He eyed me for a moment before turning his attention to the cigar pinched between his lips, flicking a lighter and turning it slowly in the flame.

In the window of a boutique, a shopgirl changed a mannequin from a blue sequined dress to a red one with a slit up to the hip. *What's the point?* You never saw anyone dressed glamorously in AC. Most people wore track suits, fanny packs, sweatpants with elastic cinched at the ankles. Dresses like that belonged to a different time.

I drifted aimlessly through the Quarter, passing the restaurant where I had gone with Tom—that felt like years ago now. I made my way to the hotel lobby, where a man was waggling his finger at a reservations agent, his wife at his side, her hands on her hips.

"Mice!" he roared. "We had fucking mice in our room! And if you don't do something about it now we're going to blast that out over the internet and this dump is going to be in even worse trouble than it already is!"

I had the urge to sob. Everything felt hopeless. Finding Peaches. Figuring out what caused these visions. Leaving. Staying here. Re-uniting with my mother. Saving the shop. It was all one big, Ru-bik's cube that I didn't know how to solve. And all the while, the image of the Tower loomed in my mind. It wasn't just Peaches who was going to face an upheaval. I felt something about my life was about to shift, to possibly break.

I sat on the concrete lip of the fountain and stared up at the false sky of the Quarter. The shapeless, smeared-looking clouds, the egg yolk–yellow sun. The tingle only lasted for half a second—a light-headedness, a strange taste in my mouth. Then a vision swallowed me up.

Movement. A woman's hand reaching for a cord, pulling on it, a lamp crashing to the ground. A man's work boot—reared back and kicked. The legs of a chair, the broken fingernails reaching toward them. The edges of the room going hazy, the light shrinking to a pinpoint, then nothing but darkness.

When I came out of it, I was on the ground, my head pounding—I must have slipped from the edge of the fountain, knocked my head against the stone. A woman perched on a scooter stared down at me, her eyes huge behind her glasses. I pushed myself up, my whole body exhausted, like waking up after a nightmare. My mouth was dry, but I swore I could smell blood. I kept bringing my hand to the sore spot on my head, expecting it to be wet.

"Hun, you okay?" the woman asked. I managed a nod. I won-dered if I had bit my tongue. I spit in my hand to see if I was bleeding—the woman's face changed from concern to disgust, but I didn't care. I forced myself to keep moving: to the bridge between the casino and the parking garage, the elevator to the ground floor, out onto the street. I knew those hands. Small, like a girl's. Peaches. I was too late. The brokenness I had felt puls-ing in this city all summer, at the center of everything that was wrong, had taken over. I had started to shake and told myself I was too cold in the air-conditioning, thought it might help to feel the sun on my face, my arms. I stood at the rails and watched a man with a metal detector make his way over the dunes, toeing at mounds of sand, searching. I gripped the rail hard, until my knuckles turned white.

I sat on an empty bench nearby, took my tarot cards from my bag. I had so many questions that I found it hard to narrow them down. Why hadn't my mother called for me yet? What was going on with Des? What had happened to them, Peaches and Victoria and Julie Zale? *What could I do to help them?* I asked. *And what do I need to do to help myself?*

The first card—the past—was the Two of Cups. Partnership. In a reading, it could stand for a romantic partnership or even a business partnership. None of the men I had been with deserved that word, *partner*. Des always called us partners, though it had been a long time since she had carried any of the weight. But still, if I thought about it, being with Des could be a little bit of a thrill. Back when I was a kid, some of her cons felt more like a game. Like the time when our water was shut off because she didn't pay the bill. We didn't fight about it, didn't worry. Instead, Des led me to the Hilton, and we snatched little bottles of shampoo from the maid's carts and snuck into the empty rooms to use their showers. Breaking in was easy—all it took was a credit card, or even a firm piece of paper, a quick slide to force the lock. But the Two of Cups was my first card; it meant that partnership was behind me. Whatever I faced from here on out, I faced alone.

The second card was the Four of Pentacles. It showed a sad man slumped over his fortune, his city in the distance behind him. This card usually meant you were too focused on money, gave it too much importance in your life. Sometimes, it could be interpreted more loosely: you were too fixated on control. I wasn't sure how to read the card—the visions, the missing women, men using me—it had been so long since I felt like I was in control.

If money wasn't that important, it meant that getting free wasn't important. I understood why the man in the picture clutched his coins close. The card seemed to imply that he'd lost his home, his relationships, because he cared too much about riches. But maybe he was like me— he wanted to see that town recede behind him. The money, like the stash under my bed, was the only thing keeping him from lapsing back into his old life, into being someone he didn't want to be.

The future, the Ten of Swords. One of the most violent cards in the deck. A man sprawled on the ground, ten swords stuck in his back. It could mean that you were literally going to be stabbed in the back, a betrayal. A crisis, a painful but inevitable end. The silver lining that I offered people when this card showed up in readings was that you couldn't control what other people did to you, but you could choose how you wanted to act in response. It could be a card about accepting your pain and having a chance to move on from it. Some people saw the dead man and thought the card was telling them they were going to die, but that wasn't it, or at least not usually. It meant that, like death, this was the final challenge—but there was peace waiting on the other side. My final challenge was still waiting for me.

I slipped the tarot cards back into their pouch and rubbed the back of my head. A bump had formed where it had struck the fountain, and it flashed with pain when I pushed my fingers against it. The visions were getting more complex, more violent, more consuming. Was that my final challenge? To overcome them? To figure out what they meant? Maybe it was too late to save Peaches and Julie, but then, what did they want from me? How was I supposed to help?

I was ravenous, but I was too anxious to eat. I headed in the direction of the shop and stopped at the 99-cent store to get myself a ginger ale, and tried to decide what to do next. At the front of the store, a row of pinwheels spun in the breeze, their metallic colors flashing. Every bone in my body was screaming *leave leave leave*. I thought of the Four of Pentacles, how happy I would be to turn my back on this city, to look back and see the skyline in the distance. I pulled the tab on my soda and wondered what I was supposed to do about the money. I was watching the pinwheels again when someone crashed into me and the soda fizzed all over my fingers, sloshed onto my shirt. It took me a minute to place him: Luis, the one who worked with Lily. Of course. Every time I saw him, something seemed to go wrong.

He held out his hands, the way people do to say *sorry* or *take it easy*.

But then I was somewhere else, outside of myself, beyond the boardwalk. Somewhere wild and untamed. Mud, and grass, a wide open field of it. A sparkle of something bright. Jewelry glinting in the light. The jewelry was attached to women. To their bodies. Their clothes looked too bright and their hair and skin was dull. There were bruises on their legs and arms. And flies. So many flies. Rings of bruises around their necks. Their faces were turned away from me, but I saw the locket, the blonde hair. Someone with Julie Zale's long runner's limbs. I could feel the flies everywhere, on every inch of my skin.

I came to, panting for breath. I had dropped the can of soda at my feet. It took all the effort I had to remain standing up. Luis stared at me, and as soon as I could catch my breath I started screaming. He held his hands out again, more insistently this time. As though he were saying *no, stop, please*. But I kept screaming, even as people gathered around us. I heard a woman mumble that they should call the cops. *No*, another voice said. *An ambulance. No*, another person said. *Look at her eyes. I think she's just strung out.* Luis edged away from me, and I fumbled for my keys, collapsed against the doorframe. I managed to stab my key into the lock of the shop door and pounded up the stairs.

I hadn't taken my own advice, hadn't listened to my own intuition. He had always given me a weird feeling—the sense that he had something to hide. But what did it matter? It didn't take back what he'd done to them, to all of them. Peaches, Victoria, Julie, and the two others who had been with them, touching hands. Was this the fearsome fate that my future held? Knowing the truth, and that I could do nothing about it? That maybe if I had paid better attention, those women could have been saved?

I curled myself into a ball on the floor of my bedroom, stayed like that until the light in the sky began to fade and the casinos turned on their signs, and everything was covered in their eerie red glow. The most I could manage was watching the colors of the light change. If this was what the Ten of Swords had been pointing to, it also meant that freedom was close. I knew one fact, consistent as a heartbeat: *I have to get out of here.* All of the others had probably thought the same.

LUIS

THE DAY AFTER HE FINDS the women, he paces the boardwalk, up and down and up and down and up and down. All the stores sell the same things—T-shirts printed with pictures of neon sunsets, wire cages filled with sad, slow hermit crabs whose shells are covered with glitter and painted designs: baseballs, moons. But at one of the shops, above the crabs, a row of cameras hangs from plastic hooks, the disposable kind in a bright yellow wrapper—his grandfather used to bring them along on their crabbing trips, or take pictures of Luis and his grandmother on the porch, his grandmother giving him a silly poke in the cheek so that he would smile, and in a few days Luis could hold the glossy images, feeling like a piece of himself was now kept safely inside. He chooses a camera from the display and brings it to the counter. He tries to control the shaking in his hands when he passes his money to the clerk. He know he's taking a risk, knows what will happen if this goes wrong. Men in black boots kicking down his door. The cops who laughed at him, coming to pick him up, cuff him, haul him away. He thinks of more words. *WOMEN, HURT, KILLED*. They are the truth, but how little help they would provide him. How little they convey. And still, he knows he needs to try. The women are there every time he closes his eyes.

He jumps at every touch, every person who passes by a little too close, every bird that swoops above him on the boardwalk, flapping its wings in a craze. He waits until he doesn't have to go to work and leaves early in the morning, when the sun has just edged over the ocean and sits low in the sky. The tips of the reeds are pale gold. He takes photos of the motel sign, the sunset that lights up one ray at a time, the parking lot to its right, the swath of marsh he cut through before. He will have to photograph his path without capturing his footprints—he hopes the police will still be able to find the way. He hopes it will be enough.

His stomach starts to flutter and twist the farther in he steps. In every breath he takes, he swears he smells it now, tastes it: The flesh. The decay. It's in his lungs, a part of him. He covers his mouth with his shirt, takes a photo looking back toward the motel, to show its size in the distance. He knows he must be close now. The mud has started to creep up his boots, sticky and thick. He takes one more deep breath to prepare himself. Mud, bodies, grass, salt.

Will it be worse? he wonders, before he parts the segment of tall reeds that hid the clearing. *Will it be worse, the second time, knowing what's there?*

It is. It is worse. What he sees makes him drop the camera, makes him run faster than before, as fast as he can.

Another girl. A fifth. Her eyes are still open. And they, too, are looking right at him.

This time, when he leaves, the rage takes over. It has tightened around his brain. He feels it spread down his spine, pressing on every inch of his skin. He kicks walls, dumpsters, cans. He buys another camera, but when he thinks about going back again he can't, can't face it, can't get over his fear, his shame. The plastic feels so small, like a toy, and he stomps the new camera under his feet, rips the film between his hands. He feels, more than ever before, the limits of who he is like a cage, a shrinking room.

Though there is another way. He could draw it, he thinks. The way his grandmother taught him before he started school. He closes his eyes and wills himself, for a minute, to think about her patient hands, the way she guided him into making images of milk cartons, sandwiches, red apples, butterflies. Innocent, simple, beautiful things. She always seemed so pleased by his work, kissing him on the head when he finished pictures of dinners he hoped to eat, pictures of places he thought she might like to go. He had liked breaking down the world that way, into line and color and shade and feeling. Pictures came easier than words, which always felt cold and barren no matter how many he learned.

He starts with the easier parts—the sign with its setting sun, the letters he remembers: the letters that could be the name of the place, *VACA CY*, the square building perched on the edge of the road. Then, grass bending in the wind, the thick, dark mud. He comforts himself by drawing a heron in flight, putting off the work he knows he has to do next. That hair, tangled with muck. Those open, staring eyes. He sketches the outlines of them first: their hands, their bare feet. He knows it's not important to the meaning of the drawing, but he feels he owes it to the women, to take the time to outline all fifty of their toes.

He hadn't thought about what he might do with it, who he will show it to. He won't take it to the cops, who could easily choose to misunderstand. Not his landlady, who had once been a friend of his grandmother's—he could never show such a horror to her. Not the girl with the red hair, who looked at him with such hatred, such fear. Maybe at work, though, there is someone who will listen. Not the girl with dark hair—he still wants to show her the note he wrote for her—*I SEE*—but this would only confuse her, get in the way. Maybe the blonde woman who helps him with supplies, the one who everyone listens to. He wonders what he will do if she gets angry, or sad, or afraid, or even calls the police. But he thinks that, of anyone he knows, she might know what to do. He folds the drawing until it's small enough to fit in his pocket, next to his matches. Another secret he's forced to wear close to his skin.

THE BLONDE girl smiles at him when he comes in the next day, then points to places he needs to clean—dust on the counters, dirt on the floors. He still feels that same buzz of energy and worry from everyone around him, everyone moving quickly, as though there is some emergency, something gone wrong. He spends the first half of his shift performing his duties with more care and attention than ever before—he knows he needs to win her, to earn her trust, before he asks her to see, to know what he knows. Sometimes the women creep into his mind, and he feels himself about to get sick again. The water in the dirty mop bucket reminds him of the color of their skin and he runs to the bathroom and heaves.

He waits until she's alone at the desk, one hand fiddling with the shining cross at her neck. Her gesture reminds him of the women—their bracelets and necklaces flashing in the sun. He takes the drawing from his pocket and unfolds it slowly, as though it could bite, and holds it in front of her. She glances at it, then looks at his face, frowning. He expects horror, anger, but she makes a face of disgust, like she stepped in a piece of dog shit. She turns to watch a woman approach the door and widens her eyes at him, nods her head in the direction of the back hall. *No.* He stands there, feeling injured, until the blonde points, her mouth making hard, angry shapes. As he steps away, he crushes the paper back into his pocket, watches her switch on a smile for the woman who's come in the door.

After that, his only comfort is the matchbook in his pocket. A few times during his shift, he steps outside to strike a match, lets it burn down until he feels a sting on his fingers. The craving for heat is huge, total. It fills him up, hollows out where other things used to be. But every time he closes his eyes, he sees the women again. Arranged, as though they are animals who have been hunted. In the back hall he tears the drawing into strips, feeling a rack of guilt as he looks at the ruined picture, the tears like additional wounds to the women's bodies. He shoves the scraps into the garbage near the coffeemaker, pushes them below the wet coffee grounds and greasy napkins and orange peels.

There are two more hours left on his shift, but for the first time in his life, he cuts out of work early. It shocks him, how easy it is. To simply walk across the parking lot behind the casino, past the dumpsters filled with the waste from the buffets: half-gnawed cobs of corns, the bones of rotting fish, a thousand crumpled paper napkins dark with grease. Past the marina, a few motorboats tied up, bobbing alongside the docks, and the overgrown bushes near the valet. The day feels both damned and filled with renewed potential. He can't save those women. Their open eyes will follow him wherever he goes. But he can set a fire, a signal. Something larger, more ruinous than ever before, that will show everyone just how cruel, how ugly and wrong this city has become.

LILY

ON FRIDAY MORNING, I GOT to the library before it opened, waited for someone to come and raise the metal grate at the front door. I wasn't the only one lingering—a woman with a cart full of plastic grocery store bags and crumpled newspapers waited with me. I shifted from foot to foot until someone came and rolled the grate up and unlocked the door.

The woman who worked on the archives, Sue, was small and tidy-looking with a neat crop of silvery hair. Once she arrived and settled in, I showed her the pictures of the paintings on my phone. At one—the diving girl done in blue—she reached out and held my wrist.

"That one. We have a photograph like that. Give me a few minutes."

She left me at a linoleum table rutted with gouged-out initials. Mil had texted me on Wednesday to say she hadn't had any luck with her husband's papers, but she hadn't gone through everything (*PACK RAT!!!* she wrote, accompanied by a frowning emoji) and would let me know if she found anything at all about the paintings. I knew Mil was doing what she could, but it seemed less and less likely that she might find something useful in her husband's notes.

Sue came back with a folder and tenderly removed a black-and-white photograph, laid it on the table in front of me. The storage conditions must have been poor, too humid, because there were flecks of mold along the edges of the frame, but the correspondence to the painting was immediately clear. The painter had adjusted the angle of the diving girl's face, gave us more of her expression, adjusted the focus on the crowd so the expressions blurred, save for a few leering smiles.

"This is one of my favorite images in the collection, but maybe the painter worked from others. It would take a long time, though, to look through the whole collection and see if there are any other matches. I can try, but it might take a few weeks. We also have photos of the Thomas England Hospital, but none of those look familiar to me."

"I'm mostly curious about figuring out who they are—the painter. Do you have any sort of record of who else has looked at these?"

"You can't check them out, like a library book, so we don't have the same information we would with a book or DVD, unfortunately. The collection, as far as archives go, is small, and we get so few visitors who ask to see them, unfortunately—I guess that's just as well now that I'm only here two days a week."

"Do you remember anyone coming to look at this photo in particular?"

She closed her eyes and rubbed her temples. "Not this one, no. We had a man who'd come in quite often, but he was a professor over at Stockton and was researching something for a book. Stiff sort, strictly a historian. And there was a woman who used to come in, every now and again. Sometimes she'd bring her grandson with her, and she'd just look through things. She'd been a nurse, so not sure how artsy she was."

"How long ago are we talking?"

"Oh God, this is the seventies. She and I got to chatting a few times. Her name was Maria. It's a shame—if I remember this correctly, she died in a house fire a few years after I met her. The boy got out, but Maria and her husband didn't. Such a sad thing. She was a lovely woman."

I felt deflated, depressed. For a moment I had thought that this woman could have been my painter—a woman, too. God, I would have loved that. But if she died in the seventies or eighties, it wasn't possible—some of those pictures were from the late eighties, early nineties. The big hair, the bulky costume jewelry, bright as candy, the saturated colors, then the entropy, the slow creep of decay. She would have missed all of that.

"Would you like to look through more of our materials? If you give me a little time, I can pull additional folders—we do have a decent collection from the war, Camp Boardwalk and all that. Not as many of the Thomas England Hospital, but you might be interested to see them." I checked the time. I was due to start my shift in half an hour. I felt on the verge of something, though. I thought that if I could only spend the day searching, thinking, locking myself away in the quiet upper room of the archives, then I would be able to make something out of it, inch toward a narrative. There were so many issues plaguing the city: corruption, addiction, recession. But I still thought that the paintings would help. They could show people what we had survived before.

"I need to get going to work, unfortunately. But maybe I can come back the next time you're here."

"If you want to email me any of those pictures, I can also try to do some more matching today." She wrote her email on a Post-it, rubbed her hands together. "It's exciting to have a project. I have to say, these archives are underused, and it breaks my heart. There's a lot to see here."

"Thanks, Sue. I'll see you on Monday." As I made my way downstairs, I thought about how the whole city felt that way. A lot to see and no one willing to look. Except for this painter, whoever they were.

I had my hand on the door when I heard a man's voice behind me.

"Excuse me, but did I hear you talking about some paintings?" he asked. I turned to see him, in his mid-thirties, tall, dark-haired. He hadn't been a part of the group waiting at the front door in the morning—he must have come in when I was with Sue.

"Yes." I tried to keep the annoyance out of my voice. I didn't want to have to explain the paintings to this eavesdropper. Words didn't do them justice.

"It's just that . . . well . . . my grandparents have always had a few of them in their house—paintings of Atlantic City—and I wonder if maybe they were done by the same person. Portraits. Mostly."

I was, despite myself and my fear of getting my hopes up, intrigued. "Like what?"

"Someone on the boardwalk. Another one of a politician in a sort of weird old hat."

"Where did they get them?"

"You know, I'm not sure. But I would be happy to ask."

"I don't suppose you have any photos of them."

"No, but I can take a few."

I tried to temper my optimism—it seemed too convenient, too much of a coincidence. And yet, what if this was it? A missing link? The thing I needed to see?

I looked down at my phone, hoping he would get the hint and move on. Clara had texted me again. *Lily, we NEED to talk. Please.*

"I'm sorry but I need to get to work. Excuse me."

"Where do you work? I could meet you after your shift?"

I turned over my shoulder and told him the name of the spa.

What was going on with Clara? News about Peaches? A blowup with Des?

"I'll try to get some photographs, soon!" he called after me.

"Okay, thanks," I said, waving as I left.

WHEN I got into the spa, Emily was leaning over the desk, trimming the brown edges from the petals of the orchids with a pair of nail scissors.

"I'm glad you're here. The visit from corporate was moved to tomorrow afternoon. Apparently Whitney needs to fly out to Tokyo early Monday morning to investigate some sort of snail sludge facial."

"When will they be here?"

"Three o'clock. Carrie's been freaking out all day. I think she's probably just locked herself in her office with a plate of loaded nachos and it's up to us now."

"So much for the captain going down with the ship. What do we need to do?"

"I know. Well, they'll be looking in every fucking corner. And I haven't seen Luis for like an hour. I've tried calling the number we have for him, but no one's picking up. It's an answering service for a social work office, and I just keep getting a recording."

"Has he ever skipped out on a shift before?"

"Not that I know of. But this glass is a wreck, and someone needs to polish the floors. And the Jacuzzi is making that weird noise again. I'm assuming Carrie never called anyone about it, so I have to get maintenance to get down here stat."

"Are they really going to turn on the Jacuzzi?"

"We have to assume they will. You've seen what it's like here. This company is all about punishment. They'll dock us points for every strand of hair curled in the shower drain."

"Points?"

"Each spa gets evaluated and scored on a hundred-point basis twice a year. We haven't been open long, so this is our first proper evaluation."

"So . . ."

"So what?"

"Emily, what do you care?"

She sighed. "Lily, this is how I spend most of my time. I know you are just buying time before you start your career over and move back to the city, but me? This is all I have. If I have to spend forty hours a week in this godforsaken shithole, then I sure as hell need something to show for it. I need to have a little pride. I don't know about you, but I feel like if I don't make something of myself, I'm going to get obliterated. I'll end up like my mother. Popping out a bunch of kids, making peanut butter sandwiches all day, up to my eyeballs in laundry. With no idea who I am anymore. People are always saying you have your whole life ahead of you, but that's not true. If you're a woman, you need to set yourself up. You need to make your path before you get steamrolled by everything everyone expects you to do. Kids, house, all that shit." Her face was steely, but her voice had gone high and thin.

"Yeah," I said. "I know what you mean." I felt it, too, a pressure bearing down on my shoulders. Every day that I wasn't doing something to build up my life was a day I felt hammered a little closer to the ground—smaller, more invisible, easier to step over and ignore. I had never heard Emily sound so upset. I thought of the day she left her student loan balance up by mistake, how that debt must be hanging over her head all the time. Emily, trapped here, when she deserved so much better, so much more—it wasn't just me who thought a part of myself would die if I didn't get out. "Want me to do a lap and see if I can find Luis?" I asked, chastened.

"Please. And here." She pressed the scissors into my hands. "Make sure the orchids in the ladies' lounge look okay."

I started my walk to the back of the spa. "No brown edges!" she called after me.

Luis wasn't in the back hallway or in any of the empty treatment rooms. I called the men's locker room attendant, who said he hadn't seen Luis for three or four hours, when he'd brought in the fresh towels from the laundry delivery service. I started on the orchids. It seemed like such a waste, with everything else going on. Clara, the missing women, those paintings without a painter. Those ridiculous, tiny scissors, doing a job that would never make any difference in the world.

I slid my phone from my pocket and texted Clara: *You okay? Working until 8. Meet at 8:30?* I wondered if she had found Peaches, if she had had a chance to ask her about the purse. After I handled all the orchids, Emily had me restock the boutique. She kept fiddling with her necklace, putting the end of the cross between her front teeth.

I was stacking jars of olive oil scrubs when I heard the big front door heave open. Emily greeted someone in her honeyed, saved-for-guests voice, and it made me smile, how quickly she could go from sardonic and arch to eager-seeming, sweet. "Checking in, sir?"

"I'm here to see someone, actually." The jar I was holding slipped from my hand onto the floor. The packaging split and there was scrub all over the tile, bright yellow oil and gritty white paste. I couldn't move to clean it up. *I must be imagining it,* I told myself. This stranger with Matthew's voice.

"A guest at the spa?"

"Ah, no. A"—a hint of a chuckle—"colleague of yours." That laugh. That's when I knew it wasn't only in my head. This new information screamed through my brain. "Lily Louten."

How had he known where to find me? And why was he here at all?

"Just a moment. Let me see if she's available." Emily's voice was cool and formal, which was how she sounded when she was mad. She stepped around the partition.

"A visitor for you?" she whispered. I knew that Matthew would be able to see our outlines through the frosted glass. A shadow performance. "Is that who you were waiting for all morning?"

"No!" I'd been keeping an eye out for Clara. She'd texted back to ask if she could meet me on my break. "I have no idea what's going on. I don't know how he even found me." My surprise must have been convincing. Her voice softened a little, and she dropped her hands from her hips.

"Well, what do you want to do? I can tell him you're busy."

"No, I'll talk to him."

Emily gave me another look then, like I had disappointed her, but I wanted to deal with this head-on. I stepped around her and made my way toward the desk.

I knew what his expression would be before I saw him: The look of mocking appraisal as he studied the lobby. Taking an orchid petal between his finger and thumb to see if it was real, the condescension in his surprise.

"Hey, Lil," he said. He always shortened my name. My father hated when people did that. He said he hadn't raised a daughter who was going to be small.

"What are you doing here, Matthew?" I forced myself to look him in the eye.

"You didn't answer my messages."

"I did, though. I told you to fuck off."

"That's not an answer. I want us to have a conversation. A real one."

"Oh, where are the cameras? The microphones? Who's documenting this now?"

"Don't worry about that. I told you. It's over."

Behind me, Emily cleared her throat. "Lily, can I remind you about our policy when it comes to dealing with personal matters at work?" Matthew eyed Emily, and I knew he was suppressing a smile. That arrogance, entitlement so thick you could feel it, like humidity.

"You need to leave, Matthew."

"Not until you talk to me."

"Fine. But I'm working now."

"Doesn't look like it."

Emily, again. "Lily, you need to finish restocking the boutique before the end of your shift. We need to completely remerchandise Face today, Body by the end of the day tomorrow."

"Stricter than Philip Louis." Matthew smiled, a smile that contracted a little when I didn't respond in kind. I knew it was an illusion or a concession, Matthew letting me feel as though I had a little bit of power.

"Meet me over there." I pointed to the Swim Club. "Eight o'clock." He looked behind us.

"Oh God, I don't have to wear a Hawaiian shirt, do I? Or drink anything out of a coconut? I've been trying to stifle all of my 'last resort' jokes since I've been here, but that kind of thing makes it really tough."

"I'll see you then," I said. I thought the Swim Club was cheesy, too, but Matthew mocking it made me angry, suddenly protective. I turned my back and walked away. I couldn't stand to smell him, to see his teeth, his arms, his neck, his hair. Already I felt my body betraying me, the way I ached for him. I wanted to touch his skin, to kiss all of his fingers. I wanted to slap him as hard as I could.

I went back to the boutique, picked up a palette of eye shadows. Autumn Auburn. Gold Leaf. Hot Cocoa. I started to stack them on a stand, to put away the summer shades that would soon go on clearance: Sandy Beach, Horizon, Caribbean Blue. I wondered if the people who named these colors ever actually experienced seasons, the feelings that they evoked. The melancholy of fall, the stifling claustrophobia of a humid summer, the despair of a long, dark winter.

"So. What's the deal there?" Emily stood over me. "Here," she said, handing me one of the metal shopping baskets to put the old products in. "This might help."

"You heard everything. We're having a drink. I didn't know he'd show up."

"So why see him at all? The guy who screwed some other woman while you were together?"

"I don't know."

Skeptical quirk of the eyebrow. She didn't believe me. "Well, don't do anything stupid."

"Like what?"

"Oh, come on, Lily. Did we not, like five minutes ago, have a conversation about being obliterated, in part, by men? About what happens when women let themselves fade into the background? Lie down for him and you'll get stepped over for the rest of your life."

"I'm not getting back together with him! It's just a drink."

"Well sometimes for you *a* drink means six. And who knows what you'll do after that."

"Thanks for the vote of confidence."

"I'm just saying, he doesn't deserve you. And yeah, that's a cliché thing women say to one another, but it's true most of the time. I know he's this hotshot artist, but he's a shitty person. And don't say I don't know him. I know enough about him from three minutes in his company to know what's up. And you're my friend. You deserve better."

I wasn't sure what made me so annoyed. Probably that I knew she was right. Despite myself, I also felt a thrill at Emily calling me her friend. "Let's not talk about what I deserve, please. We all deserve better than what we get, okay? You, me, everyone. It's really just a drink, and nothing more. I'm not reading anything into it. It's not like I agreed to marry the guy and cook his dinner every night of my life."

"Suit yourself," she said. I hated the chill in her voice.

I banged the wire basket onto the ground and turned my back, focused again on the display. Emily huffed around the corner. We went through the next few hours that way, separated by the glass partition: her at the desk, me in the boutique.

"Looks good," she said.

"Thanks." I hated that we weren't speaking, but I didn't know how to explain. We were silent until my lunch break, the only sounds the clacking of the new compacts and Emily's occasional sigh.

I was on my way to the caf when Clara intercepted me in the hall.

"Hey, what's up? Did you get my text?"

She looked terrible—violet circles under her eyes. "This can't wait until the end of your stupid shift, Lily. I told you that this is important. I shouldn't even be here. You shouldn't even be here. It's dangerous. I need your help. I mean it. I don't want him to see me." I hadn't forgotten about her text, exactly, but since Matthew came in I'd been distracted, my mind running on a single track. What would I say to him? How could I possibly try to save face? Plus, the library trip, and then all this buzz about the spa visit, Emily's voice breaking when she talked about ending up like her mom.

"Well, I'm here now. What's dangerous? Who don't you want to see you? Have you found Peaches?"

"She's . . . I think she's with the others. They're all together, Lily. Five of them."

"Together where?"

"I don't know, but they're . . . they're dead."

My breath caught. "Hold on, step back a second. How do you know that?"

"It's Luis. That guy you work with. He did it. He hurt them, Lily. I knew there was something wrong with him, but I didn't do anything about it, and now look."

"That's insane," I said automatically. But a thought jolted me—did this have something to do with why Luis was MIA? "Clara. Jesus. Okay, tell me from the beginning."

"I saw him, in front of my shop. I think he followed me there. And then I have this vision, and it's of women, five of them. All . . . all bruised up. They're like, arranged."

"What do you mean?"

"They're in the marsh somewhere. There's all this mud and grass and flies." She flinched. "And they're all in a row, lined up."

I didn't know if I couldn't picture it or if I just didn't want to. "Who are they? Peaches? Julie Zale?"

"I couldn't make out their faces, but it has to be them, Lily. Who else could it be? And I'm scared. Why did he come to me? He knows where the shop is, he knows where I live. I'm leaving. This weekend. I need to get the hell out of here, for real this time."

"Clara, I think you need to go to the cops. I mean, if what you're saying is true . . ."

"Call the cops and tell them what, exactly? Hey, I'm a psychic and I happen to know there are dead women in the marsh? You think they'll listen?"

"I don't know. I don't know how this works. You have to be able to leave an anonymous tip or something, right?"

She rubbed her eyes. "I'll think about it, but mostly I'm here to say goodbye. There's a bus heading west tomorrow, and I want to be on it."

"Just wait another day or two, okay? We can figure this out. I'm sure we can find a way to get the police involved. I just need

time to think. Promise me you won't go yet?" Maybe it was selfish, but if Clara stayed, I thought I could protect her. After all, I
knew where Luis was most of his days. I knew his schedule. And
I wasn't sure that Clara should leave without a plan—she was
still just sixteen. She'd end up somewhere else without anyone to
turn to, being exploited in the same ways.

"I'll wait until Sunday. But after that, I'm gone, Lily. I'm done.
I'm going to go home and pack now. I'm serious. He knows that I
know, I can tell. That means he'll be looking for me. I'm going to
lose my mind if I stay here." She twitched and swatted at something on her arm that I couldn't see.

"Okay. Let me think about this. About what to do. You really
think Luis did this?"

She nodded gravely. "Be careful, okay?"

"Yeah, you too."

After she left, I looked up Luis's address in the employee di-
rectory spreadsheet. Technically, Emily and Carrie were the only
ones who were supposed to access it, but it wasn't password protected, and I scrolled until I found his name: Luis Silver. I googled
the address listed—he lived right in AC. Sea Breezes Boardinghouse. If he was the one responsible for the missing women, I at
least wanted to know where he was when he wasn't at work. I
thought of the way Luis sometimes came to work with bruises,
cuts. Were they from these women, women trying to fight him
off, women trying to protect themselves? It felt unfair to jump
to that conclusion, but then I thought about the things Clara had
described. The women arranged in the marsh, the buzzing flies.
I felt like I was going to be sick.

I walked to the caf, distracted, confused. Everything around
me seemed to have dimmed. Even the jangling slots sounded
chastened. I had never seen any hint of violence from Luis, any
anger. But maybe that didn't mean anything. Only that he knew
just as well as anyone to keep his secrets stashed away. I wished

I hadn't made things weird with Emily. Or that Matthew hadn't shown up and made things weird between Emily and me. I could still ask her what she thought about Luis, if she had ever seen him do anything concerning. But then I'd need to tell her about Clara, about her visions, which I knew Emily didn't believe in. It seemed like I was failing everyone around me—Emily, who didn't trust me. Clara, who I couldn't protect. I felt overwhelmed by everything I didn't know, by how impossible it was to do the right thing when there was so much lurking in the shadows that I couldn't understand, couldn't see.

MEETING MATTHEW at the Swim Club reminded me of the night we had our first date at a Cuban restaurant in Williamsburg. Tonight he was already, at my best guess, three drinks in at the bar, murmuring to a waitress in an aqua bikini, fingering the knot on her sarong.

He sat up when he saw me, a boyish smile on his face, and offered me a shrug. He smelled like tequila. When the bartender asked what I wanted, I ordered a club soda with lime.

"Oh, come on, don't tell me you're no fun anymore."

"Let's get to the point, Matthew." I felt exhausted, impatient, after the day I'd had. The things Clara told me about from her vision hummed in the back of my mind. I looked back toward the spa, where Emily was bent forward in concentration, counting out the till. The straight line of her part, her pale hair looking almost white against her black jacket.

"I told you, I just wanted to see you." He grinned in the ingratiating way I remembered from the night we met, at the opening for a photographer Philip Louis represented. He had worn a gray blazer and jeans, his hair, as always, hanging into his eyes. He approached me to talk about buying one of the photographs: a portrait of the artist's grandmother working a strand of blue clay beads through her magnificently wrinkled hands. He didn't end up buying the picture, but he did ask me out.

"No," I said slowly. "I think it's something else. I think you can't stand that I haven't come crawling back. Is she here with you? Is this the Atlantic City episode of your little project?"

"No, she's back in New York."

"Good," I said, though I felt a pang of disappointment. I knew what I wanted from Matthew—an apology—but I still wasn't sure what I wanted from Ramona.

"So what are you doing, Lil? I mean, working as a receptionist? Hanging around in Atlantic City? Come on, this place is over. It's never coming back. You want to spend the rest of your twenties in a dying town, wasting your talent?"

"What talent? What exactly was I good at, Matthew?"

"You had an eye, Lily! And I think Philip Louis wishes every day that he could have you back. That new girl isn't nearly as organized."

"So my talent was spotting other people's talents? Keeping someone's schedule? Filing papers? Fetching dry cleaning? Making phone calls that a grown man should have been perfectly capable of making himself?" The job at the spa made me realize just how un-special I was. I was doing the same things here as in New York. Simpering and grinning and giving customers bad news in my softest, quietest voice.

"You were part of something. Working toward something. What are you a part of here? I mean, my hotel room has red carpet, for chrissakes. There's an entire wall of mirrors. I can't escape myself."

"Oh, I'd think you'd love that."

He let me have the jab, turned his glass on the bar top, rattled the ice. "Let me cut to the chase. I have a job offer for you."

I took a swig of club soda too fast and the bubbles rushed up my nose, but I was relieved, in a way, by the coughing fit that followed. It kept me from having to wonder what the hell Matthew was talking about, what he was up to. He thumped me once on the back, laughing.

"Please don't touch me," I said, though I could still feel the heat of his hand through my clothes. Could still remember the fever of being with him, of stumbling into the apartment, champagne drunk, grabbing at each other, Matthew's hands up my skirt, reaching for my bra clasp, in my hair.

"All right, just trying to help . . ." He watched me, my eyes watering from coughing.

"What's the job? Clean the apartment? Wash your sheets? I have some new skills you should know about. I've learned a lot about skincare. In fact, you are looking a little dry. You should exfoliate, then use a moisturizer with argan oil in it. A mask once a week."

"I'd like you to represent me."

I hadn't expected that. "Why?" Philip Louis was the top, a superstar. It would be career suicide to leave.

"You were always so hungry, Lil. Philip Louis is getting a little complacent. He's met a new boyfriend, this young Spanish photographer; all he wants to do is go back to the Mediterranean and drink rosé on someone's boat."

"He sure seemed to pull out all the stops for your last show."

The bartender picked up my empty glass, brought it to the soda hose for a refill. *Fuck it*, I thought. "Make that a vodka soda, please?" I looked back to the spa. Empty, the lights turned out: Emily must have left to take the deposit up. I felt less watched already and soothed, knowing that a drink was on the way.

"You're the woman for the job. It would be a great opportunity for you. Think about it: your own gallery. You would already have two clients—two clients who, if I may be as bold as to say it, have already stirred up quite a lot of attention."

Did he mean Ramona? "You want me to represent her, too?"

"Well, I figured you'd want to. You were the one who discovered her. But we can talk about that later. The point is, you'd be in charge. You'd run things, and you could hire some Lily 2.0, some smart young thing to help you with the day to day stuff. Someone to do the accounting, social media, so on and so forth."

"Matthew, is this some kind of joke?"

"Why would it be a joke?"

"Well I don't know if you realized, but that's what you took from me. You and Ramona. You took away my ability to look at anything and feel like it is real. Not only that, but I've been having anxiety attacks again. Nightmares. I don't think you understand the degree to which you've royally fucked me up."

"Lil," he said, his hand moving toward my arm, but I moved it away.

"And where am I getting the money to start this gallery, anyway?"

"I would give it to you."

"You'd be an investor."

"No, it would be yours. A single check, and then I'd step away. It wouldn't be Philip Louis kind of money. You'd probably have to set up shop in Gowanus or Bushwick, at least to start. But it would be your place. Your artists."

"Oh, come on. What's the catch?"

"No catch. Just an offer I hope you'll accept."

"Absolutely not."

"Lily! Be reasonable! Why the hell wouldn't you?"

I thrust my hand into my purse, pulled out my wallet, smoothed the paint-splattered two-dollar bill on the bar. "Because of this. Because you made my real life small. Into material. Something for you to shape. Like I'm not even real to you."

Matthew studied the bill, swallowed another sip of his drink. "I'm trying to make that up to you, Lily. I don't want to see you waste away down here. You deserve better than that."

What he was offering had been the dream I'd organized my life around. Even Brett had remembered that from high school. The Lily Louten Gallery. The space that would be sleek and clean, but also warm. Inviting. I would have the power to pluck artists from obscurity, to make careers, to bring beautiful pieces to the attention of the world. But not like this.

"Let's talk about what I deserve, Matthew. If I deserve better than this, then why did you do what you did in New York? How could you let her convince you that it would be *good* for me, that I would come to appreciate the aesthetics of it, or whatever the fuck you said? I mean, did you ever even love me? Or was I always going to be a pawn to you?"

"Did you love me?" Matthew said.

"So typical. Twist this around and make it about you."

"Did you? Look, Lily, even if you did, I wasn't the guy you were going to marry. I wasn't your forever thing. I know that. You had this whole emotional past, this emotional capacity, that I just don't have. I knew that one day you would see that. That one day, you would leave."

"What do you mean, an emotional past? And even if what you are saying is true"—and of course, as he'd said it, I knew in my bones that it was, we were never going to be a forever kind of thing—"that means you get to punish me for it? To publicly humiliate me?"

"Why do you think I always wanted to hear your stories from when you were a kid? I had—have—no idea what it is like to belong to a family like that. When I say I live in a world of ideas, I mean I *only* have ideas. How could I live up to you, emotionally, in a relationship? I know things got messed up when your dad died, with your mom and all. But still, I never would have been able to give you that kind of depth. I wouldn't be able to belong to a family like that and not screw it up one way or another. I wish I could but I can't." He ran his fingers through his hair. "Maybe some part of me doing that show was about wanting you to see that. Maybe, deep down, I thought you would leave eventually, no matter what I did. I wasn't trying to punish you, but maybe I was trying to save face, and somehow it ended up that way. But you're right. You didn't deserve it."

What had I been doing with Matthew, anyway? I thought of the other night, with Clara, the closest I had come to saying that I was with him because I couldn't have with him the same kind of relationship my parents had with each other. Matthew was sex and money and fun and glamour. He was arguments in the back seats of black cars and making up in his private elevator, gourmet coffee that cost $30 a pound, getting champagne drunk on Tuesday afternoons at someone's SoHo loft. He was moody and self-centered. He was a distraction. He was a way out of thinking about my father, about the family I had once and didn't have anymore.

We sat in silence for a moment, watched the bartender shake a drink, pour it into a tall glass, and shove a wedge of pineapple onto the rim. "Something's been bothering me. Can I ask what the deal is—with you and Ramona? Why you are pretending that you're still together? I mean, Matthew, she doesn't even like you."

He stared at me. I looked away but still felt his eyes on my lips. "You've gotten a little mean, Lily. It's kind of fun."

"I wouldn't say mean. I'd say frank. We don't really have to tiptoe around each other anymore."

Matthew sighed and studied his fingers for a moment. "Ramona and I—we wanted to keep it up until all the pieces sold—I had a few things that didn't fit into the show, and people were buying anything and everything. We didn't want to rock the boat. I could have taken the fender off of my bike and called it sculpture, and a Chinese millionaire would have dropped a cool two hundred K on it."

"How cynical."

"She's actually a complete psycho, Ramona. Decent painter. Impossible person."

I couldn't help but laugh. "Aren't you supposed to be convincing me to work with her? And I'm not sure that she's crazy. She's intense. She knows what she wants and she's ruthless about getting it. I wish I could be more like her."

"All the more reason for you to take the money. You deserve it. You have a goal, something you've been waiting to do with your life. And not just because of all that bullshit with the show."

"I'm staying here."

"*Here?* What the hell will you do here?"

"I'm working on something. A project I really care about, actually."

"What kind of project?"

"Portraits."

"That's great, but why does that mean you need to stay here? Lily, you think these people are interested in art? I've been here for twenty-four hours and let me tell you, all they care about is getting their rewards points on their stupid players' cards. They wouldn't know a Kandinsky from a Klimt."

"I think they will be interested. In the right subject, presented the right way. They need art here more than anywhere. They're losing their jobs. The casinos are failing. They're still dealing with the aftermath of the hurricane, still waiting for money from the state to rebuild their houses. Their kids are dying of heroin overdoses. You tell me they don't need art?

"During World War II Londoners lined up outside of the National Gallery for hours, in the rain, to see one painting. One goddamned painting a month, for just a few seconds at a time. They need something more than to be written off by people like you. Art won't pay for their kids' braces or new shoes or the rent on their houses. It won't stop people from shooting up. It won't bring jobs back. But I still think it's important. I think it will matter."

"I don't know, Lily. These people . . ."

"Stop saying it like that, *these people*. You mean people you think are smaller, or less than you, because you can wield a blowtorch and sell a hunk of metal for a bunch of cash. They're not smaller than you, Matthew. I'm *from* here. If you think that because you call yourself an *ideas person* you don't have to be held accountable for the damage that you do, then you've got another thing coming. Pain isn't collateral damage for art, Matthew. And I'm sorry, but humiliating women and calling it a *performance*? Come on. Women get humiliated every day, in small stupid ways and in huge, disastrous ones. It's not art. It's the most banal thing in the world." I thought about Clara, how much she must have suffered. How it lacked any beauty, any sense of purpose. "You owe me more and you know it."

"I think you're cutting off the nose to spite the face, if you ask me. You'll wither. The longer you're out of the game the harder it will be to get back." I could tell it was taking effort for him to keep his composure and was pleased to see the tips of his ears go red.

"Maybe. But I'm going to try this. And it will actually be mine. The Louten Gallery? Let's be honest. It would always have an asterisk next to it. Brought to you by Matthew Whitehall. It would always be yours, underneath it all. Now, you can either keep pouting or you can wish me luck."

He raised his glass, tilted it one way and then another so that the liquor picked up the light. "Good luck, Lily."

"Thank you." I looked down into my drink, swirled it, and finished it in three big swigs. I knew, probably before he did, that he would slide his hand up my thigh.

"Lil, Lil, Lil. How the fuck did we get here?" He swung his head, brought his face to my ear. "We had fun, though, didn't we? We had a good thing for a while. You want to come see the mirrors for yourself? For old times' sake?"

"Definitely not." Although I felt the possibility bubble up. This whole city buzzed with the promise of empty, easy, cheap sex. And yet I hadn't slept with anyone since, well, Matthew. Or maybe there was something erotic in talking about art again, feeling returned to myself a little bit.

"You're a terrible liar, Lily Louten. I think you do." He pressed the pads of his fingers into my leg, and I knew it would be the easier thing to do, to give in. But if I slept with Matthew, it would be my worst fall yet. I didn't need to seek out ways to make Clara's prophecy come true, the way I had with Luke and Rob. Opportunities to debase myself—to make my personality, my desires, subordinate to someone else's—were all too easy to come by. What I needed to do was protect myself. To remember who I was at my core.

"It doesn't matter whether I want to. It matters that I won't."

"Have it your way. I think that waitress over there likes me anyway."

"She's paid to like you, Matthew." But he wasn't listening anymore. He had reached into the hibiscus plant next to him and picked a hot pink bloom, and was twirling it in his fingers. As soon as I left I knew he would walk over and slide it behind some woman's ear and tell her, in a voice saccharine with liquor, how beautiful she was.

CLARA

I SAW THOSE WOMEN EVERY time I closed my eyes. Anytime I left the apartment, I felt overwhelmed by my senses. The blare of a car horn from a block away. The bang of a garbage collector emptying a metal trash can into the yawning mouth of his truck. Every man whose stare lingered a little too long. Every person who stepped a little too close.

I walked through the bus terminal, though in the past I tried to avoid it. At night it could be dangerous, and even during the day it gave me the creeps. Everyone there seemed damaged or deranged. People who heard voices in the silence. Men with palsied hands. Women with shopping carts full of trash and rags and muddy plastic bags. The air-conditioning was cranked all the way and it made the hairs on my arms stand up. I approached the window and asked how much a ticket to California would cost.

The woman chewed a wad of bright green gum and stared past me for so long I wondered if she forgot I was there. "Well that depends," she said finally. "Where are you trying to go?"

"Los Angeles," I said.

She clicked her mouse a few times and shook her head. "It'll take three days, with a four-hour stop in Topeka, Kansas."

"That's okay. How much?"

"Two hundred and seventy-eight dollars. Plus tax."

"I only have two hundred on me right now."

"Well, you've got two hours before the bus leaves."

Two hours—that was enough time to run home, pack some clothes, get the rest of my money. Lily insisted I stay, but I didn't think I could. I knew that she was worried, that she'd thought I was in over my head ever since she saw the burn marks. But if what she wanted was to protect me, then she needed to let me go. I knew what she meant about going to the police. Maybe I could write down what I'd seen or maybe she could talk to them for me. There had to be a solution that didn't involve me spending another minute here. I did feel guilty, though, and I wondered if everyone would simply forget about Julie and about the other women if I were to leave. Maybe I could stay just long enough for Lily and me to come up with a plan.

"Is there another one later?"

"Not today. Tomorrow. Same time."

"Okay, I'll come back soon, then."

She shrugged. I wondered what she would think if she knew about the women. If she would still sit here in her little ticket window, snapping her gum, or if she would also want to get as far away as she could.

As I walked home I came up with a list of what I wanted to bring. There was a part of me that wondered if I could do this. I didn't even have a suitcase. I had never tried to make a straight living. Never had a bank account, never finished high school. But I had told myself that in my new life I wouldn't steal, and I sure as hell wouldn't sleep with any men for money. But there was so much I didn't know about where I would live or how. But still, it seemed better to run. To start clean. Maybe that's what the Four of Pentacles meant—I could give up all of the bad things I did here, give up the money, once I was free.

When I got home there was a man leaning against the door

of the shop, a baseball cap pulled low over his eyes. Something about him felt familiar, but I couldn't say what. My memories of anything before this summer felt impossible, like something I had seen in a movie or TV show. One of my teachers? Someone Des partied with? A client for a reading? I couldn't remember. All I knew was that his calm gave me a bad feeling—the sense that there was something slippery and secretive underneath it.

"Can I help you?" I said, hoping my voice sounded mean. I was through with talking to everyone like they were the most exciting thing that had happened to me that day.

He reached into his pocket, fished out a piece of paper. I was surprised to see it was one of our business cards, creased in the middle and bent at the corners. "Do you have time for a reading?" he asked.

"Can't, sorry," I said. "All booked up today." He might be a cop, lurking around, waiting for his chance to bust us. He had that squirrely, suspicious energy about him. But I was so close to escaping, to leaving all of that trouble behind for Des to deal with for once. *Let her get caught*, I thought. *I don't even care.*

He smiled, looked at the darkened shop. I disliked him even more then. "Well, that's good news for you, then. Maybe you'll be able to fit me in next time." I hated the way he was measuring me. Probably there for a private reading, another pig Des had found at the club. I was surprised to feel the familiar tingling start up again—and then I saw a vision of a woman. Her head was turned away from him but she had a lovely curtain of shiny blonde hair. In the vision I could smell her, something floral, heavy. Roses, maybe. Or another flower I couldn't name. It was such a quick glimpse that I wondered if he even noticed a change in me. He was still staring when I came out of the vision, like he was waiting for me to speak. But I was feeling selfish—I didn't want or need to attract his attention, didn't need to flash around what I saw, this little bit of his life that he didn't even know he had given up to me.

"Yeah, well, be sure to ask for Des when you come back. She's got the real talent. I'm just an apprentice, after all."

"I'll do that," he said, and pulled on the brim of his hat, tipping it. I waited until he was half a block away to go inside, feeling a combination of relief and unease as I watched his back recede down the boardwalk. *It doesn't matter anymore*, I told myself. *You're almost out of here.*

I knew that upstairs Des would be in her last frenzy of primping before her shift—curling her eyelashes with one hand and smearing lotion along her calf with another. So I was surprised when I stepped into the apartment and it was quiet. No sound of her swearing under her breath, no clacking of compacts. If she was gone, it would be easier to slip into her room and look for my birth certificate, my Social Security card, which she had squirreled away somewhere years before. Maybe anticipating a moment like this, when I was ready to break free.

"Des? Des?" I called. I opened the fridge, studied the half-full bottles of Pepsi, the package of string cheese, closed the door again. *When I find my mother*, I thought, *I will fill our fridge with cut fruit and pink lemonade in pretty glass pitchers. When I find her she will teach me to cook, and we'll bake cakes and frost them, cakes without occasions. Cakes just because we could.*

From the kitchen, I noticed that the door to my bedroom was open a half inch. I knew right away that something was wrong, and I waited a moment before pushing it in. Des sat on top of my comforter, her legs splayed, *The Wisdom of Tarot* between her thighs. An open bottle of wine rested on my nightstand.

"What are you doing?" I asked. "Don't you have work?"

"I called out today," she said. "Figured I could use a day off."

Des had never, in my entire life, taken a day off. She didn't get sick pay, didn't get vacation. *I shake these tits rain or shine, hell or high water*, she always said. She liked me to think she was put out by this, but I knew it was a point of pride that she dragged herself into the club no matter how hungover she was.

"Are you feeling okay?" My stomach dropped. The book, the money pressed in the back pages.

"I feel great." *Please, just say it, do it*, I thought. *Scream, hit me. I'll take it. Just don't make me wait.*

"In fact, I came into a little extra money today, so I don't even mind missing out on the pay." She took a swig straight out of the wine bottle. "Great vintage. Want some?"

"Des . . ."

"Don't you *Des* me."

She slammed the book shut, sat up, and Frisbeed it across the room. I thought I heard the spine crack when it hit the wall. I winced, like I'd been hit. "What's the idea, here, Clara? Everything I do for you, and here you are, squirreling away all that money? You let me go to work every night at that shithole, while you're sitting on hundreds of bucks? I've kept you fed. I've kept a roof over your head. So, what's the big plan, huh? What do you think you're doing? You ungrateful little sneak."

"I want to get out of here, Des! I don't want to waste my whole life here. I don't want to do any of this anymore. You sold me to those guys and you knew what it would mean, what it would do to me. And then you went off and blew all of the cash!"

"Are you saying I've wasted my life? I think what you're saying is you don't want to end up like me. Come on. I'm not like you. I don't have that gift. But I know things—I see how you look at me. I know you think I ruined your life, okay?"

"I want to find her, Des. My mother." My voice sounded small, like a little girl making a wish on an eyelash.

She took another swig and some of the wine dribbled down her chin. "She's gone, okay? Anyone who could have been a mother to you is gone and doesn't exist anymore."

"That's not true. I'll find her," I said, knowing that my voice was uncertain, weak.

"You never had a vision about your mother, huh? Limits to your talents, maybe?" There was a dangerous edge to her voice, a mean smile curling the corners of her lips, and I was looking directly at something that I had tried very hard, for a very long time, not to see. "You want to go to your mother? Fine, but there's something you'll want to know first." She reached for a stack of papers that had been behind her on the bed. "Trust me, you're not going to like what you see."

I shook my head. "You just want to keep me here with you so you don't have to be miserable all by yourself. You want me to be unhappy, too."

"You want to talk unhappy? She's crazy, Clara! Okay? Your mother. She has been for a long time. She had a gift but it was like she had . . . too much. It made her head go all wrong. It started before she even left Atlantic City. It got worse around the time you were born. I told her she needed to get help and instead she up and ran away. For a long time she was like you, and then she just went haywire. Or maybe she saw something that made her brain go bad. Either way, I can tell you that she needs more help than you or I do." *She's wrong*, I told myself. *She's just lying again. This is just one more of her tricks.*

"Here," she said. "Have at it." She pushed the letters against my chest, and I had to clutch at them so they wouldn't fall. "I've been watching you lately, and something's up with you. You twitch. You hear things that aren't there. If I didn't know any better, I'd say you are just like her."

I always knew when Des was lying, so I could tell that she wasn't just angry. She meant what she said. She had thought it all along, those times I flinched, felt the creep of the flies, and she narrowed her eyes at me. What if she was right?

I slid to the floor and pulled the first letter from its envelope.

Dear Desmina and Ava,

This is for both of you. I need you to read this carefully, and please do what I say. There is a dark spirit living inside of me, in the space between my left ribs and my collarbone. I have tried everything to get rid of him but now I will need to go to the shaman in the desert, who has experience with this kind of thing. Please send me $500 for the bus ticket, and for the shaman's fee. If you cannot send the money, I think there are other ways I can barter with him. I have had visions through this spirit that worry me—

I shoved the letter back in the envelope and opened the next.

Ava,

The men I warned you about are getting closer. I have tried to come to you in your dreams but I wonder if it has been too long, if that portal between us is now shut. If you had sent me the money I asked for I could have rid myself of the spirit, but instead I must sometimes speak in his voice. Some days I don't know which voice is his and which is mine, or if they are both the same, tangled together, twisted like vines. I see so many terrible things now—wars and violence, children whose bellies are bloated with hunger. The world is full of so much evil that rushes at me like arrows. They pierce me, Ava, these things that I see. My sister is angry with me, I think. She sent me away, after all, no matter what she tells you. Please send the money if you can.

The last letter was dated three years ago. Her handwriting was so messy and frantic that I could hardly make out any of the words. One of the others was written on a Big Mac wrapper. A faded grease stain darkened the middle. The reason was always shifting, but in every letter she asked for money. I almost laughed; in that way she wasn't much different from Des. Sisters to the core. I had been a fool to think I could change my life by running away to somewhere new, that there was a different life waiting for me somewhere else. I was always telling customers about their fates, that they still could make choices when facing obstacles—but maybe I'd been wrong. Maybe fate did come for us all, slashing through our lives like a sharp knife.

At the bottom of the stack were more envelopes. The ones I had sent since I learned how to write. All of them were marked *Return to Sender: Recipient Unknown*. All of them had been opened. Des must have read each one.

"She never lived there," I said. "She made it up." All these years of pulling up the image of that guesthouse in the library, I had been hovering over someone else's life. *The Wisdom of Tarot* was splayed on the floor where Des had thrown it, but I didn't move to pick it up. The book felt more dangerous than comforting now. I had so wanted to believe that my mother had magic, that she had grace. That, once I found her, she could teach me how to redeem myself. Instead, she was a warning. I could end up the same way she did.

"You see? You want to find her, you go ahead. You think that'll make you happy? That's fine. But let me save you a little time. You're not going to like what you see. Check the homeless shelters and the park benches, okay? My guess is that she's standing on a street corner, shouting at nothing."

I couldn't see straight. I felt like someone had knocked the wind out of me. *Was* I like her? Would I go insane? Maybe it had already started—all the ways I couldn't trust my brain. Was that what the vision on the boardwalk was about, all of those women dead in the marsh? The flies? The crying child? Was it just something horrible and ugly that my mind had turned over and spit out, the way the ocean churned up driftwood and bits of glass?

Des stood and pushed her shoulders back, lifted her chin in a mean tilt. "Now excuse me," she said, walking past me and out the door, her shoulder almost brushing mine. I still thought, for a moment, that she might hug me. That she would soften and feel sorry that I had found out about my mother this way. That there might be a similar fate awaiting me, or maybe it had already begun.

I stayed up late and forced myself to look at the returned letters I'd written. They were full of bargaining, pleading hope. *If you let me come, I'll always clean my room. If I can visit you, you won't even know I'm there. Why don't I come help you with your clients? I see things, too.* Poor, stupid little girl.

THE NEXT morning, I sat in the shop, my eyes swollen with tears, turning over a few cards, tracing my fingers over the rivers, the stars. I tried to form a question in my mind, something I could ask the tarot, but couldn't come up with anything. For the first time I could remember, I didn't want to know what the universe had in store for me, what my future held.

My phone chimed. Lily: *Text me back! What's going on? We were supposed to talk . . .*

How could I face her now, when everything I said, everything I saw, might be completely wrong? It chimed again and I picked it up to turn it off, but the text wasn't from her that time. It was the man who had given me the burns.

I felt a pang of dread reading his message, but ignored it. I thought about the money Des took, about what it would take to start over again. I couldn't go to my mother, but I also couldn't stay—I would think of the marsh every single day, of those women, whether they were really there or not. Luis, skulking through the grass. Wondering when Luis would come back and find me, ready to punish me for what I knew. Wondering who he'd take next.

One night, $500. The betrayal foretold in my reading had already come true. The money I had hoarded was gone; Des had been the last person I could count on. Maybe there had to be real, physical pain before I could be free. For the price of one weekend, I could be away from Luis—his staring eyes, and whatever was in him that wanted to hurt. I could be free of Des—her moods and her pills and the bitter way the corners of her mouth turned down. I texted him back and asked where we should meet.

JANE 6

MY MOTHER WAS OBSESSED WITH my hands. *Clean fingernails are a sign of godliness*, she would say. I was to wash them twice every time I went to the restroom or if I went anywhere public or outside. Even when I walked to the mailbox and back. When I was old enough, I rebutted her—but only in my mind. Clean fingernails are a sign of a life unlived. A sign that you are a statue, an object. Lifeless. Inert.

For my birthday, she always gave me soap, lotion, scrubs rough with sea salt. My brothers got basketballs and baseball gloves. My childhood was from another time—I knew other girls didn't live this way. Preserved, scrubbed into purity. They didn't go to church for half a day in a dusty old grain warehouse forty miles east, where there was no heat, no air-conditioning, and a former car salesman who called himself Pastor Roy stood on an overturned milk crate and preached himself hoarse, folding chairs creaking and squeaking as we all shifted our weight, uncomfortable and bored. Afterward, the same group of women, my mother included, fluttered up to the pulpit to give him biscuits, cookies, cakes, flushing like schoolgirls. Desperate for approval only he could give.

By the time I turned thirteen, my mother insisted on smelling my hands before she would let me leave for church, studying them close enough that I could almost feel the flutter of her lashes when she blinked, then pressing my fingertips to the base of her nose. One inch lower and it would have been a kiss, and those years would have unraveled so differently. One fucking inch can be all that divides love from pain.

"Blood," she said, spitting the word like a bad taste, dropping my fingers so that my hands swung back, thudded against my thighs. She had probably noticed my pads in the wastebasket, carefully wrapped in toilet paper, so that my father and brothers didn't have to see them. And still I'd get sent to the sink, scrubbing until my knuckles were raw. Then my hands actually did smell of blood from all of the little cracks in my skin. My mother thought an ability to endure pain was a sign of godliness, too. At least in a woman: Pleasure corrupted. Pain improved.

My brothers went to church with dirt darkening the creases of their palms. Maybe the three of us could have been aligned, at some point, but her attention separated us, made them sheepish around me, me resentful of them. We couldn't look at one another, or if we did, our eyes met in startled gazes, as though we didn't know one another very well.

I DIDN'T do the things I did with men to get back at my mother. But her anger, her bitterness, was how I knew what to say when I met with the kind of man who wanted to be punished, who wanted the spike of my stiletto thrust into his back or to crawl across the room on his hands and knees. Those men had the freedom to crave that kind of disdain because their whole lives they had been told how good they were, how treasured and perfect and adored. Their lives kept bearing them up, granting them promotions and money and beautiful things they didn't necessarily deserve. Men for whom oppression was a novelty. I couldn't imagine a life like that.

I didn't share their desires, but I respected their dogged pursuit of pleasure, and I tried to honor that. My name was passed around in the right circles, among the bankers and doctors, and for a while, it was as reasonable a way as any to build a life. More reasonable than my mother rushing to Pastor Roy with her jam thumbprint cookies or her apple pies or her goddamned banana bread. When I see her in my mind, she's always in the kitchen wearing an apron, a red checked tea towel tucked into one of the strings, thinking she's a better person than everyone else because she never expected anything from her life, not even the smallest bit of joy.

ONE OF my clients was the first to suggest I'd make a good venture capitalist, or stockbroker, or commodities trader. *Guts and smarts.* He was right—I liked giving orders, being in charge. He ended up writing one of my school recommendations, called himself my mentor. We laughed about that, after I paddled him until he was bruised, when he was dressed and we could toggle back to our real personalities, or as close to them as we dared. *Emily is a fine young woman, ambitious, wise, and driven. I am confident of her success in Rowan University's business program.* To me, he said: *Get a job you can put on your résumé. Somewhere you can get a leg up.*

That's how I ended up at the spa. The poetic justice wasn't lost on me, a place that sold women on sanitization, body-hair removal, slathering themselves in chemicals as a way to "restore the body's natural pH levels." All that guilt-tinged bullshit promoted as self-love. But it was the only option in town, and one of the few upscale places where I didn't need to have completed my undergraduate degree. For a while, it did make me feel like I was a part of something, building something. Clipping the name tag to the lapel of my jacket, pacing the marble floors in the heels I had worn to walk along a lawyer's spine. I had moved on from meeting men in hotel rooms with my bag of whips and floggers, elbow-length gloves and garters with their fussy little clips. I was surprised by how much I missed the presence of someone else's ecstasy, facilitating it, controlling it. Giving that up felt like a loss. Not to mention the cash.

Months passed. Two more casinos shut down, and another crop of slot parlors popped up in Queens and the Poconos. The possibility that I would get a bonus was close to nil. I was already enrolled in school, queasy at the loans I'd taken out for my tuition, books, my first laptop. Not to mention rent, car payment, gas. I got a UTI and for all of its blather about wellness, the spa didn't give me health insurance. The prescription alone cost $175.

I told myself I would only meet one man a month—just enough to keep me afloat. I tried to get in touch with my former clients, but after the downturn, the wealthy men I had catered to from the Main Line, from Westchester, had taken their vices elsewhere. I couldn't blame them.

I started picking up dates at random. Called myself Delilah. My nod to Pastor Roy and his stupid milk crate sermons. To my mother and her avid, searching eyes. My father and brothers for their passive, dumb faces, and the way they pretended not to hear how my mother interrogated me—or worse, looked at me like I deserved it.

I GOT a bad feeling early on, with the last client. I could see him grinding his teeth, the way his eyes kept catching at the cross on my chest. But I thought of the bills, the humiliation of my rent check bouncing, the gas I needed, the loans that had ballooned into amounts so large they didn't seem real. After inflicting pain on the privileged, I had been naïve about the number of men who might be out there looking for women to hurt. Only once, before the last one, did someone lay a hand on me. I told Deidre I had the stomach flu and stayed home until the bruise along my jaw had faded. But that night, as soon as he got me alone, I felt my throat start to close. I was dizzy with whatever he gave me. He watched me touch the cross at my neck. The smell of his car reminded me of the baking soda pastes my mother had used to get stains out of the living room carpet: the smell of rebuke.

You call yourself a good woman? Bullshit. He jerked the chain until it broke, fell between my feet. I didn't have the strength to reach for it. There weren't enough words to explain. The cross was a reminder. But not about God. Of course, my mother would have decried as blasphemy that I wore it as a reminder to have faith in myself. To live for me.

When he put his hands around my throat, I tried to scream, but my voice was trapped in my mouth, as though my lips had been sewn shut. And there was so much I had left to do, so much I had to say. I was angry at his anger, his audacity, his desire for my pain. My flesh burned with fury like some self-immolating saint. I kept my eyes on him as long as I could, so that he might see it, feel it. I hoped my rage would brand him, sink into his skin. I wanted it to trail him through the rest of his life, like a ghost.

There was darkness after that. Darkness, water, mud, flies.

I hope when they send me back to my mother, there will be wedges of mud under my nails. My poor mother, who had God and Pastor Roy and clean hands instead of a life. I want her to see that I had at least tried to live.

LILY

I COULDN'T STOP CHECKING MY phone, but Clara wasn't texting me back. I sent one more text: *Clara, please just tell me you're okay?* I wondered if she still believed in what she'd said, now that she'd had a chance to sleep on it. About Luis, about wanting to leave. And if she was right? What were we supposed to do? My phone chimed once while I was pacing the front porch, but it was only a text from Matthew. *You think about it, Lil? I'll only ask this once . . .*

Not so long ago, I'd spent hours staring at the screen, willing him to reach out to me. It was hard, already, to believe that I had wanted him with such intensity. But what I wanted was a version of Matthew that only existed in my head: Matthew as I would have fashioned him. Penitent and sweet, adoring and humbled. A Matthew capable of remorse. I shoved my phone in my pocket without answering him. Clara would come first.

Two more hours passed and I still hadn't heard from her, so I biked down the boardwalk—something to burn through the pent-up nerves—locked my bike to the railing across from her shop. The *Open* sign was out front—no star in the corner—and I could see someone sitting at the table near the window, a bowed head, bright red hair. I pushed through that stupid beaded curtain and Des stared up at me. She looked like she hadn't slept.

Had something happened to Clara? Was it possible that she had already left?

"Ah, Lily, Come for a second reading? It looks like you have a lot on your mind. Don't worry. I can help you find the answers." She reached for her deck of tarot cards.

"I'm just looking for Clara."

"Oh, thank God," she said, in a flattened voice. "I'm hungover as all hell."

"Is she home?"

"No, your little pet is not home. I don't know where she is and frankly I don't care."

"You don't keep tabs on her when she's meeting up with clients?"

Des bit a hangnail and spit it on the floor. Both of them bit their nails. They had the same raw cuticles. "Ah, so you know about that, too, huh? She cuts me out of the money, she might gain a little cash, but she loses my protection."

"That seems harsh."

"It's her choice. I warned her about this. About turning tricks behind my back."

"So that makes you what? Her pimp?"

"It makes me nothing. That's business." Des lit a cigarette, exhaled the smoke in my direction, like she wanted to blow me away. "And I believe the proper term would be *madam*. But really, what is this to you? Our big-time New York City girl? You must think this place is so small. Clara is small, to you. A project. A game to keep you busy until you get back to your 'real life.' Tell me that's not true."

Clara had told me that Des didn't have any power to see into people the way that she did, but for someone without any psychic talents, she knew how to pin me, how to put me in my place. Was Clara a project? Was she, like the spa, like that night when we went upstairs with those two men, an experiment I was conducting? Something to give my life texture, a dinner party story I would tell one day. "The time I was sort of friends with an underage prostitute from Atlantic City. And get this: She was a psychic. She could see your deepest secrets. We got in some hairy situation together with these drunk guys from nowhere, Pennsylvania. And then we swam in the ocean in the dark." *No,* I thought. *That isn't true.* Making projects out of people was Matthew's game, not mine.

"That's not why I'm here. I . . . I . . . care about her." I could smell the booze wafting out of Des's pores, astringent and sharp. It filled me with fury. "Someone has to care about her, right?"

Des rolled her eyes. "Okay. What's her name, then?"

"Her name?" I repeated dumbly. It took me a moment to even puzzle through what Des was asking me. At first it seemed like a trick, but as soon as I understood I could have smacked myself. Of course her name wasn't Clara Voyant.

Des didn't need to say anything else. She smiled and cut the deck of cards, turned the top one over for me to see. "The Devil."

"That doesn't sound good." I looked at the card. The ugly blue-lipped creature had the tiny wings of a bat and the curved horns of a ram.

"Depends. Right side up, he means bondage, fear, addiction, materialism. Upside down, it means breaking free. What do you want to break free from, Lily? What's holding you back?"

"I thought you said you were too hungover for a reading."

She shrugged and, of course, that, too, reminded me of Clara. "The cards are just a tool. You don't need to be a psychic to ask the right questions."

"I've got to go. Will you tell Clara I stopped by? Tell her I'll be at work tomorrow?"

"Sure," Des said; the implied second half of her sentence seemed to be *If I feel like it.*

Atlantic City was a small place, but it was large enough that if someone was hiding, or missing, they could make themselves difficult to find. The honeycomb of hotel rooms. The dark nooks of the casinos. The shadowy piers. I wondered if I could call the police and leave an anonymous tip about Luis. My phone was still in my hand. I dialed a 9, deleted it. Dialed it again, then a 1. Surely they would trace my call—what if Clara was wrong? I would seem deranged. I could even get in trouble, couldn't I? But the way she had looked at me the day before. Like I was failing her. By the time I got home, it seemed like the only thing I could do was wait and hope she would text back or call.

I stopped in the driveway to pick up the newspaper, shook it from its plastic sleeve, and sat on the porch to read it. More cops and firefighters were losing their jobs. More abandoned houses had been set aflame. The governor had signed off on a new tax on fantasy sports. Hurricane season would be stirring up soon, and the paper offered tips for protecting your house. I flipped to the obituaries. A former linebacker who'd sat behind me in history class in eleventh grade had died, the obituary worded the way Steffanie's was. *Taken from us suddenly, in lieu of flowers please send donations to Drug Free NJ.* I remembered that his cheeks used to get ruddy in gym class and it seemed like it took the entire afternoon for him to lose his flush. I didn't know how his death connected to Clara's vision of the bodies in the marsh, but something brutal was still happening here—and maybe Clara knew more about it than anyone else.

I HAD a short shift that afternoon, two to eight. I was surprised to see Carrie at the desk when I arrived. She was sucking down one of her blended coffee drinks, a sludgy mess of whipped cream and chocolate syrup.

"Oh, thank God you're here," she said. "Emily pulled a no-show. I have a mind to fire her ass."

"Wait, what? And we have that meeting today? That Whitney thing."

"I know! Can you stay up front? I've gotta go prep. If you see her, send her straight back to me. Fuck, my heart is racing." I heard her swearing under her breath as she walked away from the desk.

I texted Emily. *Where are you? Carrie is flipping out! Everything okay?* I waited for her to write back, hoping for good news on her behalf. That she'd gotten a better offer somewhere else and just split without a second thought. What was going on?

Luis was back, though, and he came around the desk to polish the coffee table. I watched him while he worked. His hands, the long fingers. I tried to imagine them doing damage, tensing with rage, and couldn't. There was love, attention, in the way he touched things—it made me feel guilty. I had spent the summer thinking everything here was beneath me, that to do this job well would be some sort of a compromise of my talents, and yet there were so many people, like Luis, or even Emily, doing well at the quiet work that never won you coveted seats at restaurants, that never landed your photo in the pages of glossy magazines. I thought of the painter, too, who must have pressed on through anonymity, indifference, to create something beautiful. There was so much to admire in that.

It was stupid, maybe, to think of that as proof of Luis's innocence, an essential kindness at his core. But I believed it anyway. But what did that mean about what Clara had seen? What made her think Luis was connected? And where the hell was she? I felt hollowed out, jilted. I had thought she would at least say goodbye. No new texts. No missed calls. No Clara. No Emily either. I was bereft and lonely, and there was nothing to do but wait.

I stared at the clock on the computer screen, then googled Emily, then Clara. I don't know what I expected to find, but I couldn't stand feeling so helpless, and at least it was something to do. I googled Matthew next—at least that would offer me some small distraction. I had a feeling that something with his offer had been off. Still, the result made me gasp: "Hotshot Artist Dropped by Representation after Public Row at Downtown Opening." A fallout with Philip Louis. I could picture it perfectly, the two of them boiling up at each other with rage. Matthew flinging some reckless, horrible insult—something with too much of the truth in it, maybe. Philip Louis dropping him to save face. It explained everything. The visit, the offer. I texted Matthew a single word: *no*.

I OVERHEARD snippets of Carrie's conversations with Whitney and the passel of pastel-suited women who walked through the spa, their smiles too wide, their eyes focused and judgmental. Emily would have been such a help to her, could have charmed them and dazzled them and maybe convinced them that we actually knew what we were doing. After my shift ended I did what I had done so many other times that summer—retreated to a dingy dive bar and willed myself to go numb. By the time I ordered my first drink, I still hadn't heard anything from Clara or Emily. I was convinced my phone wasn't working and turned it off, thinking that when I turned it on again, my screen would flood with information: apologies, explanations.

Someone pushed the door open, and for a moment the light from the streetlight leaked in through the crack, and the smell of the ocean cut through the molding smell of the bar. It was the kind of night when there was so much brine in the air you felt like you could lick it from your lips. I ordered another drink, then another after that. No Emily, no Clara, and now, no gallery. I'd thought I'd feel triumphant after rejecting Matthew's money, but my mood was bleak. Also, a little voice piped up in my mind: What if I had just made the biggest mistake of my life? I ordered a fourth drink, a shot that slid down my throat, hot and tasteless. I didn't want to think about anything except that beautiful burn in my gut.

"Hey!" A hand on my elbow. A voice I recognized but couldn't place. I turned to see the man from the library.

He smelled like cigarette smoke and salt air. When I'd first arrived at the bar, the night had a cool edge to it—a hint of fall. I remembered the way it used to make me so melancholy, how hard I used to try to ignore that chill. August had only just started, but I could sense summer shutting down, autumn turning everything gray and brown. I'd noticed that already the grass at the edges of the marsh was going pale, that soon it would be the color of heather. Seeing it, I had to confront that I, who had called this a break, a stopover, a pause, was still here. And by choice, of all things. I'd chosen this. I was drunk by then, but I was also thinking that maybe, maybe I was okay. I had survived the summer. I had resisted Matthew and his offer—well, his trick.

"Can I buy you a drink?" the man from the library asked. He leaned on the stool next to mine. I focused on his hands, the tiny cuts around his knuckles.

I knew I shouldn't drink anymore—one more might make the room slide, make my thoughts slippery and words too large on my tongue. But I heard myself ask for a Maker's on the rocks.

"I talked to my grandma about those paintings," he said.

"Huh." There was something familiar about him that I couldn't place. I had the feeling I had seen him before, not at the library, but that he had been at the edge of my life in some way. He had a brawny, short body, an athletic stance, a sports watch perched on his wrist. A substitute teacher I had in high school? Someone from the beach patrol? I was too drunk to figure it out.

"She said you can come see them whenever we want."

"How 'bout now?" I asked. For the first time that day I felt a jolt of hope.

"Sure. She's a night owl. And she's excited to show them, I think." Something perked up in my chest. I was slurry, my makeup smeared, my hair a tangled mess. But the thought that the day could be redeemed, the promise of seeing more of the painter's work, was irresistible. I kept forgetting to ask the man his name. That thought and others rose and slipped, the way the strap of my purse slid from my shoulder. He had a heavy, square jaw, eyes that were both attractive and disconcerting, so pale and clear, giving his stare an incisive, pointed effect. I felt a jolt between my legs—that old confusion Matthew liked, between art and sex—and wondered if sleeping with someone else might, like seeing more paintings, be another kind of cleansing.

"Where are you parked?" I asked.

He smiled, his blue eyes gray in the dull light. "Just around the corner." I couldn't decide if I liked the way he looked or not. "I can pull around and meet you."

I paid my tab and met him out front, trying to ignore the way I wobbled from the stool. As soon as I got in the car I regretted it. I was going to be sick soon; I wanted nothing more than to get it over with, my knees braced on cold hard tile, my face on the rim of our toilet at home, drink a tall glass of ice water, and crawl in my bed with its cool, clean sheets.

As we made our way down Pacific Avenue, I asked him to tell me again what the paintings looked like.

"I told you earlier. A guy in a hat."

"What about the colors?"

"What about them?"

"The colors are what make them stand out. At least the ones I've seen."

"I can't describe them. I'm no expert. Besides, you'll see for yourself in a minute." I could tell I was annoying him, but I didn't care. He had been the one to offer to take me anyway. He rolled down the window and lit a cigarette. I wanted to ask him to stop, but I was so, so tired. My thoughts dripped.

At a stoplight, I glanced out the window. "I thought you said she lived. In. Longport." I was alert enough to know we were driving in the opposite direction, toward the city. We were on the Dorset Bridge, the water black below us. The streetlights looked hazy and huge, globes of smeared light. I thought I remembered something Clara had said. One of her visions: blurry streetlights.

"I want to go. Home," I said. "Please turn around?" He was silent. There was a strange drag on my words. I tried again, but my speech was worse. I felt ashamed, then afraid.

"I can't wait till that stuff really kicks in. You're getting on my nerves. You know, I was going to leave you alone. You weren't like the others."

"What? What stuff?" I tried to inventory the last hour in my mind—had I left my drink alone? But my thoughts were too slippery, my memory of the bar already full of black patches.

"You made an honest living, at least. You might drink a little bit, but you're not out there selling yourself, dipping into drugs. Running this place into the ground. But you seem to like sniffing around in things you don't understand. Making phone calls you shouldn't make."

I closed my eyes. Phone calls? Did he know about me calling Julie Zale's aunt? Had Emily heard more than she let on when she came back from lunch that day? Had she told someone? And then I remembered, the man in the windbreaker. Baseball cap, sunglasses. That wide-legged stance. How had I not realized he was the same person? It must have been so easy for him—I was so eager to blow him off at the library, I never even looked back. It would have been nothing for him to follow me to work, to watch and wait. And what about that night, when Clara and I swam on the beach. Clara—where was she? Why couldn't I find her? Had he gotten to her first?

"Pull over," I said. "Let me out." *There are no paintings, I realized.* The words unwieldy and slow. My vision blurred at the edges. My eyes shifted to the floor, my purse on the ground. I hadn't turned my phone on again. I kicked it closer to the seat, ignoring the way he laughed. I kicked it again, and the floor mat shifted. Something bright, almost wet-looking, caught my eye. A silver cross necklace. Just like the one Emily wore. Emily, who had pulled that no-show at work. Who hadn't answered any of my texts or phone calls. My skin burned. "Em . . . Em . . ." I tried, but couldn't force out her name. I tried to picture her, but her face was blurring with Clara's. Emily's eyes, Clara's red hair.

I reached for the door handle, weak, my fingers missing it by inches. I tried to grab it again. I had the sense that I'd just seen something important, but had already forgotten what it was. Slippery, slippery mind. I reached for the door handle once more and felt a burst of pain against the side of my head. Dampness on my face. I looked up at the hazy streetlight, the moths wobbling in the glow. I tried to open my mouth to say Emily's name one more time but instead I sank. To a place very quiet. And very dark.

CLARA

THE HOTEL SUITE WAS SO quiet that I could hear birds outside. Speedboat motors. The slam of lids on the metal garbage cans, even the occasional laugh. I don't know if that made it easier or more difficult. People were still laughing, somewhere. He had tapped a single pill onto the dresser. Looking at the perfect white pearl of it, I wondered if there were more. If I could take a whole bottle for my grand escape from this place. Not to California, but slipping out of the world, easy as a piece of silk sliding through someone's hands.

I was standing in the middle of the room. Had it been three hours? Four? I hadn't had anything to drink but had to go to the bathroom anyway. What had started as a general throb from holding it now ribboned through my torso, a sharp twinge of heat. I would ask him if I could go, but I wasn't supposed to speak. I wasn't even supposed to think. He told me that I was a terrible person, a bitch, a slut. That I was lucky all he did before was burn me, that I deserved so much worse. If I wanted to avoid being punished again, the only thing I could do was ask for forgiveness. Repent. That word was like a hammer, pounding the inside of my brain. *Repent repent repent.* I was sorry that I had been such a fool about my mother. I was sorry that I believed those visions, that I dragged Lily into it, when maybe the problem was me all along. I was sorry for all the times I stole from people who didn't deserve it for a goal that had always been impossible.

He sat in front of me reading a book. I couldn't tell what it was—something from a library, a bar code along its spine. Had he stolen a book from the library? *What about* your *sins?* I thought. He looked up at me as though he could sense my doubt beamed his way. He unpeeled a chocolate poker chip so slowly that I heard every crinkle of the wrapper. I listened as he ate it, the chocolate gumming his mouth, moving down his throat.

This was part of the deal I had made. Two days of total control. He told me it would start out simple, *easy.* Then we would work our way up to other experiments, other kinds of pain. *No more burns*, I told him. *Well, I'm paying to be the one who makes all the rules. Deal or no deal*, he said. I pictured the Ten of Swords in my mind. One more difficult thing, and then I would be free.

First I practiced mouthing the words. *May I please use the re-stroom? No, Sir, may I please use the restroom?* He looked up at the sound of my lips moving, closed his book, stood from the chair.

"Didn't I tell you," he said. "Now is the time for repenting what you've done wrong." As he pulled his arm back, in the moment before he brought it forward, his sleeve slipped again. I saw the burn scars snaking up his wrist, and then the force of his hand knocked me backward. I staggered, fell, but stood again as quickly as I could.

He went back to his chair. He flicked his cigarette lighter, and as soon as I saw the flame I jumped. He smiled and closed the lighter, slid it back into his pocket. This was a game to him, all of the ways he could scare me, make me hurt. He didn't look up when he heard the stream of urine hit the carpet. He only looked up after, when my clothes were wet and relief had flashed through me and the only sensation left was shame. I thought that must mean it'd be over soon, that it would be like before—the metallic clunk of his belt buckle and the groan as he took himself in his hand. I stood, my eyes on the carpet, and waited. But there was only silence. I had been so used to seeing into people, to thinking I understood more than most. My gift couldn't help me now. *Gift*, if I even dared to call it that anymore. I couldn't see clearly what had happened already or what would happen next—maybe I never could. I'd been so convinced that these women needed me, that they were asking for my help. But maybe none of it was real. Maybe my brain was wired badly, and now it shot off only the wrong kinds of sparks.

I was still standing, feeling woozy, waiting for whatever was going to happen to end, when I had another vision. Or, I didn't know what to call it now. The tingle surged through my body, and I saw a hand, reaching for a door handle inside of a car.

I blinked, rubbed my temples. I figured it must have been something in my brain, churned up by feeling stuck in that hotel room. Perhaps the visions were just my own wishes, my own bad dreams. My knees felt like they could buckle. My legs shook. I didn't understand the appeal of this—it hardly seemed like he was paying any attention, even—but I didn't see the appeal in a lot of things men were supposed to like. I guessed that I should have been grateful for avoiding more cigarette burns, though part of me wondered if this meant that the worst was yet to come.

Another tingle seized me, like shocks in my fingers and toes. Something silver, a necklace, with a charm in the shape of a cross against a dark background. When I came back into the room, I felt as though an hour had passed. Darkness seeped in around the edges of the blinds. I tried to track how many pages he had made it through in the book, but I was thirsty, dizzy. I couldn't trust my eyes to see things for what they were.

I was jolted into a third vision. A hand, a woman's hand again, but it was somewhere new, somewhere inside. The room had a reddish-yellow glow. I could hear that *swish, swish, swish* sound that was so familiar from other visions. Flies buzzed in my ears.

My thoughts started to race—Luis, the marsh, the glow of the room, like the neon glow of the signs. The sunset that lit up, one ray at a time. The first vision had also held something familiar. I stood as still as I could and tried to recall everything about it. The shape of the door handle. The look of the person's hands. And then: The bracelet. Lily's bracelet. The one I had stolen all those weeks ago, those little pearls, like dredging up a detail from a dream. Lily? Lily was in trouble?

No, I told myself. There would be a reason for those images. Those thoughts. That was the way I was going to live my life now. Logically. According to what I knew. Facts. That way I could hedge against whatever had made my mother's brain go wrong, poisoned by her talent. I was thinking of escape, because that's what I wanted most. A way out of my own life. There were still scraps of whatever I had seen from Luis lingering in my brain. I would learn to control those kinds of thoughts, learn to push them away.

But those women. The four—or was it five now? or more?—of them lined up together, arranged. The hungry, relentless buzz of the flies. Their blue-tinged skin.

"I have to go," I said. "You don't have to pay me, but I need to leave."

He raised an eyebrow. "That's not what the arrangement was. Remember? Total control."

"My friend needs my help."

A smile. For a second I saw it through his eyes, how ridiculous I was. A teenage girl with trembling legs, claiming she needed to run off and save someone. I stepped toward the door and heard the *thunk* of his book hitting the floor, the heaviness of his boots on the carpet. He grabbed my shoulder, pushed me into the wall, shouting insults at me—*Stupid slut. Worthless whore.* I curled into a ball, sweating, shaking. I didn't know what would be worse: ignoring the visions and the possibility of something terrible happening, or invoking this man's rage.

When I swallowed, it felt like a blade was lodged in my throat. I stood in the center of the room again and waited for my chance. Lily needed my help. He was just one man, after all. Someone who stole library books, someone who was so afraid he needed to prey on other people's fear. I would find a way to get out of there.

LUIS

HE RETURNS TO THE MOTEL one more time, unable to walk past the border where the parking lot meets the grass. He knows he needs to do something, to warn everyone, to make sure the women are found, but he thinks of all that he will lose if he is misunderstood. How dangerous it is for him to be the one who knows the truth. He sits at the edge of the lot, wondering what else he can do. A woman approaches him with a photograph of a teenage girl with bright purple hair.

For a moment the hair throws him, but then the realization lands like a punch. She's one of them. The one with the tattoo on her chest.

He waves his arms, points to the marsh over and over. He refuses to go back, but she could help him. She has a kind face, though she is startled by his gestures, and her eyes get wide. He points again, each time feeling how impossible it is to ask someone to imagine the horror, to make them understand. She reaches in her bag, pulls out a pen, and he starts to wonder if that is a good idea—something she could use as proof. Something that would show he knew about the women before anyone else—she might misunderstand. He turns his back on her, senses her behind him as he walks away and panics. At the shoulder of the road he breaks into a run.

AT HOME he puts his treasured things in a pile, should he need to leave quickly. Whether because of the fires or because someone has seen him going into the marsh or just because it's finally time. A set of clothes, the photograph of his grandmother, the sheaf of pictures his grandfather took from his hospital days. The two-dollar bill, the German bullet the doctors pulled from his grandfather's leg. The paintings along the wall eye him, the room filled with lonely stares. As though they hadn't come from him, hadn't been made with his own hands.

He looks over the canvas that he started when he realized the camera wasn't going to work, that he wouldn't be able to make himself go back and see the women again. Those frenzied nights when he'd painted until his hands were too stiff to hold a brush. If he destroyed it, who would ever know? If he didn't, someone might think he had something to do with those women. He took it off of the easel, imagined himself breaking it over his knee, making it small enough to throw away, but he couldn't bring himself to ruin it. It was another way to say: *I SEE*.

It had been so long since he painted—two years? three?—but he soon relived the pleasure of blending paint, the instant satisfaction of a slash of color against the blankness of a canvas. His grandmother teaching him, so long ago, to copy from photographs. The joy on her face when he showed her a finished picture—he always thought it was the happiest he ever saw her, when he brought her something he had made. To think, he once assumed that was how he would spend his life: Showing people what they overlooked. Making sure they didn't forget. He did paintings of the wreckage from the last hurricane, when the town got pulled apart. Paintings of the days when the casinos closed down, bits of them sold off. Men walking down the street hugging disco balls, slot machines being loaded into the beds of trucks. The portrait of the man who gave him the two-dollar bill—the only kindness Luis could offer after he died. One of a man who bought from him, a man who also sold old chairs, stacks of mismatched plates, tins of buttons. Every month Luis would bring him another picture, until one day he went back and the seller's tent was gone. He never saw him again. Another person the city simply swallowed up.

He wishes he had realized how much painting would soothe him, thinks that the fires might have been a mistake, but now it's too late. The last part of himself that the city has taken—he has become someone who thinks to ruin before he thinks to create.

HE PACES the long hallways that snake through the casino, his hand on his matches in his pocket. He feels the cameras watching him, all of those little eyes embedded in the ceiling. He starts to feel like everyone is looking at him with suspicion. The guards, the dealers, the grounds crew, the girls who carry drinks. The other day he stood behind the blonde woman while she watched a screen: eight views of the hallways and rooms. She pressed a button, and then the windows went black, disappeared.

Twice he's seen her in the spa when neither of them are meant to be there. He hates the long lines for the showers at the boardinghouse, so sometimes he sneaks in after work to enjoy the pressure, the hot stream. She emerged from the women's room in a blue dress, her mouth slicked with pink. It's one of the reasons he's so angry about her pushing him away when he wanted to show her his drawing. He thought they had an understanding— the first time she caught him, or they caught each other, she started, but then gave him a single slow nod, as if to wish him good night. But it doesn't matter now. He'll make everything burn, everyone pay.

As he slips in the back way, through the gym, and then along the dim, narrow halls, he still grapples with the strangeness of the place, its whiteness. The hallway of empty rooms. The clean smells that remind him of the medicine his grandmother rubbed on his chest when he was very small, but without comfort.

He knows it is late, that everyone is gone for the night, so he takes off his shoes, pads through the hallway to the big double door. The room has two beds in it, blankets, square vases filled with small rocks. He cracks open the cabinets, squeezes tubes of cream, unscrews the caps on all the small jars. Then he finds the candle, and it feels like a gift. Recently he can't stop thinking of his grandmother—those candles with the saints' faces she would light on the windowsill while she prayed. He had spent that evening of the fire trying to paint the glow of the saints, but the combination of dimness and light had been too difficult. He had meant to move the bottle of turpentine before he went to sleep, but frustrated by his failures to get the colors right, he'd stormed upstairs to his room. He woke to that same smell of smoke, and the flames were already raging in the hall, dividing his room from his grandparents' with an insurmountable wall of flame. He was able to escape through his bedroom window, ran to the neighbors' and pounded his fists on their doors. He remembers looking up at the cold, indifferent sky, the smoke swirling into it. By the time the fire trucks came, it was too late. His grandparents, their whole beautiful, careful life, were gone.

He finds the box of matches nearby, lights them on the countertop with shaking hands, appreciating the fire's awesome and terrible power. Wisps of smoke twist toward the ceiling. He runs a finger through the flame.

He thinks again of the women. The sight of that fifth body, her eyes on him, in the marsh. The woman from the parking lot, holding out the photograph, how he couldn't trust her to under stand. The feeling that he needs to do something erupts in him like a wave. He pulls a towel from the rack and dips a corner of it in the flame, his anger glinting, goading him on. He tells himself, as it catches, that there is still plenty of time to make it stop if he wants to—this could be the night he finally gets caught. He runs a finger through it again and the heat, the pain, feels good. His mind fills with one thought: *More.*

The flames lick along the material, more smoke rising into the air. He waits for the moment to tip, for his sense of wonder to slide into fear, but he doesn't feel afraid. It's both exciting and soothing to watch the flame eat away at the cloth, to silence his mind. Leave behind his worry about the man with the gold tooth, the cops, the people at work, the women and the flies. He drops another towel onto the ground.

He starts to feel the heat build up and expects that, at any moment, a fire alarm will flash, spray water all over the floor; the cops will come and twist his arms behind his back. But nothing happens. He thinks of the things he sees at night when he cannot sleep, the memories he has of the red-haired girl, her mouth open in terror when she saw him. For a moment a new thought flashes through him. He could step into the heat, feel all of his fear, his anger, burn away, turn to smoke, dissolve into the air.

Instead, he pulls a small pillow off of the bed, feeds it to the flames, empties one of the jars to watch the chemicals spark. He is surprised when the fire catches the base of a cabinet, when it starts to burn the edge of the wood. His stomach is flip-flopping, and there is something like promise in the way the flame contin- ues to build. The smoke is thickening and he coughs, smiling, eyes burning. The fire feels like a presence now. Its longing, its desire, is familiar. Its language one he knows well: Fury, greed. More more more.

When the smoke starts to make him dizzy, he reaches for the door handle, the metal warm, pulls it open. He hears the fire respond to the fresh oxygen with a surge of heat and light. He looks up at the cameras in the hall, and for a second, he feels sorry that the blonde girl turned them off. He wants them to see him. Wants there to be witnesses to the things that churn and burn inside him. A witness to the one thing he might have done right.

CLARA

AT FIRST, I THOUGHT THE alarms were in my head, and I felt a drop in my stomach. Something else I couldn't explain—it was different than the feeling I got about Lily. Muddled. Strange.

But then I saw him raise his eyes at me, and I knew I hadn't imagined the sound. Doors creaked open in the hallway. The tread of shoes on the carpet. Voices, sounding confused. Then a man, yelling down the hall.

"Everyone please proceed to the staircase. This is not a drill."

The man knocked a lamp from the bedside table, cut his eyes toward me, shoved his cell phone into his pocket, and pushed his way out the door. I took a deep breath. I was aware of how I smelled, the ammoniac smell of a scared animal. But I grabbed my purse and ran toward the stairs.

The lobby was a mess of people. Potbellied security guards shined flashlights in the direction of the door, tried to yell over the crowd, and couldn't make themselves heard. I ran to the revolving door and hailed a taxi. I had $20 in my purse. Probably not enough to get back, but I wouldn't worry about that. *I need to call the cops*, I thought. But how would I ask them for help before I even knew where I was going? Then, when I looked in my purse, I almost laughed. The man had made me give him my phone, had locked it in the safe. I remembered the little electric *beep beep beep* as he entered the code.

The driver looked at me, unruffled by the way my chest was heaving. "The Black Horse Pike. The motels. As fast as you can."

"Which motel?" he asked, pulling away from the curb.

"I'll know when I see." He shook his head. I knew what he was thinking—I was going to pick up a man, buy drugs, both. "Drive faster, please."

Above us the white globes of the streetlights blurred by, and I knew I was right—I had seen them before. The buildings looked even grimmer in the dark, a row of six or seven of them, wild with weeds, perched on the edge of the marsh like they might one day get sucked in. I rolled down my window, listened to the shush of the reeds. Here. We were close to Lily. To all of them.

I studied the signs, all of them with broken, missing letters. Then I saw it, down the road—that setting sun, each ray lighting up one at a time then blinking out. The Sunset Motel.

"There! There!" The driver swerved into the lot. I handed him the twenty and didn't bother to wait for my change. I stood underneath the sign and studied the motel: two floors, maybe twenty-four rooms. *I should call the cops now,* I thought, *run to the motel office and borrow their phone.* But I still didn't know what to ask for. I remembered the way the light from the sign fell on the floor at a slant in my vision. I adjusted my stance—it had to be one of the rooms on the left side. There was nothing to do but guess. From behind the door of room number 9, I heard a couple arguing about who was footing the bill. I ran to the next room, tried the knob—it swung open to an empty, dark square with two sagging beds. At the third, I looked back at the sign—this had to be it—and pressed my ear to the door: the creak of footsteps, careful and slow.

I knew the door would be locked but tried the knob anyway. Inside the room, the sound of pacing stopped. I thought again of those early years with Des, when things felt exciting and good. How with one quick flick of the wrists we would outsmart everyone and break into any room we wanted. How back then she made me feel like everything in the city was ours to claim. The motel's locks were flimsier than the casinos'— and even those didn't take more than a stiff piece of paper. I still had my business card in Victoria's purse. Whoever was on the other side would be able to see me working on the door, the card sliding through the crack in the frame. Would be able to brace themselves or arm themselves. And I hadn't used this trick in years, and this would need to be quick if it was going to work.

I worked the bottom lock, prayed that the cheap paper would hold. I heard a *thunk* and tried to stay calm, although I felt my body go cold. Another *thunk*—what was happening?—as I got the bottom lock open. Now it was just a matter of working the swing bar at the top. I eased the edge of the business card along the bar and tried to see inside the room while I worked: nothing but a slice of streetlight on beige carpet.

The lock gave, and I lunged inside. Nothing, no one, just a bathroom door to my right, open to a darkened room, the ugly twin beds with depressions in the middle, the smell of mildew. But I had heard someone! Someone had heard me. Or maybe I really was like my mother, it was true. I wasn't special, just insane. I would grow obsessed with things and people that weren't there, conjuring strange theories out of thin air. I sat on the edge of the bed, not ready to go outside again and face the long walk back to the shop, face Des, the rest of my messy, messed-up life.

And that's when I saw her, the slim curve of her wrist on the floor, the pearl bracelet glowing yellow in the low light—her arm was raised above her head—the rest of her obscured by the dust ruffle on the other side of the second bed.

When I stepped around the bed, my breath caught in my throat. She looked just like the others. Her skin was pale. There was a lump above her left eye, the size of a walnut. I kneeled on the carpet, put my hand to her wrist. Her skin was clammy, cold. Nothing, nothing, and then a gentle thump of blood under my fingertips. A pulse.

I jumped when I felt something brush against my arm, but it was only the curtain blowing in the breeze. And then I noticed the screen on the ground. The open window. The *thunk, thunk* sound. Whoever had been here was gone.

I sprinted into the parking lot just as a woman was getting out of her car. Too well dressed to be at the Sunset, too clean, she looked like a social worker, calm and safe. For a moment I wondered if, somehow, she had already been sent to help. She was startled when I yelled to her.

"Please ma'am, it's an emergency. Can I use your phone?" She stood for a moment, then nodded. Her face was sad, like she knew something I didn't understand yet.

I dialed 9-1-1. At first, when the operator picked up, the words refused to come.

"My friend needs help! My friend needs help! She's breathing, but she's not waking up. We're at the Sunset Motel. Room 10. Hurry, please!"

When I turned around, the woman's car was there, but she was gone. I stood, clutching her phone, then set it on the hood of her car. In the distance, I heard the roar of fire trucks, saw the spangle of lights at the casino.

I went back into the room, even though I didn't want to see her like that. When the police came, I decided, I would tell them about the others. I didn't know how I would explain. I just knew they were close. Closer than ever before. But now the women were silent. I didn't have any visions, didn't hear anything other than the shush of the reeds.

A siren grew closer. I saw a shadow on the floor. I braced my-self to see whoever had done this, but it was just the woman, the one from before. She was unsteady on her feet, and I wondered if I'd been wrong about her—there was a stunned look on her face. Maybe she was here for the same reasons as everyone else. She sat on the bed, folded herself in half, and let out a scream that I felt in my spine.

DEBORAH

GEORGIA'S MOTHER STOPS ONCE FOR coffee, hardly notices that it's too hot to drink until after she's finished it, when the skin peels away from the roof of her mouth and clumps on her tongue. She gets pulled over just outside Philadelphia for speeding, going eighty in a sixty-five. She accepts the ticket without a word and continues on her way. She loops around the statue in honor of Benjamin Franklin. Georgia always liked that one—history and science broken down into their core elements: the violent zigzag of the lightning, the kite, the key.

Finally she smells the ocean's cool brackishness through the dark as she crosses through the toll plaza on the way into town. Above her, billboards show women in black lingerie, holding fans of cards with long, red nails. That's the problem—men are always promised this, no matter who they are. Her daughter lost her virginity at fourteen, bragged about it during one of their fights. But what Gee didn't realize was that Deborah understood, that she could be objective. What's a woman to do other than give away what the world will snatch at, always try to take.

The city looks meager and skimpy, like the backdrop of a play that's only painted part of the way. *Why here, Gee?* she wonders. Was there nowhere else you wanted to go? She shudders. The morning is mild, but she can't seem to get warm. Georgia's instructions: *Ask for Peaches*. That's not the name of a real person, of a whole person. Not the name of her girl.

Deborah feels it now: anger, boiling up from her gut. When she finds out the whole story, finds that no-good piece of shit, Josh, she'll cut him open, split him in two. She wants to make him pay. Some men are squanderers. Some men know exactly what a woman is giving them—her future, her faith—and will use it like a lift in their shoes. She remembers his expression when she came home early one afternoon, him pressing by her to squeeze out the door as she came in, knowing she would recognize the smell on him. That smile on his face. Her jaw seizes up from the way she grits her teeth.

Deborah didn't look up the Sunset Motel online—didn't need to. She's pictured it, or places like it, on thousands of sleepless, daughterless nights. When she pulls up, she isn't surprised by the squalor: Not the filthy Astro Turf that lines the walkways outside of the rooms. Or the cluster of teenagers who watch her as she sits in her car, reaches for the photo of Georgia from her tenth grade yearbook. How they fought over that purple dye in her hair. She feels their eyes on her as she makes her way to the office but she doesn't look back—she wants to make it clear she has no plans to interfere with whatever it is they are here to do.

A bell rings when she pushes through the office door. A man stares at her, a *Playboy* open on the counter in front of him, a portable TV playing *I Love Lucy* on mute. The mold in the air makes her eyes itch. She puts the photo of Georgia on top of the magazine. The man looks at it, looks to the TV. His hair is matted to his head with grease and his white T-shirt is yellowed. She wonders how long it's been since he's showered. Days? Weeks?

Her voice is small when she speaks. "I'm looking for this girl. This woman. She goes by Peaches?"

The man runs his tongue over his teeth. The spitty sound makes her stomach churn. "Peaches ain't been here for a few days."

"How many days?"

"Don't know."

"Could you guess?"

"Two. Three."

"How'd she look? Do you remember what she was wearing?"

The man uncrosses and recrosses his arms. "Same kinda thing she always wore. Dress that barely covered that skinny ass of hers. What you want with her, anyway? She fuck your man?"

"I'm her mother. She told me she came here sometimes."

"Sure," he says. "Now and then, for a job." He seems to relish the chance to say it, leveling his gaze at her to make sure she knows what he means. His only power, his only real pleasure: to be cruel. "You want a room?"

"No," she says, as automatic as a flinch. She hitches her bag higher up her arm and steps back out of the door. She wants to show Georgia's photo to the boys who'd been gathered in the parking lot, but by this time they've scattered. She is about to get in her car when she notices a man sitting alone at the base of the motel sign. He seems agitated, is rocking back and forth on his haunches and rubbing his eyes—drugs, she assumes—but she grips the key tight in her hand, reaches for the photo with the other.

He doesn't look up at her, even when she thinks he should feel her standing there.

"Excuse me," she says, trying to bolster her voice with any semblance of steadiness, strength, she can muster. He doesn't turn. "Excuse me." Nothing. She taps him on the shoulder and he flinches, then turns to her with watering eyes.

"I'm looking for my daughter. Have you seen her? Her name is Georgia. Georgia Willis. Sometimes she goes by Peaches."

The man doesn't say anything. He acts as though he hasn't heard her. "Please," she says, her voice wavering. For the first time since Georgia called, she thinks she might start to cry. She had steeled herself against losing her daughter, but this was a feeling she had not been prepared for: hope.

The man looks at her again, then at the picture, and his face changes.

"You know her," she says. "Please, tell me anything you can. When did you see her last?"

He raises his hand and points, back in the direction of the motel.

"I know she stays there sometimes." The man can't hear, she realizes. She wonders if he can talk at all. He stands and points again, his arms trembling, his eyes wide.

"I don't understand," she says. She fishes through her purse for a piece of paper and a pen, but the man has started to walk away. She calls after him to wait, but even if he can't hear her, he knows she is following him. He reaches the shoulder of the expressway and picks up his pace, starts to run. She toes out onto the shoulder and a truck thunders past, blares its horn. Her ears ringing, she steps back into the parking lot and watches the man shrink into the distance, feeling like he has just given her something and taken something at the same time, but she couldn't say what.

SHE LEAVES the motel and drives through the city, hoping to catch sight of Georgia by chance. She thinks she sees her outside of the Knife and Fork Inn—a glimpse of yellow-blonde hair tossed over a narrow shoulder. She nearly causes an accident when she jerks the car to a halt, but as the driver behind her passes, swearing at her through his window, her stomach sinks—not Gee at all.

She parks at Caesars and wanders through the lobby with its hollow Corinthian columns and statues of helmeted men on horseback. She walks the boardwalk, the old wooden roller coaster rattling along its tracks, in the distance the shrill shouts of lifeguards' whistles directing swimmers down on the beach. But all day long she pictures the man pointing. Wondering what he could have meant.

Deborah drinks more coffee from a kiosk at the Tropicana; it tastes like it was made from dishwater, but the warmth in her gut keeps her going. She hasn't eaten since she left Eagles Mere. She sits for a second at a little wrought iron table made to look like it was imported from New Orleans. She wonders if that's why Gee chose this place: everything here was encouraged to look like something it was not. Here, Gee could be someone other than the girl Deborah raised: a girl who lives on the streets, someone without a mother worrying over her every move. Deborah's feet throb and her ankles are swelling from all the walking. She knows there will be angry red marks where her socks cut into her legs. But every second that she sits is a second that she could be looking. What if, she thinks, her daughter has changed so much in the past five years that Deborah might not recognize her anymore? *No.* A mother would always know her child. Behind all the disappointment, the anger between them, whatever these past years have wrought, Georgia would never be a stranger to her.

She waits until close to midnight to go back to the Sunset Motel, spending the evening drifting between banks of slot machines and poker tables, the occasional whoop rising from one of the players, but most gambling with grim determination, as though they are listening to an unfavorable medical diagnosis. She thinks of how strange it is, that so many things we expect to bring us pleasure end up causing pain.

As Deborah pulls into the motel parking lot, a girl with red hair runs out, tears in her eyes, begs to use her phone. She is too numb, too exhausted, to ask the girl how else she can help, to find out what exactly is wrong. She hands the girl her cell and wonders, vaguely, if she'll ever see it again, decides she doesn't care.

Later, when she talks to the police she won't be able to explain it, what made her leave the room, walk behind the motel. She won't tell them about the man who pointed, how his gestures must have solidified into instruction. She will tell them that she noticed where the grass bent in the wrong direction, where it was flattened. She will tell them about the smell. She squints into the reeds, steps from the asphalt to the edge of the marsh. Insects buzz in her ears, land on her arms, her face. The mud sticks to the bottoms of her shoes, and with each step she needs to break the suction. She has the feeling she is walking toward her own death, that she will be swallowed up, sucked in, and the prospect is more peaceful than scary: At least she won't have to worry about Gee anymore. She hears the scurry of an animal running through the grass. Her toe grazes something, and she bends to look—a disposable camera. Picking it up, she runs her thumb over the wheel, cranks it, and hits the button on top: a flash blooms in the dark. That bright light will be her last clear memory for days.

The first thing she sees when she pushes through the reeds into the clearing is her daughter's feet, the soles bare and pale, the toes she used to wash with such awe when she bathed her in the sink. Their perfection and their vulnerability. The way they curled and flexed, the delicate weight of them in her palm. But looking at these feet, these limbs, these palms upturned like they are asking for something, she does not recognize the body as Georgia's. She wonders, with what will strike her later as the dumb insistence of a record player's needle stuck in a groove, where this woman with the peach tattooed on her chest got her daughter's face. She stumbles back through the grass, into the parking lot, into the open door of a room, not caring whose it is. Her knees are about to give out, so she sits on the end of bed.

The scream starts as a pain in her gut that buckles her in two. It roars up through her lungs, rips through the air, horrible and animal. She couldn't keep Georgia happy, couldn't keep her home, couldn't keep her safe. The only thing Deborah *can* do is force sound from her mouth. She vows she won't stop screaming until everyone else feels inside of it, inside her voice, inside her pain. She pictures it like thick black smoke coming out of her, filling first this motel room, and then the parking lot, and then the entire city, making it all go dark.

LILY

I WAS SURE I'D WOKEN up in the spa: the same sharp, invasive quality to the light, the same insistent white walls. But there were noises I couldn't explain. Voices I didn't know. And my mother, in the corner, asleep in a chair, her head cranked at an uncomfortable angle. I'd never felt so tired. A dull pain erupted when I turned my head, a throbbing above my eye.

And then I remembered. The bar, the man, the way he propped me against him, carried me to the motel, the sign blinking weakly above us. Then I wondered if maybe I was dead—the room had an otherworldly quality, and I couldn't get the proportions right. Everything was shifting; distances and shapes felt impossible to resolve. The walls looked too close, and then very far away. An IV full of mysterious liquid dripped into my bloodstream, and I closed my eyes again and slept.

I FOUND out later that my mother kept the TV off, kept newspapers out of the room. But when I woke up I asked about both of them: Clara and Emily. Clara had been missing, and the flash of silver under the mat of the man's car: Emily's cross. My mother pointed to a bouquet of flowers on the bedside table. Clara had brought them while I was asleep—she tucked a little card in among the tulips.

"And Emily?" I asked. My mother's mouth gaped a little, as though she was surprised I'd asked. She shook her head, and I felt the tears seep from my eyes, down my face, hit the pillow until I fell asleep again.

ONCE I was really awake, a detective came to talk to me about what I remembered, what I could tell him. I described the man for the police, who produced a sketch based on what I said. It had the flat, lifeless quality that all police sketches have—I didn't know how to tell them the things that made him distinct. The pale blue eyes, the elegant fingers, the shape of his jaw. Those were correct, but without the anger I had seen in him, they didn't matter. I described the car, too, and eventually they found one like it, submerged in a pond in the Pine Barrens forty miles west. They searched it, but Emily's cross necklace was nowhere to be found. They couldn't recover any DNA, and the car was registered to an eighty-eight-year-old woman from Delaware who had died in 2008. I told him, too, about the paintings. How the man had been in the bar that night, how he approached me at the library, too.

"Paintings?" the detective said, sounding bemused when I told him how I had ended up in the car. I could tell he thought I was a fool.

I wished I could talk to Clara. I had no idea how to broach what we had been doing, what she had seen. I decided, in the meantime, not to mention anything about the two of us looking for the missing women, the visions, or the signs. Even now that all of Clara's hunches had proved to be true, the situation felt even more absurd. Intuition was delicate, intimate. It didn't stand up to getting passed around, submitted to scrutiny. It just was what it was. Inexplicable, beautiful. Scary and strange.

"So, do you have any idea where he went? Or who he is? There must be DNA on some of the women." I was afraid of being afraid. Of having to live the rest of my life thinking he might show up and find me. A nameless figure always lurking in the shadows.

"We're treating each woman as her own separate case. What happened to you is its own case as well."

"What does that mean?"

"Each one is being investigated independently of the others, with its own team of detectives. I'll be working on your case." The set of his mouth made me realize that he thought solving "my case" was a lost cause.

"Why? Even I know that doesn't make sense. What about what he said to me? That I wasn't like the others? Doesn't that prove he knew about them . . . and that he did it?"

He cleared his throat. "I know. But we have orders from . . . well, from higher up. No one wants to start a panic. No one wants the words *serial killer* applied to this case before we have proof."

"Proof? But they were all there, together. Isn't that proof enough?" He only shook his head in a way that seemed to say *You're right, but it doesn't matter*. Maybe they would find something that would force them to change their tack. It was too illogical, too cruel. But that night I watched a video of a press conference with the prosecutors, who rebuffed a reporter's suggestion that there was a single person behind it all. I ended the video before I could hear any more.

Later I would read articles about the women online, about the lives they came from, the places they called home, the people who mourned them. There were pictures of Emily's family, making their way from their driveway to the front door. A tall, fair-haired woman who must have been her mother. Two broad, blond boys with ramrod-straight posture, just like Emily's.

I never went back to the spa. They closed to deal with the fire damage—the fires had stopped, but that was yet another crime no one could, or would, figure out. The company issued a clichéd statement that Emily would have laughed at, about the way she helped bring more beauty into the world. I pictured her throwing her head back, her teeth gleaming with wicked delight. *Gone* was the word I used to myself for the first few days. I wasn't ready for the finality of the real word. Emily. Dead.

I WAS out of the hospital for a week before I heard from Clara. She texted me, apologizing. Said she had no cash so it had been a little while before she could add minutes to her phone, and now that I wasn't at work, she didn't know where to find me anymore. We agreed to meet in Margate, and I picked her up from the bus stop near Marvin Gardens. I jumped when she reached for the door handle: She had dyed her hair dark brown. I hadn't recognized her at all.

"Wow, I like it," I said.

"Yeah, it was time to go back. Plus, I was a little nervous with the red . . . it just makes you stick out a lot, and with everything going on . . ."

She didn't need to finish her sentence. We didn't need to talk about how afraid we both were. How I looked over my shoulder every time I heard a piece of trash rustling in the breeze. How I double-, triple-checked the locks on the door before I went to sleep. I imagined that Clara probably still felt the same way.

"Did the cops talk to you, too?"

"No," she said. "As soon as the ambulance pulled into the parking lot, I ducked behind a car. Peaches's—I mean Georgia's—mom was still there. She's the one who found them, you know. I'm sorry, Lily. I didn't want to have to talk to the cops, to tell them how I knew to get there. It would have been too weird."

"Yeah," I said. "And I read about that, with Georgia's mom." It felt strange, to use a different name for her after all that time. And then I remembered what Des had said, when I came looking for Clara at the shop. What's her name, then? Even after everything we had been through, I felt shy bringing it up. But if I didn't ask, then she would be one more part of this summer that felt unbelievable, unreal.

"I'm sorry I didn't ask this before. But what's, you know, your real name?"

"It's Ava," she said. "Same as my mom."

"That's nice," I said.

"Yeah. I guess." We pulled up to the beach, parked near the bulkhead. For a minute we listened to the screams of seagulls, the shouts of children playing in the sand.

"Can I ask you something else?" I said, as we stepped out of the car.

"Sure," she said.

"Did you ever—your visions—see anything about Emily?"

She shook her head. "That bothered me for a while. I don't know why I didn't. Some people are really closed off. I could never pick up anything from her, even when I was trying to so she'd let me into the spa. Maybe even when she died she was like that. Hard to read."

"Yeah. She was definitely"—*was*, how I hated that past tense—"closed off, that's for sure. In some ways I feel like I knew her well. I mean, we worked together all the time. But obviously I had no idea she had this other life. And I didn't know anything about her family, her childhood. Still don't, I guess." I could only piece together scraps of information from what I had read in the paper. That the killer seemed focused on sex workers in particular. *You're not like the others.* That they were in the process of interviewing other women who worked on the streets, but it was hard getting any of them to talk to the cops. I thought, too, of the way Emily had started fiddling with that necklace more and more often in those last few weeks. Those dark circles under her eyes.

Clara sighed. "I should have told you. I saw her out once. With a man. All dressed up. Different from how she was at work. The guy was like twenty years older than her. The situation was pretty clear, you know. That's why I used to get so mad at her when she'd kick us out."

I didn't know what to say. Were there clues that I had missed? I thought of my first day at work, Emily showing me all of the places to sneak a look at your cell phone, where to stash a snack. How good she was at hiding in plain sight. Would it have made a difference, if I had known? Clara must have sensed what I was thinking. "People are going to do what they're going to do, Lily."

"So what happened to her . . . you think that's fate?"

She shook her head. "I don't believe in fate as much now. We all make choices, and sometimes those choices bring us to places we never expect. Those women made choices to go with that man without any way to know he would make a choice to do something evil. I'm trying to choose a normal life. You chose to ignore that moron ex-boyfriend of yours, to go your own way. We never have total control, but we all do our best, right?"

"I guess so." We walked along the shore, let the cool waves wash over our bare feet.

"I guess you'll go back to New York now," she said.

"Actually, no. I think I'll stay here, at least for a little while."

"You're not scared?"

"I am, but I don't have a plan to go anywhere. Not really." A seagull swooped over our heads, and we both flinched. "What about you? You're being safe, right?"

"The stuff with the men, that's all over. But I am leaving. I don't know how. I actually think Des used my cash to leave town herself. I haven't seen her or heard from her in days. I mean, she goes MIA all the time when she's on a bender, or when she's met some new guy, but usually she at least comes home for a change of clothes. But I can't wait for her. I've got to get out."

We were quiet as we walked back to my car. Clara was still wearing Victoria's purse. I didn't think I could help Clara until we passed the bank. I pulled over on a side street and told her to wait. I couldn't take out more than $1,000 in one withdrawal—it was half of what I'd made so far at the spa. I had never handled that much cash before, and what overwhelmed me was the scent, that tantalizing, terrible smell of grime and paper and promise. I hoped it would be enough to hold Clara—Ava—over for a little while.

I handed it to her, told her she could only use it to go.

"I can't take this, Lily," she said.

"For once, you're not taking anything." She smiled at that. "I wish I could give you more."

"Are you sure? You might not want to get back to the city now, but maybe in a few months you'll change your mind."

"Doubt it. Plus . . . maybe this is stupid, after everything it almost cost me. But I really want to figure out the story with those paintings."

"It's not stupid at all."

"Any psychic insight you can give me on those?"

"Ha. Nothing, unfortunately. I think you've got this one, though." We were almost at the bus stop. Clara finally put the money in her purse.

"I hope you're right." I felt like there was still so much to say between us, but anything I tried to think of felt forced, melodramatic. "And hey. I never said thank you."

"You don't have to. I just wish I could have known more sooner. And I wish I hadn't said that about Luis. Whenever I saw him he gave me this feeling, like I always thought he was hiding something, but he must have been in the same boat as me. He must have seen them somehow and wondered what to do. Oh, that reminds me." She reached into the back pocket of her jeans and held out a tarot card.

"I don't know if I'm ready for another reading, Clara. I'm just going to stick to the here and now, I think. I want to rent a room somewhere here, see if I can show these paintings in town. Simple. Easy."

"Just take it, okay? It's the Moon. It stands for the part of yourself that is yet to emerge, for mystery and illusion. The version of events you can't see just yet. It's a reminder to connect with your subconscious, to trust yourself."

I took the card and slid it into the cupholder. "Thanks, Clara. I'll try my best."

"You better." A bus chugged up to the shelter.

"That's me," she said.

I leaned across the console to hug her, but I didn't want to say a real goodbye. "Text me when you know what your plans are, okay?"

"I will," she said. "Okay, better go." She waved to me from the line, and her dark hair disappeared behind the tinted windows.

Even after the bus pulled away, I sat in the car for a few minutes, feeling like there was something I could be doing, but not sure what it was. I thumbed the card. It showed a round yellow moon above a pool of water, a curving path to the horizon, a dog and a wolf raising their heads to howl at the sky. What illusions was I hanging on to? What was the version of events, the story, that I had yet to see?

Maybe I should go back to the library, talk to Sue again. But she wouldn't have anything new to tell me. I was still stuck on the idea she'd mentioned, that woman, the one who used to come looking for the photos. I wasn't ready to give her up. Something about her was relevant, close to all this. And then I felt it, the knowledge dropped like a stone in my gut.

Luis. Clara had said she felt like Luis had been hiding something. Maybe she had been right about him, but not in the way she thought. It made perfect sense. The grandson. Quiet. Stuck to her side, watching. His last name was Silver. That big, swooping S at the bottom corners of the paintings.

Luis. Of course.

THE BOARDINGHOUSE, Sea Breezes, appeared ready to collapse in on itself. All the porch spindles were broken, and sections of lattice looked like they had been kicked in. I knocked on the door and an old woman answered, her hair a nest of brown-and-gray frizz.

"Is Luis Silver here?"

"Haven't seen him today. You one of those ladies from the state?"

"From the state?"

"One of those social workers. Don't know why you bother. His grandmother raised the boy right. Never had any trouble with him at all."

"Yeah," I said. "That's right. It's just a routine visit." I felt nervous about lying to her, sneaking around on Luis. But I was worried about what he would do without his job at the spa, and he deserved so much better than this. I hoped she didn't notice the way I stammered, the way I flushed, or, God forbid, ask for a business card. "Can I see his room, please?"

"Up there, second door on your right." She moved aside to give me access to a dark, narrow staircase. I wanted to turn around and drive away, but I felt the tingle of possibility, even as the smell of cat urine stung my eyes.

I knocked once, twice. No answer. I tried the knob and the door was unlocked. I counted to three, then stepped inside, my eyes shut tight like a kid making a wish. Would he be angry at me for showing up like this? What if he wanted to keep the paintings a secret? It would be an unforgivable intrusion, inserting myself into his home, his work, if he didn't want me there.

I kept my eyes closed at first, but I could smell the paint. The mellow scent of linseed oil and the chemical tang of turpentine.

When I opened my eyes I had the same stunned feeling I always got before an anxiety attack. But instead of the tightening of my chest, the breathlessness, the clammy skin, I was dumbstruck, then filled with a warm joy.

There were canvases everywhere. They leaned against the wall, three deep. One was new, set up on an easel: the women, five of them in a single line. I knew their names now. Amanda, Grace, Julie, Victoria, Georgia. Emily had still been alive by the time Luis found Clara, when she came to see me at the spa. Another thing he'd been so desperate to show people, so relatively powerless to make them see.

There was a small pile on the bed: a book of matches, a folded shirt. Had he been planning on going away? I didn't know what I would do if he came back to find me in his room, but I couldn't resist. I started going through the paintings. There was one of a girl in what looked like a shelter, the kind the state set up during Hurricane Sandy, a Red Cross blanket draped over her shoulders. Another of a jitney driver eating lunch from a Styrofoam container. And one that I loved, of a woman praying in front of the steps of an old church. To her left was a battered rowboat at the center of a plot of earth. The boat was filled with clusters of faded impatiens and held a molded statue of the Virgin Mary in the middle. The details were stunning: from the woman's wooden rosary beads to the flecks of mold on Mary's veil.

And then I had to rub my eyes, stare at the floor for a minute, afraid that I would look again and the painting would be a mirage. But there he was, among all the gangsters and the nuns and the bartenders and the go-go dancers, the kids at the schoolyard and the pit bosses and the bodega clerks. My dad, in one of his ratty union shirts, a fingertip-sized hole at the collar. That grin like someone had just whispered a fantastic secret in his ear, his hands wrapped around a paper coffee cup, his hair wild and unbrushed, blown around from driving with the windows of his truck rolled down, even in the cold. I couldn't help it—I raised my eyes to the ceiling and laughed as I choked down a sob.

I don't know how long Luis stood in the doorway watching me stare at the painting, feeling as though something precious had been returned to me. I wanted to tell my mother. I wanted to understand *how*. I turned when the floorboards creaked. Luis raised his eyebrows at me and I held out my hands: *I'm sorry*, then gestured to the paintings—hoping he would understand my awe, my wonder for what he had made. *Wonder*. I hadn't felt it for such a long time.

Luis reached toward the small pile on the bed, moved the shirt aside, setting it down as softly as you might a baby animal, something that could be injured if handled the wrong way. He picked up something that I couldn't make out, then reached into his pocket. He held his palms out to me like an offering. A folded piece of paper and a two-dollar bill. Like the one my father had given me. Like the one Matthew had nearly destroyed.

Out of instinct I flipped it to the back, where there was a zigzag of lightning above Ben Franklin's head, traced in blue pen. The tears caught in my lashes. I unfolded the note. Two words: *I SEE.*

JANES 1, 2, 3, 4, 5, AND 6

AFTER THEY ARE FOUND, THERE is light. Bright, harsh, white like Heaven in movies. There are cameras, a battery of flashes. A large rectangle of police tape is drawn around the marsh and the Sunset Motel. There is no breeze that day. For once, the grass is somber, still, without its usually whispery *shush-shush-shush*. The marsh is filled with a quiet like the penitent silence inside a church. Without the wind, the flies are worse. Detectives and coroners are constantly slapping them away, swearing under their breath. Their boots slosh through the soft muck. Three of the men who report to the scene must step away to get sick. It's the smell. The decomposed flesh. The open eyes, staring, imploring. The vulnerability of those bare feet. The splayed hands, asking for alms. Asking for more than what they got.

All summer there have been questions in the air and the women seem to have the answers. What kind of place is Atlantic City? What is it meant to be now? A ruined dream? A tumbled-down sand castle buffed away by the tide? A nightmare?

A coroner leans over Jane #6. "Who did this to you?" he whispers. But it is one more thing sealed behind all their lips like a secret.

A dozen gloved hands touch the women. The investigation is doomed from the beginning. They will never find the man, though some of the police sketches circle his likeness—the set of his jaw, the blades of his cheekbones—yet none of them capture the pale glass of his eyes. The city won't treat the cases as the work of one person—pressure from the politicians, from the casinos; the words *serial killer* will scare off whatever tourists are left. And so they investigate each woman as her own crime, her own case, isolated from the rest. Having lain there, sisterly, so close, for so long, the women bristle at the absurdity. They thought they had seen everything this city could do to them, but even now they can still be surprised.

The other girls from the streets leave flowers, plush bears, little crosses made of plywood. But after three days, the offerings are rain-drenched and faded. The crosses tilt in the muck. In a few weeks, they'll be washed away by the September storms that drive against the coast, hurricanes thrashing up from warmer seas. Lost.

The investigators never find the seventh woman, the one he left near the rusted-out railroad tracks. They never even know to look for her, even though for weeks her dyed red hair is bright against the fading grass. The police bring in a suspect for questioning, a plumber who had been staying at the Sunset Motel when the bodies were found. They question another man—one whose apartment on the boardwalk is filled with women's shoes. But they are all the wrong guesses. The women know he's gone for good after the seventh woman. They know, too, that he'll never be caught. Who they were, their longings and dreams, their secrets and their darkest thoughts, will be lost. Time will turn them into warnings, symptoms, into stories people tell in dark corners of bars.

Seasons pass. The tides surge and recede. The moon waxes and wanes. The grass of the marsh turns green and brown and green again. One spring, the feral cats under the boardwalk are caught and taken to shelters inland. A new restaurant opens in the middle of an empty, gray block on Pacific. A section of board-walk that was ruined in a storm is nailed together again. The state buys the Sunset Motel and razes it to the ground. A new governor promises the city more funds. The lights at the Revel go on again, a glittering column at the end of the skyline. An art show draws a critic from the *New York Times*. In the *Press of Atlantic City*: "Local Painter Honored for a Lifetime of Work, Commissioned to Paint Murals Downtown." A young woman waits tables at a diner in San Diego and writes a college applica-tion essay about tarot cards and telling stories, about a boardwalk shop overlooking another sea.

The women hover above it all, presiding like ghosts. Even now, they, like everyone else in town, still believe in luck, in the change of tides, in the upswing, in the chance that they'll hit on the next deal. That something else will happen, something beau-tiful, wonderful, something that will turn it all around. They choose to believe that this isn't the end.

ACKNOWLEDGMENTS

THANK YOU—

To my agent, Sarah Bedingfield, who shaped this manuscript into the book it was meant to become with endless patience, keen editorial acumen, and unbridled enthusiasm. I can't imagine this journey without you, or our marathon breakfasts. To my editor, Kate Dresser, whose passion bowled me over from the very beginning. Thank you for embracing this project with such wholehearted gusto and for your razor-sharp insights and clear vision, which have elevated every page. To Molly Gregory and the rest of the team at Gallery for bringing this book into the world with such care and giving it a loving home.

To Susan Scarf Merrell, my very first reader, for your boundless generosity and unwavering support. I am awestruck at my great fortune to have you behind this book and its author. Thank you for making me finish the lap.

To Susie once again, along with Meg Wolitzer and the rest of the BookEnds '19 crew, for the camaraderie, motivation, and windmill sing-alongs. Gratitude in particular to Sheena Cook and Mike McGrath, whose savvy edits, honesty, and humor brought life to these pages and pushed me to be better.

To the many teachers whose life-changing support has been integral to my writing life. First, Rebecca Harlan and Susan Connolly of Mainland Regional High School, who helped a shy teenage girl realize that writing could be power. Jennifer Brice and Peter Balakian at Colgate University, for showing me the way. The wonderful, tireless faculty and staff of the Stony Brook MFA program—thank you for fostering such a smart and kind-hearted community, where much of this book was written.

To Melanie Pierce, I can't imagine the past few years without our Citarella dates, story swaps, and mutual teaching meltdowns. I am so lucky to have you as a writing buddy and, most impor-tant, as my friend.

To Scott Cheshire and Susan Minot, early readers whose keen eye, honesty, and generosity of spirit were invaluable. Thank you, too, to Paul Harding, for your gracious encouragement. I am so humbled by your support of my work and of this book.

To Lesley Williamson, Mandy Beem-Miller, and the rest of the staff and board of the Saltonstall Foundation, for providing me with essential space, time, and nourishment, as I edited this manuscript. Thank you for being the stewards of Connie's legacy. You bring a little bit of magic to your corner of Ellis Hollow.

To the many people who gave me a place to stay during long days of writing, revising, teaching, and commuting to class, particularly the Hirschhorn family, Kris and Lisa Eng, and Constance Casey.

My family, the Mullens and the Sypherds, for your bravery and brightness, along with your love. I am proud to come from all of you.

My late father, Michael Mullen. There was no better training for a future writer than those quiet mornings on the lake. The fact that you are gone still makes my breath catch in my chest, but you taught me to pay attention to the details of the world, and so there is a piece of you in everything I write.

My mother, Kimberly, who inspires me with her strength, humor, creativity, and kindness. You showed me the beauty in making things, in digging for the unexpected, and the great freedom in marching to the beat of my own drum. Thank you for leading my way.

My sisters, Lauren and Meghan. My best friends, who fill my life with so much joy and laughter, and to Sean and Jon—I can't remember our family without the two of you in it.

Spencer. Thank you for the love that makes each day brighter. For inspiring me with your incredible kindness, your great intelligence, your truly singular way of looking at the world, and for always saying *you will*.